Praise for Joseph Flynn and his novels

"Flynn is an excellent storyteller." — *Booklist*

"Flynn keeps the pages tu

"Flynn propels his plot wi
— *Publis*

Digger

"A mystery cloaked as cleverly as (and perhaps better than) any John Grisham work." — *Denver Post*

"Surefooted, suspenseful and in its breathless final moments unexpectedly heartbreaking." — *Booklist*

"An exciting, gritty, emotional page-turner."
— Robert K. Tannenbaum
New York Times Bestselling Author of *True Justice*

The Next President

"*The Next President* bears favorable comparison to such classics as *The Best Man, Advise and Consent* and *The Manchurian Candidate*."
— *Booklist*

"A thriller fast enough to read in one sitting."
— *Rocky Mountain News*

The President's Henchman

"Marvelously entertaining." — *ForeWord Magazine*

Also by Joseph Flynn

The Concrete Inquisition
Digger
The Next President
Hot Type
Farewell Performance
Gasoline, Texas
The President's Henchman

Coming soon!
Round Robin
Blood Street Punx
One False Step

The Hangman's Companion

Joseph Flynn

Stray Dog Press, Inc.
Springfield, IL
2010

Published by Stray Dog Press, Inc.
Springfield, IL 62704, U.S.A.

First Stray Dog Press, Inc. Printing, July 2010

Visit the author's web site: www.josephflynn.com

Flynn, Joseph
The Hangman's Companion / Joseph Flynn
530 p.
ISBN 978-0-9830312-0-8

Printed in the United States of America

PUBLISHER'S NOTE
This is a work of fiction. Names, characters, places, and incidents are either the product of the author's imagination or are used fictitiously; any resemblance to actual persons, living or dead, events, or locales is entirely coincidental.

Book design by Aha! Designs

Dedication

For my Godparents,
William and Virginia Flynn,
and for my aunt Ruth Leroux and
in memory of Chef Paul Leroux

Acknowledgements

My thanks to Caitie and Catherine
for the words and the pictures.

The Hangman's Companion

Pont d'Iéna, Paris, Sunday, May 17th

1

The fight under the bridge at the foot of the Eiffel Tower turned deadly when the Frenchman kicked the urn out of the American's grasp. The pewter vessel shot into the air and smashed against a bridge support, leaving a dark stain there and scattering the remainder of the ashes of the American's late wife into the Seine.

The Frenchman, Thierry Duchamp, an elite athlete, twenty-eight years old, was more than a little drunk and had been having a heated argument with a shapely blonde. Her makeup was smeared and she all but spilled out of her crimson silk blouse. The American, Glen Kinnard, forty-nine, a retired cop with a long list of excessive force complaints, had been standing on the walkway under the bridge. He'd been agonizing over whether to honor his wife's last request, when the noisy French couple made their stumbling approach.

Kinnard was bone tired after a long, turbulent flight from Chicago. He'd had to stand in a block-long line to clear customs. Then he had to make several detours to exit Charles de Gaulle Airport because of some sort of minor terrorist scare. He hadn't slept in thirty-six hours and he was jet-lagged to hell and back.

On top of all that, he wasn't a patient guy even when he was fresh.

The only thing that had kept him from telling the raucous couple to show a little respect and shut the fuck up was that the French had been surprisingly kind to him since he'd arrived.

It had started off with the taxi driver leaning against his cab at the airport. He was a tough-faced little mutt, looked like he had a glass eye, was smoking a butt that smelled like he'd fished it out of a toilet. But he saw the pain on Kinnard's face, took note of the urn the ex-cop had taken out of his suitcase. Saw how Kinnard cradled the urn like a baby. He nailed the situation at a glance.

Someone near and dear had died.

He held the door open for Kinnard like he was driving a limo not a cab. He tucked his fare's suitcase into the trunk, and slid behind the wheel. Looking over his shoulder at Kinnard, he even spoke English after a fashion.

"My regrets, m'sieur," the cabbie said. "Where may I deliver you?"

Kinnard gave the guy the name of the hotel where his daughter had booked a room for him. "The Hotel Saint Jacques." He provided the address on the Rue de Rivoli.

"I know this place. We travel with all haste."

The cabbie wasn't kidding; he put the pedal down. Slalomed through traffic like a pro. Still had time to glance in the mirror at the urn Kinnard held close.

The American knew just what the driver was wondering: Who'd kicked?

Kinnard surprised himself by answering the unspoken question. "My wife. She asked me to bring her home."

"*Elle était française?*" the driver asked.

"Yeah," Kinnard said. "Born right here in Paris."

The driver turned the meter off. Said the ride was on him.

Kinnard nodded his thanks. He looked out the window at the city and told the man, "The shame of it is I never got to see the place with her."

When they arrived at the hotel, the driver hopped out, retrieved Kinnard's bag and had a quick conversation with the doorman, who held the door for Kinnard, and then passed the word to the young woman working behind the front desk. She, in turn, spoke to a guy in a sharp suit.

If he'd had the energy, Kinnard would have been embarrassed.

He wasn't looking to come off as some Weepy Willie.

"Your name, m'sieur?" the young woman asked.

He gave it, watched her find it on a list in front of her. She turned to look at the guy in the suit and pointed the tip of her pen to a space on what Kinnard took to be a diagram of the rooms in the hotel. The guy in the suit nodded. She turned to Kinnard.

"We are sorry to say, m'sieur, all the rooms of the type you requested have been filled; we will have to offer you a suite, at no additional charge, if that is satisfactory."

Kinnard knew they were kidding him, but he played along, grateful.

"That'll be great," he said.

He signed the register and the young woman gave him her card. "If there is anything we can do to make your stay more... consoling, please let me know."

Kinnard looked at the card. The young woman's name was Emilie. Same as his daughter.

"*Merci,*" he said.

2

The suite was cozy by American standards but stylish down to the smallest detail. Suzanne would have loved the place. He would have loved to see the smile on her face had they stepped through the door together. But he had always been too busy being a cop to go to Paris, and when he hadn't been busy they'd gone places he wanted to go, Vegas or Miami. Suzi knew better than to push too hard to try to change his mind. He'd raised his hand to her often enough.

Once too often finally...and she'd divorced him.

His daughter had cheered her mother's long overdue departure.

He'd never expected to hear from Suzanne again. Certainly not after five years without a word. He almost didn't recognize her voice when she called. Her accent seemed to have faded, become more American, and she sounded old. Good reason for that. She told him she was dying, and would like to see him once more before she went.

The last thing Suzi was looking for was a reconciliation. She was thinking of Emilie. She didn't want their daughter to be left without a parent when she died. She pleaded with Kinnard to find a way to make peace with Emilie.

At the age of twenty-four, though, Emilie considered herself to be her own woman, and the last person she wanted back in her life was the prick of a father who had made her mother's life hell. If giving him another chance was what *Maman* was asking, then she was asking too much. She told Suzanne so to her face, with Kinnard in the room.

He saw the fear in his daughter's eyes. She thought he might go off on her, knock her around good, though he never had, not in his worst days. When her father failed to meet Emilie's expectation of brutality, she voiced a new suspicion.

The sonofabitch was after her mother's money. After leaving Kinnard, Suzanne had started a small, successful travel agency. Emilie was her strong right hand. The business was going to her.

Kinnard turned to Suzi and asked, "Em's your sole heir, right?

From her bed, Suzanne nodded.

"So let's put the money question to rest," he said. "Sign everything you have over to her right now. I'll cover all your expenses, medical and otherwise. You need to see a doctor, I'll take you. You need *anything*, I'll get it for you. Help any damn way I can."

Emilie had no doubt Kinnard would keep his word. To spite her.

Suzanne, though, was moved to tears. She put a hand over her mouth. She knew what she looked like. The chemo and the radiation had ravaged her. Her attempts to make herself presentable before her ex-husband arrived had only made her weep.

The damage the cancer had done to Suzanne almost made Kinnard sob, too. All the more so because it made him think of how he'd once marred her beauty. If another man had inflicted such hurt on her, he would have...

He would have to take care of her as best he could because there was no way to get revenge on a fatal illness. Thing was, as haggard and drawn as Suzanne looked, he could look past the present moment and still see her as beautiful. Her eyes were as blue as ever, and the irrepressible spirit that lay behind them was untouched by the cancer.

Suzanne wanted Emilie to have her father in her life. If that required her to forgive Kinnard for all he'd done to her, and do so in Emilie's presence, she would do it gladly.

She extended her hand to Kinnard.

"Be at peace with me," she said.

He took her hand, and now he couldn't keep his eyes from glistening with tears.

Seeing her parents look lovingly at each other made Emilie gag.

She stormed out, telling her mother to sell the business and give the money to charity.

Emilie might have been able to maintain her anger if Suzanne hadn't confounded her doctors' predictions. They'd given her a month to live, two at the most. But she hung on for a year. It was a hellish year, but Kinnard never wavered in his commitment. Emilie tried to keep her contempt for Kinnard stoked, accusing him of being too damn late in trying to act like a decent human being. But he'd shouldered most of the load Emilie had carried, giving her time to have a life of her own. He was there through the worst of it, times when Emilie had to leave her mother's room because it hurt so bad to see how she was suffering.

None of Kinnard's ministrations, though, got Emilie to discontinue her verbal abuse.

While he never said a harsh word to her.

Suzanne was the one who knocked Emilie for a loop.

She asked her daughter to be the maid of honor at her wedding.

Glen Kinnard and Suzanne LaBelle were married for the

second time one week before the bride succumbed to her affliction. She lay in bed throughout the ceremony, but clearly responded, "I do," when asked if she took this man…

Other than the judge her father secured to perform the ceremony, Emilie was the only witness present. She helped her mother place the ring on her father's finger. She kissed both her parents when the exchange of vows was completed.

Suzanne asked only one thing of Emilie: "Be kind."

Of her husband, she asked, "When I go, please take me home."

3

Kinnard tried to sleep, laying fully clothed atop the comforter on the small French bed. But he had too many demons dancing in his head to get more than a few minutes of rest at any one time. Emilie, from the front desk, called to ask if he would like to have dinner in his room. She could have the hotel's chef prepare almost anything he would like. He thanked her but declined the offer. He asked not to be disturbed before midday tomorrow.

At two a.m. he rolled off the bed, took a shower, and made a pot of coffee using the machine provided in the suite. He dressed in fresh clothes, dark shirt, pants, and windbreaker. Rubber soled shoes. Feeling the caffeine jolt of the coffee, he picked up the urn with Suzanne's ashes from the table next to the bed and left the suite.

If there was anyone on duty at the front desk, that person was not at his post when Kinnard passed through the lobby. He had to open the door to the street for himself, just as he'd hoped he would. It was two-thirty now. Early Sunday morning. Still late Saturday night to any revelers making a last stop on their rounds.

Kinnard looked right and left along the length of the Rue du 29 Juillet, on which the hotel's side entrance faced. No pedestrians were visible in either direction. He turned left and walked toward the Rue de Rivoli. He waited in the shadows at the corner of the block as a single car passed, neither the driver nor the passenger looking in his direction. He crossed the thoroughfare and entered the Tuileries Gardens.

It was only after he was well into the parklike setting and was walking in the shadows of a stand of trees that he thought he should have paused to read the signs at the gardens' entrance. He might have learned if the place was off-limits overnight, the way many American parks were. He didn't think there was much of a threat that terrorists would attempt to blow up the shrubbery. But the Louvre was just down the street. Even he hadn't been able to miss the place on the taxi ride to the hotel. If some jihadi SOBs wanted to rub the infidels noses in how corrupt their culture was, they could hide out in the trees and start launching rockets or mortar rounds at the famous museum.

That possibility had to occur to the French cops, Kinnard thought.

Had to.

Made Kinnard glad he was wearing dark clothes and running shoes.

He might not have destruction in mind, but he was a man with a mission.

He moved deeper into the trees, picked up his pace.

He had deliberately failed to inquire if it was legal to dump someone's ashes in the Seine. He didn't want to know so he could claim ignorance, if worse came to worse. Of course, the river flowed 480 miles. He could have picked a quiet spot out in the countryside somewhere, deposited Suzanne's ashes and no one would ever have been the wiser. But Suzanne had been a Parisienne and as far as Kinnard was concerned there was only one place to fulfill her wish.

Right where the Seine flowed past the Eiffel Tower.

4

The walkway under the Pont d'Iéna struck him as the perfect spot. The overarching bridge gave it a sense of privacy. A terrace of shallow steps led down to the water's edge. A support pillar ten feet out in the river shielded him from the view of anyone on the opposite bank. All he had to do to honor Suzanne's last wish was to crouch, perhaps kneel, open the urn and let the ashes swirl away with the current. They'd flow out from under the bridge right past the Eiffel Tower.

Only thing was, Kinnard just couldn't let his wife's remains go.

The last year he'd spent taking care of Suzanne had been the most meaningful of his life. He'd felt closer to her than when they had first started dating. It was the only time he'd ever cared about anyone without thinking about himself first. His selflessness had been apparent even to Emilie. In the minutes after Suzanne had passed, he'd thanked Em for playing along, pretending she'd reconciled with her father.

"I know giving me that kiss must have cost you," he said.

She shrugged. "Just trying to do what Mom asked."

"It's all right now. She's gone. You can stop acting like I'm not a total asshole."

Emilie studied him. Thought about how he'd changed over the past year.

"Maybe total is too strong." She smiled when she said that.

Almost made Kinnard cry again right there.

Emilie's forgiveness inspired him that night under the Pont d'Iéna.

Maybe the thing to do, he thought, was hold on to Suzi's ashes until he croaked. Then have Em bring the two of them back to the Seine and—No, he'd leave Suzi's remains in Paris, buy a space for them at some cemetery or something. That way, Em would have to carry only his urn with her. She could bring their ashes to where he was standing right now. Open the two urns, let their ashes mix in the air and flow away in the river.

Together forever. He'd make sure to treat Em right, live like a monk, do good works, make people forget the old Glen Kinnard. He was sure his daughter would honor his request.

The idea pleased Kinnard right down the soul he never knew he had. He didn't know how long he stood beneath the Pont d'Iéna lost in thought, but he was certain what brought him out of his reverie. An angry female voice. Screeching in French.

He looked to his left and saw a young couple approaching. The guy was having trouble keeping his balance as they walked. The woman's voice was loud; the man's was low. The man was slurring his words; the woman was bellowing hers. The woman put a foot wrong, lost her balance and started windmilling her arms. She tottered toward the water with a shriek.

The man caught a wrist and yanked her back. For a second, Kinnard thought they were going to kiss and make up, be on their way and leave him in peace. Only the guy didn't kiss her, he said something too quiet for Kinnard to hear. Whatever he said, it wasn't well received. The woman replied with a shrill rant. Her voice was enough to make Kinnard's ears ache.

Back home, on the job, he would have taken a billy club to both of them.

But he remembered where he was and how well he'd been treated up until now.

The Frenchman, though, had heard enough from the woman.

He finally raised his voice. *"Mon Dieu, ferme la bouche!"* Jesus, shut up!

Mademoiselle wasn't of a mind to turn down the volume. She planted her feet wide, put her left hand on her hip, and vigorously waved her right index finger under the guy's nose. She kept that up, Kinnard thought, things were going to take a definite turn for the worse.

As if to confirm his expectation, the guy's face grew tight with anger and he began to shake his head back and forth with increasing vigor. Kinnard was sure he was about to clock the broad: break her nose, blacken her eyes, knock out a few teeth.

The prospect of which made Kinnard's own jaw tighten. He'd learned enough about France from Suzi to know the country had a Good Samaritan law. It said people were legally obliged to come to the aid of someone in danger or distress, as long as you could help without putting your own precious backside at risk. What you couldn't do, though, was just turn your back and walk away. The least you were expected to do was call for help.

Kinnard didn't have a cell phone on him. Didn't know the police emergency number even if he could find a public phone. There wasn't a cop or anybody else in sight. So maybe he was in a legal gray area, had a loophole. Yeah, right. A gutless wonder with a microdot conscience might rationalize the situation that way. But a street cop with twenty-five years experience? No way could he split. Even if a hassle was the last thing he needed right now.

His temper climbing fast into the red zone, Kinnard was about to speak out when the Frenchman took him by surprise. Kinnard thought he'd seen it all, but this guy showed him something new. He caught the woman's wagging finger in his teeth. Bit down hard enough that she couldn't yank it free.

The woman's voice, now filled with pain, rose to operatic heights. So the guy decided to give her something more to complain about. He started whacking her with rights and lefts to the head. Openhanded blows, but hard enough to make her head jerk back and forth.

For a dizzying second, Kinnard's subconscious projected his face onto the Frenchman and Suzi's face onto the woman. He felt flush with shame. But self-loathing turned quickly into fury. The shout that erupted from his chest drowned out the sounds of the fight.

"Hey, asshole, leave her the hell alone!"

Kinnard's outburst made the French couple jump a foot into the air, the woman finally freeing her mangled finger. They both turned to gape at him. Kinnard saw it was the first time the Frenchman realized he was there. But the woman…it seemed to Kinnard almost as if she had been expecting him. Was pissed he hadn't intervened sooner.

By now the Frenchman saw who he was dealing with: a gray-haired fart holding a vase. He snarled at Kinnard, "*Va te faire foutre, papie.*" Fuck off, grandpa.

The woman tried to seize the moment to flee, but she turned an ankle and fell.

Dismissing Kinnard as inconsequential, the man turned and started to kick the woman hard. Kinnard couldn't see the guy's face just then, but nonetheless recognized himself again in the role of the pitiless bully.

Without a moment's hesitation, he joined the fray.

5

A street fighter to his core, Kinnard never worried about what was fair. He hit the Frenchman with a straight right to his cheek while the guy was still kicking the shit out of the woman. It was a good solid punch with plenty of shoulder and hip behind it, but it was a bit off target. Kinnard had been going for the hinge of the guy's jaw. Had he hit the nerve bundle there, it would have been all over. As it was, Kinnard had busted the side of the guy's face for him, but left him upright.

Well, almost. The force of the punch knocked him back into the woman lying on the walkway. The Frenchman lost his footing, but where a normal guy would have keeled over like a felled tree and smacked his head on the pavement, this SOB went horizontal in the air, spun like he was a plane doing a barrel roll, and his right leg came whipping around. As if he had it in mind all along, he locked onto the urn Kinnard cradled in the crook of his left arm. The bastard's right foot lashed out and kicked the urn free from Kinnard's grasp. Sent it rocketing into the night.

Kinnard howled, "No!"

The laws of physics ignored his plea. The urn shot out over the Seine, smashed into the bridge's support pillar and burst into innumerable pieces. Suzanne's ashes fell into the river, the portion that didn't become a dark smear on the damp bridge support.

For a moment, Kinnard could do no more than stare in stupefied disbelief.

A clatter of retreating footsteps reminded him that his business under the Pont d'Iéna remained unfinished. He turned to see the battered blonde hobbling off, her high heels resounding off the pavement. The asshole Kinnard had punched was back on his feet, running a hand over his bruised face and wincing. He wasn't done, though. He didn't give a damn about the woman now. He wanted Kinnard. Wanted to put him into the river, as lifeless as Suzanne.

But Kinnard wasn't ready to go.

Not while the French cocksucker was still drawing breath.

Kinnard watched the Frenchman as the guy moved in on him. Even drunk and with his balance less than perfect, he was light on his feet. He had his hands up, but they wouldn't be his primary weapons. The Frenchman was a kicker. That was when it came to Kinnard where he'd seen a move like the one the prick had used to kick Suzi's ashes into the river. SportsCenter. When the cable channel didn't have enough real sports highlights to show they'd put on some of those soccer trick shots. Guys doing somersaults, kicking the ball past the goalie.

So he knew what to expect: feet. Maybe a head butt. Like the guy who cracked that dago's sternum with his head in a big game a few years back. He'd been French, too. So watch for that.

The Frenchman was smiling at Kinnard, blood on his teeth from Kinnard's first shot. Looking like he was a wolf about to eat a lamb. Confident little fuck. Kinnard figured he had three inches and thirty pounds on the guy, none of it fat. Maybe it was Kinnard's gray hair that had him fooled. That was the case, hooray for gray.

The Frenchman spat out a gob of blood and started to say something.

Kinnard loved it when assholes talked. Their minds were on getting out whatever it was they had to say. Not on fighting. Kinnard shot forward and hit the prick with two lefts and a right while he was still yapping. The lefts set him back on his heels and the right lifted him off his feet.

Damn, if he didn't do a backflip instead of going down hard.

Fucker went into a roll right out of the flip and popped back up to his feet. Like he was made of rubber or something, the asshole just kept bouncing back. He was still hurting from three shots to the head, though, and Kinnard wasn't about to give him any time to recover. He closed on the guy fast.

Not fast enough. The Frenchman's right foot shot out, going for Kinnard's groin. Would have ended the fight right there if he'd connected. Kinnard would have collapsed like a sack of shit and been available for stomping. No fancy getaway moves for him. But he managed to turn just enough to take the kick on his left thigh. It felt like he'd been hit with an axe.

He staggered backward and now the frog pursued, kicking right, left, and right again. Like a boxer throwing combinations and, Jesus Christ, were his legs strong. His first two kicks were directed at Kinnard's head, only Frenchie hadn't gotten the range yet, underestimating Kinnard's height. The kicks caught Kinnard on his shoulders, felt like he'd been hit with sledgehammers. The last kick was another try for Kinnard's crotch. He managed to sidestep that one completely, get both hands around the guy's ankle, lift it high into the air, and then hold on so the fucker wouldn't be able to do any more acrobatics.

Kinnard used his grip on the Frenchman's leg to drive him straight down to the pavement. The back of the guy's head hit first, followed by his torso and keister. A series of satisfying cries of pain reached Kinnard's ears. He'd finally put some real hurt into the sonofabitch. There was a question in Kinnard's mind, though, whether that last gasp of agony might have his own.

The pain in his left leg was ratcheting up fast. God, had that bastard frog ruptured his femoral artery or something? Was he dying on his feet? Not that he was going to be standing long if the throbbing in his leg kept getting worse.

And, God Almighty, that French bastard was getting to his feet again. No fancy moves this time. He was using both hands to push himself upright. If Kinnard had had his gun with him, he would have emptied the whole clip into this guy. Then crack his skull with the barrel. But he didn't have his gun, and here came the Frenchman again.

He was trying to take a run at Kinnard but the fall had messed up his wiring. He wasn't light on his feet anymore. In fact, he was having trouble just staying upright. If Kinnard had had two good legs to work with, he could have stepped out of the way, given the guy a little shove and sent him into the river. With any luck, the prick wouldn't know how to swim.

But fancy footwork was no more available to Kinnard than his gun. Still, he was able to see what the Frenchman intended to try. No kicks this time. Not with those wobbly legs. Not with the raw hatred in those eyes. The guy was going to try to kill Kinnard with his head. He wasn't tall enough to go *tête à tête*—head to head—so he had to try to crack Kinnard's chest. Just like that other French guy in that big game.

Head butts were fight finishers, sometimes fatally so. There were only two good countermoves. The first was to get out of the way. But it was already too late for that. The second was too meet the hard surface of the attacking skull with something that could absorb the blow without damage, something that would overwhelm the integrity of the cervical spine.

The heel of Kinnard's right palm shot forward to collide with the Frenchman's thrusting forehead. The bones of Kinnard's arm were stronger than those anchoring the Frenchman's head. The smack of flesh on flesh was followed by the crack of the frog's neck breaking. He went down like he'd been shot. His legs twitched twice and then he was still.

Kinnard didn't see any of that. The jolt of hitting his opponent's head was instantly transmitted to the shoulder the Frenchman had kicked. That pain combined with the agony in his left leg was more than consciousness would tolerate. He collapsed alongside the Frenchman, his head coming to rest atop his opponent's outstretched arm.

When the cops found them two hours later it looked as if the battered American lay in the fond embrace of the Frenchman he had killed.

Washington, DC, Sunday, May 31st

1

As much as possible, which was usually not all that much, Sunday was a day of rest for President Patricia Darden Grant and her husband James J. McGill. Thing was, for the majority of the world, Sunday was not the sabbath, and there were plenty of godless cruds who worshipped only their own blood-soaked ambitions. Dealing with them, regardless of the day of the week, was the duty of the president. McGill kept more regular hours, but Saturday and Sunday were often given to maintaining paternal ties to his three young children living in Evanston, Illinois. But on that Sunday at the end of May the world's more serious miscreants were in passive mode, and Abby, Kenny, and Caitie McGill were all content to speak with their father for five minutes and pass the phone along, ending with their mother, Carolyn.

"Things really that quiet?" McGill asked his ex-wife, with whom he maintained amicable relations and a common devotion to their children.

"Abby's bottling something up," his ex said. "You'll probably be hearing from her soon."

"I'm going to London with Patti, remember."

"We'll still be able to reach you, won't we?"

"Yeah," McGill said. "All I meant was if anyone needs me, it'll take longer to get home."

McGill, a former police captain in Chicago and a former chief of police in Winnetka, Illinois, now worked private investigations under the business entity of McGill Investigations, Inc. He was between cases at the moment, conveniently allowing him to accompany his wife to that summer's G8 meeting in London. The president had told him she'd like him to be her dinner date at a little get-together the Queen of England would be hosting at Buckingham Palace.

Being a dutiful husband, McGill had, of course, accepted.

How often did a private eye get to eat with the president and the queen?

But if any of his kids really needed him, he'd have to express his regrets.

"Hold on a minute," Carolyn told him.

She must have placed her hand over the phone, but McGill could still hear muffled shouts back and forth between Carolyn and their kids.

"They said they'll be all right for the next week or so."

"Caitie want me to get something for her in London?"

"Of course. They all do. Caitie's just the only one to ask."

McGill laughed.

"I think she's got something cooking, too. She's had some secretive phone calls."

"A boyfriend already?"

"No, I don't think so. But something."

"Kenny's fine?"

"Yeah.

"How about you?"

"Just had my annual physical. All systems go."

"That's great. Say hello to Lars for me."

"Will do. Tell Patti to keep up the good work."

2

After brunch, McGill and the president repaired to the cozy room in the Residence known as McGill's Hideaway. The furnishings were two immensely comfortable leather arm chairs with hassocks and a matching sofa. The chairs were used for reading or, in season, staring at the flames in the fireplace. The sofa, eight feet in length, had been used for moments of First Couple impetuosity, after fluffy White House towels had been spread to keep the leather unblemished.

McGill and Patti had vowed to each other that such instances would never be included in either of their memoirs.

At the moment, the president's henchman was absorbed by

a story in the sports section of the *Chicago Tribune*. The Bears, the headline story said, had shocked the city by pulling off a blockbuster trade for an All-Pro quarterback. This was such an unlikely event that many of the team's faithful, including McGill, had felt it would be preceded by the return of a Republican mayor to City Hall.

Given the decades of dismal performance the team had suffered at the quarterback position, McGill, like many, was suspicious of this development. He scanned the story to see if there was any mention the incoming player had, say, turned up lame before the Bears acquired him. That, possibly, his old team was going to put the poor fellow down before they got the Chicago team to fall for a chump trade.

The *Trib* reported no physical defect in the would-be hero.

Daring to hope, McGill looked up from the paper and smiled.

He saw that Patti was looking his way. She'd been amusing herself for the last hour reading briefing books on the upcoming economic summit. There had been a lot of agonizing in the U.S. press lately about China overtaking the United States as the world's largest economy. McGill thought comparative measures were overvalued. You didn't see the Swiss sweating things like that. They kept making their chocolate and precision timepieces and yodeling in their mountains.

Individual wellbeing was more important than national aggregates, McGill thought. But what the hell did he know?

"Jim," the president said, "I'd like you to tutor me."

Apparently, he knew something.

"In what?" he asked.

"I'd like to learn some basic Dark Alley."

The anything goes, street-fighting-codified, martial art McGill's uncle had taught him. He gave Patti a look.

"You intend to kick someone's ass when you get to London?"

3

Rather than answer directly, Patti gave him a politician's bob 'n' weave.

Sometimes she couldn't help herself.

"I'll do a favor for you," she told him.

"What's that?"

"I'm dissatisfied with the lack of progress the Secret Service is making in finding out who shot Special Agent Ky."

The president, as caring a wife as a man might want, was also trying hard not to let concern for her husband's wellbeing distract her from the burdens of her office. This was despite McGill having only his driver, Leo Levy, as an armed companion. For the past six months, he'd had no Secret Service protection whatsoever.

McGill had said he'd be okay until Deke was fit to return to duty, and he'd worked several small cases in that time without so much as blistering a lip. SAC Celsus Crogher, chief of the White House security detail, however, had seen his hair go completely white from the stress of pushing the team investigating Deke's shooting—and worrying the president's husband, code name Holmes, might get his sorry ass shot.

McGill shrugged. "Patti, some cases are stainless steel whodunits."

The Secret Service had looked at all the militant antiabortionists whose ilk had been responsible for the death of Patti's first husband, philanthropist Andrew Hudson Grant, had threatened McGill's children, and when that was deemed beyond the pale had turned their hostile gaze towards the president's henchman himself. But that avenue of investigation had met a dead end. As for the possibility Deke's shooting had been the product of personal enmity, that hadn't led anywhere either. He was the dutiful son of a single mother, and almost monastic in his lifestyle.

"So you're content to let the investigation proceed under its current leadership?" the president asked.

"If your favor was to let me take the reins, no thank you."

McGill was not about to join the federal government in any capacity.

Other than being married to the woman who headed it.

"I thought you might be more motivated to bring things to a conclusion."

McGill said, "Believe me, Patti, no one could be more motivated than Deke's brother and sister agents. Look at Celsus. This thing is literally eating him up. One day soon, if we don't catch a break, there'll be nothing left of him but his scowl sitting atop his brogans."

"He worries about you, too," the president said.

"He's *pissed* at me because I won't follow orders."

The president knew she'd get nowhere debating that point.

"So will you help me? Teach me a little Dark Alley?"

"Be happy to. Sorry I can't do more."

She still hadn't told him why the best protected woman on earth felt the need to know how to personally bust someone's chops. That remained a mystery.

But he was a detective.

One who always liked a good challenge.

4

It helped that Patti was fit, well-coordinated, and possessed a fair portion of fast-twitch muscle fiber. Quickness was also McGill's greatest physical gift. But mastering Dark Alley required more than athleticism; it demanded a deep ruthlessness.

Which anyone who made it to the Oval Office, even McGill's dear wife, had in spades. Politics, though, for all its back stabbing, was a bloodless exercise. Dark Alley more often than not involved the spilling of actual corpuscles.

A primary point McGill was about to bring to the president's attention.

She stood across from him on a mat in the White House workout room. Three walls of mirrors bounced their reflections back at them. Both wore T-shirts, sweat pants and sneakers. The front of Patti's shirt bore the acronym POTUS. President of the United States. McGill's said: *Totus bonus*. Latin for "It's all good."

His only other clean T at the moment said: Eddie's Bar & Grill.

Now that he thought of it, Eddie's might have been the more apt choice.

McGill told his new student, "Dark Alley is serious stuff. The cover charge is often broken bones. The final tab might be death. You're not planning to assassinate anyone, are you?"

"Don't think so," the president said.

All right. That was as far as McGill would fish. But he did need some information.

"Well, what kind of mayhem are you looking for?"

Patti paused to formulate her needs, as if she hadn't thought it through.

Out of character for her.

Then she said, "I might need to give someone bigger than me a good jolt."

"How much bigger?" McGill asked. "Big as me?"

He was six-one, carrying one-eighty these days.

"In the neighborhood, yes."

A man most likely then, McGill decided, saying nothing.

"You want this jolt to leave the person standing or knock him down?" he asked.

"Why don't you show me both?"

McGill nodded. "You want to go for the throat? Cause a real scare?"

POTUS recoiled at the idea, horror written on her face.

"Maybe we'll save that for later," McGill said. "It's easy to go too far with that one."

Patti advanced to the spot from which she'd retreated.

"Jim, I will let you know what this is all about as soon as I can, okay?"

"Sure," he said. "Let's start with an old favorite called the foot-trap."

"One other thing," the president said, "I might have to use what you're going to teach me while there are cameras present and rolling. Whatever I do has to look like an accident."

The president's henchman nodded and took that into consideration.

Sunday Evening—Paris

5

Investigating Magistrate Yves Pruet sat on the large flower filled balcony of his apartment four floors above the Quai Anatole France quietly playing Variations from Beethoven's Seventh Symphony, Movement Number Two on his Alhambra classical guitar. It was a melancholy piece, and his playing captured perfectly both the composer's intent and his own mood. His fingers moved without conscious thought over the strings of the instrument that had been his near constant companion since his days at the Sorbonne.

Midway through the piece a large, menacing shadow fell across the tiles at Pruet's feet. He ignored it and kept playing.

"Yves, please," a deep voice said, "your virtuosity is unquestioned, but if you continue, I will begin to weep."

With a chuckle the magistrate stopped playing and looked over his shoulder. He saw his friend and police bodyguard, Odo Sacripant, a block of Corsican granite carved into eccentric planes of muscle by many a fight. Odo never wept at anything, except when his wife, Marie, presented him with another child.

"The time has come?" Pruet asked.

"As we both knew it must," Odo answered.

The magistrate placed his guitar in its stand and went to the balcony's railing. He looked out at the nearby Seine from his Left Bank vantage point. The current criticism of the Rive Gauche was that what was once the bastion of the city's artists had become the refuge of its bourgeoisie. The artists had been pushed across the river to less expensive enclaves.

Pruet took such critiques philosophically. He was still free to play his guitar here, express his art. And he appreciated his rising property value.

Odo said, "You are looking emaciated, Yves. You need to eat more."

Approaching fifty, Pruet had once been a bit plump, but now his rumpled sandy hair, smart blue eyes, and genial smile resided in and around a visage gone gaunt. His clothes hung loosely on his reduced frame.

He turned to look at Odo. "I have gone on the Alienated Wife Diet."

"Nicolette never cooked for you or anyone else," the bodyguard pointed out.

"True, but she dragged me to every expensive restaurant in Paris."

Odo took a seat at a glass-topped table.

"Whenever you are ready, *mon ami*."

Pruet reluctantly joined him at the table.

"The American is ready for you to examine," Odo said.

"There is no chance he will make things easier for me and die?"

Odo shook his head.

"Remind me of his name," Pruet said.

"Glen Kinnard from Chicago."

"And he came all the way to Paris to kill France's most celebrated football star."

"That was not his intent, he says."

"But it was the result," Pruet said. "That and to make us miserable."

"Such would seem to be our lot in life."

Pruet had become infamous for sending a former interior minister to prison. The man had been stealing government funds on a scale that couldn't be ignored. Everyone had expected the fellow to be sacked. To live out his life in disgrace in some remote outpost of French culture. But if that were allowed to happen it would have meant the thief would be allowed to take a goodly part of his booty with him and enjoy the life of a tropical potentate. Any claim that the man had been punished would have been a vile joke.

So Pruet had presented a case to the court so meticulously documented and so persuasively argued that the judge had no choice but to send the miscreant to prison for twenty years. A period likely to encapsulate the remainder of his life. Such a sentence was unprecedented in modern France. The high and the mighty were not supposed to face such harsh realities.

Once the precedent had been established, though, the thief's friends and colleagues at the top of the government and society came to fear Pruet. To loathe him. To plot his demise.

Now, he'd been presented with another disastrous case.

If his investigation were to result in this American, Glen Kinnard from Chicago, spending the remainder of his life in a French prison, that decision could very well rupture the warming relations between France and the United States.

If his investigation exculpated Kinnard, it wouldn't be only the *habitués* of the *haut monde* who would seek vengeance on Pruet. Every Frenchman who cheered for *les bleus*—the national football team—would come for him with blood in their eyes.

Pruet sighed and said, "My father wanted me to go into the family business."

"You are allergic to cheese. How could you spend your life making it?"

"I don't know," Pruet said. "But I should have tried harder."

Monday, June 1st — Washington, DC

1

The president was at her desk in the Oval Office by five a.m. She had more reading to do than a class of law school students cramming for final exams. Tomorrow, she and the circus that accompanied her everywhere she traveled would depart for the G8 summit in London. The president was routinely described as the most powerful person in the world, but the one thing she could never do was travel light. She required two highly modified Boeing 747-200Bs, known as SAM 28000 and SAM 29000, more commonly referred to as Air Force One whenever she was aboard one of them. A C-130 cargo aircraft would bring her personal helicopter, a VH60N WhiteHawk, Marine One when she was aboard, and two armored Cadillac limousines, previously called The Beasts, renamed by the president in a Seussian moment as Thing One and Thing Two.

That was just the hardware. The senior advisers, their support staff, the Secret Service contingent, the military personnel, the White House press corps, and special guests approached a number that a convention planner would have been hard put to deal with. In fact, the White House had its own travel planners. You didn't just throw together a trip for POTUS.

There was, of course, one other traveling companion for this president.

Her henchman.

Patti winced as she shifted her weight on the seat of her desk chair.

Jim had been gentle with her, showing her the Dark Alley techniques she'd asked to learn, but he had insisted she have at least some understanding of the pain she might inflict on others. Even so, Jim had stressed that knowing the damage she might do must not inhibit her from inflicting it if necessary. You did what you had to do, and reflexively, if your own precious hide was at risk.

He'd given her a wintry smile and said, "There are even times, harsh as it may sound, when you're pleased to know the price some jerk has paid for messing with you."

All in all, the president thought her husband's approach to the use of force was well considered for someone in her line of work.

With that in mind, Patti took out her personal iPhone, an instrument she'd insisted she had the right to retain, and placed a call to California, where it was still the middle of the night. She needed to talk with an old friend, a fellow former actress, who stayed up late. Her friend, the closest thing the president had to a sister, had accepted an appointment from the preceding administration as an honorary cultural ambassador to the UN. Her duties had taken her to countries around the world where her beautiful face and charming personality had made several friends for the United States. This was at a time when the occupant of the White House had been creating legions of the disaffected.

For the most part, the friend's efforts may well have created a wealth of good memories for her, but Patti had heard a rumor of one disturbing story that, if true, could have blighted the whole experience. News of the event had only a limited circulation as far as the president knew, and that was within the pinnacle of the acting community. It hadn't reached the Washington gossip mills at all. Not yet.

Patti's call was answered on the second ring, and the conversation began with a warmth usually reserved for family. It continued for the next fifteen minutes, spoken entirely in French.

Just as it was drawing to a close, there was a knock at the door.

The president, caught up in Francophony, said, "*Entrez.*"

2

Entrez?

The president was speaking French, Chief of Staff Galia Mindel wondered as she entered the Oval Office. She saw Patti was on her personal phone as she closed the door behind her. The president also had an open briefing book on her lap, one of the volumes provided to Patti that contained biographical information on the other heads of state with whom she'd be meeting at the G8 gathering in London.

Galia had been one of the people who had advocated that the president not use a personal phone, and the mere idea that Patti might have been sharing information from a presidential briefing book with someone outside the government—someone not approved of by Galia herself—it was all the chief of staff could do not to wince.

And why had the president been speaking in French?

Patti said, "*Au revoir,*" and ended her call.

Turning her attention to her chief of staff, she asked, "Everything well in hand for our departure tomorrow?"

The president closed the briefing book and put it and her iPhone in a desk drawer before Galia could see whose bio Patti had been reading.

"Yes, ma'am," Galia said, crossing the room to stand before the president. Patti nodded to a chair and the chief of staff sat. Reading Galia's expression was not a challenge.

"If all our ducks are in a row, why the frown?" the president asked.

Never one to be a shrinking violet, even when addressing the president, the chief of staff was having a hard time finding her voice. Or perhaps the right words.

"Galia, what is it?" the president wanted to know.

Despite the second prompt, it was all Galia could do just to meet the president's eye.

In a flash of intuition, Patti knew what was bothering her most senior adviser.

"Oh my God, Galia. Is this about me and Jean-Louis Severin?"

Monsieur Severin being the president of France. He'd been elected the year before Patricia Darden Grant had been sent to the White House by the American people. The two of them had spent a year together at Yale. More than that, they'd appeared together in a student-written production that ended with the two of them kissing.

They hadn't seen each other in all the years since, but *M'sieur le Président* had been the first foreign head of state to call and congratulate his old school chum on her election. In fact, he'd placed his call on Election Night before Patti had the electoral votes to put her over the top. Everyone in the Grant campaign was sure their candidate would win, but nobody dared to say so, not wanting to jinx things at the last minute. Jean-Louis Severin hadn't worried about such a trifling superstition. He knew his friend would win and wanted to be the first to say, "*Grèle au Chef.*" Hail to the Chief.

Galia hadn't wanted to let the call go through, but she knew she'd catch hell if she didn't. So the candidate renewed acquaintances with her old friend, speaking to him in French, shutting Galia out of the conversation. Not that it lasted long. But Galia detected a warmth in Patti's tone that she rarely heard outside of her speaking to James J. McGill or his children. When the conversation ended, Patti asked Galia, "Would you like to know what Jean-Louis said?"

"Of course not," Galia replied. "It was obviously a personal conversation."

"I don't intend to tell you everything, Galia. But Jean-Louis predicted Minnesota was going to fall our way and the networks would call the decision as soon as the polls closed."

Minnesota would put them over the top? But it was the incumbent's home state and hadn't voted for a Republican presidential candidate since 1972. Nonetheless, the prediction of the president of France was right on the money.

Always made Galia wonder if the man had gotten a bet down on Patti.

"Yes, Madam President," Galia said, answering the question at hand, "I'm afraid it is."

The president sighed and sat back in her chair.

"Well, people do like their fantasies," she said. "Like to project themselves into..."

Imagining they were one half of the fantasy couple, Galia understood.

Still, she said, "President Severin is recently divorced. You and he are old friends. You are both heads of state. You're going to meet in a historic city after a separation of many years."

Patti sighed. "Hollywood couldn't write a better scenario."

The chief of staff nodded. "A friend in the press gave me a confidential heads-up." Meaning the president shouldn't ask for a name. "Certain newspapers are going to give your relationship with President Severin bigger play than the G8 summit."

Without asking for the name of Galia's source, the president said, "Are we talking about the New York tabloids here?"

Galia said, "I'm sure they'll pick it up, but the English papers will take the lead."

The Fleet Street press. Scandal Central. Even when they had to fabricate one.

The president sat forward, a hard glint in her eyes.

"Well, then," she said, "it's a good thing we have our own little surprise planned. That should blow an imaginary romance right out of the news cycle."

Galia could only hope. And wonder if the president had been speaking to her old friend, *m'sieur le président.*

In French.

3

Margaret "Sweetie" Sweeney thought that the Catholic Church, if it had the least bit of smarts these days, would allow its congregants to select their own sabbaths. She almost never missed Mass at St. Al's on Sunday, but she appreciated it much more on Monday mornings when the gathering of worshipers could have fit into two pews, should they have cared to sit together. They didn't, of course. They staked out places of their own. It would have been rude for anyone who wasn't an intimate to encroach upon them.

Such a notion as personal sabbaths, of course, would be pounced on by critics as the most radical example of cafeteria Catholicism yet to come down the pike, but there were those members of the faithful, Sweetie among them, who worried that they would live to see the disappearance of the Roman Catholic Church in America, if the hierarchy didn't show some signs of flexibility.

Sweetie, from her spot near the rear of the church, could look at the handful of faithful who dotted the pews on Monday mornings and guess with fair accuracy who they were: workers choosing to spend a moment in the presence of the Divine before going to toil for Caesar; retirees, many of them present to pray for a departed spouse or more poignantly a child gone too soon; a few mavericks in faith like herself who preferred a one-to-one dialogue with the Almighty to being a bit player in a cast of thousands.

The moment the service ended with Father Agamah saying, "Go in peace," someone slipped into the pew directly behind Sweetie. Could have been a newcomer who didn't know Monday morning etiquette. But that wasn't the feeling Sweetie got. Her cop radar said the new arrival was there for a purpose: to talk with her.

Margaret Sweeney had been a cop for twenty years in Chicago, and another five in Winnetka, working both shops with Jim McGill. This wasn't the first time she'd met someone in a church, had someone slip into a pew behind her. Now, as before, her senses of smell and hearing did a scan of whom she was dealing with before she turned to look. A scent of perfume reached her, something subtle, a hint of jasmine. The creak of wood as the person sat was soft, indicating a slight weight. A woman most likely.

Giving off no tingle of hostile intent.

But Sweetie hadn't heard the woman approach.

Not until she was right there behind her.

Suggesting someone who knew how to move with stealth.

Sweetie sat tight until Father Agamah left the altar and the other communicants departed the church. She took it as a good sign that none of those leaving cast a dubious look at whoever was sitting behind her. Once the two of them were alone, Sweetie gave it a five-count before turning around.

The woman sitting behind her had a Eurasian face, mature but unlined; her clothes were stylish but not overdone for going to church.

"Help you with something?" Sweetie asked.

"Yes, I hope so," she said. "I am Musette Ky."

Sweetie knew the name. The woman was Deke Ky's mother.

She guessed why Ms. Ky had come to talk with her: to find the person who'd shot her son. The perp the Secret Service had been unable to find for the last six months. And counting.

Sweetie said, "I really can't get involved in an ongoing federal investigation."

Unperturbed, Musette Ky told her, "My son was not the target of those who shot him."

"He wasn't?" Sweetie asked. And how would Ms. Ky know that?

"I was the target," she said.

4

McGill liked to carry keys, enjoyed the feeling of unlocking a door. Nineteen months of living in the White House had all but deprived him of that pleasure. With the Secret Service and the Marine Corps guarding his place of residence, turning a deadbolt lock was not required. Having a personal driver, there was no need to carry a car key either. He had a single key to his office door, but a solitary key had no heft and didn't jingle. To feel fully dressed, he felt he should have keys jangling in his hip pocket. So he added the front door key to his house in Evanston and the key to the Honda Pilot he kept back home to his key chain.

As with many things in Washington, symbolism trumped substance.

When he got to work that morning he would meet with Sweetie and go over their accounts, receivable and payable, before he left for Europe. McGill Investigations, Inc. was operating in the black. The success he and Sweetie had had in finding and neutralizing Chana Lochlan's stalker had paid off. You did right by "the most fabulous face on television," and other people with the means and the need to hire a private investigator would beat a path to you door.

For the most part their clients' problems were mundane, an

example being the theft of a litigator's trial briefcase, a family heirloom that had conferred a talismanic confidence to three generations of legal practitioners. The suggested malefactor was the opposing counsel in the case at hand; the actual thief was the victim's second-chair colleague looking to move up at the firm.

It wasn't the stuff of song and legend, but it approximated police work and it brought in a steady stream of revenue to McGill and Sweetie, neither of whom was inclined to devolve into a sedentary way of life. Both were determined to stay sharp, mentally and physically.

McGill wasn't about to sit around the White House all day eating bonbons. But before he could leave the Executive Mansion that morning, the president's personal secretary, Edwina Byington, called him.

"The president would like to know if you can spare her a moment before you go to work this morning, Mr. McGill."

McGill said, "That might put me behind schedule, Edwina. May I borrow the president's helicopter to make up lost time?"

"I can't speak for the president or the Marine Corps, sir, but I'll be happy to give you a ride on the back of my Vespa."

McGill laughed.

Edwina was pushing seventy, but she did indeed ride a motor scooter to work when the weather permitted. Claimed she got better than 100 mpg. Her fuel economy would suffer if she had to lug McGill around with her.

"Maybe I'll just push my schedule back a little," he said. "How much of my time does the president require?"

"I have you penciled in for ten minutes, but I'll have to juggle things if you don't hurry."

"I'll be right down."

"You're a prince, Mr. McGill."

5

The prince, his wife told him in the Oval Office, would need formal wear for the Queen's soirée at Buckingham Palace. The president inquired if she had remembered to inform her husband of that necessity.

"You mean I have to wear a monkeysuit?" McGill asked.

"The invitation says white tie."

"The kind without a hand-painted hula dancer on it?"

"That's correct."

"I don't believe I have such an ensemble."

The president informed him, "We have your measurements, Mr. McGill."

"The CIA told you?" McGill asked.

"Hart Schaffner Marx," the president replied.

The company was going through reorganization, might not even survive, but they were the ones who had made the suit McGill had worn to his wedding with Patricia Darden Grant.

"Any changes in vital statistics, Mr. McGill?" the president asked.

"Not a millimeter," he said, patting a flat stomach.

"Very well. All you have to do then is commit and powerful forces will be set in motion."

"Gnomes working around the clock?"

"Fine American tailors."

McGill still had a few minutes of his allotted time left so he took a moment to examine his present circumstances.

"Our dinner with British royalty is going to be a fancy affair, you say."

"It's not asking too much of you, is it?"

He shook his head. "What I'm thinking is, these lordly people are hardly known for being spontaneous."

"Not in most circumstances, no."

"So something big must have happened. Perhaps something having an effect on our 'special relationship' with the Brits."

"The thought does occur."

McGill made a point of not intruding on presidential business, but if it required him to get dressed up and be in attendance, he couldn't help but be curious.

"Is there anything you'd care to share?" he'd asked.

"I think we'd better browse the etiquette book for dining with royalty."

Patti was playing coy again, McGill thought. First the Dark Alley, now this.

"Okay," McGill said. Finding out was half the fun.

"So you'll get dressed up and be my escort?" the president asked.

"I'll be there," McGill said.

Arlington, VA

6

"Ricky" Lanh Huu sat in his office, at the back of a storefront insurance agency in a small strip mall in Arlington, Virginia. It was a Monday and the first day of the month and Ricky was collecting money. He liked that the month was beginning on the first day of the workweek. Thought every month should start on a Monday. Be easier for him to keep track of things.

A girlfriend with a greater understanding of the calendar had once heard him express the idea and said it would require every month to be twenty-eight days long, which would also mean either adding a thirteenth month to the calendar with one day left over or keeping twelve months and having twenty-nine days left over at the end of the year.

Ricky thought twenty-nine days sounded like the right amount of vacation time for everyone to have. You could call it Happy Time. People could go crazy, just chill, or come up with new plans for making their fortunes. But nobody would have to do shit if they didn't want to.

"You think the bosses would go for that?" Ricky's girlfriend asked.

That'd be a problem, all right. Fuckin' bosses. Always grinding on everyone.

Ricky's personal taskmaster was Horatio Bao, Esquire. Bao had his law offices on 14th Street, a mile from where Ricky sat.

Bao didn't have any big name clients, but he had his thumb in most of the legitimate pies of the Viet Kieu—the Vietnamese diaspora—community in Northern Virginia. And he took a cut of every crooked game run by his ethnic kinsmen.

Ricky was Bao's bagman, his enforcer, and his recruiter for any new Viet Kieu business that opened in Bao's fiefdom. Sooner rather than later every small storefront enterprise joined the Homeland Benevolent Association. The HBA helped merchants with their bookkeeping: so much for themselves, a bit less for the association, and a plausible minimum for the taxman. The HBA also helped with insurance: business, life, health, and security. Security insurance came with a window sticker: *Protected by HBA*. No member of the Viet Kieu underworld would dare steal from an HBA-protected business. On the other hand, any proprietor foolish enough to resist Ricky's pitch was soon faced with a relentless onslaught of burglaries and stickups. If the recalcitrant fool survived commercially—or physically—he quickly came to see the light.

But HBA security extended beyond mere ethnocentric depredation. If outsiders—Italians, blacks or Latins—tried to lean on protected merchants, they were quickly set upon and sent away. If a rival thug persisted, he was sliced, diced, and served with rice to those who had sent him. Premium service for fair price was Horatio Bao's hallmark.

He also highly prized innovation.

When the *danh tu*—white Americans—grew angry at the never-ending wave of illegal immigrants flooding the country, Bao sensed it was time for new measures. He'd long been involved in smuggling his countrymen into the United States, but now it was important that the people he brought in had legitimate standing. Proper documentation. But how best to get the right papers? He consulted with his most prized adviser.

The sage, for an enormous consideration, came up with just the right answer: political persecution. That was always the ticket for legitimate admission to the United States. But how could such a claim be irrefutably proven? With a letter of condemnation and an arrest warrant issued by the Public Security Department in Hanoi, Bao's adviser told him.

The apparatchiks who maintained the Communist's grip on power in the Homeland would understandably be loath to cooperate. Issuing false documents would place their jobs and even their lives at risk. Fortunately, Bao's adviser knew those among them whose greed would overwhelm their better judgment, and a plan was devised whereby all parties prospered.

Bao was pleased with his immigration scam, assured once again there were always new ways to make money. Cash money. Disguised and dispersed around the world.

After Ricky collected Bao's local haul, his most important job was to discreetly channel the HBA money to Bao's daughter, Calanthe. She was the travel agent for her father's money, sending it on its way around the globe to foreign numbered accounts. Ricky had been at his job for five years. Underpaid, in his view, for five years. But he'd never been tempted to filch a single dollar. Bao had told him what would happen to him should he ever prove untrustworthy. Ricky wasn't afraid of much, but what Bao had said would be done to him had kept thoughts of pilferage far from his mind.

Until six months ago.

Until he'd failed to make that hit for his boss.

Of late, he'd come to feel his career had plateaued.

It might even be necessary to make a run for it soon.

Which would be a lot easier with a pile of cash to call his own.

Georgetown

7

Leo Levy drove McGill to his office on P Street just above the Rock Creek Parkway. Per the president's explicit order, Leo got out of the armored, supercharged Chevy first, took a good look around, a hand under his suit coat and on the Beretta he carried.

The building's owner, McGill's landlord, Dikki Missirian,

was out front sweeping the sidewalk. He saw Leo and said, "Good morning, my friend."

"Mornin', Dikki," Leo said in his native North Carolina twang. "Any ne'er-do-wells lurkin' in the shrubbery?"

"Not that I noticed."

The near side rear window on the Chevy slid down.

"Can I come out and play now?" McGill asked.

The president hadn't given him any orders, but she knew other means of persuasion. McGill was well aware there were crazies in the world who might enjoy doing him harm. What he doubted was that on any given day many of them would work up the energy to take a crack at him.

Then, again, it only took one.

Look at what had happened to poor Andy Grant, the president's late first husband. He'd been threatened and later killed by extremists in a vain attempt to coerce Patti to cast a vote—as a then-Member of the House of Representatives—for a piece of legislation they wanted passed.

At that time, as the chief of police in Winnetka, McGill had been the one urging caution. He would look pretty damn foolish now if he got zapped by being careless. Patti had told him she didn't want to bury another husband. His kids needed a father, too. So he waited for the all clear. Wishing Deke were back.

"Looks good, boss," Leo said.

"You do have someone waiting for you," Dikki told McGill as he exited the car. "A young lady. I gave her coffee in my office."

"She tell you her name?" McGill asked.

"Emilie LaBelle."

8

"Pardon the cliché," McGill said, "but haven't we met?"

Emilie LaBelle sat in a guest chair in McGill's office. On the way in, he'd seen that Sweetie hadn't arrived, and she was usually early to work. Sweetie was also someone who won perfect attendance awards. Something was up.

Question was what? But with a possible client on hand the question was tabled.

Emilie LaBelle looked to be in her mid-twenties, a slender young woman with dark hair cut short, brown eyes, a pert nose, and full lips that framed a smile any orthodontist would love to claim as his handiwork. But McGill seemed to remember her at a more tender age with longer hair ... and eyeglasses.

"Ten years ago," Emilie said, "at the wake for Tom Willets and Ozzie Kent."

There was no way McGill would ever forget that night. Two Chicago cops, Willets and Kent, had been ambushed by gang-bangers outside a public housing high-rise. They were acting on a tip passed to Officer Kent that a drug dealer, a fugitive wanted on a homicide warrant, was hiding out in the building.

Officer Kent had been shot and killed as he attempted to enter the building. Officer Willets had still been in his patrol unit calling for backup when Kent was shot. Hearing the gunfire and seeing his partner fall, Officer Willets ran to his aid but was cut down before he covered half the distance to the building.

The drug dealer and four other gangbangers were later killed in a shootout with the police. The dealer's girlfriend told authorities the criminal was trying to turn the tables on the police. Cops were always playing tricks to sucker fugitives into their traps, saying the chumps had won tickets to a big football game or something. So the drug dealer figured if he set up stings on the cops a few times, took down four or five of them, they wouldn't be in such a hurry to come after him.

"Dint work out like that at all," the girlfriend said with a shrug.

The funeral arrangements for the two slain officers almost came to grief as well. The widows had agreed to an ill-considered departmental suggestion to hold the wakes for both men at the same funeral home. The dead cops were both African-American so there was no problem of skin color. But there was a good deal of heated debate between the friends and families of the two cops as to which of them was to blame for their deaths.

Ozzie Kent had been a hard charger, openly ambitious for promotion and plain clothes assignments. Tom Willets' first instinct had been to use his head, think things through, and never go off halfcocked. Kent's friends blamed Willets for not having his partner's back. Willets' friends accused Kent of getting fatally ahead of the situation by not waiting for backup.

Charges of cowardice and stupidity were exchanged by two camps of armed and angry men and women. Then McGill shouted, "Hey!" And everyone took note of the two horrified widows. That problem was resolved when Glen Kinnard said, "Let's take this outside."

Bloodshed in the parking lot of Mooney's Funeral Home would have been inevitable if two cooler heads, McGill and Kinnard, had not prevailed. McGill corralled the Willets backers. Kinnard, brought his reputation as a head breaker to bear and intimidated the Kent side before it could get out of control.

Then the two peacemakers turned to regard each other.

Not a bit of love was lost between them.

Captain McGill told Sergeant Kinnard, "Take your people inside. You can have thirty minutes, and none of us will speak ill of either of our fallen comrades in front of their families."

Kinnard nodded, started to lead his people back into Mooney's, then he stopped. He belatedly remembered to give his superior officer a salute. It was right after that McGill saw a young girl standing in the doorway to the funeral home. She'd seen the whole fracas. But after meeting McGill's eyes, she ducked back inside, not holding the door for the approaching Glen Kinnard and his people.

Looking at that young girl all grown up now, McGill asked, "Are you Sergeant Kinnard's daughter?"

Emilie nodded.

"How's he doing?" McGill asked.

Emilie said, "Not so good. He killed a man in Paris."

"Paris, Illinois?"

The young woman shook her head. "France."

That was when McGill remembered hearing Kinnard's wife

had been born in France—and his daughter, Ms. LaBelle, must have taken her mother's name.

"Was your mother with your father when this happened?"

Emilie's face turned sad. "In a manner of speaking. Dad took Mom's ashes home."

McGill sighed. "I'm sorry, Emilie."

"Me, too. Thing is, Dad said the guy he killed was attacking a woman, and the French have a law that says you can't just stand by and let something like that happen."

"Really?"

Emilie nodded.

"He didn't shoot the guy, did he?"

McGill knew Europeans had a whole different attitude about handguns.

"No," Emilie said. "It was a fist fight ... though Dad said the other guy mostly kicked him."

McGill could only imagine what a bloody brawl a fight to the death must have been.

But what he didn't understand was how a charge could have been brought against Kinnard.

"I'm not sure I understand the problem," he said. "If your father was obligated to intervene, he did what was required of him, even if it went badly. Where's his legal jeopardy?"

"There are two problems," Emilie explained. "The guy Dad killed was some kind of sports star, a real big deal over there. And the woman Dad said the guy was beating, she disappeared."

Two *big* problems, McGill thought.

Kinnard clearly needed help ... and Paris wasn't very far from London.

Where, as far as he knew, White House minions would have him touring museums and glad-handing locals while Patti was doing her thing.

He wouldn't mind blowing all that off.

Thing was, though, he had never really liked Glen Kinnard.

He'd almost been involved in a fight with the guy himself.

"I hate to ask this, Emilie, but my business partner would

get on me if I don't."

"You mean money? Dad says he'll pay whatever it takes."

"He asked for me?"

"No, he just wanted an investigator. You were my suggestion. I remembered you from that night at Mooney's, and I read about what you did for Chana Lochlan. I had to persuade Dad you'd be the right choice, but it wasn't too tough a sell."

McGill thought about the situation for a moment and then came right out and asked, "Your dad still a sonofabitch?"

Emilie didn't take offense. She smiled, looked just a bit proud.

"Not nearly as bad as he used to be," she said.

Arlington, VA

9

Secret Service Special Agent Donald "Deke" Ky tried for a third pushup. The first rep had almost killed him. The second one left him bathed in sweat. The third one was making every muscle in his body twitch, like someone was passing an electric current through him. Which was far from the worst pain he'd experienced over the past six months.

When Deke had been shot last Thanksgiving night, a .223 round had passed through the right side of his chest. The result was what the docs had called a high velocity penetrating chest trauma. At the points of entry and exit he had suffered fractured ribs, but, lucky for him, the scapula hadn't been hit. The pectoral and infraspinatus muscles had been punctured. Hemopneumothorax—the presence of blood and air in the pleural cavity—followed. Deke had also been fortunate that the shooter had fired from short range. The round hadn't had the chance to start tumbling, which would have created a much larger area of damage.

His biggest break was the fucker with the rifle hadn't placed the round a couple inches to the left where his heart lay beating. He would have been dead before ... before his mother had caught him. She never did let him hit the floor. As he felt the world slipping away, he'd been aware that she grabbed him under his arms, eased him down, and cradled his head on her lap. Then with an intimacy he hoped never to experience again, she stuck a finger into the wound in his chest and pressed her palm against the exit wound in his back.

Sliding down into a deep black hole, he'd heard his cousin, Francis, the other guest at dinner, speak from what seemed a great distance. First, he called 911, demanding an ambulance. Then, with Francis's voice growing ever more faint, Deke heard his cousin begin praying for him, in English, Latin, and Vietnamese. God must have been listening in on at least one of those channels because they told him the ambulance got there in a hurry. He was on his way to the hospital with the driver going for a new land speed record once his mother told the crew he was the Secret Service agent who guarded the president's henchman. She said she never left his side until they took him into surgery.

His chest was drained, he was transfused, flooded with antibiotics and sewn back together. His bones knitted and his muscles mended. He tried to do his physical therapy with his usual discipline. But his will, which had never failed him before, was lacking.

That was when he got lucky again. His father came to visit from South Carolina, where he lived with his family and worked as an undersheriff in Charleston County. Talbert Perkins never really had a relationship with Musette Ky, not beyond saving her from a couple of drunk GIs who stumbled out of a Saigon bar as she was hurrying past. The grunts mistook Musette for a bar girl, started flashing scrip her way and making grabs at her. Tal had intervened and being bigger than the other two boys combined they didn't argue with him.

As politely as he knew how, he'd said to Musette, "If you'll allow, ma'am, I'll walk you where you're goin'. See no one else troubles you."

He hadn't known if she even spoke English, but he figured

everyone understood good manners. She smiled at him, and if that had been as far as it went he'd have been happy. But she did speak English, had understood every word he'd said.

"Thank you, sir. You may walk with me."

That was when Tal saw Musette wasn't full-on Asian. Not with those blue eyes. She had white blood in her, and her English had an accent that wasn't Vietnamese.

He smiled back, was tempted to offer his arm to her, but didn't.

They just walked along, Tal feeling like the shy boy who couldn't believe the pretty girl was letting him walk her home from school. Only they didn't go to a private home. Musette stopped in front of the Rex Hotel, a billet for U.S. military personnel with pay-grades far above Tal's. That was when he noticed how *nicely* Musette was dressed. Her *ao di* hadn't been paid for by any grunt humpin' the boonies like him.

He took a step back, as if he had finally realized he wasn't good enough for her. The frown that clouded her pretty face made him think he was right. She was going to turn on her heel and scoot. But then she grabbed his hand and led him into the hotel.

Taking him upstairs, she said quietly, "I have a very important meeting but not for an hour. Without your help I might not have made it at all."

That was her only explanation. She opened the door to a room and there was a bed. A ceiling fan was on, turning slowly. With her back to him, she started to undress. He'd never known anything like it, a woman he'd just met undressing for him—and he was engaged to a real sweet girl back home.

Looking over her now bare shoulder, Musette said, "Close the door."

He did. Locked it, too.

What he told himself, he'd been feeling real scared lately. The war was all but over, and the good guys weren't gonna win this one. Worse than that, Tal had a dread he couldn't repress that he was gonna be the last American fool to die in Vietnam.

Wasn't a bad rationalization for taking up a beautiful woman's offer.

But if it hadn't been that it would have been something else.

From their one time together, a period of less than an hour, they created a child. Not that Tal knew about his son until Deke was three years old and living in the United States. He received a photo and a letter at work. Would have been awkward explaining things to Dorothy Mills, his fiancée, except she had Dear Johned him before he got home. He was married to Eleanor Hanks Perkins now and he told her his war story. Being a wise woman, Eleanor told him to do right by his boy, but stay away from that woman.

So Tal wrote his son from the time he was little, including pictures of himself, but not his family. He always put five dollars in with the letters, ten when Deke got older, and had $11,000 saved for him by the time he was ready to go to college.

When Tal showed up at Deke's hospital room, it was only the fourth time father and son had met in person. Deke told his father about his continuing listlessness, and Tal had a question.

"These doctors a yours, they know much about gunshot wounds?"

"They put me back together pretty well, but they look like they just got out of junior high."

"You ever hear of plumbism, Donald?"

His father always used Deke's Christian name.

Deke said plumbism was a new one to him.

"It's doctor talk for lead poisoning. You got hit with a brass jacketed round, but the bullet's core is lead. Smacking into all those ribs a yours, that .223 mighta left fragments of lead behind. Get the doctors to give you a real good scan, see if they can find anything. Because if you got lead inside you, son, it can cause all sorts a trouble."

Including neurological deterioration, the doctors told him after they found and removed the fragments. Might even have killed him if they had been left in place. Deke was so relieved to be truly on the mend he didn't sue the doctors and hospital as his mother wanted him to do. He did accept a quarter-million dollar settlement, though, and sent half the money to his father. A college fund for future generations of the Perkins family.

With a grunt and the determination that no amount of pain would stop him, he began a fourth pushup.

Georgetown

10

When Sweetie showed up at the office and took a seat in one of McGill's visitor chairs, he told her they had a new client.

She said, "When it rains it pours."

"You, too?" he asked.

She nodded. "Not to take the shine off your news, but I think mine is about the biggest case we could get. I'm not even sure we can take it."

"Why not?"

"Might put us in bad with the feds."

McGill sat back in his chair and cracked a smile.

"I'm pretty well connected these days, remember?"

"Still. I'm not saying we, personally, are going to get spanked, not with Patti behind us, but it might make things awkward even for her."

McGill made a beckoning gesture with his right hand: Give.

"Deke's mother came to see me at St. Al's this morning, right after Mass finished. She said the reason the Secret Service can't get anywhere with finding Deke's assailant is because he wasn't the target … she was."

McGill sat forward. "Someone wanted to shoot Deke's *mother?* Why?"

"Just what I wanted to know. Ms. Ky said a man she knows wanted to involve her in the commission of a crime, but she refused to participate. Her refusal came after certain details of the crime had been shared with her. Knowing those details without becoming a participant in the crime made her a danger to the man.

"She also said that ninety-nine times out of a hundred, she answers her own front door. It's a hostess thing with her. Last Thanksgiving, she was just coming out of the powder room when Deke opened the door. She'd been in a hurry to get it herself because she'd heard the doorbell ring. Instead, she got to see her son get shot."

McGill took a moment to absorb all that.

Then he said, "You don't know the man's name or the nature of the crime because she didn't tell you."

"She didn't tell me, she said, because I couldn't say for sure we'd take the case."

"Without specifics," McGill said, "you don't have much to take to the cops."

"Or the feds," Sweetie said. "As it was, she asked me for a promise of confidentiality. I said okay."

"What do we know about Deke's mother?" McGill asked.

"Her name is Musette Ky. She emigrated from Vietnam not long after the fall of Saigon. She's a single mom, a successful businesswoman, owns catering, floral, and interior design shops in Northern Virginia."

"Any of those occupations seem shady to you?" McGill asked.

"Coke smugglers, at one time, used roses for a cover."

McGill remembered that. But drug runners didn't recycle old gags. It almost seemed half the fun for them was figuring out ingenious new ways to slip their products past the cops.

"I don't see it," he said. "Are any of Ms. Ky's businesses big enough to launder money for someone?"

"I never asked Deke, but the impression I got is they aren't. My feeling is, Deke's mom made good on a scale of personal affluence. Not a big money way."

"So why would someone come to her about playing a role in a crime?"

Sweetie shrugged. "Only way to find out is to commit to taking the job, but even then I think Ms. Ky is going to tell us only so much."

McGill considered the matter. Reluctant informants inevitably held back information that implicated them in some criminal act. Taking part in a crime, not just hearing about a plan and saying no thank you. He wondered exactly what Musette Ky was up to.

"You think she told you the truth?" he asked Sweetie.

She took a check from Deke's mother out of a pocket and slid it across the desk. It was made out to McGill Investigations, Inc. in the amount of $10,000.

"She's putting up a good front anyway," Sweetie said. "If we accept the job and need more money, she's willing to spend whatever it will take. If we decide not to help her, she trusts us to tear up her check."

McGill stared at the check, mulled the situation further. Musette Ky had a clear, confident signature. The upward stroke of the "y" in her last name looked like a rocket blasting off.

He said, "One thing Deke told me about his mom right after he started guarding me, she said he had to be prepared to give his life for me."

"Your point being?" Sweetie asked.

"Two points. What kind of caterer, florist or interior designer would cop an attitude like that? The other point is I don't think Ms. Ky would work productively with Celsus."

"A third point is we'd both like to catch whoever shot Deke."

"Yeah. I think we can take this case. We'd be working for a private citizen. Trying to keep her safe. If we happen to close a case for the Secret Service at the same time, good on us. If there's any heat from Celsus, I'll take it."

Sweetie smiled, as if McGill's decision was what she'd expected to hear all along.

"Ms. Ky will also bear watching here, Margaret," McGill said.

"I know," Sweetie told him. "So what's your case?"

11

"Paris," Sweetie said after hearing the story of McGill's meeting with Emilie LaBelle. "You think that might make for some jurisdictional hassles?"

"You mean you don't think I can just check in with the local coppers and go about my business?"

Sweetie laughed. "If you were an ordinary gumshoe, they'd give you the bum's rush. Maybe shanghai you into the Foreign Legion. Being Patti's husband, they'll probably let you see the sights before sending you home."

"I can be charming," McGill said.

"You can carry a tune, too," Sweetie acknowledged.

"I travel on a diplomatic passport these days."

"And you got gold stars on your report card at St. Andrew's."

"Your confidence is overwhelming," McGill said.

Sweetie put things in perspective. "Imagine a French private eye arriving in Chicago, trying to clear another French guy who had killed a Bears' superstar. You think that would go over big? Guy'd be lucky if the board of the Lyric Opera didn't do him in."

Thinking of the case in those terms did make it seem more daunting.

"Yeah, but that's Chicago," McGill said. "Don't you think the French are more...suave?"

Sweetie said, "They probably dress better, too, but I don't think that's going to make a lot of difference."

McGill shrugged. "Then there's only one thing to do. I'll have Patti put the fix in for me."

"And why would she do that?"

"I just did one favor for her and agreed to do another."

He told Sweetie about showing Patti some Dark Alley moves and agreeing to escort her to the Queen's soirée at Buckingham Palace.

"The Queen of England?" Sweetie asked, wanting to be sure.

"That's the one," McGill said.

Sweetie shook her head in disbelief.

"I know," McGill said. "The places old Chicago coppers get to go these days."

"So we're going to work both cases," Sweetie said.

"Yeah. Let Ms. Ky know you're on board, but wait until I'm out of the country to start working the case. It'll be less conspicuous that way. You can use Leo to drive you, if you want. We'll stay in touch by phone."

Sweetie asked, "You're already packed?"

McGill's answer was another excursion into the surreal.

He said, "My butler takes care of that."

The White House

12

The president's secretary, Edwina Byington, buzzed Patti the moment Galia left.

"I'm sorry to disturb you, Madam President, but SAC Crogher is here with me and he'd like to know if you might spare him a minute. On a personal matter, he says."

"Do I have the time, Edwina?"

"You do, ma'am, if you see him now and he doesn't have too much to say ... He says he doesn't."

"Send him in," the president said.

She watched the door to the Oval Office open and the chief of her security detail enter. A personal matter, Edwina had said. That caught her off guard. It had never occurred to her Celsus might have a personal life.

She gestured to a guest chair.

"Please have a seat, Celsus," she said.

She'd have left him standing if it had been a business call. He looked as if he'd have been more at ease on his feet, too, but he did as he was bid.

"What can I do for you?" Patti asked.

"Madam President, I have the greatest respect for you."

"Thank you, Celsus."

"I didn't vote for you, but I might next time."

The president repressed a smile.

"Then I'm making progress," she said.

Crogher nodded. "Even so, ma'am, I'd like to request a transfer."

This time Patti was caught unaware on a couple of levels. Heading the president's personal security detail was the crown jewel of a Secret Service career. Being the director just meant you were the top bureaucrat. So why would Celsus want to ... Well, really, she knew why. But she hadn't seen it coming. The other surprise was that by approaching her directly with his request Celsus had gone over the director's head. She would have thought SAC Crogher to be a chain-of-command man.

But maybe cutting a corner was Jim's influence, too.

"Would you care to elaborate, Celsus?" she asked.

It looked as if he wouldn't, but the SAC wasn't yet to the point of denying a direct request from the president.

Crogher said it had been more than six months since Holmes—James J. McGill's Secret Service code name—had any Secret Service protection. "I find that—"

"Unacceptable?" the president said.

"Impossible to deal with. There is no modern precedent. There's no procedure for it. There's no workaround."

The SAC pressed his lips together before he started to sputter.

But Patti could see the pressure inside him was continuing to build.

She had no answer for the man, except distraction.

"How are you doing at keeping me safe?" the president asked.

For the first time since she had met the SAC, Patti saw surprise in his eyes.

"Madam President, only an act of God will keep you from completing your term, and if He gets cranky, I'll take the lightning bolt."

This time Patti let the SAC see her smile.

But she softly said, "You would if you were still here, Celsus."

Before he could reply, she added, "You're not planning to let me go to London without you, are you?"

"No, ma'am."

"Good. Well, here are two questions you'll have to answer before I can approve your request to be transferred: Who else can I count on to take a lightning bolt for me, and who can find a workaround for that enigma Holmes?"

Sensing he'd been dismissed, Crogher got to his feet.

But the president had one last question for him.

"What was the personal aspect of all this, Celsus?"

"Telling you I'm thinking of voting for you."

"Yes, of course. I should have seen that."

"There's one other thing, ma'am."

"Yes?"

"I'm starting to do something I never let myself have time for before."

"What's that?"

"As regards Holmes, I'm starting to worry."

Georgetown

13

McGill put a call through to the White House from his office. In keeping with his hands-off politics and policy stance, he knew only a few direct phone numbers, but he could reach all of the people who mattered to him, starting with the president and working his way down to...

"Captain Welborn Yates, United States Air Force, Office of Special Investigations, detailed to the White House."

"That's quite a mouthful, Welborn, just to say hello."

There was a pause, and then the youthful voice with the South Carolina drawl asked, "Mr. McGill?"

"The same. I forgot to ask the president, but you're not traveling abroad with her, are you?"

"No, sir, I'm staying in Washington."

"You have enough to keep you busy?"

They both knew Welborn had become the president's personal—official—investigator. Personnel serving with the Air Force OSI were duly sworn federal agents. Just like the FBI, the DEA or other assorted feds. What distinguished Welborn was that if in the crush of events the president forgot to throw some work his way, he was left with too much time on his hands.

"I do have my wedding coming up," he said.

"How much fun can you have picking out floral arrangements?" McGill asked.

"Not a lot," Welborn admitted.

"How would you like to help Margaret Sweeney with something more substantial?"

Given that he reported directly to the commander in chief and had yet to see his twenty-fifth birthday, Welborn was understandably hesitant about the idea of moonlighting.

"I'm pretty sure I'd need permission to do that, sir, but I can't rightly say who should ask for it, me or you."

Celsus Crogher wasn't the only one for whom McGill caused procedural problems.

"I'll do the asking," he said. "What I'd like to know is whether you're available and interested?"

"I do have the free time, sir." He was going crazy, in fact, trying to find something useful to do, something that would legitimately excuse him from any more wedding planning. Welborn suspected that the invasion of Normandy had been a less complex exercise than what Kira had in mind for their nuptials. "This case with Ms. Sweeney, sir, it's something that would reflect well on someone with my position in the White House?"

Welborn's first case had involved an allegation of adultery in the military.

McGill said, "I think both you and the president would be pleased by a successful outcome."

There was a moment of silence and McGill could almost hear the young officer thinking. If the president was going to take notice of the case, it had to be something important. If it was something important and it involved McGill, chances were it...

"You can probably guess what the focus of the investigation is, Welborn. I'm sure the president will, too, when I ask her to let me borrow you for a week or two. But she'll be smart enough not to ask me directly. At this point, I think it would be best if you didn't either."

"Yes, sir."

"So you're in?"

"Just as soon as I get the go-ahead from the president, sir."

"Good. One more thing. The next time we talk, see if you can manage to call me Jim."

"Yes, sir. The next time."

Edwards Air Force Base

14

McGill thought it would be in keeping with the creature comforts of Air Force One if you boarded the 747-200B via an escalator instead of a flight of stairs. Of course, the American people expected to see that their leader possessed the physical vigor to climb and descend a stairway equal in height to a three-story building. In the event the electorate ever chose another wheelchair-bound giant like FDR, or a guest of the president rolled instead of walked, a ramp with a switchback was available. Neither member of the First Couple had any trouble making their way to the top, but McGill walked a half-step behind the president in case she put a foot wrong and needed catching. At the platform outside the doorway to the plane, he stayed at her side, being watchful and feeling just a bit like Celsus Crogher, as the president waved goodbye. He then let his wife enter her aircraft first, literally having her back.

McGill went to the president's private suite while Patti convened a meeting with cabinet members and other such dignitaries who were essential to the success of the trip to London. By the time the president made her way to the First Couple's private quarters, her henchman had his feet up, a beer in hand,

and was engrossed in a ninth inning drama between his beloved White Sox and the accursed Yankees. The Sox had been cellar dwellers the year before but their new manager, Robin Ventura, had the team scrapping hard in every game and they led the AL Central by two games going into New York for a three-game series. The score was tied at four with the bases loaded and two out in the top of the ninth. The batter was the wonderfully named rookie right fielder, Bobby Bang. The count was two and two. McGill knew that most of his fellow Pale Hose fans were screaming for a grand slam; the kid had the power for it.

Ever the contrarian, McGill whispered to the screen, "Lay one down, kid."

A dangerous strategy with two strikes on the batter; foul off the pitch and you were out. But what better time to catch New York flatfooted?

The batter stepped out of the box, making sure he had the signals from the third base coach right. That was when McGill saw he had company. Patti had slipped into the compartment without disturbing him. He gestured to the seat next to him, handed her his beer when she sat. Bobby Bang stepped back into the batter's box. A close shot of the batter's face showed a look of fierce determination, and McGill knew what was coming.

"Watch this," he told his wife. "This is going to be good."

She nodded, took a swig from the bottle and returned it.

The pitcher gazed down from the mound, another portrait of grit and intensity. He threw a sinker that was clocked at 98 miles per hour. Bobby Bang looked like he was running away from the plate before the ball ever arrived. But at the last instant he flicked out his bat and pushed the ball toward third base just inside the foul line. The runner on third, having left with the pitch had to skip over the ball and then dived for home. The Yankees catcher jumped over the runner, knowing he had no chance to get the man at home. He picked up the ball and fired it to first. He would have been a step too late even if the throw had been on the mark, but it sailed high, bounced off the wall separating the field from the box seats and ricocheted into right field.

Three runs scored. Sox up 7-4.

"Yes!" McGill said.

"That was exciting," Patti agreed with a smile.

McGill kissed her and turned the TV off.

"Aren't you going to watch the rest of the game?" she asked.

"Don't you need to get some sleep?" McGill asked.

"I do."

"So the choice is watching baseball or going to bed with you."

"Not a close call?"

Now McGill smiled. He stood and extended a hand.

Patti took it, stood and put her arms around McGill's waist.

He glanced at a Flight in Progress screen. They were cruising above Nuuk. He'd never heard of the place. But he recognized the shape of the map on which Nuuk appeared.

"I've never made love flying over Greenland before," he told his wife.

Over Greenland

15

Patti snuggled against McGill, their bodies still warm from their exertions. The president was on the edge of sleep, looking at McGill through slitted eyelids, saw his head reclining against a couple of pillows, his eyes open but looking at nothing in particular.

"What are you thinking?" Patti asked.

McGill said, "It'll keep. Get your rest."

The president sighed, pushed herself up on an elbow.

"You know me better than that. Talk to me or I won't get any sleep."

McGill pulled his wife close. She rested her head on his chest.

"I need a couple of favors," McGill said.

"And you didn't want me to think you made love to me just to get them."

McGill chuckled. "Foolish, I know."

"So what do you want, sailor?"

"I'd like to borrow Welborn for a week or two. Have him help Sweetie with a case."

Patti was quiet for a moment. McGill kept his breathing even to maintain a steady heartbeat. He was sure Patti was figuring out what he was up to but he didn't want her to think there would be anything risky about it. With her ear to his chest, he wanted her to hear a measured thump-thump to reassure her.

"Okay," the president said, "I'll make the call when we get up. Have Welborn take the time as a leave from official duty."

"Thank you," McGill said.

"What else? You said a couple favors."

"I got a new case this morning. Daughter of a copper I knew in Chicago wants me to clear her dad's name."

"Of what?"

"He killed a guy."

"Oh, my. Was there any justification?"

"He said he was defending a woman who was being attacked."

"That's a pretty good start on justification."

"The woman took off, hasn't been seen since the night in question."

Patti sighed. "Never easy, is it? So you need to find the woman."

"I do."

"You'll be flying back to Chicago while Sweetie's working her case in DC?"

"This is where the second favor comes in. Glen Kinnard lost his wife shortly before the trouble started. In fact, he was carrying her ashes in an urn when the fight began. He had intended to scatter them in the Seine."

Patti sat up, her eyes now opened as wide as McGill's.

"You're going to do an investigation in Paris?"

"Yeah. You think you can fix that with the French?"

The president lay back on her pillows. Thought a moment.

"Sure, I can," she said.

Tuesday, June 2nd — Approaching the United Kingdom

1

McGill was alone when he awoke. He shaved and took a shower, dressed in a freshly pressed suit for the president's arrival in the United Kingdom. An Air Force steward brought him a breakfast of two eggs over easy, two strips of crisp bacon, and a glass of orange juice, not from concentrate. A laptop computer was up and running, featuring the sports section of the *Chicago Tribune* online.

The White Sox had held on to beat the Yankees.

It would be tough to go back to flying commercial, McGill thought.

He ate carefully, didn't get a dab of yolk or a crumb of bacon on his suit.

The president joined McGill, just as he finished his breakfast and dabbed at his mouth with a linen napkin. She was dressed even more stylishly than he: a charcoal gray jacket and knee length skirt, the gray softened by a French vanilla blouse. Her shoes matched her suit. McGill judged the heels to be no more than two inches, stylish but not impractical.

There were those who thought that President Patricia Darden Grant should emulate the fashion of her recent predecessors and wear an American flag pin on her lapel. One curmudgeon of the right went so far as to ask at a press conference why she wasn't wearing the sacred accessory. Looking him in the eye, the president gave him a deadpan response.

"I don't need to wear a pin because I have a flag tattoo just above my heart."

The room became so quiet everyone could hear the questioner's jaw drop.

No one had asked to see the tattoo. Yet.

To maintain confidentiality, McGill had passed the word he'd break the nose of anyone who asked him to confirm the president's claim.

An Air Force steward came in and cleared away the breakfast dishes.

Patti sat next to her husband and said, "Buckle up. We're going to be landing soon."

A moment later, the first officer confirmed the fact over the public address system.

"You got the jump on everyone else again," McGill said, fastening his seat belt.

"I also have possession of a fact you neglected to share with me."

"What might that be?"

"Your friend Glen Kinnard—"

"He's not really a friend."

"Your client, then. He killed France's preeminent sports star, Thierry Duchamp."

"I didn't want you to toss and turn," McGill said.

She gave him a look, but then kissed his cheek.

"I would have, thank you. But you will have to tread lightly in Paris."

"I brought rubber soled shoes."

"Jim, please, I'm being serious."

"I'll be good," he promised.

"You didn't bring your handgun, did you?"

He shook his head. The president took that as a sign of good judgment.

"The Elysee Palace insists you'll have to coordinate your efforts with those of the investigating magistrate in the case."

"Do you know who that is?" McGill asked.

"His name is Yves Pruet."

"A good man? Fair and honest?"

The president considered how to respond.

"Honest to a fault," Patti finally said.

"How can honesty be faulted?" McGill asked.

"When it becomes politically inconvenient."

"Oh, yeah, that," McGill said.

Before he could inquire as to the nature of the inconvenience, Patti added, "The French also insisted that you have at least one official American bodyguard."

The president's henchman frowned. "Who?"

Patti could see McGill was imagining the worst. She patted his hand.

"The State Department's Regional Security Officer," the president said.

A fed, McGill thought. Probably a snooty one, being from State. Instead of displaying annoyance, though, he tried for a show of graciousness.

Taking Patti's hand, he said, "Thank you for all your help."

Patti laughed. "You're pretending to be a good sport."

"I am."

"You hate be saddled with anyone."

"I do."

"Might not be as bad as you think. The RSO's name is Gabriella Casale, and she shares your hometown."

An Italian girl from Chicago? McGill thought that might not be so bad after all. At the very least, she had to know where to get a good pizza in Paris. He smiled, for all of two seconds, and then he realized he'd just heard the good news.

Asking for the bad, he was told: "You get to work in France only as long as I'm working in London."

"It's not like I intended to loiter," McGill responded.

RAF Northolt

2

Air Force One landed at RAF Northolt, the military airfield west of London used by the Queen. The president's party was met by the Home Minister, the Lord Mayor of London and a gaggle of other dignitaries. Greetings and handshakes were exchanged by all the principals. McGill's grip was firm and brief, accompanied by a nod and a polite smile. He took care to remember faces and names to avoid embarrassing either the president or himself should he ever encounter any of these people again. As he added information to the old gray matter, something struck him as odd.

He whispered to Patti at the first opportunity, "Where's the prime minister? He have a dental checkup or something?"

Never losing her public smile, Patti murmured in reply, "The relationship between our countries is special, the one between Norvin Kimbrough and me leaves much to be desired."

McGill filed that away in memory, too.

He thought maybe he ought to pay a little more attention to politics.

After the formalities were out of the way, the president crossed the tarmac to Marine One. The helicopter had arrived in advance and would carry the president to Winfield House, the U.S. ambassador's residence in London. Flying there was a security measure the Secret Service had insisted on, and the Brits had agreed to it as a means to avoid traffic snarls on their motorways.

McGill kissed his wife goodbye outside the helicopter.

"You don't want to fly with me?" the president asked.

McGill said, "Thought I'd take the train to Paris. Less fuss."

He'd researched ways to get to Paris after talking with Emilie LaBelle. The Eurostar, a high-speed train, left from St. Pancras International Station in London, dived into a tunnel that had been dug under the Channel, emerged in France and concluded the trip at the Gare du Nord. He'd booked a round-trip ticket, not forgetting about dinner with the Queen.

Patti smiled. "I thought you might do something like that."

"You checked me out," McGill said. "You know exactly which train I'm on."

"I do," the president said.

"And you've arranged for someone to hold my hand so I don't get lost."

"I have. Someone to hold each hand, in fact."

At a nod from the commander in chief, two tall muscular Americans stepped out of Marine One. They wore sport coats and slacks, but their physical bearing was military and their demeanor screamed *Semper Fi.* Yielding to the inevitable, McGill extended his hand and introduced himself.

"You guys play poker?" McGill asked.

They did. The younger Marine even took a new deck of cards out of a pocket. Another detail Patti had thought of to make the trip with two bodyguards less burdensome.

McGill kissed his wife once more and whispered, "I love you, too."

3

The president's henchman wasn't the only senior member of the American party to eschew the flight on Marine One. As she stood on the tarmac, Chief of Staff Galia Mindel was approached by an Englishman of middle years wearing a black suit.

"Ms. Mindel, if you'll please accompany me, Sir Robert is waiting for you."

The driver led Galia to a black Rolls Royce Phantom and opened a rear door. The chief of staff usually took a seat emphatically, as if to announce the weightiest presence in the room had arrived. Now, she did her best to emulate an autumnal leaf drifting to earth. She managed her entrance with sufficient grace that neither the driver nor Sir Robert Reed, the Queen's personal secretary, guffawed. The driver closed the door and in a moment they were off.

A famous print ad for Rolls Royce once noted that the loudest sound the car made was the gentle ticking of its clock. That was back in analog days of springs and gears. In the digital age, there wasn't a sound to be heard as the car rolled along in complete silence. Galia thought, though, that a smile as bright as the one Sir Robert directed at her ought to generate a hum.

He was strikingly handsome. Close to her own age, Galia estimated. Late fifties. Dark hair going elegantly silver. Strong brow, nose and mouth. Chiseled cheeks, broad jaw. Skin that glowed with good health and expensive care. And dark,

dark eyes looking straight at—into—Galia.

"Countermeasures operative, sir," the driver said as they entered the motorway.

A dark glass partition slid up, dividing the front and rear of the passenger compartment.

"Countermeasures against what?" Galia asked.

"Everything but personal failings," Sir Robert replied. "Most pertinent to our situation, against eavesdroppers who might care to overhear our discussion."

He nodded to the window next to his head. Outside, Galia saw a cell tower.

Sir Robert said, "There are always blackguards about who turn useful tools to nefarious ends."

"Using cell towers to snoop on conversations in people's cars?"

"If you have a mobile phone along for the ride and it's powered up."

Galia did. She would have turned it off if the countermeasures hadn't been operative.

"That's amazing," she said.

"Only insofar as it wasn't thought of first thing. But then maybe it was. Rumor has it the notion was conceived by your NSA, and you know those chaps consider the whole world to be their personal radio program. In any case, it really wouldn't do to have anyone poking his unwashed nose into Her Majesty's private affairs."

Galia wondered which Sir Robert feared more, foreign agents or Fleet Street snoops.

"Nor the president's business," she added.

"I'm quite certain President Grant's conversations are equally protected."

Which was Sir Robert's polite way of telling her he knew things she didn't.

Galia made a mental note to become better informed on such matters.

Getting back to business, she said, "You asked to see me, Sir

Robert. To convey a message to the president, I assume."

"To convey a message and Her Majesty's gratitude ... and to avail myself of the opportunity to meet you personally."

Galia had to concentrate on the fact that her shoes were too tight to keep from blushing. This gorgeous man wanted to meet her in person? She had too good a mind to take that at face value. But up in a dusty attic corner of her consciousness a young girl was simpering.

She suspected Sir Robert with those penetrating dark eyes saw that weak-kneed child. But he was too much the gentleman to say anything.

Galia stuck to the safe path. "Her Majesty's gratitude is for the president agreeing to extend her stay in London?"

"Precisely, and the message is Her Majesty would be pleased if President Grant could join her for a private lunch at the palace on the day preceding the dinner with the other heads of state."

Galia said, "I'll be happy to extend the invitation and let you know the answer."

That was the way these things had to be done, of course, through intermediaries. If you couldn't make lunch with the queen at the palace, you didn't tell the old girl herself. You passed the word to Sir Robert—with your deepest regrets.

"You're very kind," Sir Robert told Galia.

And you're completely gorgeous, she thought, and so full of it.

Wasn't he?

Maybe it didn't matter. Either way, the guy gave her goose-bumps.

Galia graced Sir Robert with her best smile.

Aboard the Eurostar

4

Sergeant Merritt Nolan leaned forward over the table between the seats where he, Colonel Alan Ellison and McGill had been playing poker since the Eurostar train had left London and said in a quiet voice, "Permission to speak freely, sir?"

McGill deferred to the senior Marine.

"Granted."

Being a meticulous sort, the sergeant looked at McGill.

"Sir?"

"Sure, go ahead," McGill said.

"Mr. McGill, you are without a doubt the luckiest card player I have ever seen."

Not wanting to discourage the young man, McGill said, "Pretty much lucky in general."

The two Marines had won only three hands combined during the course of the two hour and twenty-five minute trip. McGill looked at Ellison.

"You feel the same way, Al?"

"Permission to speak freely, sir?"

"Absolutely."

"Mr. McGill, you are one of the sneakiest mothers I've ever had the pleasure to meet."

The sergeant sat back in his seat, clearly surprised at just how freely the field grade officer had spoken to the president's husband. But give the guy credit, he just smiled at the crack like he'd heard a good one.

Colonel Ellison continued, "You'd be a formidable opponent, sir. I'm glad you're on our side."

Sergeant Nolan sat forward again. He'd been careful to keep his voice down throughout the trip, but the Business Premier coach was sparsely filled and they really hadn't had to worry about eavesdroppers.

Looking at his superior officer, Nolan asked, "Are you saying, sir, that Mr. McGill isn't lucky?"

"Son, he played us like rubes at a carnival. We both started out looking for his tells, and he kept giving them to us, one after another, no two the same, no pattern to discern, basically none of them true, but he kept roping us in anyway. You, being younger, fell for more of them than me." The colonel paused to look McGill in the eye, and turned back to the sergeant. "You wouldn't want to get into a fight with this man; you'd never know what he might throw at you."

"That right, sir?" the sergeant asked McGill.

"Mostly I'm lucky," the president's henchman said.

The colonel snorted.

McGill had taken the two Marines for three hundred euros, a little better than four hundred dollars at that day's exchange rate. He made the two servicemen feel better about their losses by pushing most of the money back at them.

"Donate it to the Fallen Warrior Scholarship Fund," he said.

A charity dedicated to providing college funding to the children of those who had given their last full measure of devotion.

McGill kept the equivalent of fifteen dollars for himself.

Had to have something to show for his time.

The colonel said, "In Paris, that'll get you a cup of coffee, you don't go somewhere fancy."

Gare du Nord, Paris

5

The Marines relinquished custody of McGill to RSO Gabriella Casale at the bustling rail station that was Gare du Nord. As they stood off to one side, nobody paid the four Americans any special attention. The French may have liked to linger over a good meal but they scurried through transportation hubs like anyone else.

The State Department's regional security officer was tall and trim. An olive complexion deepened by the beginning of a summer tan stood in exotic contrast to her blonde hair and gray-green eyes. She wore a loose fitting cotton top over black pants and Chuck Taylors. A silk scarf was draped loosely around her neck. The scarf, shirt and sneakers were varying shades of peach, each nicely complimenting Ms. Casale's natural coloring.

After taking a good look at the RSO, Sergeant Nolan turned to Colonel Ellison and said, "I'll grant you, sir, Mr. McGill may well be sneaky, but damn me if he isn't lucky, too."

The colonel glanced at Ms. Casale and nodded. "Your argument's looking better."

The two Marines shook hands with McGill, nodded to the RSO and departed.

After they'd gone, Gabriella Casale asked McGill, "So are you?"

"Pardon."

"Sneaky and lucky."

"Pretty much. They go hand in hand."

Paris

6

McGill and RSO Casale exited the station.

"People call me Gabbi," she told McGill.

He said, "Funny name for a diplomat."

She grinned and conceded, "Ironic anyway."

As they stepped out onto the street, McGill took his first look at Paris. The sun was casting a golden light. The trees wore spring green leaves. Buildings all around, even the ones that needed touching up, had a feeling of age and a sense of place. Paris, from the little he could see of it, looked like a painting just waiting to be framed. It was no mystery why artists would thrive there.

On a less refined level of awareness, he spotted a uniformed cop standing next to a car parked at the curb. The cop was twirling a white baton by its leather loop. Engaging his own police instincts, McGill noted the car was a silver sedan, stylish, and bore a badge that identified it as a Peugeot 607.

Speaking quietly, McGill asked, "You carrying, Gabbi?"

"Discreetly."

Good answer, McGill thought. Take precautions but don't advertise them. They were both protected by diplomatic immunity, so the worst thing that could happen was—

Gabbi walking up to the cop and bussing him on each cheek?

"*Merci, Andre,*" Gabbi said to the cop who'd been watching

her car.

He saluted her and opened the passenger door of the Peugeot for McGill.

"*Bienvenue, m'sieur,*" he said to McGill.

"*Merci,*" McGill replied, exhausting ten percent of his French vocabulary.

The guy closed McGill's door as Gabbi got behind the wheel.

They drove off and he asked, "You have a good working relationship with the locals?"

Gabbi glanced at him. "With as many as I can. My job has been a lot easier since your wife's inauguration. Before that, it was a full-time job just to keep things amicable."

"You know Magistrate Yves Pruet?"

"Only by reputation and the file I read. His office is where we're heading now."

They drove along the Seine. McGill watched the tourist boats plying the river. He saw workboats moored along both banks. He wondered if anyone fished the waterway.

Before he could look for people with rods and reels, his cell phone played "Take Me Out to the Ballgame." A personal call. If Patti were calling, the ringtone would be "Hail to the Chief." The techies at the White House had set up the system for him.

"Hello," McGill said.

"Dad, it's me." His eldest child, Abbie.

"Hello, sweetheart. How are you?"

The pause that followed was long enough to answer McGill's question: not well.

"Something wrong, Abbie?"

"Dad, how would you feel if I changed my last name?"

Close to the last thing he'd ever expected to hear from Abbie—short of marriage.

But McGill did his best to play along. "To what?"

"Roberts." His ex-wife's maiden name.

"You don't like being Abigail McGill anymore?"

"I love it ... but I think it could be a problem."

"How's that?"

"It could mess up my college application," Abbie said.

"Honey, you've got stellar grades, astronomical test scores, and extracurriculars that show real compassion. How could a name throw a monkey wrench into all that?"

"I'm not worried that I *won't* get in, Dad. I'm worried that I *will* get in — because I have the same last name as the man who's married to the President of the United States. People might make the connection, you know."

"Oh," he said.

He hadn't thought of that. Another item on the long list of unanticipated consequences of being married to the occupant of the Oval Office. He didn't doubt that Abbie had it right. How many offspring of powerful politicians got clouted into elite schools? A lot.

"You want to be considered strictly on your own merit," he said to his daughter.

"Yes. I've worked hard for a long time. I've earned that right."

"You have, indeed." McGill wondered if his other two children would use the same strategy. He asked Abbie if she thought they would.

She laughed. "Kenny is going to ask Patti for a presidential appointment to West Point, and Caitie's too busy planning her future in show biz to think about college."

McGill told Abbie, "Okay, honey. Use your mom's maiden name. You could call yourself ZaSu Pitts and you'd still be my girl."

Couldn't make it any easier on her than that.

"I love you, Dad."

"I love you, too, Abbie." He said goodbye, knowing Abbie was already Googling ZaSu Pitts to see who she was.

After he clicked off, Gabbi asked, "Problem?"

"Complication. Easily resolved."

"We're here." She nodded to a well-kept low rise office building. "The lair of Pruet."

McGill blinked. He'd wanted to pay attention to the city, so he could start to find his way around. But they might have driven through Oz for all he knew. Oh, well, he thought, he'd have other opportunities to learn the Left Bank from the Right.

Better start learning the language, too, he told himself.

Winfield House—London

7

The president was continuing to work her way through the endless line of briefing books when Galia Mindel entered the suite the president would be using as her residence in London. Patti was glad to have a respite from her studies. Done right, the presidency was a real post-doc grind.

"Well, Galia, what did Sir Robert have to say, and what's your impression of him?"

"May I sit, Madam President?"

"Of course."

As her chief of staff sat in an armchair, the president saw that Galia was preoccupied, and misattributed the reason.

"Is the Queen really dying?" Patti asked.

When the request had first come from the British ambassador for the president to spend an additional day in London, Galia had immediately speculated that Her Majesty was dying, renouncing the throne or both. The chief of staff, and Jim, had pointed out correctly that the Royal Family wasn't known for acting impulsively and wouldn't bother the President of the United States with a triviality. Something was up, something big.

"No, I don't think so," Galia said.

"What changed your mind?"

"Her Majesty has invited you to a private lunch." Galia filled in the details. "I don't think she'd ask you to join her for tea and crumpets if she lay on her deathbed."

"That would be a bit macabre," the president said. "Still leaves stepping down."

"That's the way I'm leaning."

"Sir Robert gave you no clue."

"None. He's…"

The chief of staff's attention drifted away, and this time

the president saw what was in Galia's eyes. Sir Robert had set her heart aflutter. More power to him, Patti thought. Galia had been a widow for five years. In the manner of some professional women, the chief of staff had thrown herself into her work, doing her best to leave no time for grieving. But Patricia Darden Grant, herself a widow, if only briefly, knew there were times the heart would not be denied. It needed to mourn, even if the world at large would never be permitted to see.

"Galia?" the president said. "Is there anything you'd like to tell me, woman to woman?"

The chief of staff reddened, almost as if she were ashamed of what she'd been thinking.

Then her normal hard-charging persona reasserted itself. "I think, Madam President, someone in Her Majesty's government, though probably not the Queen herself, is trying to cultivate an asset close to the Oval Office."

"Meaning you," the president said, sitting forward. "Well, that would certainly be a serious matter. It's a good thing you can see through such machinations."

"Yes, it is." Galia stood up. She had work to do—and silly thoughts to disperse. "If you'll let me know when you decide to respond to Her Majesty's invitation, I'll pass the word along."

"I can tell you now. I wouldn't think of disappointing the Queen. Please let Sir Robert know I'll be happy to have lunch at the palace."

Galia nodded and turned to go.

The president stopped her. "Maybe Sir Robert just likes you, Galia."

Galia had decided not to accept that possibility, as the president could see.

"Of course," Patti said, "you could turn the tables on whoever is behind this nefarious plot and cultivate Sir Robert as an asset for us."

As a rationale for further contact with the man, the idea had appeal to Galia.

"I suppose I could do that," she said.

"Do your country proud," the president said.

Patti picked up her briefing book before Galia could see the smile on her face.

Paris

8

Gabbi parked the Peugeot in a lot adjacent to the Seine, across the Quai d'Orsay from the building housing Pruet's office.

Having had a moment to examine the edifice, McGill said, "Place looks more commercial rather than governmental."

Gabbi nodded. "Good eye. It's mostly filled with law firms."

McGill gave her an inquisitive look.

"*M'sieur le magistrat* is not your everyday *juge d'instruction,*" Gabbi told him.

"Okay," McGill said, "I'm going to need help with the language, and probably a lot of other things. But do we have time for that now?"

"Our meeting is set for any time you find convenient. Within reason, the French can be more relaxed about punctuality than Americans. So let me give you the primer on what we're facing."

McGill said, "Go ahead."

"The French have an inquisitorial system of criminal justice. Ours is—"

"Adversarial." He knew all about that.

"Right. A principal figure in the French system is the *juge d'instruction,* which usually gets translated as the examining magistrate. He's the guy who handles the big cases."

"Like the death of a national sports hero," McGill said.

"Right. Something like that … or politically sensitive cases."

McGill wagged his finger and put on a Southern drawl. "I did not have sex with that woman, Miss Whateverhernamewas."

Gabbi smiled. "Nice impression. Yeah, like that, except no French politician would ever make such a denial. He or she would say, 'It's none of your damn business who shares my bed.'"

McGill laughed. "I'd love to see someone try something like that at home."

"Anyway, the examining magistrate conducts investigations in the hot cases. He's an independent player. Prosecutors in routine cases answer to the Minister of Justice. Guys like Yves Pruet wear no shackles."

"But?" McGill asked.

"Well, they are expected to observe certain proprieties. Understand that some things just aren't done."

"Pruet did one of them anyway?"

"I don't want to give too much away," Gabbi told him.

McGill gave her a look. "Heaven forbid I should be fully informed."

"I'll give you the file on Pruet to read if you want. But it might be more useful, initially, if you draw your own conclusions."

McGill studied Ms. Casale.

"You want to see how smart I am. How much I can figure out for myself."

"It'd be good to know if you're more than just a handsome face."

That one slowed him down for a second. Nah, he decided, the RSO wasn't coming on to him. She was giving him another kind of test.

"Okay," he said, "let's see how smart I am. Is there anything else I *should* know?"

"Magistrates used to have the power of remand. Now, if they want someone locked up pending trial, they need the approval of another judge."

"Shouldn't have been hard to get in this case."

"It wasn't. But the interesting thing is, Pruet got to determine the place of custody."

McGill said, "Can't put Kinnard where France's felonious soccer fans can get at him."

"From what I'm told nobody but Pruet can get at him."

McGill thought about that. Isolation, he knew, was a double-edged sword: saved the body, destroyed the mind. Not that he was going to have a lot of time anyway, but he might need to move fast to save Kinnard from going crazy. Or confessing to a crime he didn't—

Well, he did kill the guy. He'd admitted that. But he might say his missing blonde was really a figment of his imagination, just to get better living conditions.

"One other thing," Gabbi told him. "The magistrate's job isn't to be either a prosecutor or a public defender. His obligation is to determine the truth. He's supposed to find the evidence of what happened whether it's incriminating or exculpating."

McGill had to smile. The law always sounded majestic in theory.

Theory residing over the hill and far away from reality.

9

Investigating Magistrate Yves Pruet wasn't exactly what McGill was expecting.

In fact, Pruet inspired a thought that had never occurred to McGill before: This guy could use a makeover. Maybe a couple weeks relaxing in the sun, too. The magistrate was pale and haggard. His suit needed to be pressed and his shoes needed to be shined.

But his eyes were clear, bright and blue.

Signposts for a good mind hiding behind a down-at-the-heels exterior.

McGill drew all the obvious inferences. The guy was having trouble at home. He'd been told he didn't have long to live. Somebody was stealing his copies of *GQ*.

Pruet's police bodyguard, Odo Sacripant, was as meticulous in his appearance as his boss was rumpled. Looked like he carried a lot of lean muscle, and the cast of his eyes let you know he wouldn't be afraid to use it.

The building may have been a commercial structure, but Pruet's office furnishings were governmental, and minimalist even on that scale. The magistrate worked behind an unadorned table made of polished oak. He sat on a matching chair. Two more wooden chairs were positioned opposite Pruet for visitors. Or suspects. Odo had a tiny metal desk with an upholstered office chair in a corner to the magistrate's left. In the corner to his right was a three-drawer file cabinet. Two large casement windows flooded the room with light, shining directly on McGill and Gabbi.

McGill put on his sunglasses. Gabbi contented herself to squint.

Introductions were made and Pruet said to McGill, "I must compliment you on your bodyguard, M'sieur McGill; she's far more charming than my own."

Gabbi gave Pruet a smile. McGill let Gabbi's looks speak for themselves.

Pruet asked McGill, "Do you speak French, m'sieur?"

"Sorry," McGill said. "I took four years of Latin in school. The priests pushed it. Told me it wasn't a dead language until they said it was."

Pruet smiled thinly.

He then gave McGill a quick précis of the French legal system. It matched up with what Gabbi had told him. But the magistrate added a few details. The biggie was that in France there was no plea bargaining a felony. You did the crime, you did the time. All of it.

After finishing his tutorial, Pruet asked McGill, "Are you a personal friend of M'sieur Kinnard?"

"An acquaintance," McGill said, "a former colleague. Now he's my client."

Pruet took note of the distinction between those three things and friendship.

"Do you know what interest, if any, M'sieur Kinnard might have in football?"

"He's a Chicago Bears fan."

Pruet frowned, not comprehending the response.

Gabbi explained in a French accented cognate: "Gridiron."

McGill caught the word and nodded. "Gridiron not soccer."

"No interest in *world* football at all?" Pruet asked.

"No, only the American kind," McGill said.

He didn't actually know Glen Kinnard disdained soccer, but from what he remembered of the man's Pleistocene attitudes he thought it was a pretty good bet.

"I've read a copy of M'sieur Kinnard's police record," Pruet said. "He has quite the history of brutality."

McGill responded, "Being a cop in Chicago can be a tough job. None of the excessive force complaints against my client was sustained. Many of them were filed by people with criminal records. And he didn't have any in his last three years with the department."

After talking with Emilie LaBelle, McGill had checked out Kinnard's record, too.

Pruet continued, "As you say, m'sieur, you were a colleague of M'sieur Kinnard. If you don't mind, can you tell me how many brutality complaints were lodged against you during your career with the Chicago police?"

"Two," McGill said.

"Would care to provide the details?"

"I slapped the faces of the maestro of the Chicago Symphony Orchestra and a patron of the arts—after the patron shot me."

Odo grinned and gave McGill a thumbs-up.

"Yes, well," Pruet said, "not that I would know, but I suppose being shot could shorten one's temper."

"The complaints were later withdrawn," McGill said. "But the point should be taken that a police officer in Chicago might face danger even on the stage of Orchestra Hall."

Pruet looked at Gabbi and she nodded in confirmation.

The SRO had studied McGill's bio, as much as time had permitted.

She picked up the conversation. "May I ask where M'sieur Kinnard is being held?"

"In a safe house. A measure taken to guarantee his well-being."

"Will I be able to speak with him?" McGill asked.

"Yes."

"Soon?"

"As soon as is practical."

McGill decided not to push it. For the moment.

"Thank you for your time, Magistrate Pruet," he said.

"C'est rien."

"It's nothing," Gabbi translated.

Exactly, McGill thought, but didn't say so.

"I expect we will be working together quite closely," Pruet added.

"Good to know." McGill stood and shook the magistrate's hand.

Odo escorted the two Americans out. When he returned Pruet was looking pensive.

"You see the opportunity here, don't you, Yves?" he asked.

"You refer to the opportunity to shift the blame for any unfortunate outcome?"

"Better the Amis should shoulder the burden than you."

Pruet nodded, but he didn't look greatly cheered.

Arlington, Virginia

10

When Sweetie was a kid, her mother got a real estate license so her father, a firefighter, could stop moonlighting on his days off. Actually, Mom wanted Dad to keep the pickup jobs, roofing and house-painting, and stop running into burning buildings, but the city paid better and provided great health benefits and a pension plan. So, if Dad was going to risk his life, Mom figured it would be better if he were well rested when he did. In the end, things worked out for both of them. Mom sold so many houses Dad did quit the fire department and went to work for her. Said he didn't mind her bossing him around as long as he got paid for it.

Being the child of a crack Realtor, Sweetie learned a lot

about homes and their price tags.

When she saw the house where Musette and Deke Ky lived on Dinwiddie Street in Arlington, Virginia, her informal real estate education kicked in and she ran an appraisal in her head. A frame structure with a pale pink brick facade on a quarter-acre lot. Construction date, say 1955-1960. At least four bedrooms and maybe five. Three-to-four bathrooms. Three-car garage. Solid, stable neighborhood. Equivalent schools. Close to DC. Price: a million to a million-two.

Maybe add another hundred grand for the pocket park-and-playground directly across the street. The place the sniper had set up and shot Deke. You thought about it that way—as a risk factor—maybe it knocked the price down just under a million.

A red light went on when Sweetie rang the doorbell. The camera looked down from just under the eaves and would catch the right profile of a visitor facing the front door. It was reassuring to see a precaution had been taken since the shooting. People ought to learn a lesson or two, Sweetie thought, after somebody tried to kill them.

She'd been expecting Musette to open the door for her, but Deke did.

It was the first time she'd seen him since the shooting He looked better than she'd thought he would. His color was a little less vibrant than his usual new penny hue, and his frame was a few pounds light. But his muscle tone, as displayed in a Treasury Department T-shirt, didn't look half bad. His hygiene and grooming were as meticulous as ever, always a good sign.

Sweetie smiled and said, "Special Agent Ky, good to see you."

Deke bobbed his head. "You, too, Margaret."

"I lit many a candle for you."

"Thank you. I appreciate it."

"Your mom home? She asked me to stop by."

Deke's face clouded. "She did?"

"Yeah. She bumped into me after mass yesterday."

"You go to church in Arlington?"

Sweetie shook her head. "No, this was at St. Al's in DC."

Before Deke could delve too deeply into the implications of that, his mother joined him at the door. She caressed her son's brow and kissed his cheek.

"Invite our guest inside, Donald," she said.

Deke did as his mother instructed. Ushered Sweetie inside and closed the door.

Musette told Sweetie, "I was just fixing some refreshments for us. Have Donald show you to the kitchen when the two of your are done talking."

When she was gone, Deke asked, "Has my mother hired you and Holmes?"

Using Jim McGill's Secret Service code name.

Sweetie nodded. "Me, anyway. Jim's in Paris."

"Paris?"

"Yeah. He was going to London with the president for the G8 meeting, and then a job came up in France."

"Who's protecting him?" Deke asked.

"I don't know," Sweetie said. "I imagine Patti will find someone to tag along."

Deke frowned.

Sweetie smiled. "You've got to realize something, Deke. Jim McGill is a sweet, gentle man, but if he'd been born sixty years earlier, he'd have brought John Dillinger in alive, without a shot being fired. He's going to be okay until you're up and running again."

Deke's grimace said he wasn't reassured. Sweetie chose not to argue the point.

She just asked, "Which way's the kitchen?"

11

Musette Ky extended a plate of Chocolate Marthas to Sweetie as the two women sat at her kitchen table. After Sweetie had consumed one, and her hostess had done likewise, she wondered if it would be rude to ask if she could take the other six mini-cupcakes home. Maybe give one to Putnam. Put the rest in her fridge and make them last all week. Wouldn't be gluttony that way. She could have her cake and her salvation, too. The green ice tea with mint and honey that Ms. Ky served was also sinfully good.

Sweetie's tingling taste buds made her reflect on the nature of sin. The old counterculture advice was: If it feels good, do it. But the Church's point of view always seemed to be: If it feels good, don't even *think* about it. Who had taken the fun out of being Catholic? When had that happened? Couldn't have been at the start. Jesus went to wedding parties. If the wine ran low, he took a miracle out of his pocket and made more.

The pleasantries having been observed, Musette Ky got down to business. It turned out her story involved jeopardy not just for herself but also for a member of the clergy. Questions of faith were also involved. But she began by saying, "I promised Donald I would never tell anyone what I am about to tell you."

Sweetie had to ask, "Why would you break a promise to your son?"

"It was made under duress. At the time it looked like … like Donald might die." She pushed that grim memory aside and shrugged. "Also, I am far from a perfect mother."

Sweetie reflected on that. She couldn't imagine there being a better Secret Service agent to protect Jim McGill than Deke Ky. She didn't want to learn so much about the Kys, mother and son, that it would make it impossible for Deke to resume his job.

"Do you want me to continue," Musette asked, "or should I find help elsewhere?"

Despite her misgivings, Sweetie was never one to back down.

"I'll help you," she said. "Deke isn't blood, but for Jim and me he is family."

Musette Ky inclined her head in gratitude, and offered the plate of Chocolate Marthas to Sweetie, who took one and listened closely.

"Donald has a cousin who is more like a brother to him. His name is Francis Nguyen. Reverend Francis Nguyen."

Musette took a small photographic print out of a pocket and handed it to Sweetie. It was a portrait of a young man wearing a black suit and a Roman collar. Francis Nguyen looked smart, serene, and young enough to be an altar boy.

"Francis is the child of my younger sister, Sylvie. After the war, they made their way to a refugee camp in Thailand. Francis was only four when my sister died there. I brought him to this country. He lived with Donald and me, and when the time came I paid for his years at the seminary."

Musette helped herself to another Chocolate Martha. She offered the plate to Sweetie again, but Sweetie was still hoping for leftovers and declined.

"I never thought I would love anyone as much as Donald, but there were times I thought I might love Francis more."

Sweetie noticed that Ms. Ky didn't look around to see if Deke might be nearby before she spoke, and she didn't lower her voice...but then she had said she wasn't a perfect mother.

Musette said, "Our Lord's grace shines so clearly through Francis, there are times he makes me want to fall to my knees."

"How does Deke feel about that?" Sweetie asked.

Ms. Ky smiled. "If anything, Donald loves Francis even more than I do. But there are those who do not approve of him."

Someone who didn't approve of a priest? Could be a parishioner with a gripe. If she hadn't seen Francis Nguyen's photo, it might have been—God help us—a parent with the most horrible of suspicions. But no way was someone with that face a child molester. If she was wrong about that, she'd have to hang it up. Sweetie zeroed in on what she considered a more likely target.

"Would Francis's critics be his brothers in the Church?" she asked.

Musette nodded. "Francis believes his ministry is to the faithful not the hierarchy. He will not marry gay couples, but he will bless their relationships and ask the Lord to guide them in their thoughts and deeds. He will also give Holy Communion to any Catholic—even politicians who refuse to follow the bishop's dictates on abortion."

"So he's openly disobedient," Sweetie said. "How is his bishop taking that?"

"Bishop O'Menehy has threatened to remove Francis from the priesthood, but he hasn't acted because he's afraid Francis's parish, and perhaps others, would rebel. Francis finds the thought that he might cause a schism, even a minor one, unbearable. It causes him as much pain as the idea he might be expelled from the priesthood."

Sweetie considered what she'd been told. Father Francis Nguyen was experiencing a terrible personal crisis, but so far she hadn't heard anything about the person Musette Ky thought had targeted her for death. Then things clicked into place for her.

Ms. Ky wasn't worried about the bad guys coming back to take another crack at Deke. Nor was she primarily concerned for her own welfare. She feared for her nephew, the young priest who sometimes eclipsed her own son in her feelings.

Why would that be ... unless Father Nguyen also had learned something about the criminal and his plans. And how could that have...

Good Lord. Had Father Nguyen heard the bad guy's confession?

Maybe the creep who'd shot Deke had even spilled his guts to the priest.

If that were the case, in addition to all his problems with the hierarchy, the priest would also have to protect the identity of the assassin who had shot his cousin.

Paris

12

After leaving Pruet's office, McGill had Gabbi give him a motor tour of central Paris. He saw many of the iconic sights: the Eiffel Tower, just down the street from where Pruet labored; the Arc de Triomphe; Notre Dame Cathedral. But for the president's henchman it was more than a sightseeing jaunt. He was learning a new beat just as he had when he first moved to Washington, DC. Only this time he had to try to memorize street signs written in French: *rues, allées, ruelles.*

Thank goodness French and English shared boulevards and avenues.

Still, McGill asked Gabbi to help him begin to acquire an elementary grasp of the host language. He started with obvious things, like the vehicle in which they were riding.

"How do you say car?" he asked.

"Voiture."

He also learned to count one through twenty. The colors red, white, blue and black. He learned the Seine was a *fleuve* not a *riviere,* the latter being more akin to a stream. After making a few more additions to his new vocabulary, he returned to an earlier matter.

"You want to tell me now, what was the terrible thing Pruet did? His *faux pas,* to use the vernacular."

Gabbi smiled at him. "You have a very nice accent for someone who's been in France less than a day."

"Thank you. My mother is a voice teacher. She taught me how to listen closely. There, I've shared a secret with you, so how about opening up?"

Gabbi had a good ear, too. There was just a bit of edge to McGill's voice—and he could, she supposed, have her posted somewhere a lot less appealing than Paris.

"Yves Pruet became a figure of renown, and a fair bit of loathing, when he sent Alain Gautier to prison."

McGill had never heard the name before. If he paid little attention to American politics, he paid even less to foreign wrangling. But he'd been attentive to both Gabbi and Pruet when they had explained the French legal system to him.

"Didn't I hear that investigating magistrates only refer cases to courts for trial? They don't render verdicts themselves."

"That's right," Gabbi said, sparing him a quick glance. The late afternoon traffic was increasing, growing more demanding of a driver's attention. "But what neither of us said, I guess because we both take it for granted, is when someone like Pruet refers a case for trial, there's a ninety-five percent chance the verdict will be guilty."

As a former cop, that pleased McGill.

As a PI working for Glen Kinnard, he wasn't so sure he liked the idea.

"Okay, so who's this Alain Gautier?"

"He was a former interior minister, the official who runs all the cop shops in France."

McGill whistled softly. "What'd he do?"

"Dipped his beak into the public trough. The scandal reminded me of the way things work in Chicago. But not even the boys at City Hall grab as much as Gautier did."

McGill thought about that for a moment. That had to be what Patti was talking about when she'd said Pruet was honest to a fault. And politically inconvenient.

"So the Gautier case put the kibosh on Pruet's professional reputation?"

"Made him a pariah. He terrifies much of the government elite. There are lots of people just waiting for the opportunity to knife him."

Maybe more than metaphorically, McGill thought. That would explain the presence of bodyguard Odo Sacripant at Pruet's side. It might also account for the magistrate's somber mood and unkempt appearance.

The next stop on McGill's train of thought darkened his own outlook.

"An opportunity to knife the guy?" he asked. "Like handing him the investigation of the death of Thierry Duchamp and Glen Kinnard's role in it?"

Gabbi stopped the car. Traffic had backed up for no reason visible to McGill.

She looked at him and said, "That's the way I see it. From what I've been able to find out, this is the first case Pruet has worked since he nailed Gautier."

McGill said, "It's obvious what happens to Pruet if he clears

Glen Kinnard: Everybody in France hates him, not just the pols. But what's the downside if he throws the book at Kinnard?"

Traffic began to move and Gabbi put her eyes back on the road.

"Personally, not much, if Kinnard deserves to go to jail. But Pruet has a reputation for unquestioned honesty. It would be very hard for him to sacrifice that for political expediency. In either case, though, if Kinnard gets a long sentence, it could hurt relations between France and the United States, which are better than they have been for years."

McGill sighed. Now, he understood why Pruet was gloomy.

"Having me around only complicates things, doesn't it?" he asked.

Gabbi shot him a quick look. Telling him: *C'mon, you can see what it does.*

And with that bit of prompting, McGill did.

"You're right," he said. "I might be a big help. Kinnard gets it in the head, both France and the U.S. can point the finger at me for meddling."

"Très bon," Gabbi said. "You like Kinnard?"

"Not particularly."

"So you stub a toe. Render yourself *hors de combat.* Leave the field to someone else."

McGill told her, "I've never been a quitter,"

Especially when a man's daughter asked him to help her dad.

It was too easy to identify with something like that.

Gabbi said, "Okay, as long as you know the risks."

McGill was sure he was only beginning to recognize the risks.

As if to confirm that point, Gabbi's mobile phone trilled; the call was from Pruet.

"M'sieur le magistrat says you can see Kinnard now," Gabbi told him.

Rue de Lille, Paris

13

Gabbi pulled into a parking spot in front of a well-kept residential building. There was a doorman out front. It was the kind of neighborhood, from what McGill could see, where a doorman was a standard amenity. Only this guy looked like he could be Odo Sacripant's kid brother, and he'd be just as happy to plant a foot in your backside as open a door for you.

The other thing that caught McGill's attention was the parking spot Gabbi took was the last vacant space on the block. Right in front of the place where they would have their meeting. Didn't seem like a coincidence. The tough guy had kept it clear for them.

But when he opened the car door for McGill he didn't say *bienvenue.* What he did was give McGill a once over to see if he was carrying. Probably wanted to frisk him, too. But his orders must not have allowed that. Or he got the vibe from McGill that it wouldn't be a good idea.

Gabbi handed her car keys to him and said something in French. She got a nod in response but not even a hint of a smile. McGill was about to open the door to the building when Gabbi restrained him. They waited for the doorman to do it. He took his time.

Once inside, McGill asked, "You think he used to be a waiter?"

Gabbi had another idea. "Maybe he was a fan of Thierry Duchamp."

McGill asked, "And he knows why we're here?"

"That or he used to be a waiter."

Gabbi pressed the call button for the elevator and when the car arrived it held two large plainclothes cops. French elevators being what they were, the space left for McGill and Gabbi was the approximate size of a phone booth. Under any other circumstances, McGill wouldn't want to explain having such intimate contact with the RSO to his wife. He thought about the formula for calculating earned run averages until they reached the third floor and disembarked.

Their police escorts got off with them in a hallway. An apartment door opened and they joined two more cops who waited in a comfortably furnished living room with breathing space and elbow room for all, including Glen Kinnard, who took one look at McGill and said, "I never thought I'd be so glad to see you."

14

McGill went for a more gracious hello. He extended his hand and said, "I was sorry to hear of Suzanne's passing."

His condolence was sincere and it disarmed Kinnard. He shook McGill's hand.

"Yeah, thanks. Thanks for coming, too."

"Your daughter's responsible for that," McGill said. He looked at Gabbi and asked, "You think these gentlemen could give us a little privacy?"

She made an inquiry of the oldest cop. He shook his head. She invoked Pruet's name. The cops all scowled upon hearing it, but they withdrew, a pair of them taking up position outside each of the two doors to the room. Gabbi closed each door firmly. Then she raised a finger to her lips, momentarily postponing further conversation between McGill and Kinnard.

She took two small devices out of a pocket and turned them on. One produced white noise; the other activated an MP3 file of Bob Marley's Legend album. She cranked it up. Then she took two chairs from a table and set them facing each other in the middle of the room. She gestured to McGill and Kinnard to be seated. When they were, she leaned in and said quietly, "The French love to snoop."

She stepped back, giving the two men their privacy.

Kinnard was looking at Gabbi; McGill looked at him.

His hair had gone gray, but was still full and worn in a buzz cut. His face had more lines but no fat. His body showed no signs of softening either. Kinnard still looked like what McGill had always taken him to be: a hard mean SOB.

But Kinnard had put in twenty-five years on the job and—the excessive force allegations notwithstanding—no hint of corruption had ever tainted Kinnard. That in itself distinguished him from a lot of Chicago coppers. As to Emilie LaBelle's assertion that her father had acquired a semblance of humanity, McGill would have to see about that.

Almost as if Kinnard had read his thoughts, he turned toward McGill and said in a soft voice, "You know, for most of my life I'd have thought a woman who looked like her was good for only one thing. Now, I'm a little smarter. If she's helping you, I feel better about things."

McGill nodded and said, "Tell me what happened."

Kinnard did, repeating the details of the story Emilie had told him, and then he added a few more. He was about to drop Suzanne's ashes into the Seine as she had asked him to do, but at the last minute he changed his mind.

"I wasn't going to ignore Suzanne's wishes; I just wanted to join her. Have my ashes go into the river with hers. When I die, I mean. So I thought what I'd do was take Suzi's urn back home. Then I thought, no, I'd have some funeral guy here hold them for me. Have Emilie bring my urn here after I was gone. I've patched things up enough with her, I was sure she'd do that."

Kinnard was silently explaining his new idea to his late wife's spirit when the loudmouthed couple came along and the guy started beating on the woman.

"And being who you are, you couldn't walk away?" McGill said.

Kinnard glared at him, the momentary détente between the two of them gone.

"No, I couldn't. You wouldn't have either. I read about you catching those creeps who did the president's first husband. Thought to myself that prick McGill did a righteous job, and when you told the press all those assholes should be strapped to gurneys I was so tickled I wanted to buy you a beer." The smile fell from Kinnard's face. A sheen of tears made his eyes glisten. "You got married just about the time Suzi got her diagnosis. Made me wonder about people's luck. But I wouldn't have traded any one of those last days with Suzi for anything."

Kinnard covered his face with his hands.

McGill told him, "I wouldn't have walked away either."

It was another reason he'd taken the case.

Kinnard squeegeed the tears from his eyes.

"You know about France's Good Samaritan law?" he asked.

"I've been told," McGill said. "You had no idea who you were fighting before you got into it with him?"

Kinnard shook his head.

"Was he drunk?" McGill asked.

"Smelled like he'd been drinking wine, but he fought like he was on PCP."

Angel dust. A cop's worst nightmare.

"What did the woman look like?" McGill asked.

Kinnard looked back at Gabbi. "Kind of like her, only maybe ten years younger. Not exactly smart looking, but shifty, you know. Someone who got wised up young."

"Height and weight?" McGill asked.

"Again, about like her." Kinnard said. "Maybe a little chestier."

He told McGill what the woman was wearing, as best he could remember.

"Was she drunk or high, too?" McGill asked.

The question made Kinnard sit up straight, revelation lighting his eyes. He leaned forward again. "No, she wasn't. She wasn't slurring at all. Just yelling real loud, wagging her finger at him, telling him with this nice mean edge to her voice how little his dick was. That was when the fucking guy caught her finger in his teeth."

"What?" McGill asked.

"Yeah, he bit her and wouldn't let go. Things went to hell from there, and that was when I intervened. I mean, what are you going to do, you see some asshole's about to bite a woman's finger off and he's pounding on her at the same time?"

McGill took all that in. Good Samaritan Law or not, no self-respecting cop, current or former, would have walked away. Still, Kinnard's account had raised a question in his mind.

"She said it in English?" he asked. "About the guy having a little dick."

"No, French. I picked up a fair bit from Suzanne. I understand more than I can speak." Kinnard paused. "Let's keep that between us. The frogs think I'm your standard English-only American dummy."

McGill nodded. He got up to go. Kinnard stood and looked at him.

"Probably a good thing we never got into it way back when. Doubt you'd have taken the case if we had."

"Probably not."

"Of course, you might think you'd have come out on top," Kinnard said.

McGill just shrugged.

If a guy wanted to think he was tougher than you, the best thing was to let him.

En route to Washington DC

15

Sweetie's personal car, a 1969 Chevy Malibu, was in the shop for preventive maintenance so Leo Levy had chauffeured her to Arlington and was now taking her back to the office. Sweetie had asked Leo if he'd like to come to the door with her and say hello if Deke were available. He'd declined, saying he'd prefer to renew acquaintances when Deke "was up to tippin' a glass or two."

That didn't keep him from asking, "How's Deke?" after they got rolling.

"Deke is strong in spirit," Sweetie said, "so the flesh shall surely follow."

"Love it when you talk biblical like that," Leo said with a grin. "We in any hurry to get back to town?"

Before getting into government work, Leo had driven the NASCAR circuit. He'd left professional racing because it made his mother nervous, and with her weak heart he hadn't wanted to be the death of her. Still, he enjoyed driving at high speed any time he could. With his White House credentials, it was a pleasure he could indulge knowing no cop in the country would write him up.

Even so, it was good to have a nominal reason to drop the hammer.

Sweetie said, "Time's a terrible thing to waste. Especially when neither of us is getting any younger."

"Ain't no arguin' that," Leo said.

In the blink of an eye, they were passing every other car on the road, without ruffling anyone's feathers. Most of the other drivers never saw Leo until he'd zipped past them. He moved in, out, and around cars doing the speed limit like they were gates in a slalom course and he was a downhill racer going for Olympic gold.

Sweetie thought maybe she should ask Leo for a few driving lessons.

The roar of the car's engine precluded casual conversation, giving Sweetie time to think about what she'd learned from Musette Ky. If a bad guy had bared his soul to a priest, he could feel pretty comfortable that the cleric wouldn't rat him out. But if that bad guy found out a bishop was going to kick his confessor's backside out of the priesthood, what was he going to think?

He'd made a bad mistake.

And the priest had to go.

Musette Ky had given Sweetie the bad guy's name, Horatio Bao. To the public, Bao was a respected lawyer, a pillar of the Arlington community, and a power among the Viet Kieu population. He would never stoop to shooting Donald himself, but Musette had said he had a vicious young thug named Ricky Lanh Huu working for him.

The clear implication was Ricky was the guy who'd shot Deke.

Ms. Ky had declined to reveal the exact nature of the crime in which Bao had sought to involve her. "It is too horrible to speak of. I try to push the very thought out of my mind."

Asked to characterize Deke's mother in three words, Sweetie would have said: "Tough as nails." She didn't see the woman backing down from anyone much less letting an idea bother her. Sometimes, though, working with an informant—how Sweetie was coming to think of Ms. Ky— was a dance, and you had to follow the choreography.

"Why would Horatio Bao seek your advice?" she'd asked.

Musette said, "I am a successful businesswoman. I give informal seminars on getting ahead in America. I can only think Mr. Bao thought he might turn my expertise to ... his purposes."

Sweetie saw she would get only so far pushing that line of inquiry.

So she went in another direction.

"When your son was shot, you said you rushed to his aid."

"Yes."

"And Francis was having dinner with you?"

"Yes."

"Did he run to the door to help, too?"

"Of course."

Sweetie gave it a beat then asked, "Do you think he might have looked across the street and seen the shooter?"

The question gave Musette Ky pause or at least she acted that way.

"As I recall ... the streetlight adjacent to the park was on. The park itself was partially illuminated. Francis may have seen the shooter ... or he may not."

Sweetie would bet he had. The shooter had seen he'd been spotted, and who the witness was. He'd made a point of rushing to confess his sin to Father Nguyen as soon as he could. Fearing the law's punishment far more than God's judgment.

In principle, Sweetie had trouble reconciling a loving Creator with the architect of Hell. Eternity was just too long to punish any sin. But there were people she thought should burn for a good long time, and someone who would pervert a sacrament would be prominent among them.

As she mulled the jurisprudence of mortal sin, her phone chirped, *Jesu Joy of Man's Desiring.* The caller was Putnam Shady, her lawyer, landlord and would-be suitor.

She answered by saying, "I'm too busy to save your soul right now, Putnam."

He replied, "We'll get to that after the champagne is chilled. Right now, I'm calling with a news bulletin: Erna Godfrey's first appeal of her conviction has been denied."

Erna Godfrey was the murderess of President Patricia Darden Grant's first husband, philanthropist Andrew Grant. She had perpetrated her crime with a rocket-propelled grenade. Her defense was a claim of divine justification. She'd acted to save an untold number of fetuses from abortion. A jury of her peers had found her guilty and she had been sentenced to death.

Sweetie figured she'd earned a long while in the rotisserie, too.

"How much time does that leave her," Sweetie asked, "before she's executed?"

"Figure at least five more years if someone behind the scenes isn't hurrying the process."

Meaning if the president wasn't actively seeking revenge, which Jim had assured Sweetie she wasn't. Sweetie thanked Putnam for calling, knowing better than to ask him to reveal the source of his information.

It was turning out to be quite a day. Erna Godfrey had moved closer to finding out what the Almighty really thought of her. Deke's mom had told Sweetie the names of the people behind her son's shooting. She also continued to hide the extent of her own involvement in the matter.

In Musette's favor, though, she had let Sweetie take four Chocolate Marthas home

Georgetown

16

As Sweetie entered the lobby of the building where McGill Investigations, Inc. had its offices, Dikki Missirian told her she had someone waiting to see her.

"Who?" she asked.

"Me," Captain Welborn Yates said, stepping out of Dikki's cubbyhole under the staircase. He wore casual civilian clothes. "Mr. McGill thought you might be able to use a hand. Said I might be of help liaising with the federal justice system. The president approved and gave me leave time—if you're interested."

Sweetie smiled. How thoughtful of Jim.

Giving her Welborn: her own personal FireWire into all sorts of government databases.

"Well, of course, I am, Welborn. Help is always welcome."

Winfield House, London

17

Galia knocked on the door and heard the president say, "Come in." She entered the spacious bedroom the president was using. With James J. McGill out of town, Galia didn't worry about stepping into any potentially embarrassing situation—although she already had walked in on McGill in his bath when an urgent situation required it. The chief of staff thought she might find the president reviewing yet another briefing book as she sat on the settee in the room. Perhaps she would be sneaking in a few minutes of leisure reading. Possibly, she would be moving with a dancer's flair through a tai chi sequence.

That last conjecture came closest to the mark. The president was on her feet, taking two or three normal strides and then seemingly catching her foot on some invisible obstacle. The displaced foot then came down hard, heel first. The arm on the same side was suddenly flung backward, hard enough that the president had to catch her balance.

All Galia could think of was that the president, for some inexplicable reason, was practicing a pratfall. Try as she might, Galia couldn't recall any former leader of the free world doing a Vaudeville routine.

"Madam President, may I ask, what you're doing?"

Patti turned to look at her. "You may not."

Galia kept her face blank, but instinctively felt McGill was responsible for this odd behavior. Damn the man. Seeing the president studying her, Galia knew her poker face wasn't all it might be. She moved on to the business at hand.

"You asked for word on the Russian situation, Madam President."

Russia was the only G8 nation not to be in London for the economic summit.

"Has anything changed?" Patti asked.

"The dialogue continues to be heated, but there are no significant military movements."

Patricia Darden Grant's predecessor in the Oval Office had planned to place interceptor missiles in Poland, ostensibly to keep the Iranians from nuking Central Europe. Russia interpreted the U.S. plan as a hedge against its own missiles. Patti saw the whole thing as a cowboy-versus-cossack pissing contest and canceled the missile pact with Poland, assuring Warsaw that along with all of Poland's other NATO allies, Washington would never allow Iran to rain nuclear destruction on Europe.

In a rational world, that would have been that, the status quo ante restored. But fears once raised were not easily quelled. Pride once bruised did not heal quickly. Poland, having suffered through decades of Soviet oppression, was in no mood to listen to any lectures or to tolerate any threats from the Kremlin.

"Warsaw is going to carry out its NRA plan?" the president asked.

The Polish government was initiating a plan to arm every head of household in the country with an assault rifle. With a population approaching forty million, the government had placed an enormous order with Fabrique Nationale de Herstal, the Belgian manufacturer of the F2000 assault rifle. The funds being used to arm Poland were a hundred percent domestic, but the Russians claimed that economic aid from the EU and the U.S. was allowing the Poles to create, *de facto*, the world's largest standing army.

Warsaw replied it would happily disarm if Russia did likewise, starting with its nuclear weapons. Russia said it would never disarm while the U.S. and China continued to build their arsenals. The world, as ever, grew more complicated and dangerous.

Galia reminded the president, "The Poles describe their plan as following the Swiss model."

The president said, "The Swiss allow only their soldiers to keep their rifles, and only after they've completed their military service. The soldiers who do keep their rifles have to pay out of their own pockets to have their assault rifles modified into the required civilian configuration. They also have to demonstrate continued shooting proficiency every summer. And the number of soldiers electing to keep their weapons is steadily declining."

Galia nodded, thinking what a pleasant change it was for the country to have a president who had truly mastered her coursework.

"You're right, of course, Madam President, and I believe the secretary of state has made all those points to Warsaw, and the first shipment of arms from Belgium has yet to be distributed."

"And perhaps never will be?" the president asked.

"Possibly, if the Russians dial back their rhetoric."

"The secretary of state is working on that, too?"

"He is."

"Good. Someone else should have a job nearly as awful as yours and mine."

The two women laughed, only to be interrupted by the phone ringing.

The president answered, listened for a moment and said, "Yes, thank you."

"If there's nothing else you need, Madam President," Galia said, "I'll—"

"Just a minute, Galia."

There was a knock at the door. A female Secret Service agent entered and handed an envelope to the president. After the agent left, Patti gave it to Galia.

"For you," she said. "From Buckingham Palace."

Galia's eyebrows rose, and she opened the envelope. She took out a card and read the message, then read it again as if she couldn't believe her eyes.

"What is it, Galia?" the president asked.

"An invitation." She looked at Patti. "Sir Robert Reed would like to know if he might be permitted the honor of taking me to dinner."

The president beamed.

Galia knew what Patti was thinking: Sir Robert was asking her for a date.

She shook her head and said, "The man obviously has ulterior motives."

"Most men do," the president responded. "Try to enjoy them whenever possible."

Paris

18

Gabbi left her car with a valet at a restaurant called Monsieur Henri on the Ile de la Cité.

McGill got out of the Peugeot and asked, "You made a reservation?"

She smiled and inclined her head upward. McGill saw two flats above the restaurant. "Home," Gabbi said. She led him to a doorway at the left side of the building. The lock on the door was biometrically keyed: palm print and retinal pattern. Gabbi had McGill add his bio-info to the system's memory. "Now, you have a key to the place, too," she said.

What a place it was. Gleaming wood floors throughout;

Oriental rugs; artful lighting; original oil paintings on the wall. Still lifes, landscapes, portraits. McGill walked over to one, a portrait of an old man, smiling as if his life had been one grand adventure after another. He examined the painting closely, liking it more with every detail he observed, and then he took note of the artist's signature: G. Casale.

He turned and looked at the woman to whom his welfare had been entrusted.

"My compliments," he said. He gestured at the collection of paintings. "These could hang in the Art Institute. Or any local museum."

Gabbi bobbed her head in gratitude. "Thank you. I'm an alumna of the School of the Art Institute. Came to Europe to do post-grad studies."

"But?" McGill asked.

"But I was starving, which was perfectly acceptable. What couldn't be endured was the inability to buy art supplies. I refused to ask Mom and Dad for support. Rather than sell my body, I said yes to a gentleman who walked up to me in the Tuileries Gardens one day while I was doing charcoal sketches and asked me in a whisper if I'd like to add spycraft to my portfolio."

"CIA?" McGill asked.

Gabbi nodded. "What hooked me was I thought I could fool anyone into thinking I was a native. But he spotted me for an American right away. We smoothed out my rough spots, but it turned out I really wasn't agency material. I did like the government paycheck and perks, though, and I managed to catch on with State."

McGill looked around. The apartment's furnishings were also museum quality. A government paycheck wouldn't cover the wall paint much less all the Architectural Digest goodies.

"There's more than the taxpayer's dollar at work here," McGill said.

Gabbi smiled at him and stepped behind a wet bar. "Drink?"

McGill asked for a sparkling water.

She poured him a San Pellegrino as he took a stool opposite her.

And waited for an explanation.

"My family comes from the comfortable side of middle class. Dad was a State Farm agent. Sold a fair amount of insurance. In his spare time, he was a state senator. Had things all planned out for the family."

McGill knew a cue when he heard one. "And then?"

"And then, oops, Mom got pregnant with Giancarlo. Plans had to be readjusted. I got to be Gianni's baby-sitter throughout high school, so Mom could stay on with Dad at the office as much as possible. I didn't mind—too much—because Gianni is such a sweetie."

McGill nodded and said, "He adores his big sister, and he got rich."

"He went to MIT and showed them what a genius really is. Started inventing things while he was still in school, has about a dozen patents by now. Wanted to cut me in on his stock holdings. When I said that wouldn't look good for a government employee, he found other ways to gild my lily."

"How?" McGill asked.

"Well, he made me his official 'Consultant of Cool.' He's always thought of me as being sophisticated. You know, his artist sister, living in Paris. His friends were always falling in love with me, and he appreciated that I never made fun of them.

"Instead, I gave Gianni and his pals pointers for getting along with their female classmates. I still get a thank you card whenever one of them gets married. Anyway, Gianni came to Paris and saw my old one-point-five room apartment. He wanted to buy me the Versailles Palace. I told him it would be cool for him to own his own French restaurant, and I knew a terrific young chef who needed a backer. He said great. Then he and Henri went out and found this place, and they both insisted I have the use of the two flats above the store. The title would stay in Gianni's name."

"You get free carryout from downstairs?" McGill asked.

Gabbi grinned. "Anything I want, and you wouldn't believe

the service. Well, maybe *you* would, living in the White House."

They ordered dinner. It came quickly, grilled chicken *au gratin.* So good McGill immediately wanted to share it with Patti, his kids, and everyone else he loved. He insisted on writing a thank you note to the chef.

Ever the professional, Gabbi said she'd deliver it *after* McGill left town.

The conversation then turned to the case.

"You think the French authorities would bury a body?" McGill asked.

"What do you mean?" Gabbi asked.

"Kinnard said the missing blonde woman got beat on pretty good. She might have suffered a concussion, fallen into the river and drowned. If she had been found floating somewhere, wouldn't the cops try to identify her? If they did and found she'd had a relationship with Thierry Duchamp, that would support Kinnard's story. On the other hand, if they disposed of the remains quietly, they could let the foreigner who killed their sports star go to prison for life."

Gabbi considered the possibility. In general, she had a great affection for the French, but she knew that politics everywhere favored pragmatic solutions. And nothing was more convenient than finding, or creating, a scapegoat.

"Maybe," she said. "Let me think if we should bring up the idea with Pruet."

McGill nodded. "Moving on. Do you ever remember seeing Thierry Duchamp's photo in the newspapers?"

"Not the ones I read."

"But the paparazzi thrive here?"

"Sure."

"So let's see if we can find some photos of Thierry Duchamp with a blonde on his arm who looks something like you."

"Only younger and chestier," Gabbi added.

McGill let that one lie. He'd thought she hadn't heard Kinnard's comment. He made a mental note that Ms. Casale had excellent hearing. He also got a message from his cerebral cortex. *You haven't had much sleep lately, pal. Better shut it down soon.*

He said, "Do I need to find a hotel room or is there a rollaway cot in the embassy's attic?"

Gabbi told him, "This isn't the only place in town baby brother owns."

Hart Senate Office Building, Washington, DC

19

President Patricia Darden Grant's chief political nemesis, Senator Roger Michaelson (D-OR) sat behind his office desk and asked his chief of staff Bob Merriman the question of the moment.

"Were you able to plant a spy in the president's traveling party?"

Merriman nodded.

"And has there been anything to report?"

"Not yet."

"When, damnit?" the senator asked.

He'd loathed the president ever since she'd beaten him in a race for a House seat in Illinois, sent him back to his native Oregon with his tail tucked between his legs. He'd recovered nicely, winning a Senate seat, a far more prestigious position than being one of the 435-member mob sitting in the House. But then she had left him in her dust again by winning the presidency.

If that wasn't bad enough—and it was plenty bad—her husband James J. McGill had duped Michaelson, a former college athlete, into playing a game of one-on-one basketball. The contest had been so brutal Michaelson had wound up in the hospital.

Now, if possible, Michaelson despised McGill even more than the president.

The senator reminded his hatchet man, "There's not much time before the bitch announces her plan, whatever it is." Michaelson's informal intelligence network had learned the president had asked her G8 counterparts to arrive in London a day early so she might confer with them on something that didn't fit within the parameters of the usual international trade discussion. Just what the president was up to, Michaelson's underlings had been unable to determine. But he was sure she was going to spring something big on the world. And why not? So many saps in so many places still loved the infernal woman. "If we're going to leak, distort, and sabotage her plan, we have to find out what it is, goddamnit. We can't have much time left."

Merriman nodded. "We probably don't, but rushing things won't help. The only thing worse than not hurting the president would be to hurt ourselves."

Michaelson ground his teeth, but had to agree. His machinations had come out second-best to Galia Mindel's too many times to take any unnecessary chances.

"There's no way this person you're using can be traced back to me, is there?" he asked.

Merriman shook his head. "No way to be traced to either of us."

Michaelson took a deep breath and released it slowly. He hated to be kept waiting, but in this case he would have to look to make trouble for the president elsewhere.

And Merriman came through for him.

"McGill took a train to France." Merriman's spy had learned that.

"What's he going to do there?" Michaelson asked. "Is there any way we can use this to poke a stick in his eye?"

Merriman smiled at his boss. "You know, I was just thinking about that. Getting him in trouble with the frogs, that would be fun, wouldn't it?"

Paris

20

Investigating magistrate Yves Pruet was back on his balcony softly playing his guitar with only his carefully tended floral arrangements to hear him. Someone had once advanced the theory that plants grew larger and healthier when exposed to classical music. It was an interesting concept, but he hadn't noticed any difference in the size or vibrancy of his flowers. He did think, usually when tired or having indulged in a second after dinner drink, that when his playing was especially quiet some of the blooms leaned in his direction, the better not to miss a note. He wondered if he should advance a theory of audiotropism among impatiens.

A clicking of heels, out of time with the piece he was playing, told Pruet his audience had become more diverse. He put his instrument on its stand. He looked around to see his beautiful, impeccably dressed, oh so cold wife, Nicolette, step out onto the balcony.

A small, rueful smile appeared on the magistrate's face. "Have you found a way to divorce me and make my father pay your alimony, *ma chère?*"

She shook her head. She had given exactly that matter a great deal of thought but remained stymied. Thus far.

Pruet said, "You would like nothing better than to dispossess me of this apartment and a few million euros, wouldn't you?"

She sneered at him. "I would put you and your guitar on the street corner in an instant, if I could. You could play for your supper there or on the Metro. Perhaps I would let you take a cup to collect your coins."

"I have been a disappointment to you?"

Yves Pruet had been rising steadily through the French legal system, until the Gautier case had come his way. After that, his career prospects had vanished ... and the magic had left the Pruets' marriage.

Pruet told Nicolette, "I am thinking of making peace with my father. Begging him to take me into the family cheese business. After five or ten years, perhaps I will have risen to the point where it will be worth your while to divorce me."

His wife's look of disgust became deadly. Possibly threatening to turn Pruet to stone. She said, "I have just come from drinks with a very important man in the government. He has asked me to give you guidance on the matter of the American who killed the footballer."

Unlike so many of her countrymen, Nicolette held no interest in any sport that took place outside the boudoir.

"This very important man?" Pruet asked, "are you sleeping with him?"

"Would you care if I were?"

"I would cheer the fellow on if he were to charm you away permanently."

Madam Pruet looked as if she would like to strike her husband, but she didn't.

"For once, do what is good for you, Yves. Pretend you don't have your father's money to cushion your fall. Do what a man who needed to make his own way would do. I will leave notes instructing you on how to proceed with this case. Read them. Follow them. Then burn them."

Pruet waited until his wife had left before he smiled. Notes were written. Documentary evidence of an attempt to corrupt him, to have him break the law. It was only great arrogance, either Nicolette's, her very important lover's, or theirs together, that allowed them to think he would never act against her. But if he could send his wife to prison, along with her lover, then he could be the one to initiate their divorce. Without the risk of financial penalty.

Holding that thought wondrous in mind, he listened to the traffic rushing past below him. Come the depths of the night, though, there would be relative quiet. The Pont d'Iéna was not so far away. If he'd had trouble sleeping on the night Thierry Duchamp had been killed, would he have heard the struggle? Would he have heard the football star beating the woman, the missing blonde the American had claimed to have aided? He would have to ask M'sieur Kinnard if the woman had made any outcry. If she had—if she were real—perhaps someone nearby had heard her.

Pruet picked up his guitar and resumed playing to his appreciative flowers.

La Rive Gauche, Paris

21

McGill rode with Gabbi through the narrow, winding streets of the Left Bank.

He was on his mobile phone with Glen Kinnard. He asked, "Did Thierry Duchamp know how to defend himself?"

"I got in the first punch."

Meaning Kinnard had sucker-punched the guy, McGill thought.

"Then I got in a nice combination," Kinnard added.

"He didn't know enough to keep his hands up?" McGill asked.

"Yeah, he did. He just didn't keep them high enough. Mostly, though, he did all sorts of crazy shit with his feet. Things I never saw before. Fucker had strong legs, too. That's why he hurt me as bad as he did."

McGill took a moment to recall his meeting with Kinnard.

He says, "I didn't see any sign that he hurt you."

Kinnard told him, "That's because I covered my head better than he did. But under my clothes I'm still a mass of bruises. The fucker cracked three of my ribs. Left my thighs and ass so purple I half look like an eggplant. Pain got so bad, the fucker put me down for the count without ever landing a shot to my kisser."

McGill thanked Kinnard for the information and clicked off.

Gabbi pulled the Peugeot up in front of an Irish pub, of all things. The sign on the window said The Hideaway. A muscular black man stood in the doorway.

"We're stopping for a Guinness?" McGill asked.

Gabbi gestured upward. As with the building housing Monsieur Henri's restaurant, there were two flats above the public space. As with the building where Glen Kinnard was being held, there had been a convenient parking space out front. And a tough guy at the door.

McGill was beginning to think Gabbi had the whole town wired.

"A cool place for Gianni to hang when he hits town?" McGill asked.

Gabbi nodded. "The flat is safe, quiet, and all yours for as long as you need it."

"The pub's name," McGill said, "you know, I have a room in the White House residence the president calls my hideaway."

The RSO smiled. "Maybe it's something you inspire in women."

"They want to tuck me out of sight?"

She laughed. "Or keep you all to themselves."

There was enough light remaining in the night sky for McGill to see Gabbi consider the implications of what she had said and blush.

"I'm sorry. I shouldn't have said that."

McGill waved it off. "We'll chalk it up to all your years in France. So tell me, I'm upstairs and my stomach growls, can I call down for a sandwich and a beer?"

"Whatever you like."

"Great. Listen, there's something I forgot to ask Pruet. What time were Glen Kinnard and the late M'sieur Duchamp discovered by the police? Do you know?"

"Five fifty-five a.m.," Gabbi told him.

"Let's get over to the scene of the crime at five forty tomorrow. Take a look."

Gabbi nodded. "I'll bring some coffee from my place. Before I go, let me introduce you to Harbin. He'll take you upstairs."

She beckoned and the black man at the door to the pub walked over.

Quartier Pigalle, Paris

22

The come-on guy outside the strip club on the Boulevard de

Clichy in the red-light district of Paris wore a T-shirt that made the two young jocks from North America laugh. The one from Quebec laughed upon reading the shirt's message; the one from New York laughed when he heard the translation.

The shirt said: *Je suis le type que contre lequel votre guide de touristes vous a mis en garde.* I'm the guy your tourist guide warned you about.

The come-on guy saw that the one jock, a hockey player, was fluent in French, but decided to speak English for the benefit of the other, a lacrosse player.

"Gentlemen, ten euros will get you inside and buy you a beer." He gestured to a doorway that looked like someone had pissed in it recently. "A lap dance is but twenty euros, and if you enjoy that, a fee can be negotiated for other things."

Lacrosse shrugged. "Sorry. All we have are dollars."

"American dollars?"

"Canadian," Hockey said, joking.

The come-on guy spat on the sidewalk.

The hockey player, a patriot, normally would have clocked the greasy little creep, but being in a foreign land he allowed his friend to pull him up the street.

"You broke that dumb fuck's nose," Lacrosse counseled, "he'd probably have bled AIDS all over you. With your new deal, you don't need that."

The hockey player, a bruising defenseman, had been drafted by the Calgary Flames of the NHL. He and the lacrosse player, an unstoppable attacker, were visiting the City of Light on the hockey player's signing bonus.

The two of them were best friends, having been college roommates in Boston and having found out they'd been born on the same day, exactly 21 years ago. Each of them was six-feet-two and two hundred and twenty pounds. They both had black hair and brown eyes. Their private joke was that one of their fathers had visited both of their mothers.

There weren't any big-money lacrosse leagues, so law school and professional sports management were the lacrosse player's plan. And here he was already, making sure his friend didn't bust a valuable hand on a frog's head.

The come-on guys up and down the Boulevard de Clichy often went so far as to grab passersby to get them to enter their dives. With the two big young North Americans walking shoulder to shoulder, however, more diplomatic approaches were tried. None was successful. Insults from the scorned pitchmen were ignored.

The two jocks had been schooled by upperclassmen. Go to Pigalle for a giggle. But if you actually wanted to get laid, go to Holland or Germany. Prostitution was legal in those countries; the beer was better, too. Following further words of wisdom, Lacrosse and Hockey had limited themselves to carrying a hundred dollars—American—each. Passports, credit cards, drivers licenses and other things that would be a pain in the ass to lose had been left in their hotel's safe.

So far they hadn't had any trouble spending dollars.

If they got screwed on the exchange rate, fuck it.

They were young and going places. Losing a few bucks wouldn't matter.

They'd almost left the red light district behind when the Hockey said, "Maybe we should check out at least one of these joints, so we can say we did.

Lacrosse shrugged, figuring he'd have to get used to indulging his clients' whims. Off to their right was a side street. Darker than the main drag. Ooh, *dangereux,* Hockey said, laughing. Yeah, scary, Lacrosse said. Down the side street lay yet another strip club, this one with a neon palm tree and a hula girl flickering in the window.

The two of them headed that way. There was a little man sitting on a barstool outside the entrance. Unlike all the other come-on guys, all he said was, *"Bonsoir."*

The two jocks looked at each other. Smiled. Knew they'd found something different.

Hockey told the little man, "My friend and I have been walking up and down the street for an hour. We're looking for college girls from Denmark, but nobody has any. How about you?"

The man on the stool said, "Come back tomorrow, m'sieur. We will have college girls then. But, alas, all ours come from Norway."

The two jocks laughed. The little shit had a sense of humor.

"What do you have tonight?" Lacrosse asked.

"Polish, Russian, and Algerian."

Three ethnicities unvisited by the young North Americans. They went inside. The comedian at the door didn't even ask for a cover charge.

The place was dimly lit, but that was to be expected.

Canned brasswinds crackled out of cheap speakers.

On a stage no bigger than a ping-pong table a stripper wearing only high heels, looking not too bad by available lighting, was grinding her bod against a pole for the amusement of a half-dozen men who leaned forward for a better view. Thing was, the dancer looked like she had sore feet, a bad back and maybe some other infirmity. None of the coeds the two jocks had slept with had ever made a face like that.

"Hope that's not what ecstasy looks like over here," Hockey said.

The stripper snapped a heel, cursed and kicked off her shoes, almost beaning a couple of onlookers. Her feet now as bare as the rest of her, she looked like she felt better, except maybe her back was still stiff.

"Let's get out of here," Lacrosse said.

His GPA was a full point higher than his friend's, but he was still a beat slow. An older woman, not real old, more like a mom who'd kept her figure up and didn't mind showing a lot of cleavage, appeared between them and the door.

"You gentlemen will need a table," she said.

"We're just leaving," Lacrosse told her.

"Very well, but a table fee of one hundred euros and a two-drink minimum at one hundred euros per drink is still required."

"We just got here," Hockey said, getting hot.

"As may be. You have still seen Claudine dance."

The stripper, in fact, had stopped moving. She stood leaning against the pole with one hand, her other hand pressed against the small of her back. She was watching them. What the lacrosse player didn't like was the mean little smile the stripper had on her face.

Lacrosse told the tight-bod mom, "All we have are dollars. Maybe a hundred dollars all together. You can have that."

Hockey looked at him. "Are you crazy? We aren't giving this bitch a dime."

The woman ignored him and told Lacrosse, "A credit card will do."

"Don't have any credit cards."

"Fuck this," Hockey said, "let's get outta here."

The tough broad looked off toward a dark corner and nodded. A chair creaked, a floorboard groaned. Something *big* had just gotten to its feet.

The hard-faced woman gave it one last try.

"You may leave your passports with me until you return with five hundred euros."

The stripper was smiling wide now, two gaps in her teeth showing.

"We don't have our passports with us," Hockey said, right up in the tough broad's face.

Lacrosse jerked him back when he saw a knife appear in the woman's hand.

"This is very bad," the now evil-looking mom said.

Hockey finally got the idea they were in trouble. The gawkers were retreating from their nearby tables. Still, Hockey thought, there were two of them and ... he felt it before he heard it. The floor started to bounce. There was a low rumble. Something really *huge* was getting close, and then the smell hit him.

"Jesus!" Hockey said, wrinkling his nose. "What the hell is that stink?"

The Hideaway, Paris

23

McGill lay in his borrowed bed, thinking about the case. In particular, he thought about Glen Kinnard telling him that the mystery woman had provoked the attack on her by telling Thierry Duchamp he was underendowed. Belittling a sports star's manhood was a damn good way to ... get your finger chomped in this case. Followed by a severe bruising.

Why would a seemingly sober woman do that to herself?

The only answer he could come up with was that she hadn't expected to suffer greatly. Nor for very long. Chances were she had seen Kinnard nearby when she'd delivered the cheap shot. Or her cruelly accurate assessment, as the case may be.

If the blonde were a Frenchwoman, or at least familiar with French law, she would have known that Kinnard would be obliged to come to her aid in some way. At that time of the night, with no one else around, what form could that aid have taken except personal intervention?

Had Kinnard chosen to do nothing more than call the French equivalent of 911, the woman could have died before help arrived. So had the woman judged Kinnard to be a man who would jeopardize himself to help her? If McGill had to guess, he'd say yes. But had she thought Kinnard would be able to hold his own against a professional athlete? If so, what was the basis for such a conclusion? If the woman were still alive, and Thierry Duchamp also had survived, would the blonde have come forward and brought charges against the soccer star?

Maybe not if Duchamp had been injured and were unable to pursue his sport. Now, with the soccer star dead, the sporting public would be happy to see the blonde get the chop along with Kinnard. You took a slightly different angle on the situation, though, maybe the missing woman was seriously misanthropic, had hoped to see two men beat themselves bloody. Make Duchamp suffer for whatever he'd done to piss her off and have another sap take his lumps just on general principles.

McGill considered the damage Kinnard had suffered. An experienced brawler like him should have known several defenses against kicks. But maybe, initially, he'd been put off his game by having his wife's ashes in hand. And if he'd been caring for a dying woman for any length of time, his head-busting skills had probably gotten rusty.

McGill's ruminations were interrupted when his cell phone sounded. "Hail to the Chief." Patti was calling.

She said hello by asking, "Is France still our ally?"

"As much as ever."

"Nice ambiguity. You might have a future in politics."

"My only future in politics is following your every command."

The president laughed. "Good one. You're the only person who keeps me humble. I couldn't do without that."

"Okay. But I can keep on being your henchman, can't I?"

"I'd never have anyone else. How's the case going, Jim?"

"Won't be easy to find a missing person in a place you've never visited before."

"Are the French cooperating?"

McGill said, "This guy Pruet, I'm told he's in a no-win situation. Damned domestically if he lets Glen Kinnard go; damned by the U.S. if he locks Kinnard up and throws away the key. His best hope is for me to do something dumb."

"Which, of course, you won't."

"It's not part of my plan. Once I have a plan."

"Ms. Casale is being helpful?"

"Yeah. Provided transportation, food, shelter and ... aw, damn."

"What?" the president asked.

"I left England in such a hurry I didn't bring my clothes."

"What's the address where you're staying?" Patti asked.

McGill didn't know.

He said, "I'm in a flat above an Irish pub. On the Left Bank, I think."

"A flat above a pub?" the president asked.

"It's called The Hideaway, just like at home," McGill said. "No one will find me."

"This pub and flat are owned by?"

"Ms. Casale's kid brother, Gianni, a loyal American and the next Thomas Edison."

McGill felt he'd been interrogated long enough.

He asked, "How are things in London?"

"This is the calm before the storm. I'm going to change the status quo tomorrow."

"Always a serious business," he said. Said it so she'd know he meant it. "I miss you, Madam President. I'd enjoy Paris much more if you were here with me."

"I miss you, too, loyal henchman."

McGill was just about to say goodbye when his dear wife told him, "I'll have your clothes sent 'round."

He had no doubt they would be on his doorstep before he awakened.

Wednesday, June 3rd — Paris

1

Gabbi pulled her Peugeot to the curb in front the Hideaway at 5:15 a.m. Harbin and McGill were waiting for her, and so was her parking spot. The two men shook hands, and McGill slipped into the car. Harbin went back inside.

The RSO waited until McGill was buckled in and extended a paper cup of coffee to him. It was almost too hot to hold. There was a lid on it to avoid accidental spills. As good as the coffee smelled it was a challenge to leave the lid in place. But being too eager would scald his mouth.

"There are packets of sugar and containers of cream in the console, if that's the way you like it," Gabbi said.

That was just how McGill took his coffee, but with this cup he thought he'd try it black. Once it cooled a little. He set the cup in a holder.

"I'll get to it in just a minute, thanks."

Gabbi nodded and pulled out. The traffic at that hour was light, vans making commercial deliveries to boulangeries, cafés, and other retailers. Sunrise was about a half-hour off, but the predawn light was more than enough for McGill to see the outline of the city emerging. The air held just a hint of coolness. Paris was making quite the first impression on him.

To avoid getting giddy, he said to Gabbi, "Tell me the winters here are miserable."

"Can be," she said. "Paris doesn't get really cold the way Chicago does. It's more of a wet and dreary time, chilly enough to make you want to sit by a cozy fire. Days are blink-of-an-eye short; nights go on forever. Winter here makes you want to jump on a plane and spend a month in Tahiti or the Caribbean."

McGill would bet little brother Gianni had a home in Bora Bora or St Bart's.

But it wasn't his place to pry—at least about that.

He said, "Harbin tells me he was in the *Légion étrangère*."

The Foreign Legion.

Gabbi glanced at him. "I didn't know that. And your accent really is quite good."

"Merci," McGill said. He picked up his coffee, removed the lid and sipped. "Delicious," he told Gabbi. He took a longer drink and added, "Harbin also told me he usually doesn't spend the night at the pub, but last night he did."

The RSO kept her eyes on the road.

"Is that all right with you? I asked him to do it because, if nothing else, it helped me to sleep better."

It rankled McGill when people worried about him. You put in twenty-five years as a cop, you had cat-quick reflexes, and you were the only living master of Dark Alley in the world, you liked to think you weren't an easy mark.

But as his mother had always told him, "If someone wants to do something nice for you, Jimmy, let them, and say thank you."

He'd always been a good son.

"Thank you for your concern, Ms. Casale," he told Gabbi. "I suppose if I'm going to get you up early, you'll need to sleep soundly."

Quai Branly, Paris

2

They parked in a public lot adjacent to the Seine, a short distance from the crime scene. McGill finished his coffee and said, "Gotta be something more than coffee beans in this cup."

Gabbi said, "Sure. But you don't ask French chefs how they work their magic."

They walked in companionable silence along the concrete left bank of the river. Ahead, they saw a dark-haired boy, maybe in his early teens, walking toward them. He gave them a glance, not lingering on either of them, but sizing them up all the same. McGill could tell the kid had some sort of game in mind.

He'd seen young con artists before. Alert to every person

and possibility on their side of the horizon line. The really bright ones became the hackers and phishers who stalked their prey worldwide.

"That kid's up to something," McGill told Gabbi.

Studying the boy, she said, "He's Romany, a gypsy."

McGill and Gabbi kept their eyes on the kid. He met their gaze for a second, then lowered his eyes and moved out of their way. He tensed a little as he passed by. Both McGill and Gabbi turned to watch him, saw him bend down, extend his right hand to the pavement.

The kid cried out, "*Bonté divine!*" Good heavens!

He turned to face McGill and Gabbi, took an involuntary step back when he saw they were already looking at him. Nonetheless, he showed them what he held in his hand: a gleaming gold wedding band.

"You are Americans, yes?" he asked.

"Sommes-nous?" Gabbi asked. Are we?

Her accent had the kid fooled.

"Désolé," he said. Sorry.

As the kid turned to go, McGill asked, "Would you like to make some money? Not by selling us a ring, but another way."

The kid eyed them suspiciously. McGill knew what he was thinking.

"Not sex," he said. "We need help finding someone."

The kid's bland expression said he could deal with that.

"How much money?"

McGill looked at Gabbi, "Sawbuck now, C-note if he comes through?"

The young gypsy tried to puzzle out the slang.

Gabbi nodded. She produced a 10-euro note, showed it to the boy. "This for now, ninety more if you succeed."

The kid's eyes sparkled, but otherwise he maintained a poker face.

"Who must I find?"

McGill told him about Kinnard's fight, and the woman who had been involved. He described her in outline.

Looking pensive, the kid recapitulated. Then he nodded at Gabbi.

"Like madam only younger?"

Gabbi said, *"Et plus frais."* She cupped her hands in front of her chest, which got a smile out of the kid. He took the ten euros from her.

McGill told him, "There will be an additional hundred-euro bonus if you find this woman in the next three days."

The kid bobbed his head, all business again, taking in the terms of the deal.

McGill spelled out the final details. "If you bring us just any woman with blonde hair, you will be wasting our time, and the bonus will be reduced by twenty percent for each wrong woman. Bring us three wrong women and the whole deal is off."

That didn't seem to worry the kid.

"You'll need a number to call," Gabbi told him. She wrote her office number at the American Embassy on the back of a Monsieur Henri business card and gave it to the kid.

He looked at both of them and asked McGill, "You are sure you do not wish to buy the ring for madam?"

The president's henchman said, "I'm sure."

Pont d'Iéna, Paris

3

As McGill and Gabbi drew near the bridge, they saw two figures were already standing under it. A moment later, they recognized them as Investigating Magistrate Pruet and his bodyguard, Odo Sacripant.

"Bonjour, M'sieur McGill, Mademoiselle Casale," the magistrate said. "I see our common interest has drawn us together this morning."

Without consulting with Gabbi first, McGill asked "No one has fished the body of a young blonde woman out of the Seine since the fight, have they M'sieur Pruet?"

The magistrate said, "Not to my knowledge, no."

He looked at Odo, who shook his head.

"Forgive me for asking, sir," McGill continued "but is there any chance a body might have been found and the news was kept from you?"

Rather than be offended, Pruet was grateful to hear a point raised that he hadn't considered, though he didn't say so. After another glance at Odo, he told McGill, "I will see if perhaps someone has been negligent in his reporting duties."

Then Pruet took a sheaf of photos from Odo. For the first time, McGill and Gabbi got to see Thierry Duchamp's dead body *in situ* lying next to Glenn Kinnard's unconscious form. They walked over to the spot, looked at the pavement, tried to imagine the fight as it had occurred.

McGill asked, "Would you object to a little role-playing, m'sieur?"

"Not at all," Pruet responded. "What do you have in mind?"

"I'll be the distraught American, Kinnard. Ms. Casale can play the mysterious blonde. Your colleague M'sieur Sacripant, if he doesn't mind, can play M'sieur Duchamp."

Pruet caught the spirit of the idea and liked it.

"I'll look on, an invisible observer."

They set it up so McGill stayed under the bridge with Pruet. Gabbi and Odo moved downstream a hundred feet or so and began arguing, their voices growing louder as they drew near. Pruet, following his own particular line of speculation that some passerby might have overheard the bickering voices and scurried over to have a look at the source of the unrest, kept an eye out for anyone on the adjacent Quai Branly.

On the opposite side of the street, he saw two pedestrians striding along and a man making a delivery from a commercial van. A young woman passed by on a motorbike. On the other side of the river, the Avenue de New York was empty. No one seemed to be paying any attention to the little melodrama being acted out next to the Seine.

As Gabbi and Odo neared the underpass of the bridge, Gabbi, by prearrangement, raised her voice. She shouted the insult that had set off Thierry Duchamp. Pruet looked around again. Both the girl on the motorbike and the man with the delivery van were gone. One of the pedestrians walked on, oblivious. But the other, a thin man with a youthful face but graying hair, dressed in business attire came to a stop and cocked his head.

McGill, playing Kinnard, standing under the bridge, had a ringside view of what appeared to be Odo biting Gabbi's index finger. Then, per Pruet's request, Gabbi screamed for all she was worth. Her projection was worthy of a diva, so shocking to Pruet that he thought he might indeed have heard it had he been on his balcony. Surely, someone closer must have taken notice.

The young, graying businessman, to Pruet's great approbation, was running toward the scene with his mobile phone in his hand. He was coming to the aid of a person in need, as the law required. So was McGill, as Kinnard, who yelled in a very American voice, "Hey, dickwad, knock it the hell off!"

McGill ran at the couple as if carrying an object in his left arm. The wife's urn, Pruet remembered. He was shocked once more as McGill, still advancing, yelled, "Police! Get the hell away from her!"

Police? Pruet wondered.

Would Kinnard have identified himself that way—outside of his own country?

That was when Pruet noticed that the young businessman had stopped his own advance and was craning his neck to see what was happening. He leapt a foot in the air when Pruet tapped him on the shoulder.

"Can you see what is happening?" the young man asked in French. "I am calling the police."

Pruet flashed his ID and asked for the man's name.

"Paul Leroux."

"Please wait right here, M'sieur Leroux. You will be perfectly safe and I will be back shortly."

Pruet hurried off toward McGill and Odo who seemed to be fighting with alarming authenticity ... as Gabbi, unsteady on her feet, slinked off. Odo kicked at the arm with which McGill carried his imaginary object. McGill howled and countered by sweeping Odo clean off his feet. Pruet's heart climbed into his throat as he was sure his friend's head would break against the concrete, but McGill caught Odo before that happened and pulled him back to his feet.

Then he shook Odo's hand and embraced him.

Weak with relief, Pruet turned to the businessman, Leroux, and waved him forward.

Georgetown

4

Sweetie got to the office at dawn, sat behind Jim McGill's desk, and for the next three hours read Google entries for His Excellency George O'Menehy, archbishop of Arlington, whose diocese comprised sixty-eight parishes in the twenty-one northernmost counties of the Commonwealth of Virginia. As with so many other outposts of the Universal Church, the Arlington diocese had been ensnared in the shameful scandal of enabling pedophile priests to continue their predations. As with the other dioceses, Arlington had been hit with a plague of mega-million dollar lawsuits, and had agreed to pay settlements amounting to far in excess of a year's worth of the faithful's weekly offerings.

Properties had to be sold to meet the legal liabilities.

Many people speculated it was only a matter of time before an embittered Bishop O'Menehy was retired by the Vatican. Photos of the white-haired, bespectacled, grim-faced prelate made it look as if that would not be an unwelcome development. Some observers, provocateurs obviously, put forth the notion O'Menehy's replacement might be an elevated Father Francis Nguyen—if the rebellious priest started toeing the Vatican line.

Sweetie had fallen into the habit of thinking in Latin while mulling the Byzantine turns of church politics; it was so apt to the subject. So when there was a knock at the office door she asked, "*Quid illuc?*"

There was a pause before a North Carolina accented voice replied, "That you, Ms. Sweeney? It's me, Leo. I brought you a visitor."

Sweetie switched to English. "Come in, Leo. Who's with you?"

The door swung open and Leo waved Deke into the office

He and Sweetie looked at each other.

Leo asked, "What was that you said a minute ago?"

"I asked 'who's there' in Latin."

"Huh," Leo said. "Anyway, ol' Deke here asked to see you, so I swung by his place and brought him in."

Sweetie nodded. She and Deke continued to stare at each other.

Leo said, "I'll just leave you two alone. You want to give Deke a ride home, I might just take some vacation time."

He closed the door without waiting for an answer.

5

Calling off the staring contest, Sweetie said to Deke, "You're upset. You think your mother shouldn't have broken her promise to you."

Deke nodded.

Sweetie continued, "And since your mother gave away your secret, you're about to do what, give away one or two of her secrets?"

Deke took a seat and said, "You must have been a pretty good cop."

Sweetie smiled "Back when I was in the convent, I thought I'd become a principal at a parochial grammar school. Daydreaming of how you can keep a horde of rambunctious kids in line pretty much gives you the mindset to be a good cop."

She then gave Deke the opportunity to bare his soul.

Or at least rat out his mom.

After a moment of silence, Deke said, "My mother is a schemer. That's how she makes her money. She acts as a business consultant to people who bring "hypothetical" ideas to her. She helps them see any flaws in their logic, suggests practical alternatives, and indicates where more research is needed.

"Any people in particular?" Sweetie asked. "These people your mother advises."

"They're the kind you probably locked up whenever you got the chance."

"Members of your ethnic community?"

"My mother's side of my ethnicity. The ideas she comes up with are only hypothetical, if you ask her. So she doesn't need to concern herself that they involve illegal acts. She never takes any money for her consulting services, so she can't be legally connected to anyone who puts one of those hypothetical ideas into effect. But she does receive a series of exceptionally good loans for her businesses. A lot of those loans are eventually forgiven."

Sweetie bobbed her head, impressed by the deviousness of it all.

She almost slipped back into thinking in Latin.

"How did your mother get into this line of work?"

"Consulting? She learned from my grandfather."

"He did the same thing?"

"He was a spy, a double-agent. Worked for the U.S. and the North Vietnamese."

"Ultimately for himself," Sweetie said.

"Just like Mom," Deke replied. Then he added, "You know she's playing you."

"Paying me, too. But I'll concede your point. What do you think she wants?"

"To protect Francis."

"Anything else?"

"Maybe to protect me, too."

"From what?" Sweetie didn't see the bad guys Musette had fingered, Bao and his punk, taking another shot, a deliberate one, at a federal agent.

"From myself. So I don't take out the suckers who shot me."

That sat Sweetie back in her chair.

"I know," Deke said. "The last thing you'd expect."

Well, now that he'd raised the idea, maybe not.

"You do have an interesting family," she said.

"Sometimes I get my own strange ideas. Maybe it'd be a good thing for you to wrap this whole thing up. For Francis and me. I thought it might help if you knew about Mom."

A question occurred to Sweetie. "You'd have to be in good shape to act on one of your strange ideas. So how are you feeling, really?"

"Getting stronger every day," he said, getting to his feet. "I'll find my own way home."

Arlington, VA

6

Sweetie knelt in prayer in a pew opposite the confessional booths in the Cathedral of St. John the Baptist. In the central compartment of the confessional, Bishop George O'Menehy was hearing confessions for an hour: 10:30-11:30 a.m., according to the online cathedral bulletin. Her head bowed humbly, her eyes seemingly closed, her blonde hair gleaming, her skin ruddy and flawless, her hands steepled, Sweetie was a model crying out for a Renaissance master. Or an example of the spiritual peace that came with the cleansing of a soul.

More than a few of the penitents who came out of the confessional took a pew near Sweetie to tick off their Our Fathers and Hail Marys. Two even said a whole rosary. Throughout it all, Sweetie never moved, as if her soul had already transcended earthly sorrows, and only her body remained among the living.

In truth, Sweetie was doing her absolute best to overhear the sins being confessed by those seeking the bishop's absolution. And she had very acute hearing. It was one of the things she had thought would have made her a good teaching nun—if only thoughts of the boy next door hadn't persisted long enough to make her doubt her religious vocation. Sweetie had heard admissions of missing mass and doubting papal teachings, especially as pertained to using contraceptives; doubts that a marriage could be sustained, especially if the bastard kept beating her. And if the abused woman turned the wife-beater in to the cops and he got locked up for years the way he deserved, no way could she do without a man the rest of her life.

Sweetie felt she was sinning by eavesdropping on such sorry stories. She was stealing the privacy of others. But she kept at it. Heard the doings of a despairing serial shoplifter—who *was* going to psychological counseling—but just couldn't seem to help herself. A man was having an affair with the neighbor next door, but it wasn't really his fault because he was sure the devil was in the woman. He freely admitted he was sinning by sleeping with the woman, but he knew he'd be unable to stop unless the bishop came by to cast the devil out of the woman. Then she'd just be an ordinary female to whom he wasn't particularly attracted.

Compared to the quiet voice in which Sweetie used to utter her own confessions, she was surprised by the casually accessible volumes these people used to admit their imperfections; it sounded as if they were speaking into microphones for an audience of millions. Only two men—both Vietnamese, Sweetie could see through her finely slitted eyelids—spoke too quietly to be overheard. Horatio Bao and Ricky Lanh Huu?

Seemed like a good guess to Sweetie.

Unless his excellency was confessor to Northern Virginia's whole Asian mob.

Both men had entered and left the confessional quickly, less than a minute. They both left the cathedral without kneeling to say their penance, and Sweetie hadn't heard the bishop say to either of them: "I absolve you in the Name of the Father..." They had both looked at her as they walked out of the cathedral, but Sweetie remained motionless, showing no awareness of them.

Just as they hadn't noticed Welborn Yates standing in the

shadows on the far side of the church, snapping their pictures along with all the others who had asked the bishop for forgiveness.

The two Asian men were the last to seek absolution that morning, and Sweetie was genuinely losing herself in prayer when a quiet voiced asked, "Do you have need of me, my child?"

She opened her eyes. The bishop had stepped out of the confessional and addressed her.

Sweetie told him, "I do."

She entered the confessional to enumerate her sins. Most of them.

Winfield House, London

7

Galia stepped into the sitting room of the president's suite. Patti was rereading the speech she would be giving within the hour. As with any first-rate actor, she was memorizing her lines: no Teleprompter for her. The chief of staff was the one with butterflies; Galia looked as flustered as Patti had ever seen her.

"Madam President," she said, "Jean-Louis Severin is here. He wants to see you."

Patti put her speech aside. "It's okay, Galia. I know my lines. A visitor isn't going to throw me off. Please show the president of France in."

Galia couldn't believe the president was going to accommodate the intrusion. The nerve of that Frenchman. He had to be trying to get advance word of what the president would say. The fact that he'd once had a personal relationship with Patricia Darden Grant only made it worse.

"Really, Galia, it will be all right. Jean-Louis and I go back a long way."

Exactly what worried the chief of staff.

Where the hell was James J. McGill when she needed him?

Her misgivings notwithstanding, Galia opened the door, and a smiling Jean-Louis Severin, president of France, entered.

He crossed the room to Patti, took the hand she extended and bowed to kiss it. Galia's eyebrows arched. Patti waved her out.

Severin was a darkly handsome man, an inch or so shorter than Patti. He, too, had acted, but only on stage during his student days. After graduation, politics had been his only profession. Patti gestured him to the chair opposite her.

"*M'sieur le président, s'il vous plait, asseyez-vous.*" Please be seated.

"*Oui, madame la présidente. Merci beaucoup.*"

Patti asked, "How are you, Jean-Louis?"

How was he after his divorce, they both understood.

He shrugged. "I am ... glad I still have friends."

"Friends expect less than a spouse."

"Perhaps a spouse expects too much."

"Fidelity?"

"Tell me, Patti, from a woman's point of view, which is worse, for a man to be seduced by his career or another woman?"

"Neither is pleasant, but a job doesn't leave lipstick on your collar."

For just a second, Severin's eyes darted toward his shirt.

Patti sighed. "Oh, Jean-Louis."

"You will not disown me?" he asked.

"I need you too much for that."

"I am not without my charms?"

"Not without your uses, certainly."

The president of France laughed. Patti Darden was an old friend. She had the right to needle him.

He told her, "Before she sued for divorce, Aubine said my passion for my work left none for her. Once she decided it would be foolish to ask me to resign my position, the light in her heart darkened, for me at least."

Patti asked, "Was she right? Would it have been foolish to ask you to resign?"

Jean-Louis met her eyes. "Who among us, the leaders of nations, would give up our position for a woman or a man? Would you? What would you do if your henchman came to you with such a choice?"

"You liked it when Jim called himself my henchman, didn't you?" Patti asked.

Severin beamed. "Who isn't disarmed by a winning rogue?"

Galia wasn't, the president thought. She could do without both Jim McGill and Jean-Louis Severin. But Patti knew her counterpart was still waiting for an answer to his question. A reply from one of the few people in the world who could give him a meaningful answer.

"I'd ask Jim if I could finish my first term, if he came to me with such a request."

"And if he couldn't wait?"

"Vice President Wyman is a good man. The country would be in able hands."

Severin studied his peer. "I believe you are sincere, Patricia. I also believe you are certain M'sieur McGill would never put you in such a position."

"I really can't see that he would."

Severin smiled. "Then I shall have to see that I never disappoint you either."

"Better not," Patti told him.

Washington, DC

8

Bob Merriman entered Senator Roger Michaelson's office with a wicked smile on his face and a manila envelope in his hand. Closing the door behind him, Merriman told Michaelson, "I've got him."

There was no need to identify *him*.

Michaelson pushed aside a pile of paperwork on his desk and said, "Give."

Merriman stepped around his boss's desk and handed the envelope to the senator. Michaelson opened it and saw a photo of a young woman coming out of the P Street address where McGill Investigations, Inc. had its offices. The young woman's face was clear, but the area around it was framed by fuzzy green shapes.

"What is all this stuff?" Michaelson asked, indicating the visual clutter.

"Leaves," Merriman said. "I rented an office across the street from McGill's place—in the name of a shell company. Had the tree out front pruned strategically. My place's windows are tinted so no one can see the camera setup. I thought it'd be a good idea to keep track of who is hiring McGill to be their gumshoe. Without him knowing, of course."

Michaelson smiled at his underling's deviousness, including the fact that Bob hadn't shared the news with him until now. Giving Michaelson deniability, if something had gone wrong.

"Who's the woman?" Michaelson asked.

"Emilie LaBelle. Took a little while to pin down who she is because she has no criminal record and almost no public profile," Merriman said.

"Almost none but enough for you to find something useful."

"Her father is Glen Kinnard."

It took Michaelson only a few seconds to place the name. "The guy who killed the French soccer player?"

The incident had made news on both sides of the Atlantic.

Merriman said, "Yeah. Kinnard's a former Chicago cop, just like McGill."

"Do they know each other?"

"Haven't pinned that down for sure yet. But with Kinnard's daughter going to see McGill, I'd have to think so."

"Then we know who the bastard is working for in Paris."

Merriman nodded. No way this was a coincidence.

He said, "It shouldn't be too hard to screw things up for McGill. He's trying to save Kinnard's ass? Every frog who loves his wine and cheese has to hate that. Well, they would if they knew about it. So how about a little bird tells them? McGill's case blows up in a flurry of newspaper headlines and TV stories. That ought to cause beaucoup embarrassment for the president."

Glee filled Michaelson's face. "Yeah, do it. Now, what about the direct attack on the White House?"

"We've started the whispering campaign about Patti Grant and Jean-Louis Severin being more than just friends, more than just colleagues, and it's finally reached our intended target."

"Severin's ex-wife," Michaelson says.

"Exactly," Merriman replied. "I think we should be hearing a public statement from the former Madam Severin very shortly."

"Great work, Bob. You're the best."

Merriman basked in the praise. Political destruction was an art, and he was Michelangelo.

Michaelson continued, "It's only fitting you're the first to hear."

"Hear what?" Merriman asked.

Michaelson said, "I'm going to run for president, and you're going to put me in the Oval Office."

Merriman's face went slack. His head started bobbing to a soundless beat as he considered all the ramifications of what he'd just been told. He returned to the other side of the senator's desk, slumped in a visitor's chair, and stared at his boss.

"What's wrong, Bob?" Michaelson said. "This isn't exactly the reaction I expected." Merriman pushed himself up in his chair.

"I'll get your campaign up and running, Senator. Then I'll bring in one of my people to take over. I'll backstop him when necessary."

Michaelson wasn't happy to hear that. Here he was reaching for greatness, and the guy he was counting on to see he succeeded was turning up his nose at the idea.

Michaelson asked, "Why the hell can't you just handle the whole thing?"

Bob Merriman leaned forward, a smile forming on his face.

"I'm going to be busy. Running for the senate seat you'll be leaving."

Pruet's office, Paris

9

Sitting in Pruet's office, McGill told the magistrate, "It plays for me."

McGill was referring to Kinnard's version of events, as they had been reenacted that morning.

Pruet divined the meaning of McGill's idiom, but was still mulling over his own opinion of what he'd seen. Gabbi and Odo looked on keeping their expressions neutral.

"You know the accused far better than I do" Pruet said. "That, naturally, will color your judgment. But I must confess I see the scenario as more likely than before."

McGill reminded the magistrate, "When we talked with your countryman, M'sieur Leroux, he told us he was awakened by Glen Kinnard's confrontation with Thierry Duchamp. Heard it through his open bedroom window. The one opening directly on the Quai Branly. Even if he didn't see what happened, he thought it sounded serious enough to call the cops."

Leroux's call had led to the discovery of the unconscious Kinnard and Duchamp's body. Albeit two-and-a-half hours later.

"Perhaps you're charitable enough to think an American might help as well," McGill said.

Pruet nodded. He had Paul Leroux waiting in another room for further questioning. Still unanswered was the question of whether the man had heard a woman's voice on the morning of the attack. Thus far, Leroux had said only that he'd heard the horrifying shouts of two men having a fight. If Leroux were unable to place a woman at the scene, Pruet would ask if he could provide the names of any people he would normally see in the morning when he walked along the Quai Branly.

Maybe someone else could provide a fuller account.

Pruet asked McGill, "Did M'sieur Kinnard tell you that he called out his identity as a policeman?"

McGill shook his head.

"No. But he was with the Chicago Police Department at the same time I was; he would have had the same training I did. We were taught to identify ourselves before we acted. I called out my identity as a police officer reflexively, despite the fact I'm retired. Despite the fact that I'm in Paris not Chicago. If Kinnard did the same, even if Thierry Duchamp didn't speak English, he would have recognized the word police, wouldn't he?"

Odo had been watching McGill closely and nodded. "*Oui.* I recognized it when you called out, without having to shift my thinking to English."

Pruet asked his bodyguard, "Were you thinking in French while arguing with Ms. Casale?"

Odo nodded. "Of course. That was my part."

"Were you fighting with M'sieur McGill in French as well?"

"*Oui.* But I am not a professional football player. So I doubt my kicks were as accurate."

There was a subtext here, McGill could see it on Pruet's face, but he didn't pry.

"May I ask what your next step is?" McGill asked the magistrate. "So we're not duplicating our efforts."

Pruet told McGill he would look for any possible witness to the crime, someone who did not come forth as he or she should have. "And you, Mr. McGill?"

McGill looked at Gabbi. "What's the phrase in French?"

She knew just what he wanted. "*Cherchez la femme.*"

Look for the woman.

McGill and Gabbi took their leave. Pruet turned his attention to Odo.

"You are not a footballer, so you don't know how to kick? You are a master of savate, or so you've always told me. Kicking is second nature to you."

"I used to think so," Odo said, darkening with embarrassment. "I did not see the sweep from the Ami coming. One moment I was nicely balanced on my left foot, the next I was sailing away like a kite in a gale."

"I thought I was going to lose you, *mon ami*."

"I thought so, too. But M'sieur McGill was kind enough to save me from everything but embarrassment." Odo shook his head in chagrin. "He is amazingly quick, Yves. And he knows techniques I have never seen."

"I still have great respect for your ability and your judgment, Odo. So the question I am about to ask you is entirely serious."

"Yes?"

"If it had been the president's henchman who had confronted Thierry Duchamp under the Pont d'Iéna, do you think our national sports hero would still be alive?"

Odo didn't have to think twice. "Oui. Damaged but alive. But what difference does that make?"

"It raises the question of intent. After Kinnard intervened—if there was a woman in jeopardy—did he have to fight desperately to save himself? Or was he a short-tempered fellow, further aggravated by the death of his wife, a man who decided to beat Thierry Duchamp to death simply to satisfy his own rage?"

Odo said, "His record, as furnished by his own department, indicates a frequent use of violence."

"As M'sieur McGill indicated, none of those instances was judged to merit punishment."

"Cops protecting cops."

"Probably so. But Kinnard also received commendations for valor. I would like to know who this fellow truly is. I would also like to know how closely he and Thierry Duchamp were matched as combatants."

"With Duchamp dead, we will never know."

"We may not know exactly. But if in your expert opinion M'sieur McGill would have had little trouble with Duchamp, then there is a way to reach an approximate conclusion."

Odo looked at Pruet in disbelief. "Surely, Yves, you are not suggesting—"

"I'm afraid I am," Pruet said.

Paris

10

Arno Durand, a French sportswriter at *La Bataille de Sports*—The Sports Battle—a hard-edged sports tabloid, was busy pounding out a story on his computer. He worked from a notebook, transcribing his scribbles into a story. *La Bataille's* specialty was scandal in the sports world. Durand was writing about the high-scorer of the Russian women's national basketball team being a transsexual. The tabloid made no judgments of people who changed their physical gender to match their self-image, but according to confidential sources, Mavra Baklanova had begun playing for the Russian team while still sporting the genitalia of Mikhail Baklanov.

The reporter had the documentation he needed to back up his story: dates of games in which Baklanov played preceding the date of his sex-change procedure done in a Bangkok clinic. The rebuttal of any critics of his story would be even more satisfying than the splash the breaking news would produce. A follow-up story would say that it had become necessary for league officials to do a brief but definitive examination of just what kind of crotch each "woman" possessed before allowing her to compete. He finished writing his story with a smirk on his face.

With exquisite timing, the reporter's phone headset beeped with an incoming call.

"*Oui,*" Durand grunted, answering the call.

"*Parlez-vous anglais?*" the caller's voice asked.

"Yes, of course. I cover football in England."

The English were always good for scandals. But the voice on the phone sounded American.

"This concerns the death of Thierry Duchamp."

Durand was hooked immediately. "Yes, what about it?"

"A detective has been hired to clear the American who killed him."

"A French detective?"

"No, American."

"Does the gendarmerie know of this?"

"You'll have to find out for yourself."

"What is this detective's name?"

"James J. McGill." The caller clicked off.

Durand would have dropped the phone if it hadn't been attached to his head.

The American president's henchman was investigating the death of Thierry Duchamp? That would certainly be the story of the year.

Durand knew he would have to move fast to insure that it was his alone.

Georgetown

11

Sweetie ignored Welborn as he paced in front of her desk at McGill Investigations, Inc. She read from her book of daily prayer and meditation as the young Air Force investigator paraded back and forth like a figure in an arcade game.

On Sweetie's desk lay two photos: the Vietnamese men who had briefly visited Bishop O'Menehy's confessional that morning. Each time he passed, Welborn glanced at the photos.

Without looking up, Sweetie said, "You always have so much trouble making up your mind, Welborn?"

He stopped and looked at her. "If it's all the same to you, Margaret, I'm feeling a bit conflicted. Unsure of my role here."

Sweetie marked her place and closed the book. She looked at her young companion. The two of them with their blonde hair and fair complexions look as if they could be brother and sister.

"Who sent you here, Welborn?"

"The president."

"And did Patti place any limitations on you, outside of not committing criminal acts?"

Welborn studied Sweetie. "Are you really on a first-name basis with the president?"

"Uh-huh. We're buds."

"And you don't think she'd mind my using a federal data base to help you with your case? You being a partner, if I understand things correctly, in a *private* enterprise."

"Philosophically, should any information gathered using taxpayer money ever be off-limits to taxpayers?"

Welborn said, "I'm not worried about answering to philosophers; it's courts martial that concern me."

"I think you'd be hard pressed to find an unsympathetic audience if you explain you were helping to find the assailant of a Secret Service agent."

Welborn slumped into a visitor's chair.

"Are we even supposed to be poking our noses into a Secret Service case?"

"They haven't done so well, have they?"

"Still."

"And we're only exploring an avenue brought to us by a private citizen."

"Small comfort, Margaret."

"You're going to insist on addressing me by my given name."

"It's my upbringing. As to the rest, I don't do well with ambiguity," he said.

"Me either. I'm trying to square finding Deke's shooter with fudging my confession to Bishop O'Menehy."

"You didn't tell him—" Welborn bit his tongue.

"Tell the bishop lies? No, not outright. But I shaded, I omitted. I'm worried that whatever's in the air around this town might be getting to me. I feel like I need another confession to make up for the last one. Even so, it would be nice to know if those two mugs are in fact Horatio Bao and Ricky Lanh Huu, and if so whether they have criminal records."

"And I wish I had a clue about what I should do."

"A sign?" Sweetie asked. She steepled her hands and closed her eyes, as if in prayer. A heartbeat later the phone rang. Sweetie opened her eyes and smiled.

"If that's just a coincidence," she said nodding at the phone, "the call will be for me."

The phone rang again.

"On the other hand, if it's for you..."

She picked up, answering, "McGill Investigations...Why, yes, he's right here." She extended the phone to Welborn. "A Ms. Kira Fahey, calling from the White House."

Welborn took the phone, and gave Sweetie a look.

"Hi, what? Yes, of course. Put her through."

As Welborn waited for the connection to be made, Sweetie asked, "The president?"

"Close enough. Galia Mindel."

Winfield House

12

President Patricia Darden Grant welcomed the leaders of the G8 nations, excepting Russia, and adding the president of South Korea, to Winfield House. The leaders of the world's leading economic powers were formally presented to President Grant by the U.S. ambassador to the Court of Saint James, Garret Byrne. Most of them had already had the pleasure in bilateral meetings. The handshakes were mostly cordial, correct in the case of British Prime Minister Norvin Kimbrough. There was a special twinkle in the eye of German Chancellor Erika Kirsch, the only other female leader present, when she shook Patti's hand.

The group was seated in comfortable chairs arranged in a semicircle in front of the lectern from which Patti would speak. Glasses of water had been provided for all in case President Grant's words caused anyone's throat to suddenly go dry.

French President Jean-Louis Severin sat just off-center to the left, with Norvin Kimbrough on one side of him and Erika Kirsch on the other. The leaders of France and Germany seemed to possess a foreknowledge of Patti's plans that the others lacked. Only Norvin Kimbrough gave any sign of having picked up on that. Kimbrough, a Tory, had backed one of Patti's opponents, Governor Lawrence Concannon of Massachusetts, in the Republican primary race. Kimbrough had been open in his support of Concannon, something Patti could accept as both men had been at Oxford, the governor having been a Rhodes Scholar. But after Patti had beaten Concannon, the last of her challengers to stay in the race, there had been rumors that Kimbrough had urged his friend to run as an independent. Concannon had the personal fortune to make inroads into Patti's vote count, but he was smart and knew it would damage him beyond repair, politically, to try to be a spoiler and throw the race to the Democrats. Concannon hadn't risen in the world by backing the wrong horse. He'd pledged his support to Patti and campaigned vigorously for her. That had left Kimbrough with egg on his face and a political enemy in the new American president. That blunder had also boosted the fortunes of the Labor Party in the UK, and left the prime minister vulnerable within his own party.

Kimbrough had only himself to blame for his troubles. But he didn't have the integrity to do that. He blamed Patti for getting above herself. For being a woman in what still should have been a man's world. Her and that damn Kraut, Kirsch.

As soon as all the staffers had left the room, Patti said, "Chancellor Kirsch, gentlemen, I thank you from the bottom of my heart for agreeing to meet with me here today at Winfield House. I did not extend this invitation to you lightly." Patti paused, like a cliff-diver gathering herself before taking the plunge. "What I propose to you today is that we make history."

Hart Senate Office Building

13

Senator Roger Michaelson, a member of the Senate Armed Services Committee, slammed his fist on his desk, not believing the document he'd just read.

"She can't do this, goddamnit," Michaelson ranted. "She's trying to end our status as a superpower, the only superpower.

Whatever piece of crap agreement she gets over there in London—if the goddamn Europeans are stupid enough to go for it—it will never be approved by the Senate. I'll kill it all by myself, if I have to."

Bob Merriman, who had brought the bad news to the senator, sat and pondered the situation. His initial judgment was a political one. He told Merriman, "She'll have 99% of the women in this country with her; she'll have an overwhelming percentage of liberals and voters under forty; she'll have the Libertarians and America-firsters, too." Merriman barked out a harsh laugh. "Where she'll have the most trouble is with her own damn party."

"The fucking Republicans can get in line behind me," Michaelson said.

Bob Merriman looked at his boss. The senator had heard every word he'd said and hadn't given a moment's consideration to any of them. Patti Grant had come up with a foreign policy masterstroke, as Merriman saw it, one that would allow her to proceed with domestic policy changes that would be equally profound. In the second year of her first term, she was on her way to becoming one of the great presidents of American history—and Roger Michaelson was going to kill all that?

Merriman didn't think so. Given just a few minutes to consider the situation, he wasn't even sure he wanted to thwart the president. Which was damned odd because he'd started the day wanting to destroy the Grant presidency as much as Roger Michaelson did. So what had happened to his political—his tribal—loyalty?

Could the world, and the way he looked at it, really change that fast?

The Hideaway, Paris

14

In the Irish pub below his new digs, McGill and Gabbi sat in a booth at the back of the room. Gabbi had a laptop computer sitting closed on the table between them. A waitress brought them burgers and fries. McGill had a Coke; Gabbi had a Perrier.

The waitress smiled, let her look linger on McGill a moment, then left.

"She's trying to figure out who you are," Gabbi told him.

"Character-actor types like me are always hard to place," he answered. He lifted the bun on his burger and looked at the patty.

"You're not the leading-man type?" Gabbi asked.

McGill raised his eyes and gave her a smile. "A henchman never is. Besides, I do my best work when people are looking the other way." He went back to inspecting the burger.

"Isn't it cooked properly?" Gabbi asked.

"I'm just wondering, you know, if it's really beef. I hear they eat horses over here."

Gabbi laughed. "They do, but not in this place. That's prime beef."

She picked up her burger, took a big bite. "Yum. The fries are great, too."

McGill was reassured. He took a bite and shared Gabbi's opinion of the burger. He washed it down with a sip of Coke. Popped a fry into his mouth.

"Have to bring my honey here sometime," McGill said.

"Mention my name, you'll get a good table."

McGill grinned. "You think Magistrate Pruet or his bodyguard ever come here?"

"It's more of an ex-pat place," Gabbi said.

McGill nodded, worked on his lunch.

"You don't trust Pruet?" Gabbi asked.

"I don't distrust him; I kind of like his manner. I'm just trying to sort things out. Decide what I'd do in his place."

"You don't intend to freelance, do you?"

McGill shook his head. "Can't embarrass the president. Just want to make sure I have wiggle room in case anyone tries to put the squeeze on me." He looked at Gabbi's computer. "Shall we Google the late Mr. Duchamp? See if he's been photographed in the company of someone who looks like you."

Gabbi opened her computer. But they both saw a problem before they even got started. If they remained seated where they were and wanted to see the monitor at the same time, they'd have to share the view of their research with anyone who passed by.

They looked at each other and Gabbi said, "Let me slide in next to you." She did, careful to leave six inches of space between them. She pulled up the Internet and the ubiquitous Google search engine.

McGill noticed something. "Hey, they don't have the same keyboard over here."

Gabbi smiled. "Yeah, the nerve of the French, having a keyboard of their own. Took me two weeks to learn it. Now qwerty throws me." She pulled up a list of links for Thierry Duchamp. "Only fifty-six thousand-plus possibilities. Well, maybe we'll get lucky. If it's all right with you, I'll take care of the check and get us fresh drinks so we're not disturbed."

McGill nodded, said, "Thanks." He was already into the search.

Gabbi stepped away, came back a few minutes later, wearing a frown.

McGill looked up at her and asked, "What's wrong?"

"Just got a call from the embassy. They fielded a call asking if you're in town."

"Who wants to know?" McGill asked.

"A sportswriter."

Winfield House, London

15

Patti was putting on an AV presentation. A four-color vertical bar chart appeared on a large screen next to where Patti stood at her lectern in a narrow spotlight.

"This chart shows the number of U.S. troops currently in Europe and the annual cost in dollars of maintaining those troops in their European bases."

The president clicked to the next graphic, a historical measurement.

"Here we have the numbers of troops who have served in Western Europe and the dollars that have been spent protecting the continent since the end of World War II."

The numbers of both troops and dollars were staggering.

The president looked at her peers.

"There are no charts for the number of European combat troops stationed in the United States nor a dollar amount that has been spent on them because the nations of Europe haven't had to bear the staggering burden the United States has borne. Charts similar to the first two I've shown are available to show the cost to the United States of defending Japan and the Republic of Korea.

"When I said the burden on the United States has been staggering, I was understating the situation. As the president of the United States, and the commander in chief of our armed forces, I've come to view the military commitments I inherited—essentially to protect a majority of the planet—to be unsustainable. My country and my countrymen have too many pressing needs at home to subsidize the defense of friends who have grown wealthy under the umbrella of American military protection, friends who have raced past us in many measures of national health and welfare, friends who are increasingly better able to compete in the global marketplace than we are.

"One option available to me is to return home and present to Congress a plan to bring all our military forces home and reinvest the savings in paying down our national debt and addressing critical domestic needs. But my sense is that would be too disruptive and ultimately counterproductive. So what I'm proposing to you here is a concept I call the Proportionate Forces Doctrine.

"I have to digress momentarily to let all of you know that I've been thinking of this idea for some time, before I even decided to run for president. As President Severin and Chancellor

Kirsch have been the first of your number to visit the White House since my inauguration, I've spoken to them of what I'm proposing today to all of you. Jean-Louis, to his credit, has come up with a more graphic and accessible description of what I'm proposing. He calls the plan Points of the Spear.

The president changed the video to a spear image. Three points of it were detailed.

"For purposes of this plan, we divide the spear into three parts: the tip, the grip, and the base. These parts would respectively represent: combat troops, support troops, and supply troops. In the European theater, the tip and the grip would be apportioned to member states of the European Union, the base would be the United States. In the Asian area the tip and the grip initially would rotate between Japan and the Republic of Korea. The United States would be the base. As other nations such as Australia, New Zealand, and Singapore became integrated into the structure, they would alternate as the grip and the United States would remain the base."

At this point, Prime Minister Kimbrough interrupted.

"Am I to infer, Madam President, that the United States is to become a pacifist nation?"

"Hardly, Prime Minister. We will still have continental responsibilities."

At that point, the Canadian prime minister, Gordon Kendrie, spoke up. "You're referring to North America, Madam President?"

"I am, Prime Minister. North America and the Caribbean Basin. That's where the United States will be the tip of the spear. We hope our dear friends in Canada will be the grip, and we hope to persuade Mexico and the Central American countries to join with our European and Asian friends to be the base."

"And what of the rest of the world, Madam President?" asked Italian Prime Minister Matteo Gallo.

"That we will have to work out," Patti answered.

Jean-Louis Severin added, "And when we do, we will bear in mind how much America has done for all of us through these past many years."

Several members of the group nodded. But President Ku of South Korea looked less than thrilled; Prime Minister Sugiyama of Japan was impassive. But it was only the UK's Norvin Kimbrough who gave voice to any direct criticism.

"As you said, Madam President, we are indeed witnesses to the making of history: We're witnessing the day the United States of America forsook being a superpower."

Patti gave the prime minister an arctic smile.

"Let me be the first to tell you, Norvin," Patti said, "it hasn't been all that super. But if we're smart and careful here, all of us will come out stronger."

Georgetown

16

"Madam Chief of Staff," Welborn said into Jim McGill's office phone.

"Thank you for the professional courtesy of using my title, Captain Yates, but when it's just the two of us, Ms. Mindel will do."

"Yes, ma'am. What can I do for you?"

There was a pause before Galia answers. "I'd like you to do a background check for me on Sir Robert Reed, the queen's private secretary."

Welborn wasn't quite sure what he was hearing. "The queen of England, Ms. Mindel?"

"That would be the one, captain. Look back as far as, say, his grandparents. I'd like to know everything about him, and condense the information to one hundred double-spaced pages. I'd like that as soon as possible."

Welborn still didn't have a clue what all this was about, but didn't think it his place to ask.

"What sources should I use, ma'am?" he inquired.

"Use anything you can find, from the Library of Congress to any file the intelligence community might have on Sir Robert."

This time the pause was on Welborn's end of the conversation. "On whose authority shall I base my inquiries, Ms. Mindel?"

"We both work for the president, captain. That's whom we'll be working for here."

Okay, Welborn thought. "Ms. Mindel, may I use that same authority to make another inquiry? One brought to me by Ms. Margaret Sweeney in a matter that might relate to the shooting of Secret Service Special Agent Donald Ky."

Galia quickly ran that one through her mind. She was having Sir Robert checked out because she wanted to know if a man who seemed to be developing a personal interest in her might have ulterior motives, ones that might be harmful to the president or her administration. Now Yates was asking her about a situation that had to involve the president's husband. She could simply tell the young Air Force captain to pass any information he had along to the Secret Service. But James J. McGill had made it painfully clear to her that she was not to muck about in his business, which was certainly what this had to be if Margaret Sweeney was involved.

"Go ahead, captain. But tread very lightly when you use the president's name."

London

17

Fleet Street had full-page headlines on Patti's history-making meeting before the national leaders even left Winfield House. Headlines shouted: YANKS OUT! and NATO DEAD! Television networks from around the world had already stationed reporters and cameras at the gates of Winfield House and now their numbers were doubled. Battalions of police had to clear the way for the dignitaries to depart. Only one head of state, South Korea's President Ku, had any comment, and only after he had made his way to Heathrow Airport. Asked why he was going home, he said only, "The Republic of Korea is not a member of the G8." And from the grim expression on his face, it looked dubious whether South Korea would participate in the new alliance structure.

Soon after that, the world's focal point turned to the Kremlin. The Russian foreign minister, Grigori Babin, announced that his country, in addition to not participating in that year's G8 meeting, was considering withdrawing from the forum permanently. He would also be discussing with the senior leadership of the Russian government the appropriate response to any hostile posture being adopted by any country following the lead of the United States' dangerous new plan.

Back home in the U.S., members of the House of Representatives and the Senate rose to speak critically of the president's plan. As Bob Merriman had predicted, the harshest rebukes came from members of the president's own Republican party; it was the Democrats who counseled patience, some of them even applauding President Grant's ideas.

Then the focus shifted to Paris when the website of *Le Monde* posted the headline: France Will Lead. The Elysee Palace was immediately swamped with a flood tide of questions asking how it was determined that France should be the tip of the spear. Would that be a permanent thing or would that role rotate as President Grant had said? Picking up on that question, the website for *Le Canard Enchainé* asked: Will Liechtenstein Be the Next to Lead?

All this was not the public rollout Patti had planned. Somebody had leaked her plans.

She asked Galia: "Which bastard was it, Kimbrough or Michaelson?"

Montmartre, Paris

18

Alexandru Régis and his wife Ana were fourteen and thirteen respectively and married for almost a year. Régis, of course, was their public surname. Their true names were known only to a handful of other Rom. Their families and their clan were of the entertaining arts: musicians, singers, and dancers; jugglers and acrobats; conjurers, magicians, and fortune-tellers. Ana's pure high voice, singing songs of love, was the last thing Alexandru heard at night before he fell asleep. Ana wanted very badly for Alexandru to give her a child, and he certainly wanted her to bear him many sons, and pleasure him even when a child didn't result, but Ana was as delicate as she was beautiful. He was sure if they consummated their marriage too soon—especially as big and hard as she made him—he might kill her, if not with his manhood then by snapping her in half during their passion. He'd had a dream warning him of just such a fate and he heeded it despite his desperate longing. They would wait and when Ana matured into womanly strength then they would know ecstasy such as they could not yet imagine. For her part, Ana tempered her frustration by appreciating her husband's gentleness and intelligence—and how he did let her pleasure him by throttling his great shaft until it erupted and became a soft, weak thing in her hand.

The two of them sat before Alexandru's great grandmother in the hour before midnight in her room above the storefront where she foretold the future to credulous French folk and tourist *gadje*—outsiders—as Madam Mystère. To the young couple she was Bunica—Grandmother— Anisa. As she was also the queen of their clan, they were doubly respectful. They'd come to her with the story of the *gadje* who wanted Alexandru to find a blonde woman. The *gadje* who had given Alexandru ten euros with the promise of as much as 190 more. They thought Bunica Anisa with her wisdom might know a way to get the family even more than that.

She stroked the cheeks of both children and gave them a gold-toothed smile.

"Americans, you say?" asked Bunica Anisa.

"The man definitely; the woman possibly," Alexandru replied. "Her French is perfect, including the Parisian accent. But her English is American and also perfect."

"Which part of America?" the queen asked.

She expected much of her great grandson. His intelligence was a sparkling thing.

"Television American. Also the man is a *flic*." A cop.

"But he was not with the gendarmerie?"

"No, he is here looking for the woman, who looks like the woman he is with."

"Describe this woman with the *flic*."

Alexandru did.

Bunica Anisa asked, "Is she his lover?"

Alexandru shook his head. "She works with him, I would say."

"Not *for* him?"

The young Rom reviewed his impression of the two *gadje*.

"She defers to him, but he doesn't force the respect."

Anisa took that into her calculations. Ana liked her husband's description. It matched her understanding of the way she felt about herself and Alexandru.

"This woman they seek," the queen asked, "could she be the other's sister?"

"They did not say, and I am not certain." Alexandru's face clouded with uncertainty.

"What is it, my sweet?" Bunica Anisa asked.

After only a slight hesitation, Alexandru said, "With sisters, are they likely to have different…" He cupped his hands in front of his chest.

His grandmother cackled. "It is possible, yes. Some are different, others almost alike. But what you say means the woman you saw and the one you didn't are not identical twins. More likely they are strangers with a resemblance. Let me think the night on this."

Bunica Anisa kissed each of them goodnight, but she held Alexandru back a moment. "Your wife is waiting for her marriage bed to have meaning."

Alexandru lowered his eyes. He knew Ana would never have said anything, but he believed Madam Mystère really did have the second sight

"I want nothing more, Bunica, but I have my fear."

"You are everything a young man should be, Alexandru. You and Ana will have your joy soon enough. I have seen this."

The boy lifted his gaze and smiled brightly.

"And the *gadje* with their euros?"

"That we will find out."

The Hideaway, Paris

19

McGill had the lights off in the apartment where he was staying. He looked out at the skyline of Paris. In the immediate vicinity, it was more quaint than breathtaking. Apartments and small commercial buildings. The streets below were still filled with pedestrians even as midnight approached. Tourists having a good time in Paris. Nobody thought to look up to where he stood watching them, sipping from a bottle of water.

He turned away when he heard the two bars of his cellphone ringtone: "Hail to the Chief." Patti calling.

McGill tapped the speak button and said, "I'm still thinking foreign travel is a lot more fun when you're with your honey."

"Your honey wishes she was with you right now," said the President of the United States. "Just you and me—with every last reporter on the dark side of the moon."

"Sounds good, but neither of us is a quitter when we have a job to do."

"More's the pity. I called to have you reassure me that the Dark Alley move you showed me will really work."

"Just like a charm," McGill promised.

"And if I do it right I won't look like I'm mugging someone?"

"You've been practicing right?"

"Yes."

"Then it will be devastating but entirely misleading."

"There will be lots of cameras," Patti said. "There always are, everywhere I go. Sometimes the weight of all the attention makes me tired."

McGill's curiosity about what his wife had in mind rose to new heights, and he was disturbed that she sounded almost dispirited, not like herself at all. But as far as the Dark Alley move he'd shown her went, he knew she had excellent physical coordination—a dancer's grace—and she worked hard at everything she did.

"The cameras won't matter," he said. "Do it right and they'll record just what you want them to see. Now, without me poking my nose where it doesn't belong, I really have to ask: Are you all right?"

After a moment of silence, Patti said, "Yes. I'm fine. Up to a point. If anything's bothering me, it's that I'm angry. For the first time in a long time, I'd like to smack someone."

McGill had always done his best to watch his temper when he'd been a cop. When you were given the power of arrest, a gun, and a stick, it was best to exercise conscious self-restraint. You either did that or you explained yourself to disciplinary boards and maybe the state's attorney.

His former police powers were chump change compared to the might Patti wielded. Armies marched when she gave the order. So having her angry enough to want to strike someone—and having him teach her the Dark Alley way to do just that—worried McGill.

"You know," he said, "maybe it would be better if you forgot about the physical rough stuff and had Galia show you how to politically knife whoever is bothering you."

Patti laughed. "Don't worry, I've got that part covered. And I won't beat anyone up unless I have to. The real reason I called was to hear your voice. It calms me. Makes me feel loved."

McGill's heart swelled and he told his wife, "Put the phone on your pillow. I'll sing you to sleep."

Patti said, "Do you know how long—" She stopped abruptly. McGill heard what sounded like the rustling of sheets. Then his wife's voice told him, "Okay, go."

He took a sip of water and started to sing "You'll Accomp'ny

Me."

His inflection originated two hundred miles west of Bob Seger's, but both men's voices were similarly Mid-American. And every note McGill sang in his soft sweet baritone was on key. Memories of singing lullabies to his children added to the warm glow he felt.

He finished by whispering, "*Je t'aime, ma chère.*"

He'd seen those words on a dozen T-shirts in Paris that day.

Gabbi had told him what they meant, and how to pronounce them.

Not ten seconds after clicking off with Patti, the phone sounded again. "Take Me Out to the Ballgame." This time, it was Sweetie.

"I'm not calling too late, am I?" she asked.

"Just got off the phone with Patti," he told her.

"How's she doing? After all the uproar."

McGill's pause told Sweetie he'd missed something.

"We didn't talk about business," McGill said, "hers or mine. What's going on?"

Sweetie told him about Patti's proposal to reorganize the defense structure of the globe's major industrial democracies.

"We're not going to be the world's cop anymore?" McGill asked.

"Not if enough countries go along," Sweetie told him. "And maybe even if they don't."

"Huh, I think I like it," McGill said. "How about you?"

Sweetie agreed. "We've carried the load long enough. But I think the news didn't come out the way Patti planned. There was no positive spin here at home; she's catching a lot of grief from her own party. Russia and China both think there must be booby-traps being set for them. The biggest support is coming from right where you are. The president of France is Patti's best bud."

"So somebody leaked the news, maybe hoping to wreck the whole plan, sabotage Patti's administration. And we both know who that's likely to have been."

"Roger Michaelson," Sweetie said. "But I don't think you're going to get him on a basketball court again."

McGill had delivered a savage beating to his wife's political nemesis under the cover of a one-on-one basketball game. But he didn't have the free time to deal with the junior senator from Oregon right now.

Then again maybe, with Patti asking him to teach her Dark Alley, she intended to deliver the blows personally. Sweetie then gave McGill something else to ponder.

"You remember Putnam, my landlord? He called me to say Erna Godfrey's first appeal of her death sentence has been denied."

"Huh," McGill grunted. "Any political blowback on that?"

"Might have been if Patti's news out of London hadn't smothered everything else."

McGill smiled. "So Michaelson might have inadvertently done Patti at least a small favor. But let's keep all that stuff on the back burner for now."

Taking the cue, Sweetie moved on and told McGill what was happening in her investigation of Deke's shooting.

"You told me the shot was meant for Deke's mother, right?" he asked.

"Yeah, that's what she told me. After that, Deke informed me his mother's something of a criminal mastermind, at least on a conceptual level."

"What?"

Sweetie filled him in on the details. McGill thought about what he'd heard.

"Something she did is coming back to bite her?"

"Her and maybe her nephew, Deke's cousin, the Reverend Francis Nguyen, and possibly his eminence Bishop George O'Menehy."

"This involves the church?"

"Oh, yeah. The church, at least one of its sacraments and, my guess, a lot of money." Sweetie told McGill about eavesdropping on the bishop's confessional. "Welborn snapped pictures of the two Vietnamese guys who dropped in on his eminence. He's going to run the photos through the feds' databases."

"Good. You feel comfortable handling this one alone, Margaret?"

Sweetie said, "I'm not alone. I've got Welborn and—Jim, I've got to go. I'll call you back tomorrow."

"What happened?" McGill asked, alarmed.

"It's okay. Father Francis Nguyen just dropped in for a visit."

Georgetown

20

Sweetie got to her feet as the young Asian-American cleric stepped in front of McGill's desk. She stood a good six inches taller than he did, probably outweighed him by forty pounds. But the man's stoic face, steady gaze, and sense of self-possession told her how strong he was.

"Good day, Father Francis," Sweetie said. "Please have a seat. Would you like some coffee, tea, or water?"

He gave her a small shake of his head.

"My Aunt Musette told you who I am?" he said.

"She did, and showed me a picture. A good likeness."

"May I ask what else she told you?"

Sweetie gestured to a chair, "Please, Father, if we're going to talk, have a seat."

Father Nguyen was plainly a man who didn't like to bend, but he sat. So did Sweetie.

She told the priest, "Father, I think we'd both be much better off if the two of us could speak freely. Solve our problems quickly and probably keep people from being hurt. But you have your sacramental vows to keep and I have my professional confidences to keep. We both want at least some of the same things, but the problem is, how do we talk to each other?"

The idea that Sweetie might have to be discreet about what she knew had clearly eluded the cleric. But he accepted it without complaint. "I'm sorry I bothered you. I should have realized I wasn't the only one with obligations of secrecy."

A thought entered the priest's mind, apparently an unwelcome one as Sweetie could see him struggle before yielding to it. "I don't suppose it would dissuade you from pursuing your investigation if I prevailed on my aunt to dispense with your services."

"No, Father. Not now. And I'm not the only one. Deke's not going to quit and neither will the Secret Service."

Before the priest could respond, the phone rang.

"Pardon me, Father. This might be important, but I'll try to keep it short." Sweetie picked up the phone. "McGill Investigations."

"Sweetie? It's Abbie. If you've got a minute, I need to talk with someone."

Sweetie caught the note of distress in her goddaughter's voice.

"No one's threatening you or Kenny or Caitie, are they?" she asked.

Sweetie saw Father Nguyen's head swivel toward her. He'd turned his head away to afford her a measure of privacy, but now he was looking right at her.

"No, no," Abbie said. "We're all fine. Well, I'm not. I told my dad something, and I think I might have hurt his feelings."

Father Nguyen must have overheard, Sweetie thought, because he looked away once more.

"What did you say, Abbie?" Sweetie asked.

The eldest McGill child told Sweetie about deciding to use her mother's maiden name on her college applications so she wouldn't be given undue preference in admission decisions. Sweetie saw a small smile light the priest's face. A sign of approval? If so, the good father had hearing as keen as Sweetie's.

"I don't think I should get any special treatment. I don't want it. But I don't want to hurt my dad, either. I was hoping you might have some advice."

Sweetie bobbed her head. "Abbie, not wanting an unfair advantage is exactly the right position to take. But why can't you just say so?"

"What do you mean?"

"Isn't there a place to make a personal statement on each application?"

"They all require an essay."

"There you go," Sweetie said. "Tell them what a wonderful young woman you are. Tell them how smart you are, how strong you are, how kind you are. Tell them you are also the daughter of the man who's married to the President of the United States, but if they let you in just because of that you'll use your connections to get all their federal funding yanked."

Abbie laughed, and out of the corner of her eye Sweetie saw Father Nguyen's smile brighten.

"That'd teach them," Abbie said.

"If you need a character reference, give them my name, Margaret Mary Sweeney. Tell them who I am: a former novice, a former police sergeant, and currently a private detective. If that's not good enough for them, they don't have the school for you."

"*Yeah,*" Abbie said. Then her voice softened. "I love you, Sweetie."

"Same here, kiddo."

They said their goodbyes and Sweetie put the phone down.

Father Nguyen asked her, "You had a religious calling?"

"I thought I did, briefly. Now I just try to live a good life."

The priest stood and extended his hand. Sweetie got to her feet and took it.

"I'm very glad I met you, Ms. Sweeney," Father Nguyen said.

Sweetie told him, "Let's do it again, Father."

Thursday, June 4th—Paris

1

Early morning found Magistrate Yves Pruet sitting in the backseat of his Citroën C5 saloon with Paul Leroux, the businessman who had thought to come to the aid of Ms. Casale during the reenactment of the fight under the Pont d'Iéna.

"This investigation of yours, m'sieur," Leroux said to Pruet, "it has to do with the death of Thierry Duchamp, does it not?"

Pruet's car was parked at the curb along the Quai Anatole France, less than a kilometer from the magistrate's home, and not far from where the football star had met his end. Odo sat up front in the driver's seat. Pruet nodded to a woman passing by on the sidewalk.

"Her?" the magistrate asked.

Leroux, who had the curbside seat, looked out.

"No, she is not a regular."

Having learned that Leroux hadn't seen the conflict that caused Duchamp's death, Pruet thought to take the process a step farther. The magistrate asked if Leroux saw the same cast of faces on most of his morning walks to work. The businessman said he did, and now he was seeking to point out familiar strangers, so Odo might take their names and phone numbers for later questioning.

Turning to Leroux's question, Pruet asked, "Would it matter to you if this investigation concerned Thierry Duchamp?"

Leroux adjusted his weight on the seat, seeking a more comfortable position.

Odo watched the man's reflection in the rearview mirror.

"I am not so passionate about sports as others. I do not follow football. But—" Leroux's eyes widened. "Him!"

Pruet saw two men about to draw opposite the car, one older, one younger.

"Which one?" Odo asked.

"The fellow with the garish tie."

The younger one. Odo got out of the car, caught up with the man and identified himself.

"One down, five to go," Pruet said to Leroux, "if your estimate of half-a-dozen regulars was correct."

"I told you I wasn't sure I saw all of them every day."

"We will be patient and catch such fish as swim by. You were saying you do not follow football, but..."

Leroux looked at the magistrate. "But I wonder what the repercussions would be for me if I were to aid in freeing the Ami who was arrested."

"Why should there be repercussions for correcting an injustice?"

Leroux gave the magistrate a look. Who was he trying to kid?

Pruet sighed. "You are right, of course. We will make provisions for you, if that should become necessary."

"If I have to leave Paris, there is only one other place I'd want to live."

"Tahiti, perhaps?"

"An island, yes, but not Moorea. Manhattan. I could work there."

"You said you are with Publicis?"

"That's right, an art—" Leroux stopped, leaned forward, looked past Pruet at the far side of the street where a waist-high concrete wall stood. "An art director. Where is Bertrand? I forgot all about him."

Pruet asked, "Who is Bertrand?"

"An artist, an African immigrant. He paints remarkably good cityscapes on ceramic tiles. I have been trying for the past year to think of a way to feature his work in an ad. If you've ever walked along this section of the river, you must have noticed him."

Pruet had, in fact, walked the area frequently, but in the evening not the morning.

"He must retire to the comfort of his bed by the time I'm about."

Leroux frowned. "If Bertrand has a bed, he is lucky. He would do much better selling his work if he could afford clean clothes and a regular bath."

"Is he a drug user?"

"No, he is an artist. That is an opiate in itself, believe me."

"Perhaps he provides for another as well as himself."

Leroux nodded. "More than likely. I am ashamed I didn't notice he was missing. He is usually here first thing in the morning."

Odo came back to the car just as Pruet asked, "When was the last time you remember seeing Bertrand?"

Thinking for a moment, Leroux said, "The day before Thierry Duchamp died."

"Did you ever buy any of Bertrand's art?"

The art director nodded. "I have two of his tiles at my office."

"I would like to see them, please."

Leroux said, "Of course."

"Odo, we need to take M'sieur Leroux to his office, and while we travel perhaps he can do a sketch of Bertrand for us."

Leroux took a sketch pad and pencil out of his leather folio and went to work.

St. Germain, Paris

2

McGill and Gabbi sat at a corner table inside the famous Les Deux Magots café. A waiter delivered a *citron pressé* and a *pain au chocolate* for McGill and an *expresso* for Gabbi.

Ever the gentleman, McGill sliced his chocolate croissant in two.

"Please," he said, "take half."

Gabbi sipped her drink. "I'm really not hungry."

"So, what's bothering you, my decision to see this reporter?"

"That and..." She didn't want to say at the moment. But McGill knew.

"You're worried about my safety. If this guy blabs, it might bring all sorts of creeps out of the woodwork."

"Not just creeps. Kidnappers. Killers. *L'ecumé de la terre*."

McGill needed a moment to puzzle out the French phrase. "The scum of the earth?"

Gabbi nodded.

"So you're worried about me?"

"You're a very attractive target. Me, they'd kill just to show they meant business."

"Now, that worries me. When I asked, you told me you're discreetly armed."

Gabbi didn't respond and kept her face impassive.

McGill said, "I'd be armed at home. I'd feel better if I had a firearm here, too. But I won't put you on the spot by asking for one. All I can say is, I can take care of myself pretty well. And the guy we're meeting is just a sportswriter, right?"

"Yeah," Gabbi said, but she still wasn't happy.

She'd called the U.S. Embassy to check out M'sieur Arno Durand last night. He came back clean after Gabbi had his name run through a bunch of intelligence databases, the acronyms of which she wouldn't disclose to him. But she did tip her hand a bit when McGill asked her to check Durand's phone records to see if she could find out who, if anyone, in the U.S. had called the reporter in the past seventy-two hours. When she came back with a number of a phone in Frederick, MD, that had called the Paris office of *La Bataille de Sports* only yesterday, he knew she had the juice to go to the all-hearing ear of the NSA and get an answer.

It continued to amaze McGill, the power his wedding vows had conferred on him.

After some more coaxing, he got his downcast companion to eat half the chocolate croissant.

The reporter entered the café just as she swallowed the last bite. The morning was fine, and only a handful of other indoor tables were occupied. The crowd was outside. Durand found them quickly and made his way to their table. That led McGill to think Durand had gone to the trouble of finding pictures of him on the Internet. It reassured McGill that the reporter was conscientious.

McGill stood and extended his hand.

Durand took it and said, "A great pleasure, m'sieur."

The reporter didn't use McGill's name, nor did he ask for Gabbi's. McGill liked that, too. He gestured Durand to a chair, and the waiter took his order for an *expresso*. Nobody said a word until the reporter's coffee came and the waiter left. In the meantime, Durand looked at McGill and Gabbi, both of whom understood he was trying to determine the nature of their relationship.

Gabbi began the conversation with a question: "You are carrying an audio recorder, m'sieur?"

Durand took one out of his sport coat pocket.

"And that is all?"

The reporter took a second smaller machine out of an inside pocket of the coat. A glowing red light indicated that it was functioning. Gabbi turned it off.

She said, "It would be indelicate, m'sieur, if I had to frisk you in public."

He stared at Gabbi as if daring her to try, but he soon dropped his gaze, pushed his coat back and unclipped a tiny recorder that had been attached to his belt at the hip, and put it on the table. Gabbi picked up all three recorders and dropped them into her handbag.

"She looks after me," McGill told him.

"I should have such luck," Durand said.

Gabbi got up and told McGill, "I'll take a little stroll. See if this gentleman has a friend with a directional mike or a long lens pointed our way."

"I should have such a budget," the reporter said.

He took a moment to watch Gabbi walk away and then turned to McGill.

The president's henchman told him, "I'm sure you have many questions for me, M'sieur Durand, but I'm not going to answer any of them now. Instead, I am going to make you a proposition. You can listen, and if you agree to help me, you might find yourself with a good story. Otherwise, you'll get that cup of *expresso* at my expense and that's all."

"Will I also get my recorders back?"

McGill nodded. Durand considered.

"Very well, m'sieur. Please tell me how I may be of service."

McGill said he was looking for a woman. One who looked something like mademoiselle, only younger, somewhat more obvious in her contours, and known to have kept company with Thierry Duchamp shortly before his death.

The mention of the soccer star hooked Durand, McGill saw. It also confirmed for McGill the nature of the tip Durand had been given on the phone call from Frederick, MD. *Hey, pal, how's this for a story? The American president's husband is investigating Thierry Duchamp's death.* For any reporter, a tip like that would be the equivalent of finding a winning lotto ticket.

Making McGill sure he could play the guy. He'd taken a ploy meant to embarrass Patti and subverted it. For all he knew, Durand might even be helpful.

The reporter said, "You wish me to help you find this woman? I am your man, m'sieur."

"Good. This blonde, of course, might have changed her appearance by now, have a different hair color perhaps. You might have to allow for that."

"She might not even be a woman, *n'est-ce pas? Une transvestite ou une il-elle, possibly.*"

Gabbi returned just in time to hear Durand's last remark and translated for McGill.

"A crossdresser or a he-she," Gabbi said.

Those thoughts had never crossed McGill's mind. But this was Paris.

"Maybe," he said.

Durand gave them his mobile number. Gabbi returned his recorders and provided Durand with an embassy phone number that would be forwarded to her mobile.

Winfield House, London

3

Celsus Crogher stiffened as he heard the voice in his earpiece. He'd begun to appreciate that Holly G—the president's code name—had kept him on the job when he'd wanted to pull the plug. The way things were getting crazy in London, with mobs of people marching in the streets in response to POTUS's proposed new defense plans, he'd have been beating himself bloody if he had left her well-being in anyone else's hands. But the voice now addressing him was a painful reminder that he'd always have to share that responsibility.

"How's my wife doing, Celsus?" Holmes asked.

"You should ask her directly," Crogher told him. Then a rarity occurred. The SAC had a cheerful thought. "Unless she's no longer speaking to you."

"In your dreams, Celsus," McGill told him. "What I'm looking for is an objective, professional opinion. You think you can manage that?"

Crogher took a long moment to decide if that was possible.

McGill filled the silence. "While you're making up your mind, let me tell you something you should know. In the event you need to move the president quickly anytime soon, she might be a half-step slow."

That *was* important for Crogher to know. He asked, "Is something wrong with her?"

"Her health's fine. But she has a lot on her mind. She might be a bit distracted."

Crogher processed that. Patricia Darden Grant was the sharpest politician he'd ever seen. She followed complex discussions with ease. Made intuitive leaps where others grasped for answers. And her mental acuity was coupled with an athlete's physical grace.

But if there was anyone who'd know if she was off her game—

McGill picked up the conversation once more.

"Feel free to say thanks for the tip, Celsus," he said.

"Thanks," the SAC grunted.

"Now, I'd like to do another favor for you."

"What?" Crogher asked, suspicion clear in his voice.

"You'll have to trust me on this one, but if you look back you'll see I've never lied to you."

"*What?*" Crogher repeated with an impatient tone he really shouldn't have used with the president's husband.

"Temper, temper," McGill said. "What I want you to know is you shouldn't feel bad—and my bet is you've been flogging yourself—about not finding Deke Ky's shooter. There's no way short of a miracle you could have found him."

Crogher's circuits overloaded as if a power-surge had hit him.

"*You know?* You know who shot my agent?"

"Not yet. Not for sure. But I will know soon enough."

McGill felt confident about that, but he was going to look *very* bad if Sweetie didn't come through. Then again, if he wasn't willing to put his money on Margaret Mary Sweeney, he might as well pack it in.

"You tell me what you know," Crogher ordered. "You tell me right now."

McGill chuckled. "Someone redraw the organizational table when I wasn't looking?"

The SAC ground his teeth. He *loathed* this man. But he had absolutely no lever—

The thought came like a lightning bolt to Crogher. "I'll leak what you're doing."

McGill laughed out loud this time. "You'd cut your tongue out before you gave a reporter the time of day. Now, let's be serious. I've done you two favors, so I'm going to ask you for one."

Crogher could not *believe* this guy. But he was too professional not to listen.

McGill said, "I'm going to give you the number of a public phone in a bowling alley in Frederick, Maryland. I want you to have your minions find out who was on that phone yesterday at

11:45 a.m. And before you ask why the hell you should do that, I'll tell you. You help me, and I'll make sure you're the guy who brings in Deke's shooter. How you bring him in is up to you."

Goddamn Holmes, Crogher thought.

The devil couldn't have come up with a more tempting offer.

Which was why, between grinding teeth, the SAC replied, "Okay."

Rive Gauche, Paris

4

"We'll be there shortly," McGill said into his phone. "Thank you, m'sieur."

He clicked off and turned to Gabbi who was negotiating Paris traffic, which didn't seem to him to be any worse than what he saw in Chicago or DC. From the brief exposure he'd had to London's motor routes and surface streets, he thought the traffic there was far worse.

"Should I call Pruet by his title?" McGill asked. "What is his title anyway?"

"*M'sieur le magistrat* will do, but that's for us mere mortals. Someone of your eminence can get away with informality. Also, Yves Pruet, from all I've heard, is a fairly relaxed individual."

"I'm eminent?" McGill asked. "You don't seem overawed."

Gabbi shot him a glance. "Sorry. I should be more respectful. More diplomatically courteous." She took a breath before adding, "But I'm thinking of leaving the State Department soon. My brother wants me to be the art buyer and curator for his company. Offered me a ridiculous salary. I would have left State already if President Grant hadn't been elected."

McGill smiled. "How's that?"

With a frown, Gabbi said, "Her predecessor had the department conscripting personnel for postings to Baghdad and other places."

"Because no one was volunteering?"

Gabbi nodded. "The whole damn government, the career

professionals' part, was coming apart at the seams. Not to suck up, but your wife has really helped to restore morale."

McGill made a mental note to be sure to pass that along the next time he spoke with Patti.

"Even yours?" he asked. "Even after you got stuck with me, and I'm talking to the press?"

She gave him a look. "Some assignments are tougher than others."

McGill smiled at her. "You know why I talked to Durand?"

"To get another helper looking for the mystery woman."

"That's one reason. And you know why Durand won't spill the beans right away?"

"Because he thinks there's a bigger story ahead than the one he has now."

"Right. No hints this time. What's the other reason?"

They stopped at a red light. By the time it turned green, she had it.

"Because if whoever tipped Durand doesn't get the results he expected, he'll try to make a splash somewhere else. Probably in a way guaranteed to get coverage. Possibly in a way that could backfire and hurt the president's enemies."

Gabbi took a right. They were only a block from the Rue de Lille safe-house where the police were holding Glen Kinnard.

"You're good," McGill said. "If you go to work for your brother, would you stay here or come home?"

"Stay here."

McGill nodded, looking thoughtful. "Maybe I could open my first international office. Maybe, when you weren't buying or curating art, you'd enjoy being a private eye."

Gabbi laughed as she pulled into the parking space the doorman kept open in front of the building. She looked at McGill and told him, "Whatever else I do, I'm going to paint: oils one day, watercolors the next." She paused before adding, "But if you have something interesting to investigate, maybe we could work out an informal arrangement. So what are you going to do with Mr. Kinnard now?"

"I'm going to see if I can pick a fight with him," McGill told her.

Porte Grenelle, Paris

5

Alexandru Régis—the gypsy boy hired by McGill—his wife Ana, Bunica Anisa, and a dozen other Rom, men, women, and children were convened on an old but well maintained forty-foot cabin cruiser moored at the Porte Grenelle marina on the Seine. The slip was little more than a stone's throw from the Pont d'Iéna and the Eiffel Tower.

The Seine was a magnet for tourists carrying money, jewelry, cameras, electronics and drugs, prescription and recreational. The Rom could no more ignore such booty than a hungry man could pass through an orchard without stealing an apple. The cruiser collected purloined items from clan members busy working both banks of the river, thus relieving them of the burden of possessing stolen goods. The swag was then passed along to an oncoming work barge that circulated through the Seine and the city's three canals.

But that morning the family members gathered around Alexandru and a sketch artist— whose accomplice normally pilfered the bags and picked the pockets of those sitting for a portrait. With Alexandru's guidance, the artist completed a sketch of Gabbi. He looked to the boy for comment.

"That is her," Alexandru said.

The artist told Bunica Anisa," Making this woman appear ten years younger and fuller-bodied will be no problem."

"Now, do the man," the gypsy queen ordered.

Following Alexandru's direction, the artist quickly began sketching. As the face took on definition, a Rom named Bela leaned forward for a better look. He nodded to himself. Once, and then several more times. A smile lit his face.

"Mother of God," he whispered.

That was enough to draw everyone's attention, distracting

Alexandru and the artist.

"No, no, keep working," Bela told them. "I'll be right back, but keep at it."

He went forward to the cabin he was using. Everyone watched him, until Bunica Anisa got Alexandru and the artist back to work. In minutes, the sketch was finished, the very likeness of—

"It *is* him," said Bela. He'd returned and held a newspaper in his hands.

"Who?" Bunica Anisa demanded.

Bela said, "Coming back from England yesterday, I found this newspaper. Out of boredom, I picked it up. A story I read gave me an idea for a game we might run, so I kept it."

"You can read?" the artist asked. The Rom were commonly illiterate.

"I learned so I could read the racing form." The Rom were brilliant handicappers, usually reading horses more easily than words.

Bela plunked the tabloid down and said, "Look here."

Bunica Anisa and the others crowded around the table where the paper lay. Patricia Darden Grant's face filled the front page. The headline read: Patti Comes to Visit.

"Who is she?" Bunica Anisa asked, unable to read the words. "A movie star?"

Bela said, "She was once. Now, she is president of the United States."

Everyone looked at each other, knowing this was only the first shoe to drop.

Bunica Anisa, befitting her years and status, intuitively knew what came next.

She pointed a knobby finger at the sketch of the man who'd hired Alexandru.

Bela smiled and nodded. He opened the paper to another page and there was a picture of James J. McGill. He put the paper down next to the sketch. All eyes turned to Alexandru. The boy nodded. This was the man he'd met.

Bela said, "He is the president's husband. They call him her henchman."

Bunica Anisa looked within herself and then at each of those present.

"My children," she said, "this is a rare opportunity."

The Rom would now be looking to net far more than a few hundred euros.

Salvation's Path Church, Richmond, VA

6

The Reverend Burke Godfrey's secretary, Mrs. Willa Bramleigh, according to the nameplate on her desk, had kept Benton Williams, one of the most powerful lawyers in Washington, DC waiting for over 45 minutes. She was very polite about it, offering him a cup of Kona coffee and a plate of tasty butter cookies she'd made herself. He'd partaken of both, making Mrs. Bramleigh smile with his sincere compliments. When not attending to the needs of the reverend's guest, she busied herself alphabetizing a large stack of donation pledge cards, humming "Count Your Blessings" as she worked.

Reverend Burke was gathering funds from members of his flock as seed money for the university he planned to build. Some wags had said it would be named the University of God. Campuses in Virginia and Heaven.

In any case, Reverend Godfrey was starting with small donations from the common folk. Once he had a couple hundred thousand small contributions, he would go after the fat cats and corporate money. The reverend spoke of how Harvard had the biggest endowment of any university in the country: thirty-five billion dollars. If Mammon could raise that much money, the reverend conjectured, why shouldn't a nationwide community of American faithful not exceed it, make it seem humble by comparison?

With that kind of ambition and a donor base growing exponentially, Reverend Godfrey had no trouble paying Benton

Williams' two-thousand-dollar-per-hour fee. Williams practiced appellate criminal defense law. None of the fourteen defendants Williams had represented had had his death sentence stand. Eleven of them had been resentenced to life imprisonment, but only six of those had been denied the possibility of parole. The remaining three had had their convictions overturned and were now exonerated and free.

A number of prominent movers-and-shakers in the capital had Williams on retainer, fancying that one day they might simply have to do away with political opponents, and certainly wanting to get off scot-free. With a single exception, the lawyer considered these people to be indulging themselves in fantasies of what dangerous characters they were. Nonetheless, he was happy to take their money.

It was in the same spirit that the lawyer waited patiently for the reverend to receive him; his time was always someone else's money. True, the news he brought the reverend was a challenge unlike any he'd ever faced. If genuine, he had no comprehension of it as either a lawyer or a human being. If the situation ever were to become commonplace, it would put him out of business. But he had no fear of that and even as a true anomaly, Reverend Godfrey would bear the burden of rectifying the situation. Williams would be able to help only if the evangelist did the heavy lifting.

Mrs. Bramleigh caught him woolgathering. "Mr. Williams ...Mr. Williams."

He looked up, too professional to be embarrassed.

"Reverend Godfrey, will see you now. His prayer hour is over."

The lawyer smiled and said, "Thank you. You're very kind."

Mrs. Bramleigh smiled, happy to have been a help. She closed the door behind Williams, trying not to be concerned as she heard Reverend Godfrey, his voice filled with concern, ask, "What's so urgent, Benton?"

She was back at her desk, trying to focus on the pledges when she heard such a piteous moan come from the reverend's office that all the cards she'd held in her hands shot into the air. Before the last one hit the floor, she could hear the great man sobbing.

Winfield House, London

7

Galia Mindel sat in the drawing room of Winfield House, waiting to accompany the president to Chequers, the Buckinghamshire Tudor mansion that was the official country residence of the United Kingdom's prime minister. As Norvin Kimbrough was the host for this meeting of the G8, sans Russia, he had the choice of where the meeting would be held. He'd chosen his country home.

But that wasn't what Galia had on her mind right now. She was thinking of her *date*—what else could she call it—with Sir Robert Reed the previous evening. The president had told her she'd be dining with Secretary of State Jeremy Kalman and Ambassador Garrett Byrne. After that she'd retire early. Given an unusually clear block of time, Galia had accepted Sir Robert's invitation to dine with him. Politically, Galia felt it was the right move. She might learn something that would be to the president's advantage.

Personally, she couldn't help but wonder if Sir Robert might actually have taken an interest in her as a woman. She didn't see how. They'd never met before. But Galia had appeared on television any number of times. Certainly, as the president's chief of staff, she wouldn't be unknown to the ruling class in Britain. But could an elegant aristocrat like Sir Robert have conceived an affection for someone he'd seen only in the media? Someone who could stand to lose a few pounds. Again, she didn't see how.

Games were being played. She'd read *The Irregulars,* the book that detailed how Winston Churchill had used Roald Dahl, Ian Fleming and other charming Brits to lobby the American government to enter World War Two sooner rather than later. The plan hadn't succeeded, but that hadn't stopped Churchill from trying. Who knew what machinations Sir Robert had in mind now?

For all that, Galia thought, it couldn't hurt a girl to think just a little that she might be appreciated by a blueblood whose tastes weren't reserved for clichés of feminine beauty. It was Sir Robert's hair that allowed Galia to entertain that possibility. Its cut was impeccable, but draped across his forehead was an errant wavy lock. Not a flaw overlooked by a stylist but a statement made by Sir Robert: Manners would be observed, but individuality would be preserved.

So, who knew? Maybe there was such a thing as an English aristocrat who could be infatuated with a slightly zaftig, dazzlingly brilliant American woman of high achievement.

She *still* didn't really see how, but it was fun to pretend.

And that night the man who knew just how to behave with a real queen had treated her like one. He'd taken her to—what? A restaurant so exclusive it didn't have a name. A private club with a fantastic kitchen. A property owned by Her Majesty with a royal chef doing the honors. All she knew was they went to an elegant brick townhouse in Westminster, had a private dining room to themselves, and the food and service was at least equal to that of the White House.

Sir Robert had been wonderful company, telling her stories of his boyhood, recounting the natural wonders he'd seen while traveling with the queen, complimenting President Grant on the strength of character needed to win an election so soon after the loss of her first husband. He even had kind words for James J. McGill for so quickly catching the villains who'd committed the crime—and having the forthrightness to say they should all be be executed.

"He's quite a piece of work, the president's henchman is," Galia agreed.

Sir Robert laughed. "And that's quite the sobriquet he's given himself."

At the end of the drive home, Galia hadn't expected Sir Robert to walk her to the door and give her a kiss. But the chauffeur gave them a moment alone in the Rolls.

"I had a wonderful night, Galia," he said. "You are truly a remarkable woman. President Grant and the United States are fortunate to have you looking out for them."

The guy was good, Galia thought. She felt she was looking pretty special that night, but if he'd complimented her appearance, she'd have smelled a rat. Praising her ability, though, that pressed her pleasure button. Got her to relax enough that she didn't pull back when he leaned in and kissed her.

His mouth was only slightly parted, and the contact was brief but, my God, the man's lips were as smooth as silk. She was unable to recall a kiss like that from her late husband or the handful of other boys and men who'd ever kissed her.

It almost, but not quite, made her miss the card Sir Robert deftly slipped into her hand.

A Secret Service agent stepped into the drawing room and broke her reverie.

"Ms. Mindel, the president is coming."

Aboard Marine One

8

If Galia didn't know better, she'd swear the president had gotten laid last night. She was especially sensitive to the gleam in Patti Grant's eyes because she'd entertained the possibility she might be equivalently bright eyed this morning—for the first time in more years than she cared to think about. But James J. McGill was across the Channel in France, so...

Oh, dear God, the chief of staff thought. It couldn't be that Jean-Louis Severin had crept into the president's bedroom and ... Galia couldn't bring herself to complete the thought. It was the stuff of Hollywood farce, and Washington, D.C. ruination.

Patricia Darden Grant was much too smart—and too in love with her husband, Galia grudgingly had to admit—to allow herself to become such a figure of ridicule.

Still, she had been unusually convivial—*très charmant*—

with the French president, a man who'd only recently lost his wife to divorce.

Galia probed delicately. "You had a good dinner with Secretary Kalman and Ambassador Byrne last night, Madam President?"

Patti turned away from the window of Marine One. She'd been watching the English countryside swiftly slip past below as her party flew to Chequers. The RAF had extended the courtesy of providing an aerial escort. But the British aircraft didn't crowd the president.

She told Galia, "It was a good meeting, productive."

Paying attention to her chief of staff now, Patti saw the other question in Galia's eyes, and she decided to answer it.

"I talked with Jim last night," she said with a smile. "I was feeling down about the leak and the uproar. I was displeased with Kimbrough's pissy comments. I had serious doubts about what I had done. Felt as if I'd blundered badly, might even have to abandon the plan entirely. But Jim was so kind, so reassuring, so completely confident in me that I slept as peacefully as a child. I woke up feeling strong and certain that I'm doing the right thing. For our country and our allies." The president took Galia's hand and said, "You and I, we're going to make this work."

Patti didn't say a word about Jim singing her to sleep.

If that tidbit was going into anyone's memoirs, it would be hers.

And then only if Jim consented.

"How was your night, Galia? Sir Robert showed you a good time?"

"Lovely," Galia replied.

She kept the sudden pang of envy she felt out of her voice. To have a relationship so cherished that a phone call could make you glow, it made her night on the town with an aristocrat seem like she'd spent her time doing laundry. Galia wondered for the first time since her husband had died if she would ever marry again. She didn't think it would be possible as long as she was chief of staff. There was no time for a husband. Maybe a discreet lover then, someone with his own commitments, if she could find the right man.

She repressed her personal feelings and handed a business card to Patti.

"Sir Robert gave that to me last night."

The president looked at the card. It bore only a name: Giles Pembroke.

"Who is Giles Pembroke?" Patti asked.

"He's a bookie."

Patti gave Galia a puzzled look.

"He handles the action for the American ex-pat community in London. Lets us Yanks bet on Stateside sporting events. Sir Robert said Pembroke might be someone we should keep an eye on. Him and his clientele."

Patti made the leap. "Someone from our London embassy. The source of the leak."

"The mystery solved ever so discreetly, courtesy of Her Majesty."

The discretion took the form of a social encounter between the queen's private secretary and the president's chief of staff. But what had Sir Robert hoped to gain with his kiss? That was what Galia wanted to know. Simply to make her heart go pitter-pat, put her off balance in case he should ever need something from her?

Well, he'd have to do better than that to put Galia Mindel off her game.

Rue de Lille, Paris

9

Investigating Magistrate Pruet had everyone gather in the basement of the building on the Rue de Lille. McGill, Gabbi, Kinnard, Pruet, Odo, and six Paris *flics* stood in a square space twenty feet to a side. The plaster ceiling stood ten feet above a cement floor. The walls were brick, painted white. Two small windows, both barred, rose a foot above the outside pavement and admitted daylight. But the preponderance of the illumination in the room came from four bright incandescent bulbs set in utilitarian ceiling fixtures.

Two cops covered each of the three doors to the room.

Kinnard took a few steps around the middle of the room, getting the feel of the place.

He looked at Pruet and said, "If these walls could talk, huh? I bet a lot of the poor saps who got dragged down here talked, screamed, and begged for mercy." He nodded to himself and smiled. "But whoever painted the place did a nice job of covering everything up."

The magistrate neither affirmed nor denied Kinnard's accusation. He turned to McGill and said quietly, "It would be a great embarrassment, if no great loss, if you killed this man. It would be far worse, if he so much as hurts you seriously."

McGill leaned forward and whispered, "*M'sieur le magistrat,* surely it must have entered your mind that it would be helpful to see how well Kinnard can brawl."

A rueful smile crossed Pruet's face. "You are a most perceptive man, Mr. McGill. You must serve your president well."

"Do my best," McGill replied.

"Hey, Jim," Kinnard called, "let's get this playacting on the road."

McGill looked at his former fellow copper. "Be right with you, Glen." Looking back to Pruet, he continued *sotto voce.* "Having me suggest this tussle takes you off the hook somewhat. It wasn't your idea. Now, Glen over there, he's been dying to go after me for years. So things are going to get intense. Don't let your cops jump in unless I say so."

Pruet asked, "And what will your signal be?"

McGill looked at Gabbi.

"*Au secours,*" she said quietly.

Pruet gave them a thin smile. "Very well. *Bonne chance.*"

McGill understood that.

Kinnard's patience was at an end. "Come on, McGill. Quit dickin' around."

Odo handed McGill an old aluminum coffee pot filled with a pound of loose dirt. He took it and walked over to his fellow American. Kinnard was wearing the black leather jacket he'd had on the night of his fight with Thierry Duchamp. It was torn in several places, stained with blood, and half the collar had been ripped free of its stitching. On one arm, there were clear impressions of bite marks. McGill handed the coffee pot to Kinnard.

"Your urn," McGill said. He saw real pain—and anger— in Kinnard's eyes. "Hold it the way you did that night."

Kinnard cradled the pot in the crook of his left arm.

"How far away was Thierry Duchamp when he first noticed you?" McGill asked.

"Ten, fifteen feet." Kinnard's words were clipped, his face reddening as the memories came rushing back.

McGill stepped off the appropriate distance.

"Now, you don't speak French, but did he say anything to you?" McGill said, going along with Kinnard's deception.

"Yeah, I told him that." Kinnard nodded in Pruet's direction. "I told you, too."

"Yes, you did. So tell us now how much he said to you. A few words? Or did Thierry Duchamp go off on a rant?"

Kinnard saw that McGill was trying to get at something, but he couldn't figure out what, and that only added to his foul mood.

"It wasn't a rant," Kinnard said. "I had to guess, he just cursed me out a little."

McGill had expected Kinnard's ire, but what surprised him was the appearance of tears at the corners of Kinnard's eyes. McGill had a flash of intuition. Kinnard's daughter, Emilie, had told McGill that Kinnard had cheated on her mother. At the time, McGill had the feeling she'd been holding back. Something more shameful than infidelity. A more visceral reason to be alienated from her father. Now, McGill wondered: Had Glen Kinnard been a wife beater? With his temper, it wasn't hard to imagine. That would certainly have given Emilie cause to change her last name.

If so, that night under the Pont d'Iéna, had Kinnard not only been grieving the death of his wife, had he been bleeding inside at the way he'd treated her when she'd been alive?

"So then what happened, Glen?" McGill asked, starting toward Kinnard.

"I told you both," Kinnard said, his voice descending to a growl. "The guy bit down on the broad's finger and started clubbing her. That's when I stepped in."

As McGill drew close to Kinnard, every pulse in the room began to race. McGill kept his focus on Kinnard. He said, "Sure, why shouldn't you jump in? For all you knew, Glen, this dickwad might have told you, 'Fuck off, asshole. I'll beat my woman and you beat yours.'"

Yves Pruet saw Kinnard's eyes bulge with rage. If the president's henchman hadn't somehow captured Thierry Duchamp's exact words, he'd still cut his fellow Ami to the quick.

McGill then closed in on Kinnard and kicked the coffee pot out of his embrace. A howl of agony burst from him as he watched the pot fly away, bounce off the ceiling and a wall and skid across the floor, spilling its content. Before it came to a stop, Kinnard's head whipped back toward McGill. His eyes were no longer those of a sane man.

Kinnard leaped at McGill as if he were a predatory cat, fingers extended like claws, teeth bared. McGill wanted no part of a prolonged fight. Madmen were often inhumanly strong. He stepped quickly to his left, at a forty-five degree angle to Kinnard's line of attack. He brushed Kinnard's outstretched right arm away with his left hand. Then he grabbed Kinnard's right wrist with his right hand, and pulled to accelerate his attacker's momentum. As Kinnard's head came into range, he hit him on the hinge of his jaw with a straight left hand. The nerve bundle there was so dense that hitting it a good shot—and McGill hit it a great one—was like throwing a lights-out switch, madman or not. Kinnard lost consciousness while he was still hurtling forward.

McGill caught Kinnard under the arms before his head could hit the cement floor. He lowered the man gently, turning his head so the bruised jaw was up.

Breathing hard after the adrenaline spike, McGill turned to Pruet. He said, "Imagine what might have happened to me if I hadn't gotten out of his way."

"You might have wound up as dead as Thierry Duchamp," the magistrate replied.

Rive Gauche, Paris

10

The French were considerate enough to provide McGill with an ice bag for his left hand and some ibuprofen for general pain relief. A doctor had been summoned for Kinnard. The physician insisted on taking his patient to a hospital for x-rays and proper treatment. The investigating magistrate had not objected, merely sent along a police escort and reflected on what he'd just heard and seen.

McGill decided that he liked Pruet.

As he and Gabbi were leaving the basement at the Rue de Lille building, McGill noticed that Odo was going through the sequence of McGill's move: step left, brush left, grab right, punch left. Someone else picking up his technique. Oh, well.

Gabbi started her Peugeot and asked, "Where to?"

"Lunch," McGill said. "Ebbing adrenaline always makes me hungry."

"Okay. Have something particular in mind?"

"Anything but horse."

She gave him a smile, but also shook her head. Not surprising, McGill thought. A lot of people had mixed feelings about him.

"I know a Japanese place. Quiet. If you don't like sushi, the tempura's good."

"Yeah, I like tempura. They have *crevettes?*"

This time her smile was unqualified. "You've been studying.

Yes, they have shrimp."

"Your brother own this restaurant?"

"No. I'll treat if you don't have the cash."

"I'll put it on my credit card. Lunch is on me."

"*Merci,*" Gabbi said.

As they passed by, McGill noticed a line of vendors' stalls alongside the wall lining the near bank of the Seine. Each one seemed to be offering printed material: books, magazines, newspapers, pamphlets. He asked Gabbi, "Bookstores *al fresco?*"

"*En plein air,*" she answered, translating the Italian to French. "This is a very literate part of the city. The Sorbonne is nearby."

McGill nodded. A part of him would always be a beat cop, wanting to know everything he could about his surroundings. Including the language most people spoke.

Gabbi looked at her rear view mirror, frowned, and was about to say something when McGill's phone played "Take Me Out to the Ballgame." She waited while he answered.

"Hello," McGill said.

"Dad, it's me!" Caitie, his youngest child. Her voice was filled with such high-pitched energy he couldn't tell if she was excited or terrified.

"Caitie, are you all right?" His own voice, now anxious, drew a glance from Gabbi.

"Oh, Dad, I'm great. I got an agent with William Norris! Her name's Annie Klein." This was followed by a squeal of glee.

After Caitie had watched the video of her appearance at the rally where she and Sweetie had confronted the Reverend Burke Godfrey in LaFayette Square, she'd decided her future lay in motion pictures. And what could McGill say about that? He was married to a former actress. Fortunately, his ex-wife, Carolyn, Caitie's mother, was imposing sensible restraints on their most impulsive child. An agent from a respectable firm to represent Caitie was her most basic demand.

After that, well, there would have to be acting lessons because after all—

"Dad, what's even greater, Annie got me a part. I'm going to be in a movie!" A shriek of delight followed, once again drawing Gabbi's attention.

"I hate to be a buzzkill," Gabbi said. "But maybe you better say goodbye now."

"What's wrong?" McGill asked.

"Nothing, Dad. Everything's great," Caitie said.

But Gabbi told him, "There are three young guys in a car behind us. They all look agitated, and I think the first chance they get they're going to try something."

McGill flipped down the passenger side visor and checked the vanity mirror.

He saw the car and agreed with Gabbi's assessment completely.

He felt much better when she handed him a Beretta from under her jacket.

McGill told his daughter, "Caitie, that's wonderful news, but I'll have to call you back."

Georgetown

11

Sweetie laid out six photographs on McGill's desk: Horatio Bao, Ricky Lanh Huu, Musette Ky, Deke Ky, Reverend Francis Nguyen, and Bishop George O'Menehy. She looked at Welborn, sitting across from her, and said, "Here's our cast of characters… so far."

"That fellow on my right," Welborn said. "Who's he?"

Sweetie had printed the bishop's photo off the Internet, and identified him now for Welborn. The young Air Force captain frowned.

"What?" Sweetie asked.

"My last case," Welborn reminded her, "I was snooping on colonels and generals. Now, I'm going to be investigating a bishop?"

"Maybe you'll have to write a book someday."

Welborn gave Sweetie a look.

"What did you find out about our two Vietnamese friends?" she asked.

Welborn had run Horatio Bao and Ricky Lanh Huu through his federal databases.

He now consulted his notebook. He'd used his White House password to access the computer systems of the agencies he'd queried, but he hadn't printed out the information gleaned from his inquiries. As far as anyone auditing his activities would know, he'd only looked at other peoples' files. He'd wanted to leave as light a footprint as possible.

He told Sweetie, "Horatio's given name, as far as anyone can tell, is Bao Huu; Ricky was simply Lanh Huu."

"Father and son?" Sweetie asked.

"Maybe but not because of their names. In Vietnamese, huu means very much so. Or to have much of something. Bao means protection. Lanh means, roughly, street smarts."

"For our purposes," Sweetie said, "we'll think of them as the brains and the muscle. What else do the feds have?"

Welborn told her, "Bao was supposed to be some kind of young hotshot in the old South Vietnamese government, the foreign ministry, and was a suspected big-time player in the black market and vice rackets. He got out of Vietnam early and is suspected of taking a lot of money with him. Now he's a general practice lawyer in Virginia with no criminal record. Ricky does have an arrest record but the charge was dismissed in court."

"What was the charge?" Sweetie asked.

"Manslaughter. When Ricky was 18, he used a knife to kill another kid, but it was deemed to be self-defense. The other kid had a broken bottle. Thing is, a cop I called heard a story the dead kid grabbed the bottle and broke it only after Ricky came at him with the knife."

Sweetie mulled things over.

She said, "Not too hard to imagine Ricky moving up from a knife to a gun, and if we checked to see who the lawyer who defended him was— "

"Not Bao," Welborn said. "A criminal defense guy named Peter Landeker. No blots on his record."

Sweetie said, "Well, Bao is a smart guy then. But given their histories, here and abroad, I think we can take Musette Ky's assertion that they're behind Deke's shooting as credible."

"And we can make a fair guess who pulled the trigger," Welborn added.

"Right."

"So what do we do now, Margaret?" Welborn asked.

"We ask ourselves who the weak link is," she said.

Didn't take Welborn a heartbeat. "Ricky."

"Yeah," Sweetie said, separating his picture from the others. "The youngest, most volatile, and most dangerous person on the board—but also the most likely to make a mistake."

"It'll be hard," Welborn said, "for just the two of us to watch him around the clock."

An excellent point. Sweetie thought maybe she'd made a mistake letting Leo slip away on vacation so easily. But maybe he'd been a dutiful son and had gone to visit his mother. The elderly lady with the bad heart. If things got to be more than they could handle, though, and Mom wasn't in intensive care, she'd call Leo back.

"We'll do what we can," Sweetie told Welborn. "But we are going to need one more person. Someone to join Father Nguyen's congregation and keep an eye on who drops by. You'll be busy, and the good father has seen me up close."

"Then who?" Welborn asked.

"I was thinking of your fiancée," Sweetie said.

Welborn's eyes went wide. "*Kira?*"

Washington, DC

12

Left to her own devices, Kira Fahey, Welborn's fiancée, never ate breakfast or lunch. She ate brunch and an afternoon snack.

She arrived at Tommy T's Steakhouse at 10:30 a.m. Alone. Annoyed that Welborn had been unable to join her.

She was also vexed that weekday brunch, once a prerogative Tommy T afforded to a select few, had become something of a craze among people who really should have been at their desks working: trying to cheat the government out of its money or trying to defeat those trying to cheat the government.

Kira, niece and goddaughter, of the vice-president of the United States would have had to be at her desk in the White House if the president hadn't been overseas. So who were all these people cluttering up her favorite steakhouse?

Welborn's fiancée had long made an art of being overprivileged.

Jules, the restaurant's host, was pleased to see Kira. Her star in the Washington firmament was already high, and the smart money said it would only ascend further.

Jules said warmly, "Ms. Fahey, how nice to see you again. Will Captain Yates be joining you today? Or are you dining with a lady friend?"

Kira hadn't made a reservation; some people didn't need them.

Her social standing was of no comfort to her at the moment, however.

"I'm all alone today, Jules. So maybe I'll stuff myself."

"A hearty appetite is to be commended, Ms. Fahey."

"Commended but not seen. Do you have a table for one behind a potted plant?"

"As a matter of fact. A table for two with one chair easily removed."

"I'm not the first diner who wants to eat and not be seen?"

"Far from it," he said with a twinkle in his eye. "Please follow me."

The table was, in fact, screened by foliage. Three Madagascar Dragon trees. Better yet, Jules told her, if she'd leave her credit card with him, he would run the cost of her meal as soon as she ordered. The card would be returned when her meal was served, and she could leave by the side door adjacent to the table if she wished.

Kira smiled and handed over her card. She liked the snugly placed table and the air of intrigue that came with it. She'd been to Tommy T's more times than she could remember, but she'd never noticed this table before. Thinking of the skulduggery that must go on there, both political and romantic, sent a shiver of pleasure through her.

She told Jules what she'd like to eat and to double her usual tip.

"Thank you, Ms. Fahey," he said. "I have only one other party that will be seated nearby. They won't be able to see you, and they're discreet gentlemen so their conversation is likely to be soft-spoken and shouldn't disturb you."

Kira nodded. She liked to be pampered.

As soon as Jules had left, she couldn't help but wonder what sort of lewd behavior she and Welborn might get away with at this table. He was far too proper to ever let her drop her panties and straddle him on a restaurant chair. To be fair, they were both rather energetic about such things, and she had been known to reach high C with her vocalizations. Jules might come by to inquire if all was well.

Kira's mind drifted through a series of somewhat more likely erotic fantasies. The limiting criterion was the possibility of public discovery and the potential embarrassment they might cause the president. Kira's own sense of ambition, though nuclear powered, didn't lie in the direction of ever seeking public office—too many grubby hands to shake—but she had great respect for Patricia Darden Grant. The president had ascended a pinnacle unreached by any other woman.

She wondered what unique achievement she might claim for herself. Marrying Welborn would be a good start. He'd told her that his mother had in fact invited the Queen of England to their wedding. Wouldn't that be a hoot if the old gal actually came? And why shouldn't she? Kira's uncle, the vice president of the United States, would be giving her away. The president would be there—and so would her henchman. Now, there was an interesting man. Maybe Welborn could form some sort of company with him after the president left office. Surely, he'd be bored with the military by then, and they'd need a respectable amount of money to carry them into—

A waiter appeared, bringing Kira's order and her credit card. A petite steak, blood red inside. The near rawness of the meat sometimes put Welborn off. Other times, though, watching her wolf down a steak got him going. The waiter smiled at her, but came and went without a word. What a wonderful idea, Kira thought, silent food service. She might make a permanent request for this table. It was all so peaceful...

Until Jules seated two men at the table on the other side of the Dragon trees. For a moment, she resented their presence, but she'd been warned they would be coming, and as Jules had said they kept their voices down. In fact, to Kira's keen ears, they seemed to be scheming.

Secrets were being shared. The men had no idea she was nearby. Being a DC resident and a dedicated snoop, Kira silently put her silverware down, stopped chewing, and began to eavesdrop.

13

Robert Merriman, Senator Roger Michaelson's chief of staff, was two years older than his brother Anson, one of the capital's uber-lobbyists, but in terms of ambition and ruthlessness, they were identical twins. That was why Anson was having a problem understanding what his brother had just told him.

"What do you mean you don't want to screw Patti Grant any longer?" Anson asked.

His question contained no sexual connotation. The Merriman brothers screwed people to the wall, not to beds.

Bob took a sip of water before answering.

"I know. It's not like I got religion all of sudden ... but it's not far from that, either. I was listening to Michaelson tell me he's going to run for president and—"

"He came right out and said so?" Anson asked.

Bob nodded. "Said he wants me to run the campaign that will get him the job."

"That's great. You said you would, of course."

"I said I'd get the campaign rolling, then I was going to run for the Senate seat he'd be leaving."

Anson beamed. "Even better. We'll have the White House *and* the Senate wired that way."

The brothers fell silent as a waiter approached with their meals. Anson gave the man a credit card, told him to add 25% for himself, and they wouldn't need anything else from him. He'd pick up the card on his way out.

After the waiter left, Anson asked, "Did Michaelson have any problem with your idea?"

"He can't afford to have a problem with it. He needs me too much."

"So what is the problem, this surprise appearance by your conscience? Tell it to get lost."

Bob Merriman gave a dry laugh.

"Easier said than done. I just got this feeling. It changed the way I looked at everything. Suddenly, I was absolutely certain that Patricia Darden Grant is going to make history for more than just being the first woman to sit in the Oval Office. I became absolutely certain she's going to be one of the greats. The country might actually *need* her before she's done."

Anson looked at his elder brother, a man he'd always admired, with contempt.

"Put her right up there on Rushmore, huh?"

"Maybe. But don't think I've gone soft, Junior."

Bob's tone put the younger Merriman back in his place.

"What do you mean?" Anson asked, his disdain gone.

"I mean, what would you rather do, ride a losing horse, or climb on the winner?"

"You're saying there's no way Michaelson would beat Patti Grant?"

"None," Bob said.

"So your plan is?"

"To get someone plausible to run Michaelson's campaign from the start, after I've resigned from his staff, and run my own campaign for his Senate seat."

Anson grinned. "That's more like the brother who taught me to lie, cheat, and steal. But Michaelson will learn you've betrayed him."

"Only after he's lost the race and is out of office. Only after he's a nobody."

Anson raised his glass to his brother. "Robert, I'm sorry I ever doubted you."

The Merrimans clinked glasses and sipped their mineral water.

"So you're going to protect Patti Grant's flank? Does that mean you get that English bookie to take his hooks out of that sap in the London embassy."

"That particular civil servant has had his debts paid in full this very day. Pembroke has been told to take no further wagers from him, and the quisling has been told to stop leaking McGill's doings."

"What about that frog sports reporter?"

The elder brother said, "He'll give McGill a headache. But that's okay, too."

"And that other little trick you had in store for your new favorite president?"

Bob Merriman sighed. "I'm afraid there's no stopping that one."

Behind the shelter of the Dragon trees, Kira Fahey had caught every word the Merrimans had said, and written all of them down.

And none other than Putnam Shady, Sweetie's friend and landlord, had arrived at Tommy T's. He liked an occasional early lunch. He also liked to read the seating list wherever he dined, a feat he could manage without turning the list in his direction or otherwise being obvious about it.

He found it most interesting that such notables as the Merriman brothers were dining at Tommy T's that day—and that Jules had placed Kira Fahey at the adjacent hideaway table he was planning to request.

Champs Elysées, Paris

14

Aubine Grenier Severin sat in the conference room of her divorce lawyer's offices. The space was large and light poured in through tall windows, but the room was so filled with media people Madam Severin was starting to feel claustrophobic. Print reporters from across the continent were there, including an American from the *International Herald Tribune*. TV cameras from TF1, the BBC, and CNN were on hand. All eyes, save one pair, were focused on the ex-wife of French President Jean-Louis Severin. Aubine was immaculately groomed, minimally made-up, dressed in a severely simple style, and she sat with her own eyes lowered, unwilling for the moment to engage all the attention directed at her.

Her lawyer, Marcel Choisy, sat next to his client, the two of them in matching Louis XIII armchairs. The *avocat* was equally impassive and impeccably turned out, but he saw everything, including his assistant, Giselle, as she signaled him that every member of the media who had been invited had arrived and all were ready to hear why they had been summoned. Choisy rose smoothly to his feet.

"*Mesdames et messieurs,* ladies and gentlemen of the press, my name is Marcel Choisy. It has been my honor to safeguard the interests of Aubine Grenier Severin in the dissolution of her marriage to the president of the republic, Jean-Louis Severin. In that capacity, I have been diligent in protecting my client's every interest ... based upon the information I had at the time of the divorce.

"Now, Madam Severin has presented me with new intelligence which will cause us to revisit the material disposition of the divorce, and petition the court for a revised judgment. Madam Severin will make a statement. She will not take any questions from the media, but I will."

The lawyer extended a hand to help his client rise.

Now, she took notice of the mob, and stood without her lawyer's support.

"I divorced my husband because I am a selfish woman," she said in a clear steady voice. "That is, I wished to spend at least three hours per evening with Jean-Louis, at least five days per week. I wished to see him smile at me as we enjoyed conversation and food; I wished to spend an occasional night at the theater or opera with him; I wished to have him hold me in his arms, on the dance floor or other more private places. Fifteen hours per week, that is what I selfishly demanded of him. That is what he refused me.

"I said the last time I spoke with him that I wanted no more than any decent mistress would require, but he told me his mistress was France, and she required far more of his time than any woman would. He said he gave me every minute he could spare. Being selfish, I told him the minutes he could spare were not enough, not for me. So I came to M'sieur Choisy and obtained a divorce. I was far from happy, but I had to be satisfied with my choice.

"Then I learned that my former husband had not one mistress but two."

That was the bombshell the press had been waiting for, but would it be a conventional explosion or would things go nu—

"The other woman demanding my husband's time, I have learned, was the President of the United States, Patricia Darden Grant. Now, the two of them have formed a grand new national alliance as well as a personal one. As the press has already proclaimed, 'France Shall Lead.'"

The collected media were stunned to silence, imagining

a mushroom cloud rising before their eyes, but after Marcel Choisy helped his client back to her seat and turned to face them, they shouted their questions at him en masse.

Chequers, Buckinghamshire, England

15

If looks could kill, Galia Mindel thought as she looked at Patricia Darden Grant in the president's suite at Chequers, someone somewhere should keel over dead. Presidential press secretary Aggie Wu was on the television screen in front of them, saying that the presidents of the United States and France had a cordial, professional, and entirely appropriate relationship. President Grant was a married woman who loved her husband and honored her wedding vows in every way every day. President Severin was a gentleman who respected President Grant both as a fellow head of state and as a woman. To say he would behave otherwise was a slander. To say President Grant would be party to an illicit relationship with anyone was likewise a slander.

Aggie closed by saying that both leaders had their political enemies, but for President Grant's part, if she were to find out who had started such malicious rumors, she would file a defamation of character suit against that party.

Galia liked that. The best defense was a good offense.

The press started shouting questions at Aggie as soon as she finished reading her statement.

"Turn it off, please, Galia," the president said.

The chief of staff clicked off the flat screen television. The president sat motionless, staring in the direction of the blacked out surface. For a moment, she sat there silently. Then she asked Galia a question that took her completely by surprise.

"Who made that television? Not the Brits, I'd guess."

"No, ma'am. It's a South Korean brand, but I think the assembly is done in China."

The president's frown deepened, even as she nodded.

Galia knew Patti Grant was not pleased by either South Korea's or China's responses to her new defense proposals. The South Koreans wanted to keep the deck stacked in their favor, having free access to U.S. markets and having the American taxpayer pick up the tab for keeping the DMZ between the two Koreas fortified by American GIs, while restricting the access of American products and services to their home market. The Chinese wanted to see the United States continue to overextend itself militarily, and to play one-way trade on a scale that transferred wealth to Beijing in volumes measured by the boatload.

Well, fuck them both, the president thought. We're going to change the rules of the game. Anyone doesn't like it, too damn bad. She might even come right out and say so, if they pushed back too hard.

To her chief of staff, the president said, "Start the ball rolling, Galia. Within a week after we return to Washington, I want to convene a meeting at the White House. I want the best people we have from the private, public, and educational sectors to address the question of how U.S. companies can successfully compete in the manufacture and marketing of consumer electronics, not just domestically but worldwide. Goddamnit, we're going to put Americans back to work making televisions, computers, and smart phones."

Stunned by the president's vehemence, Galia got quickly to her feet.

"Yes, ma'am, I'll get right on it."

She left Patti alone, but a moment later poked her head back into the president's quarters. "Ma'am, Prime Minister Kimbrough would like to have a minute, if you can see him."

Galia's tone told Patti that Kimbrough was waiting just the other side of the door. A Brit would think it the height of rudeness for an American to show up unannounced at his door, but Kimbrough—Oh, to hell with it, she thought. I'm not like him.

She'd kill the bastard with kindness. Or a fireplace poker, if that didn't work.

"Tell the prime minister he may come in."

Galia stepped back, and Kimbrough stepped inside, shutting the door behind him.

"Thank you for seeing me without notice, Madam President."

"What are friends for, Norvin?" It was always presumptuous to address a new English acquaintance by his first name, Patti knew. She was testing the prime minister, and he was well aware of it.

"Of course," he said, "friends." Without sounding friendly at all.

"Please have a seat," Patti said, gesturing him to an armchair opposite her.

Just as she had with Galia, Patti asked Kimbrough a question that surprised him, "These chairs we're sitting in, they're from the Victorian era?"

Kimbrough responded like a schoolboy, one proud to have mastered his lessons. "Why, yes. Thirteen years into Her Majesty's reign, 1850."

"Built by English craftsmen."

"Of course."

"And lovingly restored by the descendants of their makers?"

The prime minister didn't know what the woman was getting at, but he answered, "I can't say if there was any direct family relationship, but workers from the same part of the country did the restoration work, yes."

"How hard is it to find first-rate artisans in the United Kingdom, Norvin?"

"If you'll pardon my language, ma'am, it's a damn sight harder than when I was a lad."

The prime minister was in his mid-sixties. But he took good care of himself and could pass for a man several years younger.

"Do you know what I'm going to do with the money I save by sharing the burden of the world's defense costs with America's friends?"

Frosty now, Kimbrough replied, "No, Madam President, I

do not."

"I'm going to create a government agency to fund the training of hands-on artistry." The idea had come to her just that moment. "Something on a scale Franklin Roosevelt would have appreciated. Something to tap into the vast creative energy of the American people. I've met so many people, young and old, who express themselves in so many fantastic ways. Wouldn't it be wonderful if there were always people around who could keep chairs like these looking lovely for centuries to come?"

Poppycock, Kimbrough thought. The woman was as mad as a hat—

Or was she? England was so diverse, so polyglot now, his grandfather might mistake London for Cairo, were he to come back to life. Perhaps a government scheme that paid decent wages and conferred a measure of prestige on young blighters of all stripes for restoring traditional arts and crafts would be worthwhile as a force for assimilation and unity. The rise of national artisanal class could—good God, the damn woman had him buying into her load of claptrap.

If she had her way, Britain and every other European country would be compelled to pay more pounds sterling and euros for their own defense. The woman had come right out and said she would be shifting the burden. But she hadn't said...

"Pardon me for saying so, Madam President, but I was quite taken aback not to be given advance word of your proposal. Learning of it in the moment, so to speak, was hardly in keeping with the special relationship between our two countries."

"Neither was your blatant meddling in American politics, Norvin. You didn't really think I was going to forgive and forget, did you?"

That was just the sort of blunt, ruthless declaration that had characterized Kimbrough's rise in politics. He couldn't help but admire it—especially in so fetching a woman—but he did his best to conceal any sign of approval.

"I suppose I shouldn't have. So where does that leave us now?"

"Well, you could always reject my proposal out of hand."

"And there goes any remnant of that special relationship."

"I'm afraid so."

"It might be good for me politically to stand up to you."

"No, it wouldn't. You'd be isolating yourself. From all I've read and learned firsthand, the English relish their disdain for the French, and the only people they loathe more are the Germans. If there's to be a continental defense agreement that excludes the UK, and if London has thumbed its nose at Washington, you're going to find yourself the odd man out, cold and lonely on this Scepter'd Isle, while Paris and Berlin become much more important."

The woman was not only ruthless, she'd played him exactly as she'd needed to: Having sprung her plan without warning, she'd given him no opportunity to sabotage it before she'd brought the frogs and the krauts aboard. Now his only choice was to acquiesce.

Humiliated by a woman. Perhaps, he thought, he could return the favor.

He stood and said, "Terrible thing, these rumors concerning you and M'sieur Severin."

"They seem to be keeping a great many people on Fleet Street busy, don't they?" Patti replied evenly.

Kimbrough nodded. "So far, though, they seem to have missed out on a few facts."

"Such as?" the president asked.

"Well, you and Jean-Louis share the same birthday ... and you acted in the same theater production while the two of you were at Yale ... and I believe there was something about a cast party in New York City after a performance on your mutual birthday. Got quite licentious, I'm told."

Patti knew that she'd soon be reading about those tidbits.

She told the prime minister, "I was quite serious about suing anyone who slanders me, Norvin. *Anyone.* And you have such strict laws about that sort of thing here in England."

"Yes, we do. But even here the wheels of justice can grind

exceedingly slow. And who knows how one's spouse might react in the meantime."

A bright smile lit Patti's face.

"You mean my husband? Jim?"

Not many people would laugh at the Prime Minister of the United Kingdom to his face, not at his own country home, but the President of the United States did.

"Oh, Norvin, thank you," she said, laughing. "I really needed that. *Jim.*"

Simply saying McGill's name brought on another gale.

Kimbrough turned bright red with anger, looked for a moment as if he might do or say something truly foolish, but he held his tongue, turned on his heel and made his retreat.

Rive Gauche, Paris

16

After giving McGill her Beretta, Gabbi handed him her mobile phone and said, "Hit number one: That's speed dial to the embassy. Tell them where we are and what's happening."

McGill glanced at their surroundings. He knew from his map study they were on the Left Bank, veering swiftly away from the Seine, heading northwest he thought, cutting off traffic, swerving around slow-moving vehicles, and ignoring speed limits with an impunity only diplomatic immunity and superior driving skills could confer.

For all that, the thugs in the European minicar behind them were still on their tail. Not that they looked like diplomats. There was one other problem with Gabbi's plan.

"Sorry," McGill said. "We're going way too fast for me to comprehend street signs."

As if that wasn't bad enough, a middle-aged guy with a half-dozen baguettes under one arm and a cell phone in his opposite hand stepped into the street, oblivious to the *two* cars that were about to mow him down.

There was no way Gabbi could have stopped in time, but

there was a narrow street, maybe just an alley, at an oblique angle to her left. She shot into it, passing the heedless pedestrian closely enough to make him jump a foot into the air and send his baguettes flying. McGill turned to see if their pursuers struck the man; the second car also missed him by a whisker. But an opportunistic hand darted out of a passenger side window and grabbed a loaf of bread as it fell out of the sky.

Neat trick, McGill thought, but reflexes that quick were not a comforting quality in a potential adversary.

"Press 011," Gabbi told McGill. "The French cops'll home in on us."

McGill had another idea. There was no one in the alley. No one even looking out a window as far as he could see.

"Try to get us enough of a gap so you can hit the brakes without causing a crash," he said.

His companion flicked a glance his way, trying to determine if the man she was supposed to protect was an imminent danger to himself. No way would she—

"Come on," McGill said, sensing her resistance, "it'll be fun."

Choosing to construe that suggestion as a direct order, figuring she'd only lose her job a little sooner than she intended to leave it anyway, sincerely hoping they didn't have to kill anyone, Gabbi flicked on the car's hazard lights and goosed the accelerator at the same time. The flashing red lights caused the little car behind them to drop back; the interval between the vehicles lengthened; and Gabbi hit the brakes. McGill jumped out of the car, gun in hand, moving toward the autobug which by now had also stopped.

The driver of the pursuit vehicle looked as if he might put the bug into reverse and try to retreat, but when McGill shook his head, and Gabbi stepped up with another gun to point at them, that notion was abandoned. Following McGill's gestures with the Beretta, three oversized, over-thirty, none-too-clean men pried themselves out of the small vehicle.

McGill asked, "Who are you guys?"

Gabbi responded first. "They're Brits, soccer hooligans."

The biggest one, a red-haired lug, smiled with gray teeth and said, "That's football, if you please, miss. *Football* hooligans. What you Yanks play, that's gridiron."

Red's mates elbowed each other, chuckled, and nodded. The smallest of the three, who was well over six feet tall, bit off the end of the baguette he'd plucked out of the air.

McGill said, "Okay, now that we've got that straight, why were you chasing us?"

"Recognized you, we did," said the mid-sized one, who was missing a front tooth. "You're the bloke what married the smasher that lives in your White 'ouse."

So they actually knew who he was, McGill thought.

"Follow international politics, do you?" he asked.

That cracked all three of them up.

"All we really wants," Red told McGill, "is to buy you a pint or two. Your bird, too, if she'd care to join us."

"You chased us so you could drink with us?" Gabbi asked.

"Was you what started the stunt drivin', dearie," Breadboy said around another bite of baguette. "That just added to the excitement."

Gaptooth added, "Seein' you close like, though, I'd be happy chasin' you any time."

Another round of guffaws ensued. McGill and Gabbi exchanged a look. These three loons were drunk, and they'd led them on a chase that had almost cost a man his life.

McGill said, "Let's try this again. You know who I am, and you wanted to buy me a drink. Why did you want to buy me a drink?"

The three louts looked at each other as if the answer to the question was obvious.

"Well, yer the blighter workin' to get the copper what killed Terry the Frog Duchamp out of the nick, aint ya?" Red asked.

McGill's lag time comprehending the idiom was a half-second, and he said, "Uh-huh, and how did you know that?"

The oral exam had just gone one question too far. The three Englishmen abroad looked at one another and wordlessly decided to withdraw their offer of hospitality to McGill.

Red said, "We'll just scarper then, if you an' yer bird don't mind."

They started toward the car but stopped when McGill put his gun on Red.

"You don't really mean that, do ya?"

"Never can tell. Why take the chance?"

Without looking, McGill could feel Gabbi tense up.

Red spotted the dissent in the ranks.

"Yer bird wouldn't like it," he said.

Gabbi put her gun on him, too.

"Frogs are terrible hard on foreigners usin' guns," Gaptooth said, sounding knowledgeable.

"We have diplomatic immunity," McGill told him.

"Christ's sake, 'arold," Breadboy said to Red. "Tell 'im or I will. Let's just get the fook out of here."

Harold swallowed his pride and confessed, "I do small favors for this bookmaker in London, name of Pembroke. He told me all about you lot. Gave me yer picture. Told me yer story, helpin' the Yank what killed Terry the Frog. I thought that was brilliant. I wanted to buy you a pint with my own money, the way that fuckin' Terry was always makin' my Arsenal side look a pack of gits. But Pembroke, he paid for me and my mates to come find you. And that we did. But now I'm thinkin' it's time we get our arses back to Blighty."

Just then the man whom they'd nearly run over appeared at the far end of the alley. He'd finally come after them. Breadboy dropped his half-consumed baguette and said, "Now, we're in the shit for sure. That bugger can't but have coppers half-a-step behind."

McGill told the thugs, "Write your names and where we can find this guy Pembroke for me, and I'll square things with the French."

Gabbi provided pen and paper, and went to attend to the aggrieved local.

Harold returned the information and Gabbi's pen to McGill.

"Yer all right, mate, for a Yank. An' we won't say a word."

"Say a word about what?" McGill asked.

He nodded his head in Gabbi's direction. "You and yer bird. You have a right, what with yer missus did."

"My wife?" McGill asked. "The President of the United States?"

The three of them snickered. Breadboy said, "Her, all right."

And Gaptooth gave him a copy of a Paris tabloid he'd had in his jacket.

"Hot off the press, mate."

The front page featured a composite side-by-side photo of Patti and Jean-Louis Severin.

The headline read: Entente *Très* Cordiale.

Rive Gauche, Paris

17

Gabbi drove McGill back to his flat above the Hideaway. She said, "I'd have had some serious explaining to do if I'd let you get hurt or killed."

"Or if we'd run down that pedestrian," McGill added.

The State Department officer shook her head.

"He's a professor at the Sorbonne. Marginally tolerant of Americans at the best of times. The thing that saved us was he *really* despises the English, and he made me promise we'd have the police give the Brits a sound beating."

Gabbi had summoned the police to take the three *football* hooligans to the Gare du Nord and put them on the next Eurostar train to London. She didn't want Red getting back behind the wheel drunk. If she'd misled the aggrieved intellectual jaywalker as to the Englishmen's fate, it was probably for the best.

"You reimburse him for his baguettes?" McGill asked.

"*Bien sûr.*" Of course.

Changing the subject, McGill asked, "Can you place bets legally in France?"

Going with the flow, Gabbi said, "There's *Le Francais des*

Jeux: the lottery. There's *PariMutual Urbain:* the government monopoly on betting on horse races. And I think there are discussions going on about organizing online betting on sporting events. It gets complicated because of conflicts of interest between individual countries and the European Union as a whole."

McGill mulled that over, nodded to himself.

"Okay," he said. "How about if someone wants to get a bet down and doesn't give a damn about the law? There'll be somebody to take his action, right?"

Gabbi said, "Sure. Just like at home, crooks come in all sizes, shapes, and colors, and they run all sorts of rackets. What are you thinking?"

"Something that guy, Red, mentioned. About being glad Thierry Duchamp is dead because Thierry always beat his home team. That and Red having a connection to a bookie."

Gabbi came to a stop for a red light and looked at McGill.

"I don't understand. There's no connection between Glen Kinnard and any bookie, is there?"

"Not that I know of, but I'll check."

"And wouldn't a bookie, if he were trying to fix a game, pay off the player instead of having him killed?"

"That would be the usual way, yes."

"Then what are you thinking?"

The light turned green and Gabbi put the Peugeot in motion.

"I'm thinking there might have been a big game—a match or whatever they call it—that Thierry Duchamp had been scheduled to play in, only he met up with Glen Kinnard first."

"We can find that out."

"It would be good if we could find out if there was any unusual wagering on that match, too. Betting against Thierry's team."

Gabbi pulled over to the curb and stopped the car. She stared at McGill.

"You think Glen Kinnard was hired to kill Thierry Duchamp? As part of some gambling scheme?"

McGill shook his head. "No. Even if Thierry' Duchamp's team didn't postpone its game out of respect for his passing, I'd guess that all previous bets on the game would have been cleared and new odds posted."

"Then what are you saying?"

"What if some lowlife gamblers wanted to make a killing—ironic word, I know. But what if they hired some local muscle just to rough up Thierry. Having our missing blonde provoke Thierry into slapping her around would be the setup, but she didn't realize Kinnard wasn't the other party to the scam."

Gabbi saw it now, what McGill had in mind.

"Sure, if another guy came by, if he was in on the scheme, and if he was good enough to just, say, break Thierry's leg instead of kill him, then everything would work. The football match wouldn't be postponed, the betting line would be changed for people placing bets after the incident, but not for those who already had their money down."

McGill nodded. "It wouldn't have been the bettors' fault the sports star was a jerk who beat on a woman, and the guy who came to the rescue couldn't have been faulted. He was just doing what France's Good Samaritan law required of him."

"But why didn't the blonde know that Glen Kinnard wasn't the right guy?"

McGill told her, "If the people who set the whole thing up—assuming I'm even right—are smart, they would have used a strong arm guy the woman didn't know, someone who couldn't be connected to her in any way. So the cops wouldn't smell a conspiracy."

Gabbi regarded McGill with a look of respect. This guy was good.

She followed with what had to be the next piece of the puzzle.

"But once the woman saw things were going a lot farther than planned, she took off."

"Yeah," McGill said. "To who knows where."

Gabbi frowned at that idea, and then her expression of displeasure deepened further.

"What?" McGill asked.

"It just occurred to me. This guy who was hired to break a leg? He'd have to be a lot better fighter than Glen Kinnard. He'd have to be as good as you."

McGill understood what Gabbi was feeling now. Concern for him, and for herself. She was the one assigned to protect McGill. If they ran into the hired muscle ... McGill wondered if Sweetie was about done with her case. Whether she might enjoy a trip to Paris.

What he said to Gabbi was, "That's something to keep in mind, but if he's that good, maybe he's already made a name for himself and will be easier to find. And then there's something else to think about."

"What?" Gabbi asked, looking as if she really didn't want to know.

"That English goof, Red. He gave me a tip while you were off calming down the professor. He was sure the news about my working for Glen Kinnard would be hitting websites for soccer fans soon. He said I should be careful. Next time it might be a carload of Thierry Duchamp's fans after me."

Gabbi moaned. "Oh, God. I was so glad we didn't have to shoot anyone."

"Me, too," McGill said. "So, I'm going to need a discreet barber for a new haircut, and you're going to have to buy me some clothes that don't look so American. I'm going to have to blend, look like a whole new man."

Eighteenth Arrondissement, Paris

18

Odo Sacripant, drove Investigating Magistrate Yves Pruet slowly along the Rue des Poisonniers in northeastern Paris. The neighborhood looked as though it might have been transplanted whole from West Africa. Women shoppers wore traditional African garb. Street vendors clogged the sidewalks.

Soukous music percolated from the speakers of a music shop. In the back seat of his Citroën, Pruet had his mobile phone pressed to his ear as Odo looked for a place to park.

The bodyguard saw two men come out of a storefront. Their eyes locked onto Odo immediately. Natural enemies—a cop and crooks—regarded each other, trying to decide whether to fight or pass by. Odo took his FAMAS G2 bullpup assault rifle off the front passenger seat and placed it on the dash board. The bad guys decided to depart. They got into a gray, rusting minivan and pulled out, leaving Odo a parking space.

Catch you another day, he thought.

Pruet, meanwhile, concluded his conversation.

"Thank you, M'sieur McGill. I will see what I can do."

"The Ami is playing within the rules?" Odo asked. "Despite his exalted status?"

Odo was regarding Pruet via his rearview mirror. The magistrate noticed the weapon on the dashboard.

"We are expecting a pitched battle?" he asked. "I have forgotten my body armor."

"You never know what they might get up to in Chateau Rouge." The neighborhood's traditional name. "Street brawls are not uncommon."

"Let us hope the ceasefire holds for the duration of our visit. And, yes, the president's henchman is being most cooperative." Pruet told Odo of McGill's theory of what might have happened under the Pont d'Iéna.

Odo mulled it over. "Not a bad thing for him to think."

"*Mon ami*, do you think M'sieur McGill could have broken Thierry Duchamp's leg without having to kill him?"

"I think he could break whatever he wants. Inflict damage by degrees."

"A pleasant fellow for all that."

"You still wish to talk to the artist?" Odo asked.

"As long as we are in the neighborhood. Bring your weapon."

19

Bertrand Kalou was waiting in the open doorway to his apartment on the first floor above a shop selling clothing styled in sub-Saharan Africa, not the fashion houses of Paris. He, however, wore a workingman's pants and shirt, but his feet were bare. His hair was closely cropped and graying; his skin was wrinkled; his brown eyes were sad. But he was not as gaunt as many of the newcomers were. He'd found enough to eat in France and his accent was suitably Parisian.

"*Bonjour,*" he said, "you are from the police?"

Pruet presented his credentials.

"Come in, gentlemen," Kalou said. "I have been expecting you."

The apartment was tiny, furnished with secondhand furniture, but was clean and smelled of the flowers that the artist kept in a half-dozen vases placed about the flat. One floral arrangement sat on an artist's table placed next to a window looking out on the street.

Pruet sat on a settee with Kalou opposite him in an armchair. Odo stood guard in the hallway outside, after making sure there was no way anyone could climb in through the window.

"You are here in France legally, m'sieur?" Pruet asked.

"*Oui.* I waited many years for your embassy in Yamoussoukro to extend me the right to come here and not be afraid I'd be sent back."

"*Bon,*" Pruet said. "But now something has made you afraid. You were expecting the police."

The artist nodded. "I have read of the death of Thierry Duchamp. I fear I may be in some jeopardy."

Pruet understood why. Not complying with France's Good Samaritan law was a crime punishable by up to five years imprisonment.

He asked, "You heard him struggle with the man charged with his death?"

Kalou's eyes became sadder than usual. "I heard screams

and blows, shouts and curses such as I had not heard since I left the Cote d'Ivoire."

The man's head bobbed as if agreeing with the terrible memory playing in his mind.

"M'sieur Kalou," Pruet said, "please tell me what you saw or heard."

"The terror was mostly in my ears, and my mind. First, I heard a woman's voice, harsh with anger, sharpening to scorn and ridicule. Then came the bellow of a man's anger in response."

"French voices? Native speakers?"

The artist nodded, "*Oui.* Then the woman screamed so loudly I thought my ears would surely bleed. The sounds of flesh striking flesh followed. Again very loud. Sharp sounds. Slaps, I think."

"The man was beating the woman? With an open hand?" Pruet asked.

The artist's sad smile spoke of another memory of his homeland.

"It is ironic, I know, but there are men who will beat a woman to death while trying not to destroy her beauty. At the very least, an open-hand blow can destroy one's hearing. At most ... well, at most, a strong man can break a woman's neck with such a blow."

Pruet looked closely at Kalou now. He didn't see a man who'd delivered such a vicious strike but perhaps one whose wife—mother, sister, daughter—had met such a fate.

"You did not think to call the police then, m'sieur?" Pruet asked.

"I do not have a mobile. I walk slowly. I was starting to leave and look for a phone when I heard a second man shout, in English, and then I heard two men fighting to the death."

The immigrant looked as if he knew those sounds as well.

"But you still did not call the police," Pruet said.

"I remained in place, like an animal too frightened to move, hoping not to call any attention to myself. And then..."

"Then what, m'sieur?"

"I saw a woman move out from under the far side of the bridge, and not too long after that the sounds of the fight stopped."

"The woman appeared unharmed."

Kalou shook his head. "I saw her only from behind, but she staggered."

"Then you departed?"

"I waited. For how long I cannot say. But long enough to hope it would be safe to flee."

"And was it?"

"Another man came along. He went under the bridge where the two men and the woman had fought. I held my breath waiting for him to scream in horror at what he'd found. But he didn't make a sound. After little more than a minute, or so it seemed to me, this new man departed. After he'd gone, I also left, assuring myself that this new fellow, having regarded the terrible scene that surely must have lain at his feet, would call the police. I was safe, or so I thought. But now I see that neither of us summoned help."

Pruet considered the story. Then he asked, "Can you describe this final man who went under the bridge?"

"I can do better than that."

Kalou got slowly to his feet and shuffled over to his artist's table.

He picked up a ceramic tile and held it out to Pruet.

"I painted him."

St. Germain, Paris

20

Alexandru and his wife, Ana, walked the Boulevard St. Germain. They wore their best clothes: expensive and mainstream. They were clean and carefully groomed. Still, they wouldn't fool any cop who knew his business. He'd see their street-smart, watchful eyes and know the two of them were running some sort of game. Their olive complexions would add to a *flic's* suspicions. But the two of them holding hands in public, and Ana in a skirt that stopped above her knees, her long hair shining in the sun, would let the gendarmes know, thank all saints, that they weren't Arabs, weren't jihadis. But it would take only a heartbeat for the police to identify them: Rom. Gypsies.

On the expensive reaches of one of the city's most exclusive streets, the two of them could only be up to no good and, worse, they were straying from the precincts where their trickery with tourists was tolerated.

Alexandru had the job of watching for *flics* and steering the two of them away from trouble. Ana, seemingly chattering gaily on her mobile phone in fluent Spanish, was the photographer. If Alexandru saw a woman who might be their target, he would give Ana's hand a gentle squeeze, nod in the appropriate direction, and his wife would turn her head, laughing as if she'd just heard a wonderful joke, and use the mobile to take a picture without ever removing it from her ear: a skill she practiced regularly.

That day, Ana had photographed a dozen possibilities, always careful to include some landmark in the shot as well as the woman, so they could tell where the picture had been taken. But so far Alexandru had yet to give Ana's hand a double squeeze, the signal to photograph and follow. This one was probably the one they wanted.

After hours of walking, the young couple rested their feet sitting on a park bench, taking turns sipping from a cup of Coke. Not wanting to attract any official attention, or have a merchant chase them down the street, Alexandru had paid for the drink rather than steal it. As Ana took small sips, making sure she saved most of the drink for her husband, Alexandru cupped her mobile in one hand and scrolled through the photos Ana had taken. All of the women were in focus and within the general description of the woman they wanted, but upon inspection none was their target.

Alexandru gave the mobile back to Ana and took the cup of Coke from her.

"So many women color their hair these days," Ana said. "All of them want to be blonde."

Alexandru shrugged as he sipped.

"Would you like me to be blonde?" Ana asked.

He looked at his wife. Rom women didn't color their hair.

Not unless a scam called for it, and then only with great reluctance.

As if reading his mind, Ana said, "I could wear a wig. Only for you. Only in our bed."

Alexandru felt himself start to get excited, but he pushed the thought away.

"Maybe we could each wear one," he said. "Pretend we're Swedish."

Ana's face grew cross, thinking she was being mocked. But when Alexandru smiled at her, she had to smile back. They both laughed, and Alexandru gave her the cup back. She sipped, grateful to have a generous husband. One who loved her for who she was.

She would do everything she could to be worthy of him.

"This woman we want to find," Ana asked, "could she have been wearing a wig?"

"Not unless they make blonde wigs with dark roots."

"Dark roots?" Ana looked intently at Alexandru. "You actually saw her? When?"

"Early in the morning. I couldn't sleep. I went for a walk along the river, hoping I might find some tourist droppings." Tourists lost the most amazing things, quite on their own. In the natural order of things, scavengers followed along close behind them. "I did not find anything of value, but I did see the blonde woman. That's why I was able to see how much she looked like the one with the American."

"Why didn't you tell me before now?" Ana demanded.

She had wondered if her husband leaving their bed had somehow been her fault.

"Grandmother taught me I must save my secrets as carefully as I do my gold."

Ana felt great relief. The call of fortune, she decided, had compelled her husband to go out early, not any failing on her part. She kissed her husband's cheek, a public display of affection a Rom woman would normally not even consider, especially where passing *gadje* —outsiders—could easily see it.

"The woman I saw had a small rhinestone on the right side of her nose," Alexandru added, pointing to a spot on his own nose. "But it was small, might have just been stuck on."

Ana beamed at her husband. "You are giving us the best chance to find her."

"Bunica Anisa will reward us if any of our tribe finds this woman and brings us riches. But if we find her ourselves, the reward will be even greater."

Ana couldn't help herself. She kissed her husband again. On his mouth.

Alexandru yielded to his wife's passion. He told himself it would be excellent cover for two Rom pretending to be *gadje*. Almost as excellent as the kiss itself.

Warm and wet and tasting of Coke.

Ana set the cup on the pavement and put her mobile on her lap. She took both of Alexandru's hands in hers and looked him in the eye.

"If there is anything else about this woman you did not tell the others, you must tell me now, so I might know if I see her while you are watching for the *flics.*"

Alexandru looked away, his complexion darkening. Ana didn't realize what she was seeing for a moment; she had never seen her husband blush before. Once she understood he was embarrassed, though, she pulled him close.

"What?" she demanded. "What did you see?"

In a quiet voice, he said, "I could not help but see. Her shirt was torn, hanging very low."

Ana took but a second to form the picture in her mind.

"Her breasts? What about them?"

"She was not born with them; she did not grow into them. She—"

"Bought them?"

Alexandru nodded.

"Big?" Ana asked. She was waiting, praying, for her own development.

"Yes, big," Alexandru said. And ashamed now that he would have noticed such a detail, he added, "With the right one sitting just a bit higher than the left."

Rue de Rivoli, Paris

21

Arno Durand, the sports reporter McGill had recruited, joined McGill and Gabbi at a table in a café just up the street from the Louvre. McGill had asked Gabbi to place a call to Durand through the embassy. Durand brought a small black leather portfolio with him. He made no move to open it as a waiter approached. The reporter ordered a glass of red wine. Service was prompt and when the waiter departed Durand put all three of his audio recorders on the table.

Gabbi stared at the reporter and told him, "I'm going to be very disappointed if you try to play any tricks on us."

The Frenchman looked back at her, trying for indignation, but saying nothing.

"I'm going outside," Gabbi told McGill. "See if I gave him any ideas last time about bringing some help along." Turning to Durand, she continued, "And don't tell me you don't have the money. You'd find it."

As Gabbi got up to go, the reporter sighed and took out his mobile. He tapped a button.

"*Pierre, faites signe de la main à mes amis.*" Wave to my friends.

A scruffy young guy on a motorbike across the street waved his hand. With a nod, Durand sent him on his way. He stuck his phone back in his pocket.

Gabbi put both hands on the table and leaned in close to the Frenchman.

"Too obvious," she said. Looking at Jim, she added, "Be careful what you say."

Both men watched her go. Durand sighed.

"I am trying to decide if one such as her would be worth the trouble," he said.

McGill told him, "My guess is she's already known a journalist."

"That would explain a great deal." He shrugged and opened his portfolio, spinning it around so McGill could see. "These are the women Thierry Duchamp has been linked to by the media in the past twelve months. Each of them is either an actress in European cinema or a model for a fashion house here in Paris or in Milan."

"He didn't care for goalkeepers on women's football teams?" McGill asked.

The Frenchman laughed. "No, m'sieur, that was not his style."

"Would you mind turning the pages?" the president's henchman asked.

He didn't have to say he wasn't going to leave his fingerprints on the portfolio.

"Of course," Durand said, and McGill studied the faces of eight beautiful young women who'd achieved public notice on Thierry Duchamp's arm in the past year.

McGill looked up and told Durand, "I don't see her, the one who bears a resemblance to my suspicious friend."

"Nor did I," Durand said.

"All of these women, they'd all acquired a measure of fame on their own by the time they'd met Thierry?"

"Yes. The publicity they received from his company added to their appeal, but as you Americans would say, they were already on their way."

"What about unknowns? Was there anyone he liked to spend time with outside of the spotlight's glare?"

Durand smiled in genuine appreciation. "You are very intuitive, m'sieur. I am told Thierry Duchamp liked an occasional woman he didn't have to treat with…sensitivity."

"He liked it rough," McGill said.

"At least some of the time."

"And a tough girl, she might give Thierry a hard time in public, say, under a bridge."

"You must have been quite the *flic* in your day, m'sieur."

"I had my moments," McGill admitted. "So there were nights when Thierry liked it rough, but he'd still want a looker."

The reporter needed a beat to understand the idiom. Then he smiled and nodded, "*Oui*, a looker."

"An office girl or a sales clerk," McGill speculated. Uneasily, he added, "A female cop?"

Durand shook his head. "My information is he liked a stripper or two when he wasn't with someone whose face he dared not bruise."

McGill nodded. The guy sounded like a real jerk. A girl who pole-danced for a living, she could be bought off fairly cheap if she got roughed up. The president's henchman felt better about helping Glen Kinnard. Felt less judgmental about Kinnard beating the life out of the guy.

"You've eliminated the possibility we're looking for a transvestite or a transsexual?" he asked.

The reporter nodded. "I've turned up no source to say Thierry was drawn to anyone but women."

Durand told McGill where he would go looking for the blonde woman now.

"Let me ask you something else that might figure into this," McGill said. "Does France allow mixed martial arts fighting?"

He was following up on Gabbi's notion that a thug hired to break Thierry Duchamp's leg would have to be as good as he was. Which implied a wide range of skills.

The reporter nodded. "This is a quite recent export from your country. Of course, being French, we had to civilize the barbarism a little."

"How's that?" McGill asked.

"Here, matches must take place in a ring, not a cage. When

one man is on the mat, the other must not kick, knee, or elbow-strike his head."

"But you can go after the body?" McGill asked.

"*Oui*. If that were outlawed, what would the appeal be?"

"Might as well watch golf," McGill replied.

Durand laughed again, and asked, "What is your interest here, m'sieur?"

McGill wanted to keep the reporter interested, but he didn't want to give everything away. He said, "I'm just considering possibilities. Who's the national champion, heavyweight class?"

"Henri Bonard, a very fierce fellow." Durand studied McGill's face; the reporter was also an intuitive fellow. He saw something lurking in McGill's eyes. A secret, perhaps the center of this whole affair. "There is one man who is said to be even more fearsome than Bonard."

"Who's that?"

"His real name he keeps secret. He simply calls himself *L'Entrepreneur*."

"The businessman?" McGill asked, not sure he had it right.

Durand said, "His full title would be *l'entrepreneur de pompes funèbres:* the businessman of funerary affairs. Colloquially, The Undertaker. I have not seen him fight, but he is said to be like your American boxer, Tyson. Only less restrained."

McGill blinked and asked, "Mike Tyson?"

"*Oui*," the reporter said. "The Undertaker will not be bound by any rules. The sports authorities will not have him."

"They're afraid he'll kill someone?"

Arno Durand nodded. "*Exactement.*"

The reporter was actually frightening himself a little now, that he and a creature such as The Undertaker should both be involved in the same drama, but he was more certain than ever this was going to be the biggest story of his career.

McGill was thinking: *Less restrained than Mike Tyson?* The guy who'd bitten off a chunk of Evander Holyfield's ear *during* a championship fight.

Gabbi returned and saw the two men sitting at the table lost in thought.

"What'd I miss?" she asked.

Rive Gauche, Paris

22

On the way back to The Hideaway for the night, McGill told Gabbi of his conversation with Arno Durand.

She said, "If this Undertaker creep pops up, I hope you'd shoot him."

"I thought that was the last thing you wanted," McGill said.

"The last thing I want is for you to die. Joined at the hip to that is for me to die."

"Reasonable."

McGill looked out the window. They were driving along the Seine. He liked the way central Paris was organized around the river. He hadn't read a history of the city, but he'd bet that the body of water was what drew the original settlers. Just like Lake Michigan was Chicago's reason for being. They rolled past the outdoor periodical vendors stationed along the riverfront. He decided he'd have to check out their stalls before he left town. A cosmopolitan place like Paris, some of the vendors were bound to offer a few English language publications.

Gabbi interrupted his reverie. "What I was getting at, you wouldn't feel obliged to fight such an opponent barehanded?"

"I try not fight at all. If it's inevitable, my only obligation is to come out on top. Using any means necessary."

"No rules for you either?"

"Only the one I just mentioned."

She nodded. "You think this creep is like you then? In that way, I mean."

McGill smiled inwardly. Gabbi was starting to sound a bit like Sweetie. Less like a diplomat. Made him feel good.

"Sounds like he is. Might be even more extreme."

"How could that be?"

"Well, let's say he's strong and skilled and ruthless. But

maybe he's also one of those brutes who likes his stew seasoned with steroids, amphetamines and PCP. My uncle, the guy who taught me how to fight, warned me you have to be on the lookout for all sorts of crazies."

Gabbi glanced at him. "Yeah, what did your uncle say you should do with crazy people?"

"Shoot them if you have to. Cut them if you can. Drop rocks on their heads. If no other alternative presents itself, outrun them until they double-up in exhaustion, and then go back and finish them off."

"Interesting guy, your uncle."

"He was a government employee, too: U.S. Navy."

Gabbi looked at McGill and when he smiled at her she smiled back.

"My compliments to the president," Gabbi said.

"On what?" McGill asked.

Gabbi pulled up in front of The Hideaway.

"Her choice of henchmen," she said.

The Hideaway, Paris

23

"Jim?" the president asked, a note of uncertainty in her voice.

McGill had answered his cell phone, in the apartment above the Irish pub, with his mouth filled with corned beef, spicy mustard, and rye bread. When Gabbi had dropped him off he'd stopped for a few words with Harbin. He'd assured McGill that he'd yet to meet a troublemaker who could make trouble for him. Even an angel-duster? Harbin pulled his jacket open. McGill's first thought was Harbin was going to show him a gun. Instead, he saw two cylindrical sticks, a half-inch in diameter, maybe twenty inches long: escrima sticks. Filipino martial art tools. Bone breakers. Even King Kong in high dudgeon would settle down once he got his skull busted. McGill didn't insult Harbin by asking if he was any good with the sticks. He only requested that the kitchen send up a corned beef sandwich and a bottle of Harp Lager. McGill swallowed the bite of sandwich in his mouth, helped it along with a swig of beer, and tried answering his wife's call once more.

"Hello, Madam President," McGill said. "Pardon me for talking while I was eating."

"Is that what it was? I thought you were all choked up to hear from me."

"I would be, if you were calling from downstairs and on your way up."

"I have your address now," Patti said. "Do you?"

McGill didn't. But he couldn't let his wife think he was a complete rube. "I bet I could find my way here from the airport by now."

It did his heart good to hear he'd made the president laugh.

"You feel safe in your new digs, Jim?" Patti asked.

"There's a guy with sticks guarding the door."

"I'll sleep better knowing that," the president said.

Each of them knew and accepted that the other was engaged in dangerous work. The president of the United States, upon the tallying of 270 or more electoral votes, automatically became a target for an unknowable number of enemies and loons. The Secret Service had agents whose only jobs were to read, evaluate, archive, and investigate threats made against the president. As for McGill, the nature of his work dictated that he poke his nose into places where it might meet ballistic resistance: the range of possibilities including a fist, a bat, or a bullet.

If the awareness of those realities wasn't enough, they shared still painful memories of the death of Patti's first husband. McGill had tried and failed to protect Andy Grant from militant antiabortionists. Andy had died in the master bedroom of his lakefront mansion, the means of his demise being a rocket-propelled grenade fired from a boat on Lake Michigan.

McGill had caught the perpetrators the very next day, but the underlying truth of the tragedy remained vivid. If a rich man, living in a walled estate, wasn't safe in his own bedroom, who was safe anywhere?

Even so, McGill told Patti, "I intend to keep our date to meet the queen."

"Safe and sound? Looking as much like Rory Calhoun as ever?"

"I might change my look a little."

That took his wife by surprise. "To what?"

"I was thinking Belmondo."

"The father or the son?" Patti asked.

"Belmondo had a father?" McGill asked.

"Paul Belmondo was a famous sculptor; his son Jean-Paul is a famous actor."

"The actor," McGill said. "Have to keep my motif intact."

Patti laughed again and asked, "You know what Jean-Paul Belmondo was famous for?"

"A winning smile?"

"Good guess, but my point was, he did all his own stunts."

"Me, too."

"As well I know." Then the president said. "Jim, there's something I have to tell you."

"I already know, and I don't believe a word of it."

Following a beat of silence, Patti said, "The French media have picked up the story, of course."

"Yeah." McGill told her the story of the soccer hooligans and the tabloid they had with them. What Patti picked up on, though, was when her husband mentioned the name Pembroke.

"Pembroke is the name of the man behind the leak of my new defense."

McGill said, "The no-good bleep."

Patti told him, "It's okay if you swear with me, if the context justifies."

"I don't want to come off lowbrow when Galia's tapes are transcribed."

It was a running joke between the two of them. McGill had once suspected that Patti's chief of staff had bugged the offices of McGill Investigations, Inc. He didn't actually think Galia would bug the president's communications, but it didn't hurt to keep Patti on her toes.

"Meanwhile," Patti said, "about Mr. Pembroke..."

"You mean, whom do we know who'd use a Brit bookie to both embarrass you and deliver a good thumping to me? The answer is obvious."

"Senator Roger Michaelson."

"The Brit hooligans wanted to take me out drinking to celebrate the demise of Thierry Duchamp. Just a guess: Doing that in Paris might lead to strong differences of opinion with the local fandom."

"But you were too smooth for them."

"More than that," McGill said. "I've already set Celsus to tracking down a link between Michaelson and the Old World. Your full-service henchman at work."

"You are a marvel," Patti said, but the compliment was followed by a sigh.

A cue any married man in the world might pick up on. "What?"

"Nothing ... a president shouldn't whine."

McGill said, "I'm the only one who will know, and I won't tell. So go ahead."

"Right now," his wife told him, "feeling you hold me would do me more good than anything else. The fate of the free world might depend on it."

McGill asked, "Want me to abandon Glen Kinnard to his fate?"

"You wouldn't."

"For you and the kids, anything," he said.

"Okay, you *shouldn't*, but you are very sweet."

Although on a scale infinitesimal by comparison, and of a vastly simpler nature, McGill actually had more executive experience than his wife: five years as the chief of police of the Village of Winnetka, Illinois. This inclined him every so often to push her in a direction of his choosing.

"Sweet but occasionally demanding," McGill told her. "After

you're done in London, I want two, no, three days with you here in Paris. It would be crazy for us not to see it together when we're right in the neighborhood."

There was a moment of silence, but McGill could imagine the thoughts racing through his wife's mind: How many demands on her time would she have to forsake to enjoy an impromptu respite with him? What might the substantive consequences be? What might the political cost be?

Whatever the considerations, McGill's heart was warmed by Patti's response.

"Valiant henchman, I shall be at your disposal for three days."

McGill cleared his throat. "Now, I'm all choked up."

Chequers, Buckinghamshire, England

24

The President of the United States sat sideways on a sofa in her suite at Chequers, her knees drawn up, a legal pad resting against her legs, a pen in her hand. She was doing a rewrite. A former actress in feature films, she was well acquainted with scripts being rewritten up to the very moment the camera rolled. If done for a good reason by a gifted, unflappable writer, the result was an improved, more memorable scene. Possibly a moment indispensable to the fabric of the story.

It was nearly midnight now, but having talked with Jim, hearing him express his unquestioning, unshakable faith in her, she felt renewed in her energy, her self-confidence. It had never occurred to Jim to tell her she needn't worry about him and Regional Security Officer Gabriella Casale. Having lost one beloved husband—Andy Grant—to a violent death, the president wasn't shy about acquiring all pertinent information regarding the personnel safeguarding James J. McGill. Ms. Casale's dossier included a photo and a biography. She was highly regarded, multilingual, an altogether striking woman. A perfect foil for a tabloid headline: *The President's Henchman's Mistress*. Jim might have—probably had—thought of the possibility he might be used in such a way. But he hadn't thought it worth mentioning to her that she had nothing to worry about. He expected her to have the same faith in him that he had in her.

Patti started to think what she and Jim might do together in Paris...

But her self-indulgence lasted only a moment. Then she summoned the discipline to return her focus to China and Japan and the Republic of Korea. East Asia in general. That was where her new defense plan had the greatest chance of going awry. Awry being a euphemism for leading to war, the deaths of millions, and—

No. Rewriting her plan to include a major war involving China didn't work for her, made no sense. In the old days, when China was still an underdeveloped nation, still a militantly Maoist country, the risk of war would have been far greater. Now that China's economy was fast catching up to Japan's as the second largest in the world, Beijing had too much to lose to start a serious war—one with the possibility of going nuclear— or even to be lured into such a conflict without existential provocation.

Even so, great tensions would be released when the United States took a step back. The burner would be turned up under the historic feelings of enmity that always simmered between Japan and both China and South Korea. And relaxing the steady pressure of a robust U.S. military presence in the region might embolden the Chinese military. With its rapidly growing navy, China might take the disastrous misstep of invading Taiwan. Measures had to be taken to prevent that and other catastrophes.

The president picked up a fresh pad of paper and began to outline her ideas. Formulate her vision for a better world. Never thinking of herself as someone given to megalomania. A reporter for the New York Times had once asked her about the power of the presidency and if the occupant of the Oval Office didn't have to be a little crazy to exercise that power to its full extent. Patti had answered it was the fear of not doing everything she could to safeguard the United States that kept her awake at night.

She didn't know if she'd been busy remaking the world for minutes or hours when there was a knock at her door. At this hour, she thought, it couldn't be good news.

Celsus Crogher stepped into the room. The president saw his face was blank, as usual. That was a small measure of comfort. Jim had told her how Celsus had cried while telling him Deke Ky had been shot. So chances were nobody close to Celsus—and therefore her—had been killed.

"I saw you had your light on, ma'am," he said.

"Yes, Celsus," she said. "What is it?"

"The president of France, ma'am."

"Yes?"

"He'd like to know if it's too late to pay you a visit."

Patti saw a tiny flicker of disapproval in the SAC's eyes.

"Please send him in, Celsus," the president said.

Pigalle, Paris

25

Gabbi Casale's dad had warned her never to visit the red-light district of Paris. Had warned her more than once, in fact. The first time had been when Gabbi was fourteen. She had just finished her freshman year at Maine East High School in the Chicago suburb of Park Ridge.

The family was taking its first trip abroad. Mom—Marianne Rogers—was the most popular language teacher at Maine East and had been invited to participate in a six-week teacher exchange with a school in Neuilly-sur-Seine, an upscale suburb on the western boundary of Paris. Dad—State Senator Tomaso (Tom) Casale of Illinois's 33rd senatorial district and a top-earning State Farm agent—had appointed himself director of planning and security for the trip.

To his credit, Dad had everything organized to a fare-thee-well. Their passports—with photos everyone actually liked—

were in hand; the limo to take them to the airport was waiting when they stepped out the front door; the flight—miracle of miracles—departed O'Hare on time and arrived punctually at Charles de Gaulle airport; a pleasant driver found them as soon as they cleared customs and took them to the apartment Dad had rented.

Once inside, he kissed his wife, his daughter, his infant son, Gianni, and told them all, "... and on the seventh day, Senator Casale rested."

The senator retired to his bedroom and slept through till the next morning. He then took his family to breakfast. He took his wife to her new school and met—inspected—her new colleagues. He took his children to the U.S. Embassy on the Avenue Gabriel.

Tom Casale was a close political ally of the governor of Illinois, who in turn was great friends with the U.S. ambassador to France. After meeting the eminent diplomat and introducing his children to him, Tom was turned over to a counselor of commercial affairs. The two men planned to stroll in the nearby Jardin des Tuileries, Tom pushing Gianni in the pram that had been waiting for them at their new French apartment, and discuss the business possibilities available in France to a preeminent American insurance company—State Farm.

Gabbi was left to tour some of the city's cultural venues in the care of a Dartmouth student doing a summer internship at the embassy. The intern, Daniel Ahearn, passed paternal muster from a visual standpoint, but just in case his judgment was spotty, the senator told him, "Keep her away from Pigalle."

"Yes, sir," young Ahearn said promptly.

For emphasis, Tom Casale turned to his daughter. "No Pigalle."

"Sì, padre."

That made the senator smile. Gabbi's mother had been teaching her French from the time she was in diapers. Tom had lost the Italian he'd learned as a child from his mother, but Gabbi, on her own, had sought out Nonna Casale to learn

Italian. Tom knew his daughter used Italian when she wanted to butter him up, but he loved it anyway.

With a goodbye kiss on Gabbi's cheek, father and daughter went their separate ways on that sunny morning in Paris. As soon as it was safe to speak freely, Gabbi asked her escort, "May I call you Danny?"

"Sure," he replied.

She asked that he call her Gabbi, and he agreed to that, too.

"*Parlez-vous francais, Danny?*"

"*Oui, ma mère est du Québec.*" My mom's from Quebec.

Gabbi was pleased to hear that and from that point forward, except at the embassy or when the senator was around, she and Danny conversed in French. The better to fit in with their surroundings.

"My father has never been to France before," she told Danny.

"No?"

"No. So what can he know about this Pigalle place?"

"Your dad seems pretty well prepared. A guy who does his homework."

Gabbi had to agree with that, and she was impressed that Danny had sized him up so fast.

"Yeah," she said. "He probably did a lot of reading. So Pigalle's a dangerous place?"

Danny looked down at her. He had a height advantage of several inches. Then he looked away as if trying to decide how to respond.

"You can tell me the truth," Gabbi said. "I know how to keep a secret."

Danny looked back at her and smiled. "Yeah? That's a good thing to know."

"So, tell me."

"How old are you?"

"Fourteen. How old are you?"

"Twenty. You ever have a boyfriend?"

"No." Gabbi had to sacrifice a measure of pride to admit that. She'd *wanted* to have a boyfriend for a couple years now.

She asked, "You have a girlfriend?"

Danny nodded and showed Gabbi a picture. His girlfriend was gorgeous. Red hair, green eyes, a great smile and the kind of figure Gabbi could only hope she'd have someday.

"Do you miss her?" she asked.

"Yeah. But she's coming over to see me my last couple of weeks here. We're going to have a *good* time."

Gabbi was too young to know exactly what that meant, but just the way Danny had said it almost made her swoon. Before she got too carried away, she moved back on point.

"So what's all this got to do with Pigalle, and me?"

"Well," Danny said, "let's say my girl had told me if I went away to do an internship in Paris, we were finished. And let's say I came anyway and was over here feeling lonely, maybe even a little angry at my ex-girlfriend."

"Yeah?"

"I might go to Pigalle, if I were that kind of guy."

"I don't get it."

"Pigalle is the kind of place where a guy can find a new girlfriend—for money."

26

Gabbi had been innocent enough at the time that she still hadn't understood. What did money have to do with friendship? But Danny had been too nice a guy to explain. He'd only told her the light would dawn as she got older, and if someone was going to take the fall for wising her up, it wasn't going to be him.

Now as she walked briskly along the Boulevard de Clichy after midnight, Gabbi thought one visit to Pigalle was more than enough to be wised up. She'd returned to Paris following her sophomore year at the School of the Art Institute to do her own summer internship at the U.S. embassy, and she tacked a semester abroad on to that. Once again, Dad had told her: "Stay away from Pigalle. Now more than ever."

By that time, Gabbi had learned about the intersection of

intimacy and commerce. Not that she understood why any guy who wasn't an ogre or over forty had to pay for sex. The way the college girls she knew were giving it away, there had to be a glut on the market. Especially if a guy was a painter. Good God, to be rendered in oil on canvas, girls couldn't get out of their clothes fast enough. It didn't matter whether the guy wielding the brush had any real talent. And what happened while the paint dried was only natural.

It was also to be expected that a college coed, an adult before the law, a woman in body and somewhat in mind, should not acquiesce to paternal demands as easily as a young girl had.

"Dad," Gabbi had said, "Pigalle was named for Jean-Baptiste Pigalle, a sculptor. Toulouse-Lautrec, Picasso, and Van Gogh all lived there. Pigalle has a museum honoring Salvador Dali."

She'd thought about mentioning the Moulin Rouge being there as well. But she'd heard a story from Mom about Dad walking out on a revue in Las Vegas when the chorus line pranced in topless. That was when a moment of epiphany hit Gabbi: Jeez, was that what her father was afraid of, that she'd be tempted to dance with her boobs bare in a French girly-show?

All her father had said was, "Remember who's paying your freight, kiddo."

She growled at him, with an Italian undertone to let him know she was serious.

For her first six months in Paris, she performed her embassy chores with a dedication that won glowing letters of commendation. In the tiny rented room she called her own, she painted like a madwoman and sold several small pieces she'd later wish she had back. Being an overachiever, she even tutored children of foreign diplomats in American English, saving every sous she earned. At the end of the semester, she sent her father a letter and a photocopy of the bank account she'd opened in her own name. The balance was the equivalent of $5,000. She told him with the contacts she'd made, and the letters of references she'd earned, she'd be able to find work in Paris, and she was thinking of applying for permanent residence in France.

She would make her decision after she visited Pigalle.

The senator replied by express mail.

"Congratulations on becoming an adult. I'm sure you'll make wise choices. Mom and Gianni say hello."

27

At the time she received it, that bit of paternal jiujitsu had infuriated her. But after visiting Pigalle she better understood Mark Twain's words. She was astonished how much her father had learned since the time she was fourteen.

The excursion to Pigalle had left her feeling depressed. The neighborhood might have once been home to some of the greatest names in art, but what drew the tourists by the busload was a profession even older that the paintings done in the Cave of Lascaux. There were streetwalkers on the district's side streets—the *girlfriends* Danny Ahearn had mentioned. On the main drag, the Boulevard de Clichy, the merchandising of sex approached hypermarket scales. Any carnal thought that could be imagined had been given form, and usually substance, too. Nude revues, strip clubs with less costuming and choreography, videos, peep shows, pornography, toys.

It was all too much. Way too much. Gabbi had come to think of herself as a liberated woman, and she was making her way in the world. But she had yet to find any time for a serious boyfriend. When she did, though, she didn't want it to be with any guy who'd look at her like the guys on the street leering at the photos of nudes in the windows. Any guy who tried—

To grab her. Someone reached out right there on the street and grabbed her wrist, started saying something about her being a rare find. That was as far as he got before her training kicked in. Once the family had returned from their first trip to France, Dad had enrolled her in aikido lessons. He'd said she would need it to keep all the high school jocks honest. But that night in Paris it worked just fine on the greasy guy with the toothpick in his mouth. She broke his grip while he was still trying to talk, and then she put him in an arm lock that brought him to his knees.

He was screaming by that time, making what sounded like threats in some language Gabbi didn't recognize. She decided immediately that she had to finish what she'd started. She increased the pressure on his arm and proned him out. Then she stepped on the back of his right knee, got a nice big popping sound. The guy would have a hell of a time just standing on that leg now; no way was he going to chase after her.

Gabbi left him lying there still yelling at her. As she quickly walked away, she thought she heard him call her a *putain*, a whore. Was that what he had been looking for, someone to sell him sex? But then Gabbi saw on the opposite side of the street two young women who to her eye probably were hookers. They were pointing and laughing at the man Gabbi had hurt, as if his comeuppance had a personal meaning to them. That notion was reinforced when both of them blew kisses at Gabbi and called out, "*Vive les femmes fortes!*"

In American: You go, girl!

Which made Gabbi wonder if her assailant hadn't been a john but a pimp looking to add to his roster of talent. The thought made Gabbi shudder and start to run.

She never told her father of the incident, but she thanked God she'd had him to look out for her. And she felt sorry for all the girls who never had such a man in their lives.

Yet here she was cruising Pigalle alone once again.

Not only wouldn't her father like it, she was sure the president's henchman would feel the same displeasure. He was an involved dad, too. She'd heard it in his voice when he took the calls from his daughters.

But Gabbi had the idea that if she looked something like the blonde who'd been under the Pont d'Iéna with Glen Kinnard and Thierry Duchamp, and if that blonde had worked as a stripper, as Arno Durand had suggested to McGill, then maybe one of the creeps who worked the door of some sex club in Pigalle would mistake her for the missing woman.

Call out to her, "Hey, Josette." Or Marie. Or Cerise.

Establish himself as a link to the woman McGill wanted to find.

And if the creep tried to lay a hand on her when she ignored him, well, she had experience with that. Only now she was older, stronger, better trained, and a whole lot more wised up.

Even so, she missed the two Gypsy kids, Alexandru and Ana creeping along behind her. They'd spotted her ten minutes ago and had been tailing her ever since.

Georgetown

28

Sweetie looked at the Caller ID and answered the office phone. "McGill Investigations, Inc. We make house calls."

"You solve cases by dint of shoe leather, not navel gazing?" McGill asked.

"We usually pray for divine intervention. Sometimes, we even get it."

"Close to the Almighty, are you?"

"Not badly positioned for a sinner," Sweetie answered. "How are you doing?"

McGill told her, "I beat up my client."

"I can't let you go anywhere."

"The investigating magistrate seems to like me, and his bodyguard is studying my moves."

"Never pass up an opportunity to learn something new." Sweetie gave it a beat then asked, "You see what the newsies are saying about Patti?"

McGill said, "I saw a local tabloid. I talked with Patti a little while ago. Told her I didn't believe a word of it."

"Me neither. But I had to wonder if it wasn't inevitable that someone would attack her that way. What with her background in modeling and acting."

McGill mused on the notion a moment. "It might go beyond that. Maybe now that the gender line has been crossed in the Oval Office, any female president who doesn't look like Golda Meir will have to be very guarded about any display of affection. Not give a sliver of opportunity for misinterpretation, lest the sleaze merchants pounce."

Sweetie asked, "What about you? You doing anything that could be misconstrued?"

"My new bodyguard is a good-looking woman from the State Department's Bureau of Diplomatic Security."

"How good looking?"

"Like she could be your cousin, only with a European flair."

"Some guys have all the luck. Patti, me, and now a knockout State Department cop."

McGill had never worried about anybody daring to suggest any impropriety between him and Sweetie. The honest reporters had too much respect for Margaret Mary Sweeney; the sleazy ones were too afraid she'd beat the snot out of them. Gabbi Casale, however, was an unknown quantity, unlikely to inspire the awe Sweetie did.

"I'm being careful," McGill said, "but thanks for the reminder."

"Other than bruising Glen Kinnard, how's the case going?" Sweetie asked.

McGill brought her up to date, and Sweetie snorted.

"The Undertaker, huh?"

"*L'Entrepeneur,* if you prefer the French."

"In this case, I do. Definitely cooler. And you've got a French sports reporter and a gypsy kid working for you?"

"I'm an equal opportunity employer," McGill told her.

Sweetie was quiet for a moment. McGill knew she was processing what he'd told her, was working out a thought. They were comfortable with such silences.

"I think you may be overestimating the bad guys," Sweetie said.

"How's that?" McGill asked.

"Well, you're operating on the idea that your missing woman and The Undertaker don't know each other, right?"

"That'd be the smart thing to do."

"Yeah, but if you're right, the whole thing started as some sort of sports betting scam, and it involves a stripper and a brawler, and the whole thing blows up when Glen Kinnard accidentally gets in the way. That doesn't sound like a work of criminal genius to me. Sounds more like a low budget plan with marginal players and a lot of room for error."

McGill asked, "Why would the missing woman set things in motion if she knew The Undertaker? She'd have seen Kinnard wasn't the guy she was expecting."

Sweetie said, "Maybe the hired muscle was late. Maybe she was getting impatient or had to pee, and figured things could work out with Kinnard. He's a big guy. You know these mopes, Jim. If they were conscientious workers, they wouldn't be lowlifes."

McGill could see Sweetie was right. "Damn, I must be getting old."

"You're working a new beat," Sweetie told him. "We'll chalk it up to that and jet lag."

"Well, at least I had it in mind to ask if you'd have the time soon to come over here and lend a hand."

Sweetie told him she still had work to do at home, and recapitulated where things stood in the matter of Deke Ky's shooting. This time it was McGill who was silent, thinking hard, and on to something.

McGill asked, "How did Deke's mother describe what had happened when she said her son took the bullet for her?"

Sweetie told him, "She said they were just about to sit down to Thanksgiving dinner: Deke, his mom, his cousin, Father Francis. Ms. Ky excused herself to use the powder room. While she was there, the doorbell rang. So Deke went to see who'd come calling."

"And he got shot for his troubles," McGill said. "By a sniper, we were told. A guy with a rifle, right?"

"Yeah. So?"

"So who rang the doorbell?" McGill asked. "Not the guy

waiting to take the shot."

McGill heard Sweetie mutter under her breath. He had never heard her curse aloud, but he thought there were times when profanities butted up against the backside of her teeth.

"Maybe you and I shouldn't work cases unless we're holding hands," she said.

McGill laughed. "Wouldn't that be a picture for the scandal sheets?"

"Yeah, I guess it would," Sweetie said with a sigh. "I still like this creep Ricky Lanh Huu as the shooter. Ms. Ky fingered him, he's got one DB on his rap sheet, and I've seen that he goes to confession in a Catholic church."

"I think you're right," McGill said. "But I don't think the other guy, what's his name..."

"Horatio Bao."

McGill was quiet again, a new thought running through his mind.

"Okay," he said, "We both know Bao is the brains in your case. So no way is he going to be anywhere near the shooting, but he's not going to farm it out to anyone who might turn on him. That means he trusts Ricky, and whoever rang the doorbell—"

"Has to be somebody close, too," Sweetie finished.

"A longtime associate," McGill said.

"Maybe even family."

"Maybe. Gives you a place to look."

"But if Ms. Ky was right and she was the target, why shoot Deke?" Sweetie asked.

"No pun intended, but maybe it was a bang-bang situation. Door opens, shot is taken. The deed is done before anyone can see a mistake has been made. Or maybe Deke stepping onto the bull's-eye was an opportunity to send a warning. Talk and we'll kill everyone you love. Or the shooter was just ticked off his real target wasn't available. So he took the shot he had. You know how these mopes can be."

"Yes, I do," Sweetie said. "I'll see if Horatio Bao has a wife, somebody who could have rung the bell but can't be made to testify against him."

"See about a girlfriend, too. One who might be expendable."

"Good thought," Sweetie told him. "You've still got your A-game."

"Huh," McGill said, unwilling to let go of his own failings. "Maybe we're each seeing the other's case more clearly from a distance."

"Yeah."

"Might have a good commercial for a phone company here," McGill said. "Reach out and collar someone."

Pigalle, Paris

29

Having had no luck so far, Gabbi tried to think how a stripper might walk. One foot directly in front of the other, like a runway model? Get the hips swinging. Throw the shoulders back. Push the chest out. A look of hauteur obvious in the eyes and mouth. Or someone with feet tired from boogying on concrete for too many hours in do-me pumps. With a sore back from torquing her spine too hard on a pole. Wondering if the creep with the long fingernails had infected her when he scratched her abdomen stuffing a euro-note, that was also probably none too clean, into her G-string.

She eschewed either of those possibilities, going with the springy, light step of an athlete who'd had some ballet lessons. Basically, her normal stride, with a little bit extra toe-push to give her modest bust a bit more bounce, her hair a bit more swing. Her regard for her surroundings was alert but not forbidding. For the right guy, she might...

Well, she wasn't going to find the right guy in Pigalle; Dad didn't have to worry about that. In fact, there weren't any takers at all on the Boulevard de Clichy. She had cruised by the marquee places like the Moulin Rouge and the Sexodrome without raising a wolf-whistle or even a second glance. The lack of response was enough to make a girl think: It was late, the creeps were tired, their eyes were bleary from drink, or they possessed barely enough brain cells to realize she was far too good for the likes of them.

Certainement, ce n'etait pas de sa faulte. Certainly, the fault wasn't hers.

She hoped.

Not having any success on the main drag of the red-light district, she headed for the side streets, and hoped she wouldn't have any trouble with streetwalkers who might think she was encroaching on their turf.

To move off an arterial street in Paris always made Gabbi feel like she was stepping back in time. Even after all her years abroad, a child of Chicago's suburbs, she felt taken aback to find herself on a passageway that hadn't been designed for automotive traffic. Adding to the archaic feeling of the narrow lanes, the wattage of the streetlights always seemed to drop by half. Torches placed in sconces might do as well. Shadows were everywhere and houses and shops that were old before America had declared its independence slouched against one another like companionable drunks. At any moment, she expected a *tumbril* to appear around a curve, hurrying off with its cargo of shackled royalty to keep an appointment with Madam Guillotine.

The discordant elements to this historic vision were the neon lights of still more sex shops and strip joints, and hookers whose public raiment—miniskirts, hot pants, and halter tops with plunging necklines—was far more meager than the undergarments of courtesans of old. The prostitutes, standing in knots on the pavement or pairs in doorways, didn't fail to notice Gabbi. The appearance of an attractive white woman walking by herself was a rarity, as the creep who had grabbed Gabbi's arm years ago had observed. The hookers, now, Gabbi saw, were more often than not black, immigrants from France's former African possessions.

If these women, plying their dangerous trade, had any

means to protect themselves—or their commercial interests—it would likely be in the form of sharpened steel. It was simple economics: People who couldn't afford guns used knives. Besides the monetary consideration, it would be more politically acceptable to the police, the public, and the pimps who ran the girls for a hooker to cut a john who gave her trouble than to shoot him. Gabbi had a gun, had it in her hand inside her purse, but she didn't want to shoot anyone either.

She stepped clear of any gathering of working girls well before she came to them. She heard muttered insults as she passed, sometimes in French, which she understood perfectly, sometimes in an unfamiliar tongue, whose tone was nonetheless unmistakably scornful. The commentary she did understand gave her the likely reason none of the guys working the doors at the clubs and shops had given her any verbal recognition.

"*Regardez la salope snob avec ses vètements chic.*" Look at the stuck-up bitch in her fancy clothes.

Gabbi had considered that her manner of dress could be a defect in her plan, but she was a State Department professional of no small standing. She couldn't and wouldn't dress like a hooker. That probably diminished her chances of being mistaken for the missing stripper, but it was likely also the reason the prostitutes didn't see her as a direct threat and confront her with their knives. Or hatchets. Or whatever else they carried these days.

Like everything else in life, her choice was a tradeoff.

But she was getting tired, physically, mentally, spiritually. She wanted to be somewhere else. Somewhere love was more than a four-letter word, and not measured in euros per minute for whatever got you off. She didn't want to walk back the way she came, run the gamut of the same women. They might think she'd taken offense at their insults and was challenging them. She'd loop around back to the Boulevard de Clichy and—

"*Diana!*" A man's voice, using French pronunciation.

Out of the corner of her eye, to her right, she saw a man standing in a doorway waving to her. He was a middle-aged bantamweight with bandy legs standing in the doorway of yet another strip club, this one with a green neon palm tree shading a pink topless hula dancer. Glowing blue neon letters said: *Paradis Trouvé*. Paradise Found. The property, no doubt, of a sex merchant who could enjoy a joke at Milton's expense.

Gabbi turned to face the man. He pulled his head back when he got a good look at her. Then he tapped the fingers of his right hand to his forehead. My mistake.

"*Désolé.*" Sorry.

"*De rien.*" No problem.

Gabbi continued on her way, both her step and her heartbeat quickening. It might be just a coincidence, of course, the little guy in the doorway of the strip club mistaking her for someone named Diana, but she didn't think so. She'd tell McGill when she saw him, let him decide, but she felt certain this was the break she'd been looking for.

If she had been any more self-preoccupied, she wouldn't have heard the soft voice speak up behind her. A man speaking English with a French accent. "A woman such as you shouldn't be down here alone."

But she did hear. And when she whirled to face the guy she had her gun out and pointing directly at his head. He immediately squeezed his eyes shut and put his hands in the air.

Arno Durand. McGill's French sports reporter.

He told her, "I have often thought I might die at the hands of a beautiful woman, but one I had known intimately, and I would be undone in the boudoir, not on the street. With poison in my wine perhaps, or even on my lover's breast, but never a gun."

"Open your eyes," Gabbi told him.

Being cautious, Durand opened only his right eye. It was enough to see that Gabbi had put her gun away and turned her back to walk off. He hurried to catch up.

"You were here, of course, looking for someone," he said.

Gabbi didn't reply.

"So was I," Durand volunteered. "Who were you looking for?"

Gabbi picked up her pace, continuing to say nothing. Durand struggled to keep up, thinking maybe he should give up smoking.

"Perhaps you were looking for the little fellow in the doorway back there," Durand suggested. "Not that you knew it until he spoke up."

Gabbi cut him a quick pointed looked, remaining mute.

Durand continued, "He mistook you for someone else, *n'est-ce pas?* Say the missing woman from under the bridge. The one M'sieur McGill says resembles you."

Gabbi winced at having her plan so easily penetrated.

"No, no," Durand said with sympathy. "It was a very good idea."

"Yeah," Gabbi said, finally speaking, "so brilliant even you could figure it out."

"*Mais non,* I was working another angle. Did you wonder why such a small fellow was working as the bouncer back there?"

Gabbi hadn't, and now that the anomaly had been pointed out she was even more annoyed, and said, "No."

"It is a ruse to encourage the foolhardy to feel they have the advantage. They see the little fellow and think, 'If that's the best this place can do, I have no worries. I might even walk out without paying my check.'"

Gabbi saw where Durand was headed. "But it's not like that."

The reporter shook his head. "Inside, there lurks a monster."

He waited to see if Gabbi could make the connection.

"The Undertaker?" she asked.

The reporter nodded with a smile. He appreciated a woman with a good mind, as long as she had all the usual attractions.

"To exit the club, I had to empty my wallet, and charge a credit card to the maximum." Durand smiled. "Fortunately, it was a company card, but I was lucky I didn't have to sign away the title to my apartment."

Gabbi ignored that and said, "The Undertaker working the same club where the stripper does her thing? That's not the way Jim McGill figured it."

Durand gave her a Gallic shrug. "Who among us is perfect?"

The reporter's smirk suggested he just might be the one.

Then he added, "I am without a euro for the Metro. May I have a ride home?"

Rue Anatole France, Paris

30

Investigating Magistrate Yves Pruet sat on the balcony of his apartment overlooking the Seine, picking out the notes of a melancholy tune on his guitar. Playing had always come easily to him. His fingers always had the dexterity and the instinct to find their way to the right strings and frets. More important, he had the ear and the composer's intuition to understand a melody the first time he heard it. He had taken lessons briefly, for the purpose of learning to read notation. After that, he explored on his own, using his playing as a meditation.

If he had one failing with his guitar it was the lack of daring to think he could ever make his living with it. He had to smile, at least to himself, when recalling Nicolette telling him he should play on the Metro. Perhaps he would. Or find a small club where he might play under an assumed name, perhaps wearing dark glasses, for free drinks. Some place where his father would never hear of what he was doing. Augustin Pruet, cheese magnate, the son and grandson of successful businessmen, had tolerated his son's love of music only because Yves said it helped him in the study of law. The senior Pruet was pleased by his son's goal of becoming a magistrate rather than be content to work as a money-grubbing *avocat*. In the magistrate's position, he told his son, there was the dignity of ridding the city of its verminous criminals.

"*Oui, mon père*," Pruet would think, "I am an exterminator of distinction."

Augustin, though, hadn't anticipated that his son's zeal would extend to holding a criminal highly placed in government to the bar of justice. He had to admire Yves' courage for making it impossible for the government to do anything but convict the larcenous interior minister, even though the affair would bring his son's career to a permanent halt. In recognition of that courage, Augustin had permitted his son to continue to reside in the apartment he'd bought for Yves and Nicolette. He had intended to deed the place outright to the married couple on their wedding day, but Yves had asked him to keep the title in his own name.

"Why?" Augustin had asked.

"There may be some small chance my bride-to-be loves me for a reason other than my guitar playing," he'd responded.

The senior Pruet had snorted, but he thought his son's decision showed the wisdom of an older man. Augustin appreciated looking at the lovely Nicolette, but he loved his son far more than his daughter-in-law. One was blood; the other was not.

As Pruet continued to play, he wondered, "*What would you have me do now, Papa? Throw the American to the mob and be done with the whole affair? I am sorry to say that does not look like the right thing to do.*"

Pruet glanced at the painting on the ceramic tile he'd bought from Bertrand Kalou. The one that showed the menacing figure who had ventured under the Pont d'Iéna after Glen Kinnard had fought Thierry Duchamp to the death. The image was of a man seen from a distance, none of his features distinguishable. But in scale with his surroundings, the fellow was something of a giant. And his fists—accurately rendered, according to the artist—were clenched as he approached the bridge; his shoulders leaned forward; his whole manner was aggressive.

The magistrate wouldn't want to see such a fellow approaching him, not unless Odo were with him, not unless Odo had his assault rifle aimed and ready to fire.

That was when Pruet realized he wasn't alone. Someone was standing behind him. From the scent the breeze carried to him, Cacharel Liberté, it was his wife. Nicolette.

She recognized he had become aware of her and asked, "What is that you are playing? A piece from Bach?"

Pruet put his guitar down and turned to her with a smile. "The arrangement is my own. But the composer is Steve Winwood. 'Can't Find My Way Home.'"

She looked at him without comprehension, then with the suspicion he was playing her for a fool, finally with acceptance he was telling her the truth. "Popular music? You are reduced to playing rock 'n' roll?"

"I am a man of reduced circumstances," he told her, his smile growing rueful. He picked up his instrument and looked back at the city, a scattering of lights still shining in the darkness. Nicolette stepped forward, leaning against the balcony railing, regarding him bleakly.

"You've been ignoring the notes I gave you," she said. "On how to proceed with your investigation."

"I'm an obstinate fellow. Beyond that, your notes were no more instructive than fortune cookies." Pruet had been sorely disappointed by Nicolette's puerile jottings.

—Do what you know is best.

—There is only one path forward.

—Those who love you won't lead you astray.

How was he supposed to use drivel such as that in a divorce proceeding against his wife? She hadn't even had the decency to append her signature to the banalities.

"I'm sure you can read between the lines," Nicolette said, her eyes reduced to slits.

"There was something between the lines?" asked Pruet, whose vision was perfect. "I will have Odo take me to an eye doctor at the first opportunity. In the meantime, perhaps you could write what you need from me with great specificity and in large block letters, and please sign your full name in a clear hand in case I forget the source of the advice."

Nicolette looked as if she would like to hurl him off the balcony. Pruet had much the same thought about her, and she was so much closer to the edge. But he contented himself by saying, "You know, my dear, though I often seem preoccupied by my work, I do take note of the world at large."

"Meaning what?"

"Well, I've noticed, over the years, the appearances of the women Jean-Louis Severin has escorted to various public functions, up to and including his former wife, Aubine. And none of them has had quite the same look as you. So I am relieved to say I no longer think that you are sleeping with our esteemed president."

Nicolette knew he was mocking her, and for his part, Pruet was glad he had his guitar to shield him from her.

"I've noticed something else from time to time," he continued. "I've seen you comfort, right here in our apartment, various of your friends who've had grievances with their husbands. In each instance, as I recall, your advice was to skin the bastard alive. So I suppose I should take some comfort that you only wish to see me play for my supper on the Metro. But it also occurs to me, that through your friends, you must know some of Paris's best divorce lawyers. Perhaps you even know Marcel Choisy, the *avocat* for Aubine Severin who held his press conference the other day. Possibly, you hope to obtain his services someday for your personal benefit."

The magistrate was startled when his wife actually hissed at him. A snake poised to strike. Nonetheless, he took her reaction as confirmation of his surmise. Pushing off against the balcony railing, she'd had enough of his company for one night. She started off on her way to wherever she slept these days. But Pruet caught her by the wrist and held on tight.

When she finally looked at him, he told her. "There is no love left to lose between us, Nicolette, but I tell you now you are swimming in a treacherous current."

He let her go. She looked at him, not with affection but the fear that he might be right. But her decision had been made and moments later he heard the door slam as she departed.

Pruet started to play, idly dancing his fingers through runs of notes. All of them were complementary, pleasing to the ear, but none suggested a theme he might turn into a pop tune to make him famous and wealthy. He thought he should do a broader study of the American blues canon. Frenchmen, indisputably, also knew times of heartache and reversals of fortune. Perhaps that was where his future as a composer lay. French blues. *Les bleus Francais.*

That speculation was interrupted by the ringing of the telephone.

On the other end was James J. McGill, the president's henchman.

Another fellow whose wife wasn't at his side, and had yet to go to bed.

Washington, DC

31

Sweetie said grace before eating dinner with friends and finished with, "... and thank you for our gracious host."

That one caught Putnam Shady by surprise. In all his thirty-five years, he never remembered anyone thanking God for him. Certainly not his parents. But Welborn Yates and Kira Fahey joined Sweetie in saying, "Amen."

The four of them sat at the breakfast bar in the kitchen of Putnam's townhouse on Florida Avenue. For their dining pleasure he'd had a couple dozen soft shell crabs brought in from Great Catch, his favorite seafood restaurant in Baltimore. Yes, he'd paid to have the restaurant's top chef come to town to cook the crabs on site, and steam eight ears of corn, artfully throw together a green salad, and bake a tray of brownies that were an invitation to gluttony.

But all of the hard work—the driving and the cooking—the credit for that belonged to the person who had done the work: Chef LuAnne Bisby Scott. All he'd done, as usual, was to put out some money to impress people. Clearly, he'd impressed Margaret, and he was grateful for that, but he felt guilty about publicly being acknowledged before God when he had done so little. Okay, he had poured the Moët Cuvee he and Kira were drinking, put out an Aviator Lager for Welborn and a Poland Spring for Margaret. Even so, he'd have to do better, and...

That was when it hit him.

Margaret, in her pious way, was manipulating him. The same way she'd gotten him to risk his precious backside when he'd accompanied her to that rally of religious zealots in Lafayette Square, where she had stood up to the Reverend Burke Godfrey. Where little Caitie McGill had shown impressive courage, too. Heck, where he had grabbed the wrist of a yahoo who might have caused a riot by trying to assault Margaret.

He and Margaret had dined out for the first and only time after that epic confrontation. Normally, that would have been the perfect opportunity for Putnam to make a move on his date. Instead, he'd been happy simply to dine with Margaret, to listen to her as she revealed a little bit of her life. He'd responded by telling her a carefully edited bit of his own childhood. Losing his brother. He'd never told any casual acquaintance about that before. But at the end of the night he'd felt wonderful. Laying his head on his pillow, still feeling Margaret's lips on his cheek from a kiss as chaste as it was memorable. The kiss and Margaret saying, "Thanks for coming with me."

Okay, so now she'd thanked God for him, and that could only mean—

Sweetie nudged him and asked, "You going to start eating?"

—she was going to get him to do something risky again.

"Yeah, sure," he answered. He speared a forkful of salad.

"This is a very nice kitchen, Mr. Shady," Kira told him.

The room was a spacious composition of polished oak cabinets and stainless steel appliances. The floor was slate, and during the day the room was flooded with sunlight. An unlikely place for a conspiracy. After Putnam had learned of the Merriman brothers' lunch at Tommy T's., he'd called Margaret at the offices of McGill Investigations, Inc. Told her of Ms. Fahey dining within earshot of two of the president's foremost nemeses. He had suggested they get together for drinks, discuss the possibility Ms. Fahey might have overheard something interesting. Margaret had said she'd already heard from Captain Yates that Kira would like to speak with her. Putnam had thought that would put the kibosh on his chances of going out with Margaret, but then she'd told him she'd like to speak with him and Kira and Captain Yates in a setting where they wouldn't have to worry about anyone eavesdropping. Putnam had immediately volunteered his home, and since it sounded to him like it would be a work-oriented gathering, they could dine in his kitchen.

"Thank you, Ms. Fahey," Putnam said, "and by the time we finish this bottle of wine, let's call each other Kira and Putnam."

The last thing he wanted to do was ... well, maybe he did want to try to outflank whatever maneuver Margaret had in mind for him. But he didn't want to come on too strong to the vice-president's niece, especially with her fiancé in the room and doing his best not to frown or punch Putnam in the nose.

Dousing that fire before it could grow, the host said, "Let's see if we can all use our given names. When you're eating crabs and corn with your fingers, Mr. and Ms. seems a bit much."

Everyone smiled at that, and the meal and small talk proceeded with everyone growing more relaxed, even Margaret, who in her own mysterious way seemed able to get a buzz going from sparkling water. Putnam wondered if she was able to change it into wine on the way down.

He insisted on rinsing all the dishes and stacking them in the dishwasher; he let Margaret dish up the brownies, with whipped cream and fresh strawberry slices for Kira, Margaret and him, straight up for Welborn. Milk for Welborn and Margaret, the last of the bubbly for Kira and him.

At that point, Sweetie took over the discussion, saying, "Welborn and I are working a case."

"Unofficially and *sub rosa* for me," Welborn said.

"True, but with his customary zeal," Sweetie said. "The case is getting complicated, to a point where we could use some extra help."

Everyone knew what was coming next. Putnam could see Kira was almost trembling in anticipation. He, meanwhile, was trying to keep the whipped cream in his mouth from curdling.

Leaning forward, Kira asked Sweetie, "There's something I can do to help?" She turned to Welborn. "Really?"

Now, it was the young Air Force captain's turn to look dismayed. "I have nightmares about what the president, the vice president, and our respective mothers would do to me if I let any harm come to you. And that's nothing compared to what I'd do to myself."

Kira sat back and looked at her beau. Her eyes sheened with moisture, but her jaw firmed with resolve. "I'm tougher than I look, you know." She flexed her right arm.

Sweetie gave her a thumb's up.

Whereupon Kira had second thoughts. "It's not *too* dangerous, what you have in mind for me, is it?"

Welborn said, "We'd like you to pretend to be a Catholic. Does that prospect fill you with dread?"

Kira's face got tight. She thought Welborn was teasing her.

But Sweetie said: "A particularly pious Catholic. One who can pray for *hours*. Without calling attention to herself."

"This isn't a joke?" Kira asked Sweetie.

"No. What you'd be doing is working a stakeout. We'd like you to spend as much time as reasonably possible in a Virginia church. We'd like you to make mental notes about anyone who visits the pastor, Reverend Francis Nguyen."

"That's it? Sit, kneel, and pray in a church?"

"Light a candle when you arrive, and gather intelligence," Sweetie said. "These guys we're after, I'm pretty sure they're behind the shooting of Deke Ky."

Kira drew a sharp breath.

And Putnam gagged on the brownie he was eating.

He had to clear the obstruction with champagne.

Everyone looked at him, and he held up a hand to indicate he was okay.

Turning back to Kira, Sweetie said, "These are seriously bad people, but a woman praying in the public setting of a church, a person they've never seen, should be perfectly safe. We'd have to tone down your appearance, though. You sparkle a bit too much now."

Kira glanced at Welborn, wanting to say something but reluctant, as if not wanting to reveal a secret to her betrothed. Finally, she admitted, "I can look plain if I want to."

Welborn said, "I seriously doubt that."

An expression of disbelief that earned him a peck on the cheek.

Sweetie continued, "It would also be good if you had something to really pray for. Father Nguyen, if he sees you, will likely stop by and ask if there's anything he can do for you. He's almost certain to see through any deceit."

To everyone's surprise, Kira's face crumpled, and the tears hinted at earlier came in a rush now. Welborn took Kira's hand and asked, "What is it?"

He, too, now appeared as stricken, thinking she'd kept some grim secret from him.

Kira patted his hand in reassurance and said, "I lost my dad when I was little. He died in a fire. Most of the time, I hardly think of him at all. I have to look at photos to remember what he looked like. But lately ... with my wedding coming up..." She turned to look at Welborn. "I really wish he were here to walk me down the aisle. I want him to see how lucky I am."

Welborn put an arm around Kira's shoulders.

Sweetie said, "I don't know what your beliefs are, but you could pray for a sign that your father does know how lucky you are, that he will be with you in spirit when you marry."

Kira nodded and asked the others to excuse her. Welborn left the room with her.

A moment passed in silence before Putnam said, "Poor kid."

Sweetie looked at him.

"She's not up to it," he said, "I can do the church stakeout."

Sweetie told him, "I've got other plans for you."

Chequers, Buckinghamshire, England

32

The presidents of the United States and France sat next to each other on a sofa in Patti's suite at Chequers and looked at the jumbled sheets of paper on the coffee table in front of them. Each sheet was filled with handwritten sentences, strikethroughs, revisions, and marginal notes. Each of them had taken turns writing and editing. The document was written in both English and French. The whole might never have cohered if they hadn't taken the precaution of writing a page number in the top right corner of each sheet.

Having already decided to turn the world's major military defense alliances inside out, Patricia Darden Grant and Jean-Louis Severin had decided to take the next step and deny the planet's most violent strongmen their means of seizing and holding on to power—and their plan was making the two presidents distinctly nervous.

The French president looked at his old friend. "What we are attempting here is to seize a bone from the mouth of a very bad-tempered dog."

Patti had to smile. "You do have a way with metaphor, Jean-Louis."

"Billions of dollars and euros, then, if you wish me to speak like an accountant."

She patted his hand and got up. "I want you only to be yourself. More water?"

He shook his head as Patti picked up the two empty Schweppes bottles from the table. She tossed them in a recycling bin and took another bottle out of a mini-fridge for herself. She returned to the sofa and unscrewed the cap.

"I'm tempted not to use the coaster," she told Jean-Louis.

He laughed and replied, "It is enough that we formulate our plans under Norvin Kimbrough's roof. There is no need to be gauche. May I have a sip?"

Patti grinned and handed the bottle to him.

"How about we call this idea The Plowshare Initiative?" she asked.

Jean-Louis lowered the bottle from his mouth and gave it back.

"*Bon*," he said. "I like it."

"There will certainly have to be retooling plans before we can announce this," Patti said.

"And many economic, medical, and educational aid plans to devise."

Patti nodded to their paperwork. "A lot more scribbling to do."

"Fortunately, we have the time. You have more than two years left on your first term and I have four on mine."

"And we better get this one right if either of us wants to be reelected."

Jean-Louis nodded. Then he squeezed Patti's hand and stood up. "We have made a good start. I thank you, Madam President, for the great opportunity of working with you."

Patti said, "Could you give me just a moment more of your time, Jean-Louis?"

He took his seat again and waited to hear what his friend had to say.

"Jim and I would like to spend three days, possibly more, together in Paris, after our meetings here in England are over. We'd like to do it as quietly as possible. No formal state affairs. Just a married couple visiting a beautiful city. Passing through like phantoms, if possible."

A bemused smile appeared on the French president's face.

"Being phantoms is impossible, of course. Your Secret Service is too corporeal. But it is a beautiful idea, positively cinematic. And for a dear friend and an invaluable colleague, I will tell you this: I will do my best; France will do its best."

The president of France kissed the hand of the president of the United States.

At that exact moment, the phone rang.

Jean-Louis looked up from Patti's hand and asked, "Your parents or mine?"

She laughed, reclaimed her hand, and picked up the phone. "Yes?"

After listening for a moment, she said, "*Oui. Il est ici. Un moment.*" Turning to Jean-Louis, she offered him the phone. "For you. Your friend Pruet."

Winfield House, London

33

Galia Mindel thanked the Marine who extended a hand to help her board the president's helicopter, known as Marine One when the commander in chief was aboard. When the White House chief of staff was the sole passenger, it had a different call sign. Hardass One, Galia suspected. She had borrowed the aircraft to return to London to read the report Captain Welborn Yates had prepared for her on the life and times of the Queen's private secretary, and was now returning to Chequers.

Sir Robert Reed, it turned out, was a Canadian. That had made Galia chuckle to herself. She wondered if Her Majesty had gotten any grief for outsourcing the job to a foreigner.

Maybe Sir Robert would get a pass from the English public. After all, he had graduated from the Royal Military Academy Sandhurst. Had served a dozen years in the royal army. The interesting thing about his military service was that its nature was classified. Kept so tightly secret that even the American intelligence community didn't know what he'd been up to. Galia's assumption was that he'd been seconded to the Secret Intelligence Service, MI6.

She could have learned the available details of Sir Robert's life without having to travel to London, but Captain Yates had suggested she read the report in a secure location. Meaning where there was no chance it would fall into British hands.

Yates was a real find, Galia thought, a diamond in the rough fast gaining polish. Some of that refinement was due to the personal tutelage of James J. McGill. An irksome fact, but tolerable because it was not necessary to acknowledge publicly.

Sir Robert's foreign birth wasn't the only interesting tidbit the captain had unearthed. The man had a connection to another famous Canadian who'd served the British Empire. Sir Robert's mother had worked for William Stephenson during World War II. Stephenson, code named Intrepid, had been London's chief spymaster and propagandist in the Americas—and according to Ian Fleming the real life model for James Bond.

If that wasn't a dashing enough family history, Sir Robert's father, whose actual identity had never been determined, at least in any database that Captain Yates had been able to access, was thought to have been a clandestine operative trained at Camp X in Whitby, Ontario, the first training facility for spies in North America, and the finishing school for five future directors of the CIA.

The likelihood of Sir Robert carrying on the family trade—snooping on others—fit neatly with the fact that shortly after President Grant's inauguration, Galia's government file had been probed by computer hackers working out of Hong Kong. That prying could have come from the Chinese, of course. But Captain Yates's research had picked up on the eavesdropping on Galia's file and he'd diligently noted in his report that Hong Kong had been a British colony for 155 years. So London might have done the probe, using an Asian facade so as not to disrupt its *special* relationship with Washington. Or it could have been a cooperative venture between the British and the Chinese, giving each party deniability by allowing one to point the finger at the other.

Galia, who had studied both Niccolo Machiavelli and Lavrenti Beria, had anticipated such an attack, and had larded the cyberfiles of all senior White House personnel with disinformation, and thus wasn't upset when she learned of the probe. On the contrary, she would be pleased if the information gleaned were taken at face value.

On the other side of the coin, she had to consider the possibility that the information she'd obtained on Sir Robert Reed was also a concoction of … well, someone who liked to read James Bond novels.

If it was accurate, though, it raised an intriguing question.

What was Her Majesty doing with a spy for a private secretary?

Friday, June 5—Paris

1

McGill was having an excellent croissant with the best raspberry preserves he'd ever tasted—not bad for an Irish pub's kitchen—when he heard two men start to shout downstairs. Possessing a keen and well-tuned ear, he recognized both voices: Harbin the chiseled doorman of The Hideaway and ... Jesus, could it really be Celsus Crogher?

The chance that it was scared him silly. He jumped up from the breakfast table, flung the door to the flat open and descended the staircase in three bounds, yelling at the top of his best cop voice: "Knock it off!"

Not that the two men confronting each other had actually started to exchange blows, but McGill was sure violence would have ensued if he hadn't intervened. Both men—and Celsus *was* one of them—looked his way, and each of them took a step back, allowing McGill to interpose himself between them.

"This man..." Harbin began. But that was all the English his temper would allow for at the moment. He had both of his escrima sticks held tightly in his right hand.

A glance at the Secret Service SAC showed McGill that Celsus had a hand inside his suit coat. A gun would beat sticks, but only if it could be drawn, pointed, and fired. McGill wasn't sure Celsus would have had time for all that before Harbin started breaking bones. And wouldn't that be a fine mess?

McGill put up the palm of a hand to each man, a traffic cop preventing a collision. It was only then he heard in his ears how hard his own heart was beating. Taking a deep breath and letting it out slowly, he was able to speak again.

"M'sieur Harbin," he began, "may I introduce Mr. Celsus Crogher. Celsus, M'sieur Harbin. Each of you is in the same line of work: protecting others. So cut each other some slack."

McGill looked at the doorman, who, after a beat, nodded his agreement.

The president's henchman had to glare at Crogher before he did the same.

Then McGill took the SAC by the arm, and led him outside, saying, "Let's take a walk."

Crogher yanked his arm free but went along with McGill. They weren't ten paces down the sidewalk, heading toward the Seine, when McGill said to Crogher, "Please tell me it isn't Patti or one of my kids."

The moment McGill had heard the SAC's voice, the first thing that had leaped to mind was last Thanksgiving night. Celsus summoning him from the dinner table to tell him that Deke had been shot. He couldn't imagine Celsus coming to see him in Paris unless something terrible had happened. But to whom?

Far from the most sensitive of people, the SAC nevertheless intuited McGill's apprehension. This time, he was the one who held up a hand, putting the brakes on McGill's fears.

"It's not like that," Crogher said. "Nobody's been hurt."

McGill sagged in relief, his heart sliding down his throat and back into his chest.

On the rebound now, he had to wonder what the hell the SAC was doing in Paris.

Crogher saw that, too, and said, "Give me a minute, okay?"

McGill nodded. The two of them continued walking toward the Seine. The morning was sunny and pleasantly warm; the sky was delft blue, fronted by a few puffy white clouds. The light was a painter's dream. But Crogher saw none of that. He'd slipped into professional mode. James J. McGill was the *package*, and Crogher was the *bullet-catcher.* As such, the SAC was busy checking out pedestrians, automotive traffic; watching doorways, windows and rooftops.

A former cop, McGill also surveyed his surroundings, though he was somewhat more subtle in his watchfulness.

"We're okay for the moment, Celsus."

The SAC was unwilling to make that concession.

The two of them walked along the row of book and magazine stalls lining the river wall. McGill noticed that most of the publications were in French, but several were in English, and many were in a variety of other languages, not only from Europe but around the world.

The U.N. of the printed word, McGill thought. It gave him hope for civilization.

"We see things," Crogher began. "That's the basis of our jobs."

The Secret Service, McGill understood. He nodded.

"A lot of the time, we see things we'd just as soon not," Crogher continued. "But you can't know that in advance, so you have to watch for everything. Most things go into reports, into the data banks. But some we keep to ourselves, and we try to forget them."

Again, there were similarities with cops, but McGill remained silent. This was Celsus's story.

"We're not really supposed to have feelings about the people we protect. Mostly, that's so we don't wind up hating them, which would make us hesitate to … well, you know."

Catch the bullet, McGill knew.

"But there are others, a precious few, we have to be careful we don't like them too much, because then you spend your time watching them instead of the perimeter."

Celsus wasn't having a bit of trouble not looking at McGill.

"The president is someone who's very easy to like," her henchman said.

The SAC nodded. Still avoiding eye contact with McGill.

McGill continued, "So where you and your people would normally be the souls of discretion and would never mention a straying spouse to an offended spouse, now you feel there's something I should know."

For the first time since he'd known the man, McGill saw a blush of color appear on Crogher's chalk white cheeks. He wasn't sure if the cause was embarrassment or anger. If he had to bet, though, he'd go with anger at McGill anticipating his spiel.

"Celsus, forget the threat horizon for just a second and look at me."

The SAC uneasily gave him a moment's attention.

McGill told him, "I trust the president completely. If you saw something between her and, say, the president of France, I'm sure there's an innocent explanation. I thank you for your extraordinary concern and the thought that I should know about whatever you saw, but I don't want to hear it. I'd feel much better if you got back to England as fast as possible and watched over the real threats to my wife."

Crogher nodded, and went back to looking for threats to McGill.

He said to his package, "You know, you won't always be able to walk around like this. You're a target, too."

"You think I should have a gun?"

"I think you should have a full detail of my people. I think you should follow procedure. But I was wondering if you'd ask me for a weapon when you saw me."

"Did you bring one for me?"

Crogher gave McGill a brief look, but didn't answer. He did see McGill smile, though.

"Sonofabitch," the SAC said. "You've already got one."

McGill didn't respond. Except to say, "Tell the president not to worry about me."

"Yeah. I'll be getting back now."

"That favor I asked of you?" McGill said.

"Still working on it."

"I figured out who was behind the call from Frederick, Maryland to Paris. Bob Merriman, Senator Roger Michaelson's chief of staff. He used a middleman, no doubt, but he's the big fish."

Crogher couldn't help himself; he had to look at McGill again.

"How'd you—" The SAC bit his tongue. He wouldn't tell McGill his methods, and the president's henchman wasn't about to reveal his secrets either.

McGill stopped abruptly, putting Crogher on alert. But Mc-

Gill didn't duck for cover. He strode over to a stall. He picked up a magazine. On the cover, two fighters were beating each other bloody. Looming over them in the background, arms folded over his chest, was a brutal looking hulk who had to be at least seven feet tall. A banner above the giant said: *Le Champion Tacit.*

The stall owner approached. McGill held up the magazine and asked, "*Combien?*"

An essential word to know when visiting France: How much?

"*Quatre euros, m'sieur.*"

McGill gave him a fiver and got a single euro coin in return.

The merchant said, "*Merci.*"

Crogher glanced at the magazine cover as they resumed walking.

"Something special about those guys?"

"I think the big lug might be someone I'm looking for."

"Sonofabitch," Crogher said.

"Me or him?" McGill asked.

"Take your pick."

McGill smiled. It was good to be back on a familiar footing with the SAC.

Arlington, VA

2

At three a.m., Deke Ky sat up straight in bed. He thought he'd been dreaming, that his mother had come to his bedside, kissed his cheek, and said something to him in Vietnamese. After arriving in the United States, Deke had never wanted to be anything less than 100% American, and he'd let his Vietnamese erode in favor of learning English. But he still remembered: *Tù biét ai cùa toi con trai ca*. Goodbye, my son.

Actually, Goodbye, my son and heir.

His mother had twice left him with his Aunt Sylvie, Francis's late mother, when he was a toddler and each time he'd been terrified he would never see her again. He remembered the instances clearly because he'd been inconsolable despite his aunt's gentle ministrations. The only things that had gotten him to stop crying were pleas not to wake baby Francis.

His mother had come back for him each time, and he'd clung to her until he had to be fed or put to bed for the night. Now, all these years later, and having been awake for a minute, he knew she was gone again. And just as when he'd been little she'd come to him and said goodbye.

Tù biét ai cùa toi con trai ca.

He placed his fingertips to his cheek, where he'd felt his mother kiss him. Turning on the bed table lamp and bringing his hand in front of his face, he could see traces of red on his fingers. Lipstick.

Musette Ky was the daughter of a master spy. She had left Vietnam with her son ahead of the North's victorious push into Saigon. She had later told Deke it would have been dangerous to stay at the time. She had learned secrets from her father that remaining in Saigon would have been embarrassing to many people who would soon be taking power in the South. To spare themselves the embarrassment, these people would have been only too happy to do away with Musette and her son.

But times and circumstances changed. Washington and Hanoi had made peace with each other. Those who had assumed power in the aftermath of the war had been displaced by age and the ambitions of others. Nike had set up factories for Vietnamese workers to make running shoes for the masses. And Musette Ky had renewed and nurtured contacts with old friends and had made new ones in the land of her birth.

Deke got out of bed and walked naked through his mother's house, something he never would have done if he had any doubt she hadn't gone. Room after room was empty. His mother's closet was bare, and with all the clothes she had, she must have been packing, shipping, and making other preparations for some time.

In her home office, on her desk, he found the deed to her

house. Ownership had been transferred to him. A card for a lawyer whose name he didn't recognize lay next to the deed. On the back of the card, in his mother's hand were the words: *If you ever need money...*

Deke returned to his bed and lay staring at the ceiling, trying to decide what he should do. He was able to think of only one thing. He called his cousin Francis.

The two of them now having lost their mothers.

Chateau Rouge, Paris

3

The kidnapping went off without a hitch. The stripper, stage name Honi Moon, real name Diana Martel, thought she'd hit the jackpot. A sleek black Mercedes limousine pulled up outside the fleabag hotel on the Rue des Poisonniers where she'd been hiding. The rear door opened and she came scurrying out. She all but dived into the back seat. The door closed and the Mercedes departed at the legally mandated 50 kph.

The hour was half past nine, the sky was bright, and the sidewalks were filled with pedestrians. Any number of people saw the stripper's departure, but in Chateau Rouge people knew better than to pry into the affairs of others. The person who took the greatest interest was an immigrant sitting in front of a nearby second-story window. He'd been in the country for years but was endlessly fascinated by watching the great city come to life each morning.

That morning, the presence of the gleaming limousine on his shabby street was like a visit from some passing nobleman, a dark prince perhaps. And then the white woman appeared. She ran clumsily to the car, but how could anyone run properly in such ridiculous spike-heeled shoes? He wasn't quite sure if she jumped into the car or fell into it. What was obvious, though, as her short skirt flew up, was that she had a fine bare derriere. Oh so white and round. The sight was as brief as it was memorable.

The long, black car departed immediately

The immigrant made note of its license plate number.

He knew there was a Nigerian fellow, a most unpleasant individual, running whores out of the hotel from which the woman had fled. But he'd never seen a white whore in the neighborhood before. While he didn't know the white woman was with the procurer, who but a *putain* would enter a fine automobile in such an undignified fashion? *Sans lingerie.*

The immigrant, Bertrand Kalou, didn't want to let go of the fleeting image.

He picked up a ceramic tile, and a brush. He dabbed the brush in black acrylic paint. He'd start with the car and the woman. Work while his memory was still fresh. The background of the painting was available to him any time he cared to look out the window.

At the top right corner of his art table he noticed the business card the investigating magistrate had left with him. Yves Pruet. And his phone number.

He wondered if such an important man, one with the murder of Thierry Duchamp to occupy his time, would be interested in a trifle such as he had seen. He doubted it.

He outlined the shape of the car and cleaned his brush.

Now he'd start on the woman.

Organize her figure around that fine derriere.

4

The backside that Bertrand Kalou was immortalizing in paint sat astride the lap of the literate Rom known as Bela, the fellow who had led Bunica Anisa and the other members of his tribe to know that the man who wanted the *putain* sticking her tongue into his ear was none other than the husband of the President of the United States of America, James J. McGill.

The fellow known as the president's henchman.

How much he would pay for this creature remained to be seen.

But someone in his position doubtless had a fortune at his

command.

Bela, by tribal prejudice, did not like *gadje* women. To know one was to pollute one's manhood. Still, he was human, and the way this one was grinding herself against him, the predictable result was being produced. Soon he would foul himself and the car. The latter point was important to avoid. Bela was aware of what *flics* could do with DNA these days. He often tried to explain American television crime shows to his kinsmen but they rarely bothered to listen.

He asked the woman, "*Voulez-vous du champagne?*"

She pulled her tongue out of his ear and looked at him with a smile.

"*Oui.*"

He patted the leather seat to his left. She climbed off him, and to his relief the involuntary excitement he'd felt began to wane. The cleanup of the car would be easier now, and he wouldn't have to burn his best slacks.

He produced a bottle and two crystal flutes from a mini-fridge. He handed the stemware to the woman while he opened the bottle. He was careful with the cork, not letting it shoot off, and he kept the wine within the bottle until he poured, and then he was careful not to spill any.

For a moment, the woman looked at the glasses in her hand, examining them closely. Keeping the sudden trill of fear he felt off his face, Bela wondered if this dim creature could possibly suspect what he hand in mind. Keeping his voice steady, he asked, "Is something wrong?"

"In some ways I am very generous," she said, giving him a wink. "In others I'm quite selfish."

He looked at her without understanding the second part of her comment. Then he saw she was comparing the measure of wine in each glass. She handed him the one that was a millimeter less full.

"*A votre santé,*" she said raising her glass.

He clinked his glass to hers and they drank. Both glasses had been coated with Amytal. Soon both he and Honi would be sound asleep. She would be on her way to confinement and, Bela fervently hoped, he and his tribe would reap a magnificent ransom. Meanwhile, falling unconscious, he would be rid of her repellent company.

He shuddered to think where that vile thing she'd been rubbing against him had been.

5

"Where do you think you're going, kid?" the doorman at *Paradis Trouvé* asked.

In most cases, he greeted customers with a smile and bonhomie. His job was to lure as many suckers as he could. When a derelict without a *centime* or a young fool with nothing more than fuzz on his peaches presented himself, however, P'tit Henri sent him swiftly on his way. True, Henri was not large, but in his hand a knife became a blur, blood appeared, and scars followed.

"I am looking for a woman," Alexandru said honestly. "I have searched all of Pigalle."

That was true, too. He and Ana had gone home to nap after searching St. Germain. Then late in the evening they had headed out to Pigalle. Having learned from Alexandru that the woman they sought had large false breasts, not artfully done, Ana said she must be a sex worker of some sort. Where better to look for one such as that than Pigalle?

They'd walked for hours, staring at display posters of dancers, strippers, and peep show models, looking closely at any woman on the street who might be a possibility, Ana photographing them with her phone. All they got for their trouble were tired legs, aching feet, and the feeling that something more than what they'd seen had to be available to people who really loved each other. They didn't know how to articulate their feelings, so they simply felt depressed.

Until Alexandru gently nudged his wife.

"There she is," he said quietly.

Ana's fatigue disappeared immediately and she whispered,

"The woman we want?"

"No, the one with the man who hired us." He nodded up the street. "The blonde."

Ana saw her turn off the Boulevard de Clichy. "Do you think she knows?"

Where to find their quarry, Ana meant.

Alexandru said, "Let's see. If she does, maybe we'll have to steal the woman from her."

It never occurred to the two young gypsies, their combined weight barely two hundred pounds, that they'd be unable to overcome the resistance of two grown women. They followed Gabbi, hanging well back, their plan being they would embrace and kiss, leaning against the nearest stationary object, should they see their quarry start to turn around.

She didn't, and Ana said, "She looks as tired as us."

Alexandru nodded. Then he saw the bouncer at the strip club take notice of Gabbi, look surprised, and call out to her.

"What did he say?" Alexandru asked his wife.

"He called her Diana." Ana's ears were the sharpest in the tribe.

They held their position, watched Gabbi tell the fellow he'd made a mistake. She walked off. Another fellow, coming out of the club, caught up to her, and stared down the barrel of a gun for his trouble. The two young gypsies gave each other a long look: a good thing they hadn't tried any of their tricks on Gabbi. When they looked around, Gabbi and the man were turning a corner, no violence done.

They didn't know what that meant, but Alexandru had quickly figured out one thing.

"The little man on the door, he knows the woman we want."

A bright smile lit Alexandru's face.

"What are you thinking?" Ana asked him.

"Remember my joke? About us pretending to be Swedes?"

She nodded, and he told her his plan …

P'tit Henri told Alexandru, "You must have no money, *mon ami.* There are women in Pigalle who will pleasure young boys for the right price."

Alexandru kept the irritation of being called a boy off his face.

"I am sure you're right, m'sieur," he said, "but I am looking for *this* woman."

He showed P'tit Henri the sketch the gypsy artist had done of their quarry.

The man recognized the drawing. Alexandru saw that at once. But P'tit Henri scowled. "This one does *not* pleasure children."

"M'sieur, I mean the lady no disrespect. I do not seek her for myself but for my employer."

"Who is that?"

"His name is Magnusson. Swedish. He saw the lady dance, but he cannot remember where. He had too much to drink. He would like to hire her."

"For the night?" P'tit Henri asked.

"For three months, sir." When the bouncer's eyebrows rose, Alexandru continued. "M'sieur Magnusson is very rich. A businessman. Each summer he takes himself and his friends on a cruise aboard his yacht. The Mediterranean. The gentleman needs ladies to ... dance. To keep him and his friends entertained. The ladies will be well paid and everything will be first rate. If you do not know this lady, I apologize, and I must be on my way to look for her."

Alexandru started to leave, but P'tit Henri caught his arm.

"How much money for the woman?" he asked.

"I do not know exactly, but thousands of euros certainly."

"For three months?"

"Per month, m'sieur."

Alexandru saw the bouncer had risen to the bait.

P'tit Henri was well aware that many customers of *Paradis Trouvé* and other strip clubs often had foggy memories. The drugs slipped into their drinks saw to that, made them far easier to rob. What surprised the little man was that this Magnusson fellow had any memory of Diana at all. But he knew that Diana was hiding out, knew *where* she was hiding. And if he were to put her on to a job that both took her away from Paris for three months and paid her a small fortune, he would be in for a big cut. Of course, if she got too much money, she might decide to stay away. So he would have to tell Diana he would find her and render her a gargoyle with his knife if she didn't mail at least a third of her windfall to him by year's end.

He nodded to himself and patted Alexandru on the shoulder.

"Where would your boss like to meet Diana?"

"That is the lady's name? I will give you a mobile number, m'sieur. If the lady is interested, M'sieur Magnusson will send his limousine to pick her up wherever she likes."

"His limousine?" P'tit Henri asked.

"It goes with his yacht, and his helicopter, and his jet."

"Give me the number, boy," P'tit Henri told Alexandru.

He did.

And now Alexandru looked at the woman the president's henchman had set him to find. She was indeed on a boat. Not a yacht on the Mediterranean, but a barge moored on the Canal St. Denis. Sleeping peacefully. To be confined in relative comfort until every last euro could be squeezed out of James J. McGill for her delivery to him.

Bunica Anisa had been delighted with her grandson's scheme, how well it had worked.

As for Alexandru, he was also well pleased, thinking his future was bright. That morning, he decided, he would go home to Ana and consummate his marriage.

The Hideaway, Paris

6

Gabbi brought a hair stylist and a garment bag holding locally purchased clothes with her when she showed up at the pub. By that time, McGill was downstairs at the bar, having a cup of coffee, with just a drop of Jameson, trying to puzzle his way through the morning copy of *Le Monde*. Side by side photos of Patti and Jean-Louis Severin appeared on the front page above the fold. But as far as McGill was able to discern the paper was interested in what the two heads of state had planned for the world rather than each other.

Harbin, as ever, was at his post, apparently still a bit grumpy from his encounter with Celsus Crogher, a not uncommon reaction. But even Harbin had to smile after Gabbi bussed him on each cheek. And when the young sylph Gabbi had brought along got up on tiptoe and did the same, McGill could see a twinkle in Harbin's eye. Ah, Pah-ree.

Gabbi walked over to McGill, gave him a smile but no kiss, and introduced him to her companion. "M'sieur Smith, Mademoiselle Caresse Montaigne."

"Caress?" McGill asked, going with the flow on his new alias.

"With an e on the end, means endearing," Gabbi explained.

The young woman beamed at him. She had dark brown hair with red highlights done in a pixie cut. She carried a leather bag slung on a strap over her right shoulder. She offered McGill her hand and he took it.

"*Enchanté*," he said.

The stylist put her other hand over his. "*Enchanté, m'sieur. Parlez-vous francais?*"

"*Seulement un peu.*" Only a little.

"*Plus de chaque jour*," Gabbi said, and off McGill's look: "More every day."

Caresse let go of McGill's hand, gently took him by the chin, turned his head to her left and right. Studied his haircut, the shape of his face. Was tactful enough not to criticize the work of Eddie the Barber back in D.C.

"Belmondo?" she asked.

"Jean-Paul," McGill specified.

"*Naturellement. Couleur?*"

"No," McGill said. No color. A cut would be enough. But he didn't know how to say that.

Meanwhile, Gabbi overrode him. "*Oui, couleur.*"

And remembering Celsus Crogher's warning that he wouldn't always be able to stroll down the sidewalk like an average Joe, McGill reconsidered.

"*Couleur,*" he said with a nod.

Who could say? Maybe Patti would like it.

Caresse led him upstairs to begin his makeover.

7

"*Très beau,*" Caresse said, after she'd finished her work on McGill and he'd changed into French jeans, white polo shirt, and charcoal suede sport coat. His shoes were sporty black leather, comfortable as kid gloves, with rubber soles that would be good for running.

"Very handsome," Gabbi agreed.

McGill slipped on a pair of Bulgari gunmetal sunglasses.

"*Ooh, la, la,*" Caresse said.

McGill laughed. He looked at himself in the mirror Caresse held up for him. It *was* a new look, he decided. He wanted Patti to see it, and almost said so, but he remembered he was M'sieur Smith to his stylist and refrained. Still, he'd have to ask Patti to give him an ooh, la, la every once in a while. It was good for a middle-aged guy's ego.

The president's henchman leaned in to Gabbi and whispered, "You've taken very good care of the young lady?"

"*Mais oui,*" she replied softly.

McGill took Caresse's right hand in both of his, "*Merci beaucoup.*"

She kissed both his cheeks. "*Mon plaisir.*"

Caresse gave Gabbi a wink and left with a bounce in her step.

McGill lowered his glasses to the tip of his nose and looked at Gabbi.

"She thinks we're…what?"

"Who knows what young people think?" Gabbi said. "But she doesn't have a clue you're married to the President of the

United States."

Then she reached over and popped his shirt collar for a bit more continental flair.

Quai d'Orsay, Paris

8

"*Paradis Trouvé?*" McGill asked as Gabbi drove him to a meeting with Yves Pruet at the magistrate's office.

"Your accent really is very good for someone just starting out, but you don't pronounce the s at the end of a word unless it's followed by a vowel."

McGill made a mental note of the rule.

Returning to the story he'd just heard from his new partner, he said, "And you ran into Arno Durand after he came out of this strip club?"

Gabbi didn't mention pulling her gun on the reporter, only said, "He caught up to me as I was walking away from the place."

"But the club's bouncer called out to you first, from across the street?"

"*Oui.*"

McGill considered everything she'd told him.

Keeping her eyes on the road, Gabbi asked, "You think I made a mistake?"

"Not you. Me ... and probably Durand."

Gabbi said, "Your mistake was not thinking the girl and the beast knew each other."

McGill nodded. "My partner back home disabused me of that notion in a phone call last night."

He told Gabbi of Sweetie's reasoning.

"She's smart," Gabbi said.

"Just one of her many virtues."

"What was Durand's mistake?" Gabbi asked.

McGill told her, "Maybe it's different over here, but at home these days, any newspaper reporter of any weight—politics, sports, you name the beat—does TV work, too. Guys and gals who used to be perfectly anonymous scribes now have much higher public profiles. So if you were a creep involved in the death of a star athlete, and you saw a big-time sports reporter drop into your strip club, wouldn't you get just a bit suspicious?"

Gabbi pulled up at a red light. She stared off into space.

When the light turned green, Gabbi nodded to herself and put the car in motion.

"Durand told me he had to max out a credit card to get out of the strip club. Said he was lucky he didn't have to sign over his apartment. Read between the lines on that and—"

"Maybe The Undertaker was looking to grab him right there," McGill said.

"But he couldn't be sure Durand hadn't just come in looking for a cheap thrill or a little action, and if he did need to be taken out better to do it away from his place of business."

Gabbi pulled up in front of Pruet's office building.

Just then, McGill had a moment of doubt. He'd already made one incorrect assumption about the case. Maybe going after this stripper was another mistake. He asked, "You think this woman, Diana Martel, is really the person Glen Kinnard saw under the Pont d'Iéna?"

"You tell me," Gabbi replied. She pulled a manila envelope from under her seat. "*Paradis Trouvé* has a website with pictures of its dancers. I printed out the only one I thought resembled me at all."

McGill opened the envelope and pulled out an eight-by-ten color image printed on photo stock. The resolution wasn't great, but it was good enough for a rough comparison. The dancer was younger than Gabbi, and fuller, some of that obviously the work of a surgeon. Honi Moon's eyes didn't reflect an intelligence that would ever land her a spot in the French Foreign Ministry. But her dyed hair was close to the shade of blonde Gabbi had naturally. The shape of her face was oval as was Gabbi's, and the placement and size of her features was similar.

"My gene pool from the wrong side of the *chemin de fer*," Gabbi said.

"Wrong side of the tracks?" McGill asked.

"Yeah."

McGill slipped the picture back into the envelope. His doubt had vanished. Kinnard had been the one, unprompted, who'd told McGill the blonde he'd seen resembled Gabbi. He'd even made accurate distinctions between the two. SOB or not, Kinnard had a veteran cop's eye for detail. Diana Martel was the woman they wanted.

"I'll show the picture to Pruet," McGill said. "See if he can find out if the lady ever posed for a police photographer."

"And I'll call Durand," Gabbi said. "Tell him to be careful."

Annandale, VA

9

Ricky Lanh Huu bopped down the street on his way to St. Magnus Church. He was thinking maybe it was time to think of a new surname for himself. Lanh Huu was just too *Asian*. He'd have to come up with something new that sounded tough and meant the same thing: street smart.

Cutter was cool—Ricky Cutter—especially for someone good with a knife.

But that didn't say anything about being smart.

Maybe *Slick* Ricky Cutter. Okay, that might be too much.

Keep working on it, he told himself. The right name would come.

He'd given the matter of choosing the right first name considerable thought. His first inclination had been to name himself after a soldier, some special forces dude who greased bad guys by the battalion. Then he realized that most of the bad guys in the media spotlight these days were either Arabs or Asians, the latter looking a whole lot like him. The special ops dudes were mostly whites, with a sprinkling of blacks and Latinos.

That led him to think maybe he ought to swipe a movie star's name. But look at what those dudes had for names these days: Ashton, Heath, Keanu. What the hell was with that? Even the older stars, the ones with all the action blockbusters, what did they have for names? Arnold, Sylvester, and Bruce. Damn!

Not willing to forsake popular culture entirely, he looked next at rock stars. Again he was dismayed by the current possibilities: Gruff, Colm, and Thurston. It was enough to make him think he ought to move to France. Call himself Gaspar.

But then he remembered there used to be cool names in music. Back in the old days. This time he struck gold: Elvis, Conway, and Ricky. Elvis was the coolest, of course, and if he'd had an American face, he'd have gone with it and not thought twice. Being who he was, though, he thought Elvis would be too much of a reach. He'd get a lot of shit about it and wind up killing someone. He liked Conway a lot, too, but then he found out it was pretty much a country name, and he was pure city, born in Saigon, just learning to walk and steal from fruit stands before the city fell. That left Ricky—as in Nelson. He had the hair for it. He had the sleepy-eyed look the guy had used, too. Set the suckers up, thinking he was about to nod off and, zip, he'd have 'em by their throats.

So Ricky it was. After six months, he still liked his choice.

He climbed the steps of St. Magnus with a spring in his step. Passing through the front doors, he dipped his hand in the holy water, made the sign of the cross. He figured he was fucked as far as God was concerned. But who knew? Maybe good manners counted for something.

All thoughts of salvation departed as he stepped into the church proper; he cased the place as if he were entering a restaurant where a gang shootout was about to erupt. Half a dozen women were scattered among a couple hundred pews, the best he could tell. Damn Father Nguyen kept the lights low when he wasn't saying mass. Saving on electricity, Ricky had been told. The parish operated on a tight budget. Also, he'd been told the low light was good for prayer and reflection.

That's what all the ladies were doing, as far as he could see. Praying. Five Vietnamese women, four in American clothes, one granny in an *ao dai* that even in the dim light looked as old as she was. Maybe her wedding dress. Worn to pray for her dead husband, no doubt.

When the sun was out, Ricky didn't mind too much the lights being low, but on a cloudy day like today, with all the shadows in the church, it was too easy to imagine somebody lying in wait to ambush him. Someone could step out from behind a pillar and shoot him in the back. Not be bothered at all by killing someone in a church. It wouldn't bother Ricky to do it. The notion became so real to him he could see it all in his mind. In slow motion. The muzzle flash, him falling, the blood pooling. The granny hobbling over, horrified, the hem of her dress soaking up the blood. Her scream bringing Father Nguyen rushing in. The priest stopping short when he saw Ricky. Refusing to hear Ricky's last confession or give him absolution.

Ricky would die and go from the church straight to hell. He thought a lot about dying. When he wasn't thinking about killing. Or sex or food. All the basics of life. Like...

Who was that? The sixth woman in the church. American, this one. She knelt in a pew just to the rear of the confessional booths. There was enough light to see that she wore a green scarf over red hair and a pale white face. Her features were ... he couldn't decide if she was plain or pretty. Might go either way depending on how she was feeling, and if you fixed her up.

Right now, maybe she leaned more toward plain because you'd have to turn off all the lights in the church not to see how sad she was. Ricky thought he could see the track of a tear on her left cheek. Despair meant vulnerability and, to Ricky, nothing was more enticing than a defenseless woman. He started to drift toward the red-haired woman, thinking, yes, she was young enough for him. Not bad looking at all really. And so wrapped up in her own sorrow that—

A hand fell hard on Ricky's shoulder. He jumped a foot in the air, hating that he had been taken by surprise, his hand reaching for his knife even as he came down. Before he could grab the weapon, a small, hard fist hit him in the solar plexus with enough force to make him go numb, take all the fight out of him. He was marched to the back of the church, and that was when he saw his assailant was Father Nguyen.

He was relieved that he wasn't about to die, but he was angered that a priest had gotten the drop on him, was leading him along like a child grasped by his ear. Ricky pulled free as they entered the church's vestibule.

He turned to confront the priest, saying, "I should kill you."

Father Nguyen extended his hands to his sides, offering an open target.

When no attack came, the priest told Ricky, "You are not welcome in my church, and you will never again disturb the piety of any of my parishioners."

"Mr. Bao wants to see you," Ricky told the priest.

"He, also, is not welcome here."

"Not here," Ricky said.

"Nor will I see him anywhere else."

The priest's hands were still in a submissive position. The whole centerline of his body from throat to groin was available to be slashed. If Ricky was quick enough.

"What kind of priest are you?" he asked indignantly. "How do you know Mr. Bao is not in need of your sacraments?"

"He and you have already abused the Church's mercy," Father Nguyen said. "I see no sign of repentance in you; I doubt I would see any in him. If I am wrong, I will plead for forgiveness."

Ricky glared at the priest. "You'll be pleading for mercy."

The priest didn't respond, even when Ricky pulled his knife and flicked it open.

But Ricky didn't attack; he used the weapon to cover his retreat.

Once he was gone, Father Nguyen went to see if he might be of help to the woman Ricky had been about to harass. The unfamiliar woman with the red hair. The priest wondered what the appearance of someone new among his congregation might portend.

10

Father Nguyen didn't bother the woman, who was still praying. As Ricky had noticed, he also saw signs that she had been crying. In silence, he asked the Savior to comfort the woman, bring her peace. Then he moved past her, went to the altar, took a cotton cloth out of his pocket and began to dust the altar. The priest made it a point of respect to both the Almighty and his flock to keep his church immaculately clean; he made it an exercise in humility to participate in the cleaning, right down to scrubbing the floor on his hands and knees. At the moment, though, dusting was sufficient. When he turned around he saw the red-haired woman was on her feet, in an aisle, watching him.

He walked over to her and extended his hand.

"Hello. I am Francis Nguyen."

She took his hand. "I'm Kay."

Kira wasn't lying. Her mother had named her, but her father had always called her Kay. She couldn't remember the last time she'd used Daddy's pet name, hadn't even told Welborn of its existence. But with the priest, using it felt right.

"Is there some way I might be of help?" Father Nguyen asked.

Kira started to cry. Father Nguyen took the dust cloth out of his pocket. He shook it and extended it to her. It was all he had to offer. Kira took it with a sad smile.

"I could use a miracle, Father," Kira told him drying her eyes. "You wouldn't have one up your sleeve, would you?"

Keeping his expression deadpan, the priest checked one sleeve and then the other.

"Maybe later," he said.

Kira laughed, keeping it quiet in deference to her surroundings.

Father Nguyen smiled.

"Thank you, Father. You've already made me feel better."

She took another swipe at her face with the cloth and gingerly handed it back. The priest casually put it back in his pocket, not concerned with the moisture Kira had added.

"If you'd care to join me in the rectory for a cup of tea, perhaps I might be of help. Or..."

He nodded to the confessional booths.

"The tea would be lovely."

Father Nguyen gestured to a door off the sacristy and led the young woman in that direction.

"What's troubling you, Kay?" he asked.

"I'm getting married soon," she said.

And she told him why that was a problem.

Washington, DC

11

Putnam Shady arrived at work before dawn and got his billable hours in by one p.m.; helping Sweetie was all very well, but no way he could neglect his day job. A partner in his law firm, albeit the junior one, he had responsibilities to meet. But as the up and coming rainmaker in the office, his senior colleagues gave him a good deal of flexibility. As long as he got his quota of billable hours in and spent the requisite time schmoozing business prospects, they were happy.

Just make money, baby, they'd say, paraphrasing Al Davis.

Now, Putnam was adding Junior G-Man to his portfolio. Given his personal history, there was a rich irony. For anyone but Margaret, it would have been unthinkable. But it was for Margaret, and the way she got him to do the damnedest things, he thought he might wake up one day and not recognize himself.

While his secretary was out—and all his legal colleagues had departed for business lunches, shopping for high-end indulgences, or trysts with their mistresses or boyfriends—Putnam took his personal laptop out of his briefcase and booted it up. He never used one of the firm's computers for anything he wouldn't want the FBI to read, another legacy from his early years. His personal machine's files were all password protected and encrypted. No one was going to follow his footsteps across cyberspace without his permission.

Putnam pulled up the website for the Virginia State Bar. He did a membership search for the creep Margaret had sicced him on: Horatio Bao. Found him with no trouble. He looked to see if the VSB had taken any disciplinary action against Bao. They hadn't. But the state bar did note that Mr. Bao engaged in the private practice of law without the benefit of having malpractice insurance. Interesting. The guy must be really sure of himself. Or he was certain none of his clients was ever going to complain even if he did screw up. That, of course, would imply Bao had another type of insurance policy in force.

Putnam looked for and found a website for lawyer Horatio Bao. A studio portrait of the esteemed attorney was front and center on his home page. Bao was late middle-aged, well groomed, conservatively dressed: just what you'd want from your legal counsel. But the guy had a merciless stare that belonged to a villain right out of *Terry and the Pirates*.

Someone the previous administration might have used as its counsel on water-boarding. If that was Bao's public image, Putnam thought, who the heck knew how he partied when the curtains were drawn?

Putnam began to look for court filings with Bao's name on them.

See whom he'd had for clients the past four or five years.

Putnam paused for a moment of reflection. He could be immersing himself in deep water here. As a favor for Margaret. So it only seemed right that if danger came calling she should stay very close to him. She might even have to move upstairs for the duration of this little adventure.

Comfort him should he become fearful.

Spank him should he turn naughty.

Thinking about the possibilities made Putnam tremble in anticipation.

Arlington, VA

12

Sweetie was sitting in her car and talking with Caitie McGill when her BlackBerry beeped to signal another call waiting to be answered.

"Just a minute, Caitie. I've got another call coming in. Might be your dad."

It wasn't. Putnam was on the line, telling her, "I just sent you an e-mail."

That was it. No cute comment. Not even a goodbye. Well, he could have been busy at work. Had just enough time to alert her to a waiting message. Or, Good Lord, she hadn't put him in a bad spot, had she? She had told him—firmly—not to get anywhere near Horatio Bao, but Putnam, like any overage adolescent, might have acted impulsively. Had just enough time to phone her before he had to beat feet.

Sweetie murmured a quick prayer before clicking back to Caitie.

"Was it Dad?" the youngest McGill child asked.

"No, honey. It was a business call. Remind me, why did you call?"

"Annie said she'd talk to Dad, but she can't reach him."

"And Annie is?"

"Annie Klein. My new agent at William Norris. She got me a part in a movie, but Mom says I've got to get Dad's permission. Annie said she'd give Dad all the details, but she says his phone just rings and rings and he never answers. I'm getting scared." A tremor entered Caitie's voice. "Sweetie, is Dad okay?"

"Yes, I talked with him yesterday. Did your agent use her own phone to make the call?"

"Sure, I guess. What other phone would she use?"

"Caitie, your dad's phone only takes calls from certain people: Patti, your mom, you, your sister and brother, and me. That way he doesn't get bothered by other people."

There was a pause, and then Caitie asked, "Can I get a phone like that?"

"Maybe when you're president." Sweetie was still worried about Putnam, wanted to read the e-mail he'd sent. "Tell you what. You're worried your dad won't let you be in this movie, right?"

"Yeah," Caitie said, sounding glum now.

"You trust me?"

"Of course, Sweetie. We were at Lafayette Square together."

Spoken like one Rough Rider to another, recalling the charge up San Juan Hill. But Caitie's presence the night they confronted the Reverend Burke Godfrey and his congregants had taken no small amount of courage for a ten-year-old.

"Then here's what we'll do. I'll see if this movie's right for you. If it is, I'll have your dad call Annie Klein. Deal?"

"That'd be great, Sweetie! You want me to tell you about the movie?"

"Not now, kiddo. What you do, have your agent send me the script."

That problem resolved, Sweetie picked up Putnam's e-mail on her BlackBerry.

Stakeouts had gone 21st century.

13

Sweetie's car was a 1969 Chevy Malibu coupe with polished but faded Fathom Blue Metallic paint. She'd parked up the street from Horatio Bao's law office in Arlington, Virginia. Stakeouts were usually a deadly dull business, but Sweetie never got antsy, never felt anything but peaceful sitting in the Malibu.

The car had belonged to her cousin, Michael Quigley. He'd left it in her care when he went to Vietnam. She was only eight years old at the time, but she'd promised to wash and wax the car and keep it clean inside, too. When her dad had confided in her, without going into specifics, that Michael was in a dangerous situation and she should keep him in her prayers, Sweetie had hung a picture of the Sacred Heart from the Malibu's rear view mirror. At least once a day, every day, she got into the car and prayed that Michael would come home safe and sound.

He did. Skinnier than Sweetie remembered. Looking a lot older than a young man who'd been away for only a year. But he was able to smile when he saw her.

"How's my car?" Michael asked.

Sweetie took his hand and said, "Come and see."

She led him out to the garage where the car had been stored.

The Malibu gleamed like it was sitting on a showroom floor. Michael picked up Sweetie in his arms and kissed her cheek. He rocked back and forth for a moment, almost as if they were dancing, before putting her down.

"You know, Margaret Mary, a lot of guys I was with in the army, they wanted to get home to their girls. Thinking of their sweethearts was what kept them going. But maybe half of them got the letter."

"What letter?" Sweetie asked.

"The one that said their girls found other guys."

At nine, Sweetie could only imagine some horrible form letter that—

"But not me," Michael said. "What kept me going was thinking about this car. Knowing that you'd keep it sparkling, just the way it is now. I'd come home and drive down Lake Shore Drive with the radio up high, and even if it was cold as hell, I'd have the windows open."

Sweetie understood that perfectly, and beamed at her cousin.

"The inside clean?" Michael asked.

Sweetie yanked open the driver's door.

Michael eased inside, ran a hand over the steering wheel—and stopped short when he saw the picture of the Sacred Heart hanging from the rear view mirror.

"This is new," he said, looking at his young cousin.

Sweetie shrugged, her face turning red. "Dad said..." Another shrug. "I came here and prayed you'd be okay."

Michael Quigley looked at her, his eyes getting big and filling with tears. Sweetie was dismayed. She hadn't thought she'd done anything wrong. Her eyes started to fill, too.

But then Michael stepped out, embraced her and said, "Thank you, thank you."

It was several years before Michael told her in detail of his wartime experiences, but at that moment he said, "I was the luckiest damn grunt in the 25th Infantry. I should have been dead half-a-dozen times. Each time I got away clean. I thought for sure the next time I was going to die. I got more and more scared. Even when I got on the plane to come home, I was sure it would get shot down or crash. The only comfort I could find was thinking of this car. Feeling that somehow I'd get back to it."

Sweetie slipped past him, reached inside the Malibu. She handed him the picture of the Sacred Heart. And Michael gave her the keys to the car.

Even as a youngster, she knew that wouldn't be the right time to argue with Michael. She was sure the time would come when he'd ask for the keys back, and she'd wink and hand them over, letting him know she'd known all along how it would work out.

But Michael never did ask for the keys back. He went out and bought another Malibu, a 1970 model. The picture of the Sacred Heart didn't fit around the new rear-view mirror, so he kept it in the sun visor. All these years later, his luck still held, and he still drove that car.

It was the experience of praying for Michael and having her prayers answered that led Sweetie to think she had a religious vocation. But it was driving, and more specifically parking, the Malibu with her one high school boyfriend, an adolescent romance she hadn't been able to get out of her mind no matter how hard she'd prayed, that caused her to leave the convent. When she returned home from the convent, her father gave back the keys to the Malibu that she'd given him.

The Lord moved in mysterious ways.

But in the end the signs were usually clear.

She wondered if Kira Fahey would be given a sign about her

father being present at her wedding. Maybe, maybe not. But if she had to bet, she knew where she'd put her money.

She'd been watching for Horatio Bao for two hours, thinking it had seemed like mere minutes, when a young woman came out of his storefront office. She was slim, of Asian heritage, and wearing a business suit with a skirt that showed off shapely legs. She carried a bundle of manila and number ten envelopes. Despite the burden, she locked the door to Bao's offices without difficulty. She walked with an athletic stride, approaching a new Nissan Altima parked at the curb out front. About to move out from behind the Nissan and into the street, she had to quickly retreat to avoid a fast moving car. The high heels she wore didn't inhibit her fancy footwork.

She entered the Nissan with grace and an economy of motion, slipping inside and pulling the door closed a heartbeat before the next car zoomed past.

Sweetie remembered what Jim had said. Someone had to ring Ms. Ky's doorbell for the sniper who had shot Deke. She and Jim had also speculated about how the person who rang the bell might be related to Bao, thinking she might be a wife or a girlfriend.

Sweetie waited for an opening in traffic, and made a U-turn to follow the young woman in the Nissan.

To Sweetie's eye, she wasn't tailing a wife or girlfriend. A girlfriend was unlikely to be toting the office mail, unless she was also Bao's secretary. But the feeling Sweetie got from the young woman, having a key to the office, she had some sort of executive capacity. A wife would either be an older, trusted companion, or young and flashy, a trophy model. The woman Sweetie was following was young, but stylish rather than flashy.

Putnam's e-mail had included a copy of the photo Horatio Bao used on his website; it was a match for the shot Welborn had taken of the man coming out of Bishop O'Menehy's confessional. Putnam's message said Bao ran a sole practitioner's office.

Sweetie felt sure he would keep his business all in the family.

Making a dutiful daughter as trustworthy an assistant as Sweetie could imagine.

And one who moved well, she'd be a natural to ring Musette Ky's doorbell.

Sweetie followed the young woman to a local post office. Took her picture with the BlackBerry. Got her license plate number. Felt the investigation gaining momentum.

Pruet's office, Paris

14

Odo admitted McGill to the investigating magistrate's office. He took in McGill's new appearance at a glance, looked as if he might comment on it, decided silence was the better course. Without the magistrate present at the moment, McGill focused on something he'd barely noticed before. There was a picture—a headshot— of the president of France on the wall.

Jean-Louis Severin. The guy was good looking, McGill thought, and he had been able to discern from his perusal of *Le Monde* that old Jean-Louis had recently been divorced by his wife. Guys who had been put through that wringer often went looking for ... what? Affirmation that they hadn't become ogres? And what better way to do that than to find a welcoming woman?

Thing was, looking at *M'sieur Le President's* photo, McGill couldn't quite imagine Patti getting together with him. Not even if he hadn't been the man in Patti's life. Sure, the two of them could be—hell, they were—friends. But they were, if anything, too much alike. They'd wind up coming at each other head on, if they tried to pair up. A good match called for complementary qualities. Strengths and weaknesses that meshed like finely machined gears. That was why Patti had been happy with Andy Grant, why she was happy with him. They hadn't duplicated, didn't duplicate, each other. They filled in each other's gaps. Completed each other, if you wanted to get sappy about it.

"M'sieur McGill?" Odo said.

From his tone, McGill knew he'd missed the first time he'd been addressed.

"Yes," he said, turning to look at Odo.

"*M'sieur le magistrat* will be with you shortly. May I get you a drink?"

"Perrier," McGill said.

"Champagne?"

"The sparkly water kind," McGill said.

"*Oui, bon.*" Odo turned to leave.

McGill stopped him. "Odo, would you mind telling me something?"

"What, m'sieur?"

"Your primary martial art is savate?"

Odo's face took on a measure of reserve.

"*Oui.*"

"But my guess is you're familiar with other disciplines."

Odo hesitated before responding, "I know some Brazilian jiujitsu."

McGill nodded. He knew he'd gone as far as he could for the moment. McGill wouldn't want to give away all his secrets either. But he had one more question.

"Do you think it would take long for the two of us—and maybe one other fellow—to be able to work out a coordinated attack?"

A new expression appeared on Odo's face: interest. An opportunity to learn something new might be presented to him.

"This other fellow, he is skilled?"

"I haven't seen a demonstration," McGill admitted, "but my educated guess would be yes."

"How many men would we be facing, and how would they be armed?"

"One man, probably barehanded. He might have a blunt object, possibly a blade."

"Three of us, skilled fighters, against one man without a gun?"

"He's a pretty big guy."

Odo nodded, his interest now fully engaged. "I will get your Perrier, m'sieur, and have an answer for you when I return."

"*Merci,*" McGill told him.

As Odo opened the office door, Pruet was there, about to enter. The two men exchanged several words in French that McGill couldn't follow.

Pruet stepped inside his office and looked at the president's henchman.

"You've gotten my bodyguard excited," he said. "Always a risky thing with a Corsican."

15

McGill sat opposite Pruet, the magistrate's old table between them. Pruet was more forthcoming than Odo had been about the makeover the president's henchman had undergone.

"You've had your hair cut and colored," he said.

"Remind you of Belmondo?" McGill asked.

The magistrate sat back and considered. "Perhaps, somewhat. You are also wearing French clothing, not American."

"I have new sunglasses, too." McGill modeled them for just a moment.

"So you are affecting a disguise."

"My wife worries," McGill said. He told Pruet of the English louts following him and Gabbi. He left out Celsus's visit and the warning that he'd someday need greater protection.

Pruet told McGill, "I had the pleasure of speaking ever so briefly with *Madam la Présidente* last night."

That caught McGill by surprise. Maybe Patti had a thing for Frenchmen after all.

The magistrate continued, "She took my call and passed the phone to President Severin."

"Who happened to be conveniently at hand?" McGill asked.

"*Oui.* I apologized to my president for interrupting his business with your wife."

McGill kept his expression neutral.

"Jean-Louis is a good fellow," Pruet went on. "I have known him since we were at school together; we corresponded during his year at Yale."

"He was at Yale?" McGill hadn't known that.

"Yes, that is where he met Patricia Darden."

McGill saw that he was being led down the garden path and asked, "Would you care to cut to the chase, *m'sieur le magistrat?*"

"I am telling you all this because my wife, Nicolette, also knows these details. I have proof—her fingerprints and DNA—that she has read my confidential files, doubtless in the hope of learning something that might be of use to her in divorcing me. Included in my files are the letters Jean-Louis sent to me from America."

Which begged the question as to what had been in those letters. But McGill didn't ask. It was none of his business what Patti and any of her boyfriends had done years before he'd even met her. Some things were better left unexplored.

Pruet nodded, approving of McGill's restraint.

He continued, "I believe Nicolette shared what she learned with Aubine Severin, the former wife of *M'sieur le President.* I don't know if Nicolette played any role in instigating the Severins' divorce, but I believe she used a long-ago affection and a current working relationship to conjure an illusory affair between two heads of state, and aggravated matters for everyone."

"Why would she do that?" McGill asked.

Pruet said, "I have disappointed Nicolette in many ways. I have been insufficiently ambitious. I have been politically maladroit. I have declined to give her access to my family money. I would rather play my guitar alone on my balcony than be her escort in high society. In short, I am a failure as a husband."

"You haven't given her any other reason to be angry?"

Pruet required a moment to understand. When he did, he smiled ruefully.

"Another woman? No, m'sieur. Having one seek my ruin is more than enough."

"But how does your wife's anger at you apply to France's president?"

Pruet said, "As I mentioned, Jean-Louis and I are *confreres.* A plot that would undo us both would please Nicolette and—"

"Your president's political enemies. Those who might accuse him of following his heart rather than his country's best interests when he aligns France with the United States."

It was a guess, but it made sense, McGill thought. If Patti had Roger Michaelson looking to undermine her at home, why shouldn't Jean-Louis Severin have people who wanted to do him in, too?

"Bravo, m'sieur." The magistrate applauded McGill's insight.

"That's only half the riddle from my point of view," McGill said. "How are you undone if your president falls?"

"As you probably know, I made the mistake of calling a former interior minister a thief. Then I made things far worse by sending him to jail for his crimes. Such things are not supposed to be done. So his friends sent me into exile." Pruet opened his hands, gesturing to his present humble surroundings. "My career was effectively over. If I were a less stubborn man, I would now be working for my father selling cheese."

McGill understood, more than what Pruet had just told him.

"You'd also be out on your derriere if you didn't have Jean-Louis covering it. So, if he goes, you go, too."

Pruet nodded.

McGill said, "In Chicago, we have a saying when something like this happens to a cop. We say somebody put a brick on him."

"A brick?" Pruet said. "*Tellement approprié.*" How appropriate.

"They kept you idle, right? Hoping you'd go away."

"The better part of a year, but I am still here."

"And then you were handed the Glen Kinnard case. And got me as a bonus."

The magistrate shrugged.

The door to Pruet's office opened. Odo was back with a tray bearing two green bottles of Perrier and two glasses. He set his burden down on the magistrate's desk, and poured for both McGill and Pruet.

Then, without being specific, Odo told the president's henchman, "Two days to prepare would be best; one will do; if necessary, improvisation is possible, but not advised."

Pruet looked at the two of them and asked, "Do I even want to know?"

Chequers, Buckinghamshire, England

16

The shape of the G8 conference table at Chequers had been changed from round to oblong. Prime Minister of the UK Norvin Kimbrough sat at its head. To his immediate right was Gordon Kendrie of Canada; to his left was Ichiro Sugiyama of Japan. Next to Kendrie was Matteo Gallo of Italy. Across from Gallo was an empty chair in case the president of Russia decided to drop in.

These four leaders were, nominally, the Kimbrough bloc, though only Kendrie, a Tory at heart, was committed to his friend from London. Sugiyama faced a tough problem in assuming more military responsibility for Japan without scaring the wits out of all his neighbors. He had yet to come to grips with the necessity of apologizing for Japan's atrocities during World War II. Gallo was simply being wily, biding his time. Russia hadn't sent in an absentee ballot.

The task of the Kimbrough bloc, as the prime minister saw it, was to persuade or coerce the United States into reversing course and maintaining its historic burden of financing the overwhelming majority of the civilized world's defense costs.

Distant from Kimbrough, to his right, were Erika Kirsch of Germany and Jean-Louis Severin of France. Across from Severin, isolated by the empty chair held open for Russia was Patricia Darden Grant of the United States.

Some world leaders might have considered it an affront to

be placed beyond an empty chair, but President Grant appeared unruffled.

As Kimbrough droned on about the press announcement they would make shortly, lauding the agreement they had reached on the phasing out of agricultural subsidies and import restrictions, Patti picked up the small American flag placed on the table in front of her and used it to fan herself. The agricultural agreement was actually a milestone achievement, and having developed nations buy food products from developing nations would be critical to the success of the Plowshare Initiative that Patti and Jean-Louis were hatching, but there was no getting around the fact that Norvin Kimbrough was a gasbag.

Jean-Louis and Erika grinned at Patti as she fanned herself.

Three heads of state cutting up like kids at the back of a classroom.

Even Matteo Gallo smiled with them.

When Kimbrough finally noticed he took umbrage. "Something wrong, Madam President? A hot flash perhaps?"

Before Patti could respond to the insult, there was a knock at the door. A woman on Kimbrough's staff poked her head in and told him, "Fifteen minutes until you go on, sir. Five minutes until all of you are needed in makeup."

Taking advantage of the open door, Galia Mindel slipped in behind Kimbrough's staffer, crossed quickly to Patti, handed her a note, and retreated as swiftly as she'd come. Patti read the message at a glance and her face hardened. Jean-Louis and Erika looked at her with concern.

Kimbrough asked, "Something your friends might help with, Madam President?"

Patti composed herself and said, "No thank you, Prime Minister. It's purely a domestic matter."

She stuck Galia's note in a pocket.

"Very well then. I believe we're all ready to make our announcement, and the gentlemen amongst us, at least, could do with an extra minute or two with our makeup artists."

Kimbrough rose and led the way out of the room.

Arlington, VA

17

Mrs. Eva Novak, the personal secretary of Bishop George O'Menehy, looked across her small outer office to where Father Francis Nguyen sat in a guest chair. Next to the priest, standing on a pedestal, was a small statue modeled after the portrait of Our Lady of Czestochowa. It was hard for Mrs. Novak to decide whether Father Nguyen or Our Lady looked more serene.

The priest had his eyes closed and his palms rested on his thighs. He barely seemed to be breathing, but his color was good so Mrs. Novak didn't worry that his soul had been taken to heaven right in front of her. Though that would be no less than what Father Nguyen deserved, in her opinion. Such a good man. He'd remembered to bring the rosary he'd promised to Mrs. Novak's mother, Agneta. Mom was near the end now, had been worried that she hadn't done enough to deserve God's mercy, and feared dying. Mrs. Novak had asked Father Nguyen to visit Mom and reassure her, even though he wasn't Mom's parish priest. He had gone to see Mom and the peace of mind he'd brought to her was nothing short of a miracle; hearing her confession and counseling her on how to spend her remaining time had dispelled her anxiety.

As a grace note, he'd promised to send her a rosary to which he had given his blessing.

Mom had asked to have Father Nguyen say her funeral mass, but Mrs. Novak didn't know if that would be possible. Eva Novak wasn't a snoop, not at all, but there were times she couldn't help but overhear Bishop O'Menehy. Times when he'd been on the phone with the president of the National Conference of Catholic Bishops and the two men had discussed the possibility of removing Father Nguyen from the priesthood.

That would be a tragedy in Mrs. Novak's opinion.

A self-inflicted wound for the Church.

And Bishop O'Menehy keeping the good father waiting now. It was beginning to annoy Mrs. Novak. Then her intercom buzzed, the signal that the bishop would receive his visitor.

Keeping her voice soft, she said, "Father, he'll see you now."

Father Nguyen opened his eyes and smiled at Mrs. Novak. He appreciated that she hadn't jarred him to attention. He got to his feet.

Mrs. Novak said, "Thank you again for remembering the rosary for my mother."

The priest took Eva's hand. "Agneta told me it's just a shame I'm not Polish."

Mrs. Novak's cheeks turned red, but when Father smiled, she laughed.

"Your mother is a wonderful woman, Eva. Our Lord's company will be far the richer for her presence."

Tears welled in Mrs. Novak's eyes. She, too, felt at peace, not doubting for a moment that Father Nguyen had it exactly right.

He' knocked on the bishop's door and stepped into his office, shutting the door behind him. Bishop O'Menehy sat behind his desk and gestured the priest to a chair.

"Please sit down, Father Nguyen."

The priest did as he was bid.

O'Menehy removed his glasses and asked, "How may I help you?"

Father Nguyen was sure his Excellency would love to hear him ask for permission to go on a retreat and renew his vow of obedience; to ask for reassignment to another diocese; even to announce that he was leaving the priesthood.

Well, maybe not that last one. The church had relied on immigrants to fill the ranks of the priesthood for a very long time. The Irish and the Poles had answered the call early on in America. They'd been followed by the Latinos. Now, it was the turn of the Asians and Africans. If those last two groups faltered, Holy Mother Church would be in dire trouble.

Or it would finally have to change its doctrine and permit priests to marry. Maybe even ordain women. But with the hardline conservatives in charge at the Vatican that was unlikely.

"I have a problem, your Excellency," Father Nguyen said. "Yesterday, I was confronted in my church by a young man who brandished a knife."

O'Menehy was stunned. "A robbery? Were you hurt? Was *anyone* hurt?"

These days, the hierarchy had to think not only of their flock's moral well being, but of their own legal liability. The Church had been sued more often in the past twenty years than in the previous two thousand. There was a clerical joke, a play on Shakespeare, on the strategy the Church should pursue: First, we excommunicate all the lawyers.

Then they could claim all the lawsuits were an anti-Catholic plot.

Father Nguyen answered the bishop, "I escorted the young man into the vestibule and told him not to return. No one was harmed."

O'Menehy's gaze turned thoughtful. Father Nguyen was a force in the diocese in so many ways, and now he'd made short work of a man with a knife?

"Is there more to this story, Father?"

"That is why I'm here, your Excellency. I've heard this young man's confession, but his deeds say he is far from truly penitent. In fact, I know he has used the sacrament to insulate himself from punishment."

"Whose punishment?" the bishop asked.

"The state's, your Excellency. The Commonwealth of Virginia."

"That is none of our concern," O'Menehy said.

The bishop felt his words congeal in his throat, almost making him choke. He firmly believed in what he had said, but by ignoring, or worse, covering up, sexual assaults by members of the clergy on the children of the faithful, the Church had placed itself in great jeopardy.

The Lord would surely mete out appropriate punishment to those who had sinned so grievously. But there was no longer any question in civil society that Divine judgment could not be substituted for jail sentences handed down by secular courts.

"This young man," Father Nguyen continued, "works for a powerful figure in the Vietnamese immigrant community."

"You learned this in confession?"

"No," Father Nguyen said. "It is common knowledge."

The bishop nodded. The matter was suitable for discussion in that case.

Even so, his Excellency was far from comfortable with what he knew was coming next.

"This powerful figure is Horatio Bao, a lawyer," Father Nguyen said. "He has a sinister reputation, but he is also a congregant of yours, and a generous contributor to Church charities. The young man with the knife demanded that I accompany him to see Bao."

The bishop paled. "What did you say?"

"I refused."

O'Menehy slumped with relief. Realizing his posture constituted a confession of sorts, the possession of guilty knowledge, he straightened up.

He wasn't fast enough for Father Nguyen to miss the correction.

"I came here, your Excellency, because I am sorely troubled by an evil abuse of the sacrament of Confession," the priest said. "I thought you might offer me guidance. If you are Horatio Bao's confessor, you might even have direct empathy for me."

"That's enough, Father," the bishop said, his voice stern. "You've not revealed any of the substance of this young man's confession to me, and I'll not say *anything* about any confession I've ever heard."

The two clerics sat in silence, looking past each other, for what seemed like a long time.

Finally, the bishop spoke. "Francis, you've been at odds with the teachings of the church for some time."

Father Nguyen said, "I feel that those among the faithful who are in error would best be helped by drawing them closer to God, not pushing them away."

O'Menehy leaned forward, "Even if that were so, it is not *your* place to decide. And you just told me you banished this young fellow from your church. You did so with justification from what you told me, but you gave him the boot nonetheless."

Father Nguyen bowed his head. "I am far from heaven myself."

"As so many of us are. But you are not to raise this matter of false confessions to me again. The seal of the confessional is absolute."

The priest nodded. He completely agreed that the privacy of a sincere confession should be inviolable. But using a sacrament to gag a witness to a crime was an abomination. Of course, if you told the faithful in advance that their priest would be the one to judge the sincerity of their remorse, and would feel free to reveal anything he deemed to be insincere, that would be the end of the sacrament.

These were indeed troubling times for the Church.

Bishop O'Menehy came out from behind his desk, and Father Nguyen dropped to one knee to receive his blessing.

The priest left the bishop's office feeling certain Horatio Bao had confessed a crime to O'Menehy, as Ricky Lanh Huu had done with him. He'd seen it on the bishop's face. But he didn't reveal to the bishop that the former novice, Margaret Sweeney, who now worked with the president's henchman was investigating a matter that might unmask the crimes confessed to both of them.

A development that would likely result in more shame for the Church.

But the bishop had said he wanted to hear no more about it.

18

As Father Nguyen walked to his car, two men and a woman approached him. It was a measure of the situation in which he found himself that he was glad they were Caucasian, not members of his own ethnic community. He was further reassured when all three smiled at him.

The elder man asked, "Father Francis Nguyen?"

The priest nodded.

"I'm John Kinsale. This is my wife, Georgine, and our son, Patrick."

"Hello," Nguyen said.

"We've heard great things about you, Father."

"Exaggerations, I'm sure."

"Not from our sources, Father. We also heard you've had some difficulties with your superiors. Might even become subject to severe discipline. Or worse."

Francis Nguyen took a step back and examined the three people. He was sure he had never seen any of them before. The husband and wife didn't look like anyone who'd followed a religious vocation in the past, and the son ... well, young white men were far more likely to offer their lives in combat these days than offer them to God. They looked like what they had told him they were: a family.

Father Nguyen asked. "What do you want?"

The woman told him, "We're from Massachusetts, Father."

The son added, "We have a church there."

The father summed things up. "We're looking for a pastor."

Magistrate Pruet's Office, Paris

19

Yves Pruet showed McGill his find: the ceramic tile painted by the immigrant artist, Bertrand Kalou. He pointed out a figure in the painting. And a straight thin vertical line next to it.

"M'sieur Kalou painted this figure of a third man who ventured under the Pont d'Iéna shortly after the fight between M'sieur Kinnard and Thierry Duchamp ended."

"An eyewitness?" McGill asked. "Did he see the blonde woman?"

"He did, but at a distance, and only from behind."

McGill looked at the tile again. The view was from an elevated spot, looking down at the Seine and the walkway under the bridge where the fight had occurred. The figure of the third man was in the foreground on the near side of the bridge. It was more a suggestion of a man than a detailed likeness. Still, it managed to convey a sense of both bulk and menace.

The president's henchman pointed at the straight line next to the figure of the man.

"The artist added that? Some sort of scale of measure?"

Pruet nodded. "M'sieur Kalou said the line would indicate the height of an average white Frenchman, approximately 177 centimeters. About five feet ten inches."

McGill saw that the figure of the man was significantly taller than the line. He looked to Pruet for the numerical difference.

The magistrate told him just over 223 centimeters. "Approximately seven feet four inches."

"This painter has a good eye for proportion?" McGill asked.

Pruet told him, "I had a friend at the Musée D'Orsay look at his work. He told me M'sieur Kalou has an excellent eye and a respectable talent. He recommended our witness's work to a gallery he values."

"Glad something good came out of this," McGill said.

He looked at the painting again. The artist had, in a few strokes, captured the feeling of a real brute. Someone who would use his size to get whatever he damn well pleased.

Odo, who had been standing by silently, asked, "Is this the big fellow you spoke of earlier, m'sieur? The one who would require more than one opponent?"

McGill took the magazine he'd bought that morning at the riverside stall out of the manila envelope Gabbi had given him.

He tossed the magazine on Pruet's desk and said, "Here's a better look at him."

Odo looked over Pruet's shoulder at the magazine cover. *Le Champion Tacit.* The magistrate opened the magazine to the article inside, but most of the text, as Gabbi had told him, had to do with the other two fighters on the cover. The monster got just a throw away line as the man who could turn the whole sport upside down, if the authorities ever dared to let him compete, and he could find an opponent brave enough to enter the ring with him. The writer of the piece identified the monster only by his *nom de guerre.*

"The Undertaker," Pruet said. Turning to McGill, he added. "Perhaps you'll need a fourth man to defeat this one."

"Or an elephant gun," Odo offered.

McGill grinned. "If I were at home with this guy, I'd be inclined to use a firearm myself. But over here, I thought I'd better tread lightly."

Pruet told McGill, "France appreciates your consideration, m'sieur. Perhaps, if we are fortunate, the police will have a net large enough to throw over this fellow."

"That'd be nice," McGill agreed, "if we can get him to do something stupid in front of a bunch of cops who are ready for him."

"*Touché,*" the magistrate said.

"Just the fact, though, that he was on the scene where Thierry Duchamp died is enough to make an American cop suspicious."

Pruet nodded, and Odo confirmed, "A French *flic,* as well."

"So did you find out if there was a football match coming up where Thierry Duchamp's absence would affect the betting line?" McGill asked.

Pruet steepled his hands and looked at the president's henchman.

"It is more complicated than that," he said, "and perhaps to you it will seem absurd."

"Try me," McGill said.

"Thierry Duchamp's team, the Paris Football Club, has qualified to play for the Champions League Winner's Cup."

McGill gave the magistrate a blank look. The two Frenchmen exchanged a glance and shrugged. *Americans.*

Odo explained, "International competition, best team from each country."

"From Dublin to Moscow," Pruet specified. "Normally,

France would be uniformly exhilarated by the good fortune of the Paris team."

"Except?" McGill asked.

"Except Thierry Duchamp, in many ways, had upset the old order. He was a scoring machine—which was entirely contrary to the normal style of French teams."

Odo, the Corsican, made a rude noise in his throat.

The magistrate shrugged. "I am not a great football fan, so I cannot judge. France's usual style of play was to emphasize defense. Some people ..." He glanced at Odo. "... perhaps many, find this approach less than entertaining. But an equal number are wedded to the old way. They would consider a team that won the Cup by virtue of offense to be a triumph of burlesque."

McGill, a Chicago White Sox fan, had long despaired of ever seeing his team win a World Series. When they finally did win in 2005, he wouldn't have cared if they'd scored all their runs by dint of bases on balls, fielding errors, and hit batsmen.

"Yeah," he said, "that is hard for me to understand. Very hard to believe it would be worth the taking of a man's life."

Odo leaned forward. "As you yourself suggested, we do not believe that was the original intent."

"Our theory," the magistrate said, "is that this Undertaker fellow was meant to do no more than hobble Thierry Duchamp. Slow him down to play at the traditional pace."

McGill laughed, then held up a placatory hand.

"Gentlemen, please believe me, I'm not laughing at you. I had a similar idea myself. But now that we've seen a photo of The Undertaker, would either of you hire him to hurt someone just a little? I was pretty much told he'd bite your head off as soon as look at you."

The two Frenchmen looked at the behemoth's picture again.

Pruet said, "I would not enter into *any* business arrangement with such a fellow. But we will be closer to knowing the truth once we find the blonde woman."

McGill reached into the envelope again. He took out the photo Gabbi had given him and tossed it on Pruet's desk.

"Great," he said. "Let me introduce you to The Undertaker's girlfriend."

Le Marais, Paris

20

The literate gypsy known as Bela, using a public phone outside a Chinese restaurant, called the telephone number for the United States embassy he had found in the Metropolitan Directory.

Marjorie Jean (MarJean) Mathers of Austin, Texas, employed by the State Department for three months and beginning her second week in Paris, answered, "*Ambassade des Etats-Unis.*"

"I speak English," Bela said. He did not want his meaning to get lost in translation.

"How nice," MarJean replied, "so do I. How may I help you?"

"I wish to speak with the president's henchman."

MarJean knew immediately whom the man meant: James Jackson McGill, formally the First Gentleman of the United States. She knew all that, but at her pay grade she had no idea he was in Paris. She could only make an assumption of where he might be.

"I'm sorry, but he's in Washington, D.C."

"He is?"

"That's where he works."

"Nowhere else?"

Bela began to think his kinsmen might have been taken in by someone in their own line of work, conning the gullible. Had he kidnapped that horrible *gadjo* woman for no good reason? Would there be no huge ransom?

"I haven't heard that Mr. McGill works abroad," MarJean said

She was unsure now how much she should speculate about the activities of the president's husband. She thought maybe she should call her supervisor, but if the man on the phone was just a crank, she would be expected to dispose of him by herself.

"Perhaps if you can tell me what this is all about ..." Wouldn't hurt to fish a little bit.

Bela recognized a baited hook when one was dangled in front of him. But what choice did he have, if there were still some gain to be had. Perhaps he was only dealing with a fool here.

The gypsy said, "I have the woman he wants."

Okay, now it was getting weird, MarJean thought. Her caller ID had automatically tagged the guy's phone number once she connected to it. Now, she brought up the phone's location on a city map. He was calling from a public phone in Le Marais—wherever that was.

All calls to the embassy were recorded for security purposes, so MarJean had to be careful how she phrased the thought at the front of her mind.

"Are you saying, sir, that Mr. James J. McGill is here in Paris and he asked you to procure a woman for him?"

The woman *was* a fool, Bela thought. She thought ... well, he did say he had a woman for a man. And if the woman he did have wasn't a *putain*, he wasn't a Rom. Still, there had to be more to it than that. If an important man simply wanted sex, any pretty woman would do, and the boy, Alexandru, had said the president's henchman already had an attractive woman with him. So—

"It is not like that," Bela said.

"Well, what is it like, sir?"

"I don't know!"

MarJean, unruffled, summarized, "You have a woman for Mr. McGill, but you don't know why you have her?"

The infuriating *gadjo* woman was right, Bela thought. He didn't know why he'd kidnapped the *putain*. He should be angry only at himself. *He* was the fool here.

"I hope, sir," MarJean said, pressing a button to alert embassy security, "that the woman you have for Mr. McGill without knowing why is with you voluntarily. If she isn't, I urge you to release her immediately."

The embassy woman's words were softly spoken, but they raised the hair on Bela's neck. She was not a fool at all. She understood criminal activity was at play in his call. He looked around to see if a squad of *flics* was closing in on him. But he saw only a bovine crowd of milling *gadje* tourists. Still, the police might be just around the corner.

Bela instructed the embassy woman firmly, "Listen to me. I have the woman the president's henchman wants. He knows why he wants her even if I do not. If he does not pay me well for her in the next twenty-four hours, I will throw her in the Seine."

"But, sir—"

Bela hung up on MarJean.

It was only then he realized he had not given the embassy woman a way for the president's henchman to contact him. He would have to call back.

But not now. Now, he had to get away.

Magistrate Pruet's Office

21

Glen Kinnard's jaw was wired and his hands were cuffed behind his back when Odo brought him into Pruet's office. McGill stood as the men entered and he winced when he saw what he'd done to Kinnard. Dark Alley tended to be a frightfully effective way to defend yourself. Comfort came in the form of the oldest rationale in the book: Better him than me.

Odo said, "I took the precaution of restraining the prisoner."

In case he felt like taking another run at McGill.

"Glen?" McGill asked.

Kinnard shook his head.

"You sure?"

He nodded.

McGill looked at Pruet. "I'd appreciate it if you would unhook him."

The magistrate gestured to his bodyguard. Kinnard's hands

were freed.

"Have a seat, Glen," McGill said.

He took the chair to McGill's left. The president's henchman returned to his seat. Odo stood behind Kinnard. Which was okay with McGill. Some people you could trust only so far.

Kinnard glanced at McGill and then turned to Pruet.

"You are being treated well, m'sieur?" the magistrate asked.

Kinnard nodded.

"You have no complaints?"

Through compressed lips, Kinnard mumbled, "I'm missing the baseball season."

Pruet looked at McGill, uncertain of what he'd heard.

"Everyone's a kidder," McGill said. "He'd like to go home."

The magistrate turned back to Kinnard. "Our investigation is making progress, m'sieur. And now, if you don't mind, we would like to have your assistance."

Kinnard's eyes narrowed with suspicion and he turned them on McGill.

"Relax, Glen. You're not being set up. We just want you to look at a six-pack. You think you can do that?"

He continued to stare at McGill for a moment, then nodded.

"*M'sieur le magistrat*," the president's henchman said.

At McGill's suggestion, Pruet had sent Odo out to see if the photo of Diana the stripper could be matched to someone who had a criminal record. They'd found an indisputable match, according to the facial recognition software. Their perp had a record for prostitution, public drunkenness, and cutting a man with a knife. The last charge was dropped when the victim admitted he'd tried to have his way without first paying for it.

There was something in Ms. Martel's file that had made Pruet frown when he read it; McGill practiced a moment of self-restraint and didn't inquire what the problem was. If the magistrate chose not to tell him, he'd write it off as purely a French thing.

Diana Martel's mugshot was put along with those of five

other similar looking women in a 3x2 cardboard grid. Pruet took out the photo array and placed it on his desk in front of Glen Kinnard. McGill wondered just how good a look Kinnard had gotten of the woman in the low light under the Pont d'Iéna, and how well he retained his visual impression after the beating he'd suffered—two beatings, now that McGill had clocked him—and the passage of the intervening days. Glen might pick the wrong woman, and then where would they be?

But McGill's misgivings were quickly dispelled. Kinnard tapped his right index finger on Diana's photo without a moment's hesitation.

Even so, Pruet asked, "You are sure, m'sieur?"

Kinnard hit the picture hard two more times, then sat back.

"Thank you, m'sieur. We are looking for this woman right now."

Kinnard held his hands out as if to say, "Well?"

Pruet responded, "We will move you to more comfortable quarters, m'sieur. But we cannot release you for the time being."

McGill said, "The magistrate will find the woman for you, Glen. You still want me to stay on the case?"

Kinnard nodded emphatically.

"It's costing your daughter a fair amount of money."

Kinnard tapped his chest with his right hand.

"You want me to put you on the clock and take her off?"

"Yeah," the ex-cop grunted.

"Anything else we can do for you?"

Kinnard voiced something Pruet couldn't understand.

"What was that he said?" the magistrate asked.

"Satellite TV," McGill told Pruet. "He really would like to watch some baseball."

While that was being negotiated, McGill's thoughts turned in another direction.

He wondered where the heck was Gabbi after all this time.

Fifth Arrondissement, Paris

22

The moment Gabbi Casale pulled up in front of Arno Durand's building on a side street off the Rue Mouffetard she knew something was wrong. The three casement windows at the front of the sports reporter's flat were open. Durand had told her the preceding night, after she'd given him a lift home, that when he had female companionship and the night air was pleasant he left his windows open. So that the music of his lovemaking might be added to the soundtrack of the city: the jazz, pop, and reggae coming from other apartments; the rush of traffic from Rue Mouffetard; the polyglot conversations rising from the streets of the Latin Quarter. When he was alone, though, all that noise kept him from getting his sleep and he kept his windows closed.

As Gabbi had declined Durand's offer to spend the night with him, the windows should have been shut. Of course, he easily could have gone out after she had left and found another woman. After having been aroused by the soiled flowers of Pigalle, that might have been the expected thing for Durand to do.

Only there was a far more ominous sign that all was not well. To the right of the shuttered ground floor restaurant, the door to the stairway leading to the two flats above hung open, kept standing only by its bottom hinge.

Paris was not a town where people left their doors unlocked.

Much less hanging open. A sign too clear to miss.

A big predator had fed and the scavengers were welcome.

In normal circumstances, Gabbi would not have hesitated to call 17, the police emergency number. But her situation was anything but normal. She was working with James J. McGill, and McGill had involved Durand in this affair. If things had gone badly for the reporter, the fallout might land on the husband of the president. An event of this sort had not been covered by her State Department training but she couldn't see that letting bad publicity happen would be a good thing.

She took another look at the building and at the street

nearby. Apparently, the ground floor restaurant relied on the dinner trade and no one had arrived for work yet. The flat immediately above the restaurant appeared to be vacant. Durand had told her it was tied up in a probate fight. No pedestrians were nearby. She slid out of the Peugeot, taking her handgun out of her pocket and holding it pressed against her leg.

She crossed to Durand's displaced door and peered through the opening. The staircase, in stark contrast to the door, was unblemished. Polished oak stairs were covered with a plush wine red runner. She thought she ought to be able to tiptoe up that without making a sound. Still, she was going to be bummed if her actions got her declared *persona non grata* and kicked out of France.

Of course, Mom, Dad, and Gianni would be *really* depressed if she came home in a box.

That thought was sobering enough to make her stop and think: Maybe what she ought to do was call McGill. If he was with her and they ran into trouble, he'd take the weight … she was pretty sure. He had the clout to absorb the blow without getting hurt. He'd shield her.

Of course, all that was looking at things from a selfish point of view.

Arno Durand might have a different take on things. He could be upstairs in his flat, busted up as bad as his front door. If she waited for McGill to arrive, Durand might die while she was taking the time to cover her ass. She didn't like the reporter, but she wasn't sure she could live with that.

She quietly muttered, "*Merde*," and slipped past the dangling door, taking care not to make any noise or impale herself on projecting splinters.

Once inside, she noticed two things. She could hear her heart beating like a kettle drum, and she could smell a body odor so powerful and offensive it was almost a physical assault. It made her eyes start to water. God! Contrary to U.S. stereotyping, the French people she knew were scrupulously clean, but this guy could start folk tales all by himself.

There was no question in her mind who she was facing here: The Undertaker.

She hoped to hell if she had to confront the SOB, it didn't take more than a whole clip to kill him. Of course, as bad as the stench was, maybe she'd pass out before she got a shot off.

To lessen the chance of that happening, she clicked off the safety and extended the weapon in front of her as she began her climb. She fixed her eyes on what lay above; a skylight banished any shadow big enough to hide someone lying in wait. None of the stairs betrayed her with a creak or groan. She was grateful for small favors, but she could still feel beads of sweat rappelling down her spine.

Approaching the first floor landing, Gabbi lowered her gaze to look at the door to the vacant flat. It stood squarely in its frame, no sign of being disturbed. Caution dictated trying the doorknob to see if the door was locked, but that might give her away.

It didn't seem likely to her that a brute who had torn one door off its hinge would have a change of heart and neatly close another behind him. Still, it wouldn't do to be faked out by the monster she was dealing with here. Then she came up with a solution to the problem—but the very thought of it made her wince.

She'd reasoned that a huge hunk of stink couldn't possibly be hiding behind that door without the density of the stench being increased by a factor of ten. Steeling herself, Gabbi crept close and drew a deep breath. It almost made her choke, but the reaction came only from gulping the air instead of sipping it. The Undertaker wasn't lurking in the vacant apartment.

Sure that she would never recover to smell another rose, Gabbi was nonetheless onto something. She sniffed her way up to Arno Durand's flat, noticing no increase in the general stink. She had to hold the pistol with both hands now as her palms grew damp. The door to the reporter's apartment, she saw, had been knocked completely out of its frame. It lay on an oriental carpet like a corpse awaiting the medical examiner.

More important, though, the BO level held steady.

Gabbi entered the flat in a crouch, suddenly no longer aware of any scent. Her sensory input had been reduced to painfully acute vision and a steady high-pitched tone ringing in her ears. She took in an apartment whose furnishings were suspiciously undisturbed. She'd expected a shambles, with Durand's body lying prostrate in the thick of it. Instead, the only thing that caught her eye was a window in the kitchen at the rear of the flat. Just like the ones in the living room at the front of the place, it was wide open. Unlike the others, the kitchen window didn't have a screen to keep out flying bugs.

She crept forward keeping low, her field of vision rounding into a literal tunnel, the tinnitus in her ears sounding like a tuning fork struck with a sledgehammer. She was so low when she entered the kitchen she was duck-walking. She swung her pistol in a one-hundred-and-eighty degree arc, and then back again. Then a sudden wisp of fear that The Undertaker might somehow be sneaking up behind her made her pivot and fall to her knees. It was from that supplicatory posture she pointed the weapon back the way she had come.

The flat remained as empty as ever. That left her only one thing to do.

She got up, knowing she was already too late. She saw now that the kitchen window's screen, like the two doors, had been forced out of place. She leaned against the casement next to the opening, stuck her head out and looked down.

There he was, Arno Durand, lying face down in the alley thirty feet below. It looked to her as if he had jumped, escaping the murderous intent and vile stench of the creature that had battered its way into his home. Had The Undertaker thrown Durand out the window, she was sure he would have flown farther, perhaps to the roof of the two-story building across the alley.

McGill had been right about the danger the reporter had faced.

Poor, sad, lecherous—

Gabbi saw a puddle forming on the pavement between Durand's legs.

Wasn't there a moment ago.

It took a second, but she realized the man had just peed.

Dead men didn't do that. They voided on expiration.

Oh, Christ! Had he just died?

The back door was bolted. Gabbi had to undo three locks before she could race down the stairs to see if she could aid Durand.

France's Good Samaritan law required no less of her.

Chequers, Buckinghamshire, England

23

The Secret Service agents who guarded the president and the detective constables from Scotland Yard who protected the British prime minister were ready for anything—except a vaudeville routine between their two principals.

The seven heads of government present at Chequers stood in an anteroom, making small talk as they waited for the cue to make their public appearance. The day was so gloriously fine that Norvin Kimbrough had decided that the G8 leaders would make their momentous announcement on the phasing out of crop subsidies on a terrace in full sunlight. A mob of reporters, photographers, and videographers was already in place, and growing restless in the surprising warmth of the day.

The media people had been firmly instructed that their questions would be limited to the substance of the new agreement, an exercise in diplomacy that would materially improve the lives of millions of people in developing nations. Contrary to that, no questions would be taken concerning the gossip involving the presidents of the United States and France.

Of course, England being a free country and having a tradition of brash reporting, should any of the newsies have the temerity to overstep their bounds, well, they couldn't exactly be thrown into the Tower of London, could they?

Presidents Grant and Severin would simply have to stand in front of the world's press stone faced until the offending buggers were removed. And if the miscreants chose to make a spectacle of their ejections, well, that would only prolong the embarrassment.

Exactly what Norvin Kimbrough hoped to see.

Then his minions would leak the detail of the Darden-Severin romance at Yale.

Who knew what mischief that might cause?

But Kimbrough was sure his position would be enhanced as theirs were diminished.

The usual protocol for the type of appearance the G8 leaders were about to make would have the leader of the host nation introduced first. He would then greet his visiting colleagues one by one as they were introduced and took their respective places in a lineup of smiling faces for the benefit of the media and their respective populaces. So when Norvin Kimbrough approached Patti and Erika Kirsch with a novel suggestion before the show got started, Patti smelled a rat.

"Madam President, Madam Chancellor, I have it in mind that we might do with a bit of gallantry today, and let the ladies lead the way. Put our best faces forward, so to speak, before we bring out the chaps. Would that be acceptable to both of you?"

The prime minister had asked his question with a bright smile.

His makeup had been applied far too heavily, Patti thought, giving him a seamless vinyl finish. Made him look like a Norvin Kimbrough action figure. The prime minister wasn't at all a bad looking man, but today he was trying too hard to look too young. And while modern makeup stood up quite nicely to the heat of television lights, a moment too long in direct summer sunlight could make it run like wax under a flame.

Patti had done her own makeup—far more lightly—and that of Erika and Jean-Louis.

The president said, "If that's your wish, Prime Minister."

The chancellor nodded impassively. Erika was also suspicious.

Out of the corner of her eye, Patti could see Jean-Louis. He couldn't quite conceal his merriment. He knew Kimbrough was about to attempt some sort of prank and, apparently, he had every confidence his friends would rise above it.

So they formed up with the two women in the group standing side by side at the head of the line. Kimbrough came next, followed in single file by Gordon Kendrie, Ichiro Sugiyama, Matteo Gallo, and Jean-Louis Severin. A member of Kimbrough's staff, standing outside, raised a hand to indicate all was ready. The Secret Service and Scotland Yard seconded that appraisal.

"Ladies, if you please," Kimbrough said.

The president and the chancellor spared each other a glance, nodded, and stepped outside. The temptation was for the two women to march, as if heading a wedding or graduation processional, but Patti let Erika have a half-step lead on her. The chancellor understood intuitively what her friend had done and maintained her small advance. The two of them strolled at a comfortable pace, looking natural, not like drum majorettes.

The walked along a cobblestone path toward a stage thirty meters distant; the media mob gathered behind a rope-line ten meters farther on. Both women were glad they had worn shoes with low heels. Walking the stones in high heels would have been treacherous. As it was, there were two patches of shade cast by trees where everyone had to watch his or her step as the light level fell and rose.

A voice speaking over a public address system announced, "Ladies and gentlemen, the leaders of the G8. *Mesdames et messieurs...*"

The newsies normally responded with pro forma applause. Today, however, having received press handouts detailing the fact that the politicians had actually accomplished something of substance, the media broke with tradition and cheered.

Every pol in the world knew how to respond to that: a smile and a hand held high in recognition, and implicitly calling for the cheers to continue.

But as both the president and the chancellor were about to emerge from the second patch of shade, each woman dropped her raised hand just enough to shade her eyes. Erika's step faltered ever so slightly as her foot searched for a secure landing on the next cobblestone. Instinctively, Patti's left hand moved out to steady her friend.

That was when she felt a hand reach out to her. Not to help her maintain equilibrium, but to grope her. Norvin Kimbrough was feeling her ass. Not in any way that could be passed off as brief, accidental contact. His hand slid from cheek to inner thigh.

The bastard had to think he would get away with it. Her ass and his hand were still in shade. No one would see. If she jumped or even shrieked, it would be attributed to a misstep like the one Erika had almost taken. Of course, he also had to count on Patti not turning to confront him then and there, creating an international scandal at a moment of diplomatic triumph.

He was right on that point. Patti was not about to undermine what they had achieved. But a point of white-hot flame had ignited inside her.

Nobody laid a hand on the President of the United States.

She remembered what Jim had told her about executing a foot-trap. She'd practiced it privately many times. Had mastered the move precisely. Now, though, she had to appear to take a pratfall.

Instead of jumping up or forward, she let her left ankle roll outward as if she had turned it on one of the stones. Looking for balance, her right foot took a half step back. It came down right where she wanted: on Kimbrough's foot. She ground his toes under her heel. Managed not to laugh when she heard *his* shriek. But she wasn't done with him yet, not by a long shot.

Jim had told her the most interesting thing about Dark Alley was the way it allowed you to improvise. Once you had successfully countered an opponent's attack, a world of possible responses presented themselves. You only had to instinctively pick out the one you liked best. Of course, the choice you made revealed just how vicious you were.

Patti felt particularly heartless. The right arm she had held up to shield her eyes from the sun swung backward, as if it were following her foot in the search for balance. Her elbow drove hard into Kimbrough's cheek and nose. The blow forced him backward, but his foot was still trapped under Patti's heel. Jim said this kind of contradiction of forces did terrible soft-tissue damage. That was confirmed by a dreadful high-pitched whine that exited the prime minister's throat.

There were also unintended injuries. The back of Kimbrough's head, as he fell, clipped Gordon Kendrie of Canada smartly on the chin, dropping him like a Sunday punch. Patti let go of Kimbrough's foot at that point, lest any other collateral damage be done. She turned the release into a spin and a stumble, winding up on her backside, her outstretched hands keeping her semi-erect. Her back was toward the media mob and its wall of cameras.

The first face she saw belonged to Ichiro Sugiyama. Japan's prime minister was not looking at his fallen colleagues, but at her. He was studying Patti. More than that, he was replaying what he'd seen in his mind. Analyzing her movements. Each head of government present had read the others' *curricula vitae*. So Patti knew Sugiyama held an advanced black belt in aikido.

She was sure he'd never come out and say the President of the United States had attacked the Prime Minister of the United Kingdom. But he would have an insight into her the others would lack—and he would never walk too closely behind her.

Hearing men racing her way now, Patti shifted her gaze. Gordon Kendrie looked as if he'd curled up on the path for an afternoon nap. She thought she could even hear him snore softly. Norvin Kimbrough, on the other hand, lay on his side with his eyes closed and his mouth open and dripping blood. Patti's elbow had cleared a wide trough through Kimbrough's makeup, creating the effect that half of his face had been pushed up against his nose, itself displaced at an odd angle.

Patti hoped she hadn't killed the bastard.

Before she could explore that notion any farther, Jean-Louis and Erika were kneeling next to her, each of them supporting her with a hand on her back.

"*Mein Gott,* Patti, are you all right?"

Jean-Louis just looked at her, his eyes bright with concern—and admiration.

Patti wanted to say she was fine, but that wasn't what the script called for.

Letting her eyes go out of focus, she asked, "What happened?"

Georgetown

24

There was a knock on the outer door of McGill Investigations, Inc. Sweetie had left it locked while she worked in Jim's office. You never knew when a loon off some nearby pond might light on your doorstep. Sweetie thought she should talk with Dikki Missirian about installing surveillance cameras.

She didn't pick up her handgun, but from out of the line of fire she called out, "Who's there?"

A voice with a thick brogue responded, "It's yer landlord, missus. The rent's o'erdue a week now, an' I'll soon be puttin' yer things on the street."

Putnam had her fooled for a moment. She hadn't known he could do impressions.

"That's okay," she said. "I'm going back to the convent."

"If that's the case, I'll be puttin' me head in the oven."

Sweetie had to laugh. She went into the outer office and unlocked the door. Putnam was there with a briefcase and a bag of food from a place called Little Saigon.

"I can't have your death on my conscience," she told him. "I'll stay in the apartment. And I'm sorry I forgot about the rent." He'd been right about that. "I'll write the check right now."

But after she'd let him in, she relocked the door first.

They went into Jim's office. Sweetie sat behind the desk; Putnam took a visitor's chair. He placed the bag of food on the desk. Ever thoughtful, he placed it atop a copy of the Washington Times he'd also brought along.

"I didn't have lunch yet," he said, "so I stopped for carry-out: sesame chicken, egg rolls, steamed rice, and iced green tea. There's enough for two, if you're hungry."

Sweetie wrote a check, ripped it from its pad and handed it over.

Then she opened a desk drawer, took out a pair of lacquered chopsticks, a geisha painted on each one, and clicked them together in anticipation of the food.

Putnam asked, "Are those Mr. McGill's?"

"Yeah, but Jim won't mind. I mean, I've bled all over the guy and he didn't wince. I wash off his sticks, it won't bother him a bit I used them. But don't let that get around, okay?"

Putnam took all that in and had to ask, "Margaret, I'm happy to help you, and I'd like to think I wouldn't object if you bled on me … but is there any chance what I'm doing for you might lead me to do any bleeding of my own?"

Sweetie gave the question serious consideration as she set out the food. She seized a piece of chicken with Jim's sticks, dipped it in ginger sauce, popped it in her mouth and chewed. Followed it with a swig of tea.

"Up till now, you've been safe, Putnam. But you raise a good point. I was going to ask you to do something for me, but maybe I'll look for another approach."

They ate in silence for several minutes.

Then Putnam said, "Horatio Bao has several clients with criminal records."

"What kind of criminal records?"

"Strong-arm thuggery. Extortion. Robbery. Carjacking."

"No homicides?"

"Only the manslaughter charge filed and dropped on Ricky Lanh Huu"

"I thought Mr. Bao didn't do criminal defense."

Putnam said, "He doesn't. He does real estate mostly."

Margaret arched an eyebrow to indicate the contradiction in Putnam's testimony and ask for clarification.

He told her, "Bao has helped his ex-cons become propertied people. At least, he's the lawyer of record on purchases of real property by a bunch of former jailbirds."

"What kind of property?"

"Single family homes. Nice ones. Nothing big or fancy, but pleasantly middle class."

"How many?"

"Six that I found so far."

"Iffy neighborhoods?" Sweetie asked.

She was thinking: rock houses given a veneer of respectability. Make things less obvious to the narcotics squads.

But Putnam shook his head. "All of them are in nice, quiet neighborhoods. Good school districts. Libraries and parks. Where a lot of people would be happy to live."

Sweetie shook her head. "Street creeps don't live in those places, and they certainly don't have the money or the credit history to buy homes like that. So what's the angle?"

Putnam looked down and went back to eating, but not before Sweetie caught the look of guilt in his eyes.

"Putnam," she said, "what did you do?"

He sighed and looked up. "I drove out to Virginia to check out one of the houses. See if I could get a glimpse at who lived there. I felt the same way you do: street-level bad guys don't live in nice places."

"And what did you find?"

He took a digital camera out of his briefcase.

"I'll show you," he told Sweetie.

Marine One, in flight

25

White House physician Artemus Nicolaides directed a beam of light at the president's eyes as they flew back to London aboard Marine One. Chief of Staff Galia Mindel looked over Nick's shoulder as he conducted his exam. A private hospital in London had been alerted, should the president's condition require lab work, radiology, or surgery.

But Nick said, "Madam President, I am very relieved to say your eyes are equal in size and reactive to light. You pulse and heart rate are within normal range. For a twenty-five-year-old, even."

Patti favored Nick with a small smile, and the physician's own well being improved. Even Galia let herself relax, to the extent that her shoulders sagged.

"You are sure you didn't hit your head?" Nick asked.

He'd yet to see the video that would be replayed for years to come.

"Yes, I'm sure, but I did hit Norvin Kimbrough's head a pretty good shot," she said, rubbing her right elbow.

"Let me see that." He helped the president remove her suit coat and examined the arm. "Considerable swelling. Can you bend your arm?"

Gingerly, the president tried. She hadn't gotten far before she started to grimace. Nick turned to the helicopter's Marine crew chief, standing nearby in his dress blues.

"Please bring me a cold-pack for the president's arm."

"Yes, sir."

While the Marine went to the aircraft's medical supply locker, Patti said quietly, "If it weren't so embarrassing, I'd ask Sergeant Kendricks for another cold-pack to sit on."

Nick smiled, but he said, "If the pain persists, we'll do an MRI."

He cleaned and disinfected the abrasions on the president's palms. When the cold-pack arrived, he secured it to Patti's arm.

"You gave us all a terrible scare today, Madam President. But you appear to have come through the incident with only minor trauma. But I will visit you hourly for the next four hours, and every two hours after that for the next twenty-four hours. Your affairs of state will have to allow for my presence. Don't hesitate to take the ibuprofen I provided, if your elbow—or anything else—causes you discomfort."

"Yes, Nick. Thank you very much."

He nodded and went aft. Galia took the seat next to the president.

She asked, "Just how hard did you land on your anything else?"

"Hard enough that if I have to forgo sitting on a cold pack, I'd love a hot bath. Do we have any word yet on Prime Minister Kimbrough or Prime Minister Kendrie?"

"Kimbrough is having surgery. You broke a cheekbone and his nose. And some toes. And he may be concussed. Other than that, he's fine. When Gordon Kendrie came to, he thought he'd gotten knocked out in a hockey fight. The idea cheered him greatly. He's promised to take his skates and stick out of mothballs. He should be fine."

The president smiled. "Old footwear never fits," she said. "Make a note to send Prime Minister Kendrie a new pair of skates and a half-dozen sticks with my best wishes."

Galia waited a beat, and then she asked, "And Kimbrough?"

"I'll think of something for Norvin. Who handled the G8 announcement? The show did go on, didn't it?"

"Yes, Erika Kirsch, Matteo Gallo, and Ichiro Sugiyama did the honors. The Fleet Street crowd was less than amused not to have you and President Severin to feast upon. They've already started making wisecracks about the new policy being an Axis plot."

"They would," Patti said.

"Her Majesty called."

"She did? Herself?"

Galia nodded. "She's very concerned about your well-being. She asked me to call the palace and let her know your condition."

"I'll return the call personally. After we reach Winfield House. After I've bathed. Have you figured out what Sir Robert Reed is up to?"

"I think so. I have a few more people to call, then I should have it nailed down."

"Would you care to share or should I be patient?"

"On this one, patience."

"How nice," she said. She took the ibuprofen Nick had left for her. Her bottom was hurting even worse that her elbow. Be a damn fine joke if the president of the United States wound up with her ass in a sling. Patti closed her eyes, telling her chief of staff, "I really would like a long, hot bath. And maybe a nap."

"You had another call, Madam President," Galia said.

The president opened her eyes.

"Mr. McGill called. Before your mishap. He said he phoned me because he has information bearing on your presidency, but he didn't want to interrupt your G8 meeting. So he asked me to pass the word to you at an opportune moment."

"But he didn't tell you what the word was, did he?"

"No, and much as I hated to, I didn't ask."

"I know that was hard for you, Galia, but thank you."

"Yes, Madam President. You haven't forgotten the note I passed to you, have you? That the full Supreme Court has agreed to hear Erna Godfrey's petition that she be executed without delay."

The president closed her eyes again.

"No, Galia, I haven't forgotten that."

U.S. Embassy, Paris

26

In the fluid world of modern media, the Double Bump at Chequers, as the video had quickly come to be called, had made its way to ESPN with a pair of expert commentators, a gymnast and a figure skater, doing analysis with a SportsCenter host.

"See, see right there," the skater said. "That's where the president turned her ankle; that's where she lost her balance."

An optical move pushed in tight on the presidential ankle and froze the president's motion. The skater drew a telestrated circle to emphasize her point. Six video cams from the media menagerie present at Norvin Kimbrough's summer home had caught the action, but none had captured anything unique.

An unknown number of cellphones had also shot video of the moment, but their content had yet to be made public.

The gymnast said, "Let's back it up just a little."

The ESPN video marched seven of the most powerful people in the world backward.

"Stop right there," the gymnast said.

Along with millions of his fellow countrymen, Paul Legard, the United States ambassador to France, watched the video in his office overlooking the Place de la Concorde. Unlike Glen Kinnard, he already enjoyed the privilege of watching American sports on satellite television.

"You see," the gymnast continued, "that's when the other lady—"

"The German chancellor," the SportsCenter host said. "Erika Kirsch."

"Yeah, her. She broke stride, almost seemed to draw back."

"Good call," the skater conceded. "And there goes President Grant's hand to steady her."

"The president's smooth with that move, still in good control, but she must've taken her eye off where she was going because—"

"The ankle roll is coming right up," the skater said.

"Wait a minute," called the host. "Back it up a few frames, Charlie." The video clicked back frame by frame. "Stop. There, look at that. Not the president or the chancellor, but behind them. The British prime minister, he looks like he's already leaning forward to break the president's fall—it's hard to tell because of the shadow—but she hasn't even lost her balance yet."

The two analysts grunted.

"Got a good jump on the ball," the gymnast offered.

"Maybe he'd tripped around there himself," the skater suggested.

"Looks to me like he's copping a feel," Ambassador Legard

muttered to himself.

He couldn't tell for sure. What he knew for a certainty, though, the video of the Double Bump at Chequers would be studied as intensely as the Zapruder film of the Kennedy assassination.

There was a knock at his door. He clicked the TV off and said, "Come in."

Clarence Lee, Minister-Counselor of Management Affairs, the embassy's number two man, entered. He was accompanied by a young woman with butterscotch blonde hair and a visibly nervous manner. Either a college student whose boyfriend was in a French jail, the ambassador decided, or—

"Sir, may I present Ms. Marjorie Jean Mathers of Austin, Texas. She's the embassy's newest employee, with us just over two weeks now."

That was going to be Legard's next guess.

He was tickled, but kept a straight face, when Ms. Mathers curtsied to him. Then she realized what she'd done and blushed. Her anxiety became more pronounced.

"Please be seated, Ms. Mathers," the ambassador said.

Clarence guided her to a guest chair and took the adjacent one for himself. The ambassador, with a gentle paternal air, poured a glass of water for each of his guests. A few sips seemed to calm the young woman.

"You're all right now?" Legard asked.

"Yes, sir."

"Good." The ambassador took his seat behind his desk and looked at his number two.

"Ms. Mathers works at the switchboard. Her French is impeccable, and her Texas accent is *crème fraîche* on strawberries."

MarJean's face began to color once more, but Minister Lee moved on.

"Unhappily, Marjorie took a rather unnerving call today. She dutifully reported it to her supervisor, and the story has been rising through the hierarchy ever since. Please tell the ambassador, Marjorie."

MarJean told her story, and waited for the same questions she'd been hearing for hours now. But the ambassador came up with a new one.

"Have you ever heard a real threat of violence before today, young lady?"

Those words snapped MarJean right back to Texas. Made her forget all about her current discomfiture in Paris.

"Yes, sir, I have."

The scene appeared in her mind like a movie trailer. Wayne Hotchkiss, a linebacker on her high school football team, popping out of the dark the moment she and Lucy Winger had come out of the library after a night of studying for midterms. Wayne looked and smelled like he'd been drinking.

He told them, "You girls're gonna step over here with me where nobody can see us, and I'm gonna have me a cheerleader sandwich."

Both girls stood where they were, petrified.

Wayne fed off their fear, smiled, and took out a knife. Beckoned them with the blade. "Come on, now, 'fore I git mad an' cut you. An' I git mad real easy these days."

There had been several fights on the football practice field that season. Teammates going at it. 'Roid rage, all the rumors said. Wayne waved the knife and snarled, "Git over here before I have to hurt you."

Lucy started to whimper—and took a step forward.

That broke the spell for MarJean. She wasn't going to let an asshole like Wayne hurt her or her friend. MarJean stepped in front of Lucy. Wayne mistook that for eagerness. MarJean's right foot shot up. She tried to kick Wayne's balls all the way to Oklahoma, but she missed. As her foot continued its upward arc, she tried for his chin, but she missed that, too. She was in a bad spot just then, her right foot up over her head, and Wayne still holding his knife.

Wayne grinned real big, liking this new view of MarJean. He took a step forward and that was his undoing. MarJean's heel came down, slammed into his nose, taking the skin off from bridge to tip. Mashed it flat, too. Sent the football player sprawling.

The girls ran off and, despite fearing retribution, never told their parents or anyone else what had happened. It was to their great relief that Wayne attributed his injuries to a fall and never so much as looked at them again.

Now, MarJean was afraid Ambassador Legard was going to ask her the nature of the threat she had experienced. He very well might have if he hadn't seen the powerful emotions he had stirred in the young woman.

So he asked, "How did the threat you heard today compare to the one you just recalled?"

Looking at things through the lens of her own history, and fully realizing for the first time just how lucky she had been, MarJean said, "It was just as serious, sir. There's a poor woman out there in real trouble."

Hôpital Saint-Antoine, Paris

27

Gabbi drove so close to the bumper of the ambulance carrying Arno Durand to the hospital she felt she was pushing the damn thing. Psychologically, if the ambulance driver checked his mirror, she probably was. At least, the ambulance never slowed down, not until the driver turned the light bar off and his hazard lights on to let her know they were approaching the hospital and he would have to slow down to make the turn into the emergency entrance.

As there was a police car hard on Gabbi's bumper, she put her own flashers on. The three vehicles glided off the street and onto the hospital grounds. The ambulance continued on to the emergency entrance where a medical team stood waiting. Gabbi and the cops peeled off into a parking area.

The cop car sealed Gabbi's vehicle into its parking space and two cops jumped out. Neither drew his weapon, but each had his hand resting on it. One of them moved to each side of her car. They hadn't been in the alley behind Durand's apartment, hadn't seen she was the Good Samaritan who had called for medical help. She had knelt next to the reporter's body and could hear the thin, ragged thread of his respiration even before she found the pulse in his neck. Not knowing whether Durand had suffered spinal injury, she hadn't dared to move him. She just whispered to him to hang on.

"*Soyez fort. L'aide vient.*" Be strong. Help is coming.

She repeated the admonition in as many ways as she could conceive.

Not believing how long the damn ambulance was taking. Had they stopped at a café for a meal? Was the crew new to the city and couldn't find its way? What the hell was the problem?

Giving in to her frustration at one point, she muttered, "*Merde, merde, merde.*"

That was when Durand opened one eye and looked at her.

"*La bète fétide,*" he murmured. The foul beast. The Undertaker.

Then his eyelid slid shut, scaring the hell out of her once more that he'd died. But she found his pulse, though it seemed to be weaker. Just as she was about to fall into despair, the damn ambulance finally came, and when she looked at her watch, she saw that it had been under ten minutes in arriving. She quickly backed out of the emergency team's way, and a moment later ran around to the front of the building and got into her car.

There was a police vehicle—the one now blocking her car—at the mouth of the alley halting traffic so the ambulance might make an unhindered exit. Gabbi timed her move perfectly, letting the ambulance enter traffic and flashing around the police barricade the moment it had. The cops, startled by her maneuver and uncertain of her intent, were on her tail in a heartbeat.

And now two more patrol units arrived, these cars discharging gendarmes with automatic weapons. All of them neatly pointed her way.

Gabbi had her driver's window down and extended her official ID in her left hand.

"*Je suis diplomate américaine.*" I'm an American diplomat.

Not a weapon was lowered.

"*J'ai telephone à l'ambulance.*" I called the ambulance.

That eased the tension a little.

"*Vérifez mes mots avec le magistrat Pruet.*" Check with Magistrate Pruet.

The cops sighed in unison and lowered their firearms.

Annandale/Arlington, VA

28

"I do like this car, Margaret," Putnam said.

Sweetie was driving her Malibu, taking her landlord to see how Deke Ky was mending, but they were swinging by Annandale first to take a look at the residence of Edward and Marilyn Vinh.

"Must be worth more than the original sticker price," Putnam added.

Sweetie thought of how much the car meant to her.

"It's more valuable than I can tell you," she said.

Putnam understood. The car was more valuable than she cared to tell him, at least right now. He could live with that. He intended to outwait Margaret on a lot of things. He turned the conversation to a new topic.

"You don't think the Vinhs might recognize me?" Putnam asked.

Sweetie glanced at him. He was wearing sunglasses and a Washington Nationals baseball cap. She said, "Let me ask you something, and I'm in no way implying you're a bigot."

"That's good," Putnam told her, "because after my parents abandoned me as a child, I was raised by black people."

Sweetie came to a stop for a red light. Gave him a long look.

Like he'd said he'd been raised by wolves or something.

Putnam only smiled. Letting her know, okay, she might have secrets about her car and what it meant to her, but he had stories about his past, too.

Sweetie understood. Didn't pry. She could be patient, too.

The light turned green and she put the Malibu in motion.

She told him, "What I was getting at is this: Today, you saw the Vinhs, and you took pictures of them. Tomorrow, if one of them passed you on the street in D.C., would you recognize him?"

Putnam thought about it. "The kids, no. They're pretty young, fall into a generic Asian kid picture in my mind. The dad, probably not him either. Nothing about him struck me as memorable. The mom, though, she was pretty nice. I think I'd remember her."

If Putnam was trying to bait Sweetie, she didn't rise to it.

"What if Mom was wearing sunglasses and a scarf?" Sweetie asked.

Putnam tried to compose the image in his mind. He couldn't.

"Okay, you got me. So what's your point?"

"My point is, why do you think the Vinhs would remember what you look like for more than ten minutes? Why do you think they'd recognize you when you're wearing shades and a baseball cap. One of the most disappointing things a new cop learns is how unreliable eyewitness testimony is. People hardly ever see things in detail, and even when they do, few of them have the vocabulary to express just what it was they saw."

"And me being a white boy and the Vinhs being Asian, political correctness be damned, we all look alike to each other?" Putnam asked.

"Not so much alike, just a lot harder to process."

"Is that cop lore or a scientific fact?"

"Both. Cops have known it for a long time and science has caught up. There was a recent study done in a Boston children's hospital. It showed that as infants learn to specialize in recognizing the faces they see most often the ability to recognize other kinds of faces diminishes."

Sweetie turned onto a block of neat frame houses with large front lawns and mature trees. She pulled the Malibu to the curb a half-block distant and on the opposite side of the street from the Vinh house. MapQuest had led them every inch of the way. Sweetie had made the choice of parking in the shade of an oak on her own.

"So I shouldn't sweat being recognized," Putnam said.

"No, not specifically you. But if Mr. Vinh, say, was paying enough attention to see you snapping pictures, he might be on the look out for *any* strangers. That's a much easier visual task."

"That's why you parked in the shade," said Putnam.

"You always take whatever cover you can get."

Sweetie took a pair of Bushnell Compact Zoom binoculars out of the glove box and focused them on the Vinh house. No one was working or playing in front of the house. No bicycles or toys had been left on the neatly cut lawn. No pruning shears had been left in a flowerbed. The garage door was down. The curtains were closed tight on every window facing the street. Sweetie had the feeling that if the Vinh house had come with a drawbridge, it would be raised.

The Vinhs' defenses certainly had been.

She looked at Putnam. "Let's go over those photos you took."

Putnam pulled his camera from his briefcase and they looked at the display screen. He narrated, "Dad was washing the car; Mom was weeding the flower bed; the kids were playing marbles in that little patch of dirt in the corner of the lawn. I hadn't seen anyone doing that in years."

Sweetie nodded. The composite feeling of the photos was of a family at ease, enjoying the fine weather outside their peaceful home. Now, they were either hiding inside or had locked up tight before jumping in the car for parts unknown. Raising the question of what had happened.

"You took the pictures out the driver side window from this side of the street, right?"

"Just up there, by that pale yellow house," Putnam said.

Sweetie looked and estimated the distance between the yellow house and the Vinh house. Maybe sixty feet. Pretty close if one of the subjects of Putnam's portraiture, Dad or Mom, had reason to be watchful. Neither would have had to get a good look at Putnam himself to realize a stranger was taking pictures of them from his car. Putnam had even photographed the kids, which would be enough to alarm any parent. But maybe the Vinhs, with their connection to Horatio Bao, had other reasons to feel anxious.

If the Vinhs had gotten in touch with Bao, maybe he was feeling threatened, too.

Sweetie handed the binoculars to Putnam. He returned them to the glove box as she put the Malibu in reverse, backed into a nearby driveway and drove off the way they came, never passing in front of the Vinh house.

"Did I screw up?" Putnam asked.

"Probably."

"Shit."

Sweetie normally had little tolerance of vulgarity, but she didn't reprimand Putnam.

"Could work out," she said.

"How's that?"

"If I'm right, you called attention to yourself."

"That's good?"

"Like you said, you're a white boy. That's what the other side will be looking for. And they'll be puzzled what a white boy would be doing looking at the Vinhs. Meanwhile..."

"Meanwhile, what?"

"We bring in somebody who doesn't look like you at all."

29

Special Agent Donald "Deke" Ky opened the door to his mother's home, but only after the security camera mounted under the eaves identified the visitors. Sweetie was taken by how much better Deke looked than only a couple of days ago.

"You been drinking protein shakes?" she asked.

"Nice to see you, too, Margaret." Deke was looking at Putnam, evaluating his threat potential. He admitted both visitors to his mother's home.

"Mom here?" Sweetie asked.

Deke shook his head. He could get closed-mouth like that, Sweetie knew.

She introduced Putnam. The two men shook hands.

"You mind if we sit down?" Sweetie asked. "I'd like to talk with you about something?"

"What?" Deke asked.

"I think I might have found the person who rang your doorbell the night you got shot."

Deke's eyes narrowed to slits, a razor's edge of blue pupil gleaming from each one. He gestured to a sofa in the living room. Sweetie and Putnam sat next to each other. Deke took an armchair opposite them.

Sweetie told Deke straight out what they'd found out about Horatio Bao and Ricky Lanh Huu.

"That guy," Deke said. "Little jerk came to Francis's church. Tried to coerce Francis into going to see Bao, threatened him with a knife."

"Some guys just set themselves up for a fall," Sweetie said, shaking her head. "But I'm kind of surprised Father Francis shared with you."

"He wanted me to know in case anything happened to him."

Had the priest, in effect, sicced Deke on Ricky? If the creep had confessed shooting Deke to Father Francis, he couldn't do anything about that. But if Father Francis, himself, should fall victim to Ricky's predation, Deke would know just who to ... well, whatever Deke decided was fitting.

If that should fall outside the bounds of morality, Deke could always confess his sin.

It would be poetic. But Sweetie had her own ideas.

She said, "Let me tell you what we found out. Actually, Putnam found out, so I'll let him tell you."

Putnam told Deke about Horatio Bao's collection of jailbird homebuyers, and how when he went to look at one of the homes, he found a nice Viet-American family living there.

Deke took that in and asked Putnam, "How'd you find out

who the family is?"

Putnam turned red, looked at Sweetie. She nodded.

"I photographed his car, got the license plate. I used that to determine identity."

Access to the Virginia DMV database was supposed to be restricted to law enforcement personnel working with a valid need to know. Use of the database outside of those parameters was a crime—but Deke was on disability leave and didn't push the matter. He wanted to hear what else Margaret's friend had to say.

Putnam saw the federal agent's tacit acceptance of his transgression and continued. "Once I had Edward Vinh's name and address, it was easy to do a credit check. He's an auto mechanic at a service station in Alexandria, makes about 35K a year. His wife Marilyn adds another 15K working part time as a cook in a Chinese restaurant. They have two children, Thomas, age seven and Sarah, age six. The kids go to a parochial school in Annandale."

Deke had been processing the information as Putnam provided it.

"Working class family in a white-collar neighborhood."

"Median income 110K, more than twice what the Vinhs bring home." Putnam, being a lawyer, had thought to look into that.

"The guy who bought the house where this family lives, what's his rap sheet say?"

"Extortion, shaking down Viet immigrant businesses, and strong-arm robbery."

"What's the going rent for a house like the one where the Vinh's live?"

Putnam had looked that up, too. "Two grand to twenty-five hundred per month."

"Takes most if not all of Dad's after-tax income. These people look like they're scraping by?" Deke asked.

Putnam shook his head. "Looked like they fit into their neighborhood. Mr. Vinh was washing a late model Hyundai sedan out front. Mrs. Vinh was tending some nice landscaping. Kids were nicely dressed."

"Maybe they just know how to stretch a dollar," Sweetie said, deadpan.

Deke grunted. He asked Putnam, "You check how long the Vinhs have held their jobs?"

"No."

"Might be interesting to know. See if maybe there's unreported income."

"Cash," Sweetie said. "And Putnam came up with five more felons who used Bao to buy homes. You think you might be up to checking them out. See if they're renting to nice families, too. Maybe at a discount."

Deke nodded. "I've been needing to get out of the house."

"Maybe you can check out Bao's office lady, too. I'm pretty sure she's your bell-ringer."

"I could do that."

Sweetie told him, "I'd feel awful if I misjudged your health and you got hurt again."

"You want me clear this with SAC Crogher?"

Sweetie shook her head. "I'm just saying. You're not feeling up to snuff, I'll work out something else."

"Margaret, I start feeling faint, I'll get a protein shake. I would appreciate Mr. Shady's help with background checks and the like, seeing as he's so well connected."

Sweetie looked at Putnam, who nodded.

"We'll keep all this from your mother, all right?" Sweetie asked.

Deke said, "No problem there. Anything else, Margaret?"

"Just this. If there are other nice hardworking families in the other houses Bao's thugs bought…"

"Yeah?" Deke said.

"See if all their kids go to Catholic schools."

Hôpital Saint-Antoine, Paris

30

Arno Durand had suffered a concussion, two broken wrists, two dislocated shoulders, and two fractured knees. His doctors considered it a miracle he was alive and had incurred no spinal damage. But with all four limbs encased in plaster casts and his head bandaged, he looked like what he was: a man who would be a long time healing.

After he regained consciousness in his private hospital room, he had not only Gabbi for company, but also McGill, Pruet, and Odo. Durand chose to look at the Americans and avoid the eyes of his countrymen.

Gabbi asked, "You fought the law of gravity, and the law won?"

Everyone saw that Durand wanted to shrug, but that was beyond him.

He said, "Gravity was by far the lesser of my opponents. I tried to land like a cat. I extended my hands and arched my back, but I couldn't manage to point my toes."

"You survived," Gabbi said.

"Yes, thanks to you, I am told. *Merci.*"

McGill said, "Just to be clear, it was The Undertaker who broke into your apartment?"

"*Oui.* I would hate to think there was another like him."

Pruet said, "Please describe the incident as it happened."

The idea of visiting that memory made the reporter shudder under the weight of his casts.

"M'sieur, it was a nightmare from which there was no waking. I am alive, in part, because hunger visited me shortly before the monster did. I was in the kitchen at the rear of my apartment. I had only just taken an iron pan in hand to make an omelet when I heard what sounded like a clap of thunder. Moments later, there was another explosion and my front door burst from its frame."

McGill said, "Once you saw who'd broken into your flat, you

had no doubt your life was in jeopardy?"

Taking things very slowly, Durand shook his head.

"To see that face, m'sieur, was to understand there would be no mercy. For one lunatic moment, I thought I might bash the brute with the pan I held."

"You discarded the idea?" Odo asked.

"I improvised on it. I threw the pan at the bastard. It bounced off his head, possibly denting the pan but drawing not a drop of blood."

"Why didn't you run out your back door?" Pruet asked.

"There are three locks on it, m'sieur. I had no time to open them all."

"So you jumped," McGill said.

"I did, happy to have a window big enough to permit me to take flight. When I hit the ground, the pain literally blinded me, and I don't remember hearing anything either. But I knew I was still alive. I could feel blood bubbling out my nose as I breathed. But I thought I must have presented a fairly good likeness of a corpse, so I did my best to hold still. Sometime after that, I lost all awareness, and for all I knew I had died."

The reporter took a deep breath.

"It was an experience to make a man reflect on his life."

Gabbi's mobile phone sounded: Stars and Stripes Forever.

"Excuse me," she told the others. "I've got to take this."

She stepped out of the room. McGill moved closer to the reporter.

"If you'd had a chance to run," he asked, "do you think you could have outpaced him?"

Despite his injuries, the question amused Durand.

"I very much would have preferred running to jumping, and I cannot imagine a cheetah catching me, as frightened as I was."

McGill nodded. "A guy as big as that, I can't see him running too far before losing steam, either."

The sports reporter considered. "He might have a burst for twenty meters. He might keep up a slow run for half-a-kilometer. I don't see him going past that. His own mass would be the one opponent he couldn't defeat."

McGill and Odo exchanged a look. They both filed Durand's words in memory.

Gabbi came back into the room, concern clear on her face. She gently took McGill by the arm and pulled him into a far corner of the room.

"What's up?" he asked.

She whispered, "The president has put the prime minister of the UK in the hospital."

"And the president herself?" he asked.

"A sore elbow."

McGill repressed a smile.

Gabbi added, "And a sore backside."

McGill drew his head back, hearing that.

"There's video playing nonstop and worldwide," Gabbi told him.

Before he could respond to that, Gabbi turned to Pruet.

"*M'sieur le magistrat,*" she said, "the United States embassy received a call today asking for Mr. McGill. The operator who took the call assumed he was still in the United States. When she told the caller that, he informed her that he'd kidnapped the woman for whom Mr. McGill is searching—the missing Diana Martel, I presume. He said if Mr. McGill doesn't pay him handsomely for the woman, he will throw her into the Seine."

Durand's eyes bugged out. Here was the story he'd been hoping to get.

And now he had no way to write it.

Gabbi took notice and moved to his bedside.

"We'll work out something, maybe not the whole story, but you'll get something to publish." She looked at McGill and Pruet and got nods of approval. Turning back to the reporter, she said, "But I have one more question about The Undertaker. When I came to your apartment, there was an awful stench. How could he smell that badly and work in a strip club?"

Durand said, "He possessed no foul odor there."

"Then why did he stink to high hell at your place?"

"I have heard a story," Durand said. "I gave it no credence. That is why I did not mention it to you."

"What story?" McGill asked.

"It is said that The Undertaker, when he becomes frustrated for lack of a fellow his own size to fight, sometimes he grapples with bears."

"Bears?" Pruet asked in disbelief.

"It would explain the rank scent, *n'est-ce pas?*" Durand asked.

"Well, that's great," McGill said. "Grizzly Adams goes French."

31

McGill and Pruet stepped out of Durand's hospital room and moved down the hall, away from the two *flics* guarding the reporter's door.

The magistrate asked McGill, "Who is Grizzly Adams?"

"An American frontiersman of the nineteenth century. He lived in the mountains of the West and kept grizzly bears for pets."

Pruet asked, "This is a myth?"

"Supposed to be true. He'd wrestle the bears for fun. But one of the animals got cantankerous and split Adams' head open, exposing his brain."

"He was killed?"

"Not until later. Another head injury, incurred while training a monkey for P.T. Barnum."

"Now, you jest," Pruet said.

McGill shrugged. "I'm not saying that's what happened, but that's the way it's written."

The magistrate sighed. He walked farther down the hall, McGill keeping pace. The doors to all the other rooms were closed, and there were no medical personnel bustling about. The place was silent, peaceful. McGill got the feeling this was a wing reserved for very important patients, not doing much business at the moment.

"I am considering having you withdraw from this affair, m'sieur," the magistrate told the president's henchman.

McGill said, "Fine. Release Glen Kinnard, rescue Diana Martel, and my job here is done."

Pruet looked at McGill and frowned. "It would be premature to release M'sieur Kinnard at the moment."

"Yeah, but asking was worth a try, as long as you're trying to get rid of me."

The magistrate smiled. "It is not that I do not enjoy your company, but I worry what would become of me if I let you meet your end in Paris. I do not think even Jean-Louis could save me."

"You're probably right. My wife might bring some pressure to … I was going to say bear, but that would have been a terrible pun."

Pruet nodded, smiling again.

"Do you think," Pruet asked, "that this Undertaker fellow truly tests himself against wild animals?"

"Not with any success. But it's a good story; look how anxious it's made you."

"A brute with wiles." The magistrate shook his head.

"Yeah, it's better when they're dumb," McGill agreed. "You have to hand it to the guy. Who'd want to get in the way of someone who smells like a seven-foot pile of manure?"

Pruet's expression turned rueful. "I fear you would."

"Maybe with a ten-foot pole," McGill said.

"You have experience using such an object to defend yourself?"

"I'm pretty good with anything that comes to hand."

"You do not make things easy for me, m'sieur."

They came to the end of the hallway and stopped. A window looked out on the city. McGill thought Paris was quiet compared to big American cities. Fewer helicopters, sirens, cars roaring by with the stereo cranked high. Of course, the French blew up unattended bags left in public places. There was always something to disturb people's sleep.

Pruet told McGill, "Besides my concern about losing you, I also worry about having another American kill another Frenchman, even one who is an obvious villain."

McGill asked, "And what would you do in my place, *m'sieur le magistrat?*"

Pruet looked at his American counterpart. "Your accent really is quite good. As for me, I am also quite stubborn. That is why I am in my current predicament." He started walking back toward Durand's room, and McGill fell in step with him once more. Pruet said, "I will sleep on the matter. Perhaps I will awaken a glimmer more brilliant than I am today."

McGill extended his hand and Pruet shook it.

"*Et je, aussi, mon ami,*" McGill said. Me, too, friend.

The Hideaway, Paris

32

Regional Security Officer Gabriella Casale insisted that she sleep over at McGill's borrowed apartment. Her reasons were entirely pragmatic.

"For one thing," she told McGill on the drive over to the Hideaway, "it might take the two of us to gun down The Undertaker, if he comes to pay a visit."

"And you could claim to have fired the fatal round?" McGill asked.

"I will claim to have fired *all* the rounds."

"Two-gun Gabbi? An American legend is born. Can I play the part of McGill in the movie?"

"Sorry, you look too French."

McGill laughed. "I'm told I can do a good Rory Calhoun."

Gabbi had to smile. "We'll see. There's another reason we should stay together."

"Okay."

"You don't want to know what it is?"

"I'm sure you'll tell me."

"I will. The embassy is going to forward any new call regarding the ransom of Diana Martel to me. If the kidnapper insists on talking with you—"

"I'll be right at hand."

"Exactly. You know who has to have her, of course."

"Gypsies. Our kid probably found her, then the grownups screwed things up."

They pulled up in front of the pub. It was closed now, but Harbin stood watch behind the front door, waiting for them. At Gabbi's suggestion, he'd supplemented his customary escrima sticks with a bit more firepower: a Benelli Supersport shotgun. Harbin's precaution and Gabbi's presence were deemed necessary in case Arno Durand, in an exercise of reporter's guile, had learned where McGill was staying, and a written record of that information had passed to The Undertaker when he'd come calling.

Harbin opened the door for them and said, *"M'sieur, ma'amselle."*

"Bonsoir," McGill said.

Gabbi asked if everyone else at the pub had gone home.

"Oui."

McGill told Harbin, "We don't know if The Undertaker will come tonight, but if he does, use the gun. Don't try to use the sticks."

Harbin only nodded. McGill could see he didn't like the idea that there might be someone he couldn't put down with his favored weapon.

"Seriously," McGill said, "use the gun. Shoot him from behind, if you have to."

Harbin stiffened at the perceived insult. Gabbi placed her hands on Harbin's shoulders and whispered something to him in French. He relaxed visibly. He nodded again, and Gabbi kissed him on both cheeks.

McGill and his government chaperone headed upstairs. He waited until they were inside the flat and had the door closed and locked before he said anything.

"You told our friend down there that he wouldn't want any of The Undertaker's B.O. rubbing off on him?"

Gabbi smiled. "You really are smart, aren't you?"

"More than just a pretty face."

"I thought you might give me an argument about staying with you."

McGill shook his head. "You can even have the first shower. Just leave me some hot water."

"But make it long enough for you to make a phone call?"

"You're pretty sharp yourself."

Gabbi kissed McGill on each of his cheeks. That alone, McGill thought, would have been enough to calm him down, had he been displeased.

But as an extra measure of comfort, Gabbi told him, "There's another shotgun in the kitchen."

Magistrate Pruet's residence

33

"You don't wish me to come up with you, Yves?" Odo asked Pruet.

The two of them sat in Pruet's Citroën in front of the magistrate's residence on the Rue Anatole France. Passing traffic was light, a trickle of gourmands heading home from their favorite haunts.

"I will be all right, and you should spend at least a few minutes with your family."

"That would be pleasant. You are carrying the gun I gave you?"

The magistrate pulled the weapon part way out of his coat pocket, a Ruger SR9. Pruet hadn't wanted to carry a gun, but Odo said it would reassure him, let him do a better job protecting Pruet. Odo had been wise enough to select a weapon that was slim, light and stylish. Let his friend rationalize he was carrying a fashion accessory rather than a firearm.

But style had come with a caveat: "In normal circumstances," Odo had said, "a 9mm cartridge doesn't have the best stopping power."

"We certainly can't have that," Pruet had responded with a straight face.

"Which is why the cartridges for your gun will come from me and not the factory."

"You are in the munitions business?" the magistrate asked.

"Since I was a boy," the bodyguard replied. "Would you prefer an explosive round or one tipped with poison?"

Remaining deadpan, Pruet asked, "I can't have both?"

"You have a point. I will alternate the loads in the magazine."

"A perfect compromise."

Pruet had been joking, and he'd humored Odo further by taking target practice until he could hit the figure of a villain in the chest with regularity at a distance of five meters. Carrying the gun had filled the magistrate with a sense of regret rather than one of power. That the world and his place in it should have come to this ...*quelle honte.*

What a shame.

Tonight, though, his misgivings were mixed with the cold comfort of feeling the gun in his hand. Monsters were afoot, and he lived at a greater remove from the pavement than Arno Durand did. If he were to take flight from his balcony, likely there would be no resurrection for him. Better to—

"Remember," Odo said, "before you fire, you must disengage the safety."

Pruet nodded soberly. "I will try not to shoot myself in the foot."

The bodyguard frowned. "I hope to have you speak at my funeral; if I let you die, I would be far too embarrassed to speak at yours."

The magistrate said, "Perhaps M'sieur McGill might say a word or two." Getting out of the car, he added, "*Jusqu'a demain, mon ami.*"

Until tomorrow, my friend.

34

The stink rushed out to assault Pruet the moment he pushed opened the door to his building's lobby. He took a half-step back and turned to call Odo, but the bodyguard had driven off down the street, his car already turning onto the Boulevard St. Germain. The magistrate waved frantically, but Odo did not see his gesticulations.

"*Merde*," Pruet muttered.

He turned his head back to the entryway. His nose wrinkled as the stench hit it full on ... but he sniffed an underlying odor as well. He stepped back outside and let the lobby door swing shut. The smell of fresh air was almost intoxicating. The stink was gone, but the underlying scent was still present. In his mind, at least.

The familiar fragrance defined itself. Cacharel Liberté. His wife's choice of perfumes. Nicolette had been wearing it for as long as he could remember. She would be wearing it, he imagined, long after she had left him.

That was, if she hadn't already encountered The Undertaker.

The admixture of reek and bouquet suggested she had.

Pruet was surprised when he took notice that the Ruger was already in his hand and pointed at the entrance to his building. He was further amazed to see that he'd thumbed the weapon's safety off. Having done so blindly, he considered himself lucky not to have hit the nearby magazine release, scattering Odo's lethal projectiles all over the sidewalk.

Un moment, ma chère. One moment, my dear. I will be up to rescue you the instant I have collected all my bullets.

Pruet as hero was the stuff of farce, Pruet told himself. He took his iPhone out of his pocket. Odo was on speed dial. Regretfully, the bodyguard's reunion with his family would have to wait. Of course, if the Corsican bastard had turned off his mobile, he would have to—

His iPhone informed him its battery was all but depleted and it shut down.

The magistrate thumbed it back to life, a period lasting no more than three seconds before it shut down again. Pruet was ready to hurl the damn thing into the Seine, except it was even more stylish than his Ruger and had been a birthday gift from his favorite niece. He jammed the phone back into his pocket, and looked up at his balcony.

Darkness prevailed there. No light from his apartment filtered outside. Nicolette was not screaming bloody murder, which she would be doing unless she was already dead. But if she were dead, there would be no point rushing inside to meet what would likely be his own demise. As to his possessions, there was nothing he really couldn't do without.

Except his guitar.

The instrument had been with him longer than his wife, and their relationship had been happier, even when he broke a string. He would hate to lose his guitar.

Pruet looked up and down the block. Not a pedestrian in sight on either side of the street. The few cars that passed by took advantage of the light traffic to drive as though they were trying to qualify at Le Mans. If he ran into the street, especially with a gun in hand, he would leave the better part of himself in the treads of the car that ran him over.

Another farce.

With a sudden pang, Pruet wished he had the president's henchman with him.

The irony of wanting to dismiss McGill only an hour earlier was palpable.

To have to face The Undertaker alone was no less than he deserved. He pushed open the door to the lobby with his left hand. As Odo had trained him, since his gun was not on a target, his finger was not on the trigger. It really wouldn't do to shoot himself in the foot. Not with the rounds Odo had loaded into the Ruger.

Moving into the building, Pruet asked himself: *How would James J. McGill do this?*

The Hideaway

35

As soon as McGill heard Gabbi's shower come on, he called the President of the United States. If Patti wasn't off saving the world, she'd pick up by the fourth ring, or he'd hang up and try back later. That was the current protocol. As it was, she picked up on the third ring...

A heartbeat after Gabbi started singing in the shower.

"La Vie en Rose." In French. On key.

Before McGill could say hello, his wife asked him a question.

"Is that Edith Piaf you have with you?"

"I believe she passed on some time ago," he said.

"You're right. So who's the chanteuse?"

His wife's hearing was acute, McGill thought.

"That would be one of your underlings, my State Department bodyguard."

"A singing bodyguard, now there's a multi-tasker. But what's that static?"

So her hearing was excellent but not infallible.

"That would be the water from her shower."

"Ah," the president said. "The Secret Service hasn't used that tactic with me yet."

"She left me a shotgun for company."

"To supplement the fellow downstairs with the sticks."

McGill said, "He has a shotgun now, too."

There was a pause before Patti asked, "Anything you care to tell me?"

"My relationship with Ms. Casale is strictly platonic."

The president snorted. "I was referring to the need for shotguns."

"Well, there's this fellow." He told her about The Undertaker. "Magistrate Pruet is thinking of sending me packing."

The pause this time was far longer. Long enough for McGill to fill the silence.

"The guy is big as a house," he told his wife. "I'm sure I can outrun him."

"If you say so. But running really isn't your style, is it?"

"No, but if you don't mind my saying so, I think I know what's bothering you."

"And what might that be?" the president asked.

"You once told me you don't want to bury another husband. And I know my kids would hate to see me go. Even my ex-wife would shed some tears."

Sweetie, on the other hand, McGill knew, would come seeking vengeance.

"You're a well regarded fellow, that's for sure," Patti said.

"I won't do anything stupid. And I tend to see things coming from a long way off."

McGill was thinking how his first wife, Carolyn, had left him because she couldn't take the stress of being a cop's wife, and she hadn't lost her first husband to violence the way Patti had. But as long as Patti held the presidency she'd have more people gunning for her than McGill would ever have hunting him. He had to live with that.

But for each of them there were times that sorely tried one's faith.

Patti cleared her throat and said, "The singing has stopped, and so has the shower, I believe."

McGill hadn't noticed. Maybe someone could sneak up on him.

But he said, "Ms. Casale is a diplomat. She won't interrupt our conversation."

As if on cue, a hair dryer began roaring. McGill had to put a finger in his open ear.

The President of the United States told him, "Jim, I'm sorry if I wasn't encouraging just now. You do what you need to do. You have my unqualified support."

"Thank you. And you have mine. By the way, how's your elbow?"

He was pleased to hear her laugh. "It hurts like hell, but not as bad as my backside."

"Like that, is it? Maybe even with our magic phones we'd better save this conversation until we see each other next."

"That would be best, but you left a message for me with Galia, remember? So you must have something you can tell me now."

"I do."

McGill told her the source of the rumors about her and Jean-Louis Severin.

Nicolette Pruet, the alienated wife of Magistrate Yves Pruet.

Pruet, the longtime friend of the president of France.

Pen-pals, in fact, during their college days.

One last pause followed. McGill could imagine Patti putting a hand to her head.

"Jean-Louis wrote letters?" she asked. "While he was at Yale?"

"While the two of you were there," McGill said.

Magistrate Pruet's apartment

36

Yves Pruet took the elevator up to his apartment. The choice involved a number of considerations: shooting angles—straight on was better than shooting up a flight of stairs; lighting —the elevator car was brightly lit, the staircase more softly illuminated; most of all, the elevator car smelled of cut roses—the stairway stank of ...unwashed bear, if American legend were to be believed.

The elevator was operated either by a key from the lobby or sent from the top floor, inside Pruet's dwelling. There were no stops in between. Augustin Pruet had economized wherever he could, and at age 80 didn't mind climbing the stairs to the lower floors. The two flats below the magistrate's were used by family when they visited central Paris for an evening or a weekend, but they were currently unoccupied.

Pruet's plan was to take the elevator to his apartment's level and wait there with the doors closed. If The Undertaker were nearby, he would certainly hear the elevator's arrival, and when the doors didn't open, the brute would become curious. Likely, he would consider the closed car an ominous thing; he might even begin pounding on the doors in an attempt to break in.

In that case, Pruet would immediately send the car down to the lobby. Where he would wait with the doors closed. If the monster followed him down the stairs in pursuit, the magistrate would send the car to the top of the building again. If pursuit continued, down he would go again. Pruet's plan was to run the fetid fellow ragged without ever confronting him directly. At least not until he was exhausted.

Hardly a heroic plan, but it had the virtue of preserving Pruet's skin.

Except it did not work out at all as he envisioned.

The elevator car rose to the level of his apartment, whirring loudly enough for anyone inside the flat to hear, came to a stop, and nothing happened. Pruet waited ... and waited ... and no oversized fists beat against the car doors. Not a floorboard creaked under the weight of a 200-kilogram miscreant. There was no stentorian breathing nearby. No stink pervaded the magistrate's refuge. No menacing trill of violins portended the coming of doom.

Pruet considered the possibility that The Undertaker had the animal cunning to outwait his prey. If that were the case, he would have a long wait indeed. Pruet was a patient man. He'd stared down many a suspect, maintaining a stony, unblinking silence until the villain confessed.

But this time was different. He didn't have Odo's forbidding presence close at hand; he was alone. In an elevator car that seemed to grow hotter by the moment. Holding a gun that grew heavier by the second. Fear infiltrating his mind that somehow a hulk of a street criminal was outsmarting him.

And then he thought he heard Nicolette whimper.

At once, the scene became a fantasy conjured by the devil. The treacherous, faithless wife, constantly threatening divorce, lies at the mercy of a fiend. All one has to do is wait for fate take its course. The shrew is gone and being rid of her costs not a sou. What more could a fellow ask?

Perhaps to level one's gaze at a mirror without cringing from that day forward.

Sacré bleu, but the cost of maintaining one's self-esteem was high.

With his left hand, the magistrate keyed the elevator doors open. Doing so, he backed off and dropped into a crouch. If the monster wanted to seize him now, he would have to bend to do it. Pruet, meanwhile, would fire at least two rounds—one poisonous, one explosive—into The Undertaker. With his luck, he would kill the beast, which would then fall on him and crush the life from him. Or, worse, vengefully pin him and asphyxiate him with its stench.

But no vision from a nightmare presented itself to Pruet as the doors opened. All he saw were the shadowed outlines of his home and its furnishings. The door leading from the stairway to the foyer was open, soft light coming from a sconce on the staircase wall. The Undertaker's point of entry had not been subject to any brute violence … which meant that a door normally kept locked had been unbolted, perhaps even left ajar.

The Undertaker had buzzed Pruet's apartment? Nicolette had thought it was her deficient husband, having forgotten his keys, and she'd decided to let him climb the stairs rather than send the elevator? Must have been quite the surprise when she'd found out who had come calling.

Nicolette whimpered again. This time there was no doubt the sound was real. One of self-pity, not of terror or pain.

Pruet wanted to tell the damn woman to be quiet. He had more important sounds for which to cock his ear. The thump of heavy footfalls, a hair-raising snarl. But he could not silence Nicolette without giving himself away. Even at a time like this, his wife was a source of frustration to him.

The magistrate crept out of the elevator car, looking quickly to his left and to his right. He saw no intruder, large or small. But the smell was so bad now his eyes began to water. He blinked furiously to clear them. He placed his left hand over his nose and began breathing through his mouth, hoping his throat wouldn't close.

He moved out of the foyer into his living room. The glass doors leading to the balcony were open. Ambient light from the city presented a sight that pierced the magistrate's heart. His beautiful Alhambra guitar, bought when he was still a student, earned by working for Papa, by saving money from eating but once a day, lay in a thousand jagged shards of cedar and rosewood, strings broken and curled as if in agony. The sense of loss Pruet felt was greater than—

Nicolette whimpered yet again, and Pruet knew: She had done this.

Not The Undertaker. Her.

He moved through the apartment at an almost reckless speed now. There was no way the monster could conceal himself. If he were present, the closer one came to him the more vile the reek would become. If at any point Pruet felt his gorge begin to rise, he would empty his gun in the appropriate direction. Out of simple diligence, the magistrate went from the living room to check the dining room, the kitchen, the pantry, the wine room, the study, the library, both bathrooms, and all three bedrooms. No Undertaker in any of them, though his vile emanations lingered everywhere. The villain had been thorough in his trespass of Pruet's home.

But he hadn't wrecked anything other than the air quality.

The Undertaker was a killer but not a vandal.

The only physical damage he had done was to dent the door of the safe room.

Adjacent to the master bedroom, the safe room lay behind what looked like a closet door, only the door and its frame were five centimeters thick and made of steel. The structure was bullet and blast resistant. Papa originally had insisted that the room be built in case *les Boches* turned militaristic again. After decades of peace with Germany, Papa said the room might still be useful in the event of a terrorist attack, and while it was unlikely The Undertaker was motivated by either politics or religion, there was no doubt he inspired terror in his victims.

Bravo, Papa.

Nicolette whimpered once more. Pruet looked to his right. The sound came from the speaker of the phone answering machine on the nightstand adjacent to the magistrate's bed. What used to be his and Nicolette's bed. When Pruet had first shown his wife the safe room and she had seen that it was equipped with two cots, a chemical toilet, dehydrated rations, and bottled water, she had turned up her nose.

"I would rather die with a glass of wine in my hand," she'd said.

Upon The Undertaker's arrival, she obviously had changed her mind. And now some part of her was pressing against the intercom button that let those inside the room speak with those outside. This communication channel was a safeguard in case the door mechanism malfunctioned, turning the safe room into a cell.

For The Undertaker not to have pinpointed the direction of Nicolette's mewling, the man had to suffer from a hearing deficit of some sort. Perhaps a useful thing to know.

Pruet said in a quiet voice, "I have come for you, my dear."

A heartbeat of silence was followed by a shriek of fear that lifted Pruet a foot into the air.

"Yves, please, I am so sorry..." Nicolette was all but hysterical.

He could guess why: "You smashed my guitar."

"Yes, yes. That and everything else!"

Everything else? Snooping his files, he knew about that. Destroying his guitar, she had just made that confession. But what else?

"Please, Yves, don't let that thing kill me. I never would have suspected you'd send such an animal to devour me. I am your wife!"

She thought he had sent The Undertaker? *Très intéressant.* But he didn't like the note of indignation in her voice when she had reminded him they were still married.

How would McGill respond to that? What would an American say? Oh, yes.

"A man must do what a man must do."

The whimpering flowed in a steady stream from the safe room.

"You will destroy me, Yves?"

"What is my alternative?"

For a moment, there was silence. Then: "I will tell you *everything.*"

Pruet sensed there was a rare opportunity to be claimed here.

"You will also give me a divorce and make no claim on me whatsoever."

"*Oui.*"

"And you will put everything in writing," he added.

Silence.

"Very well," Pruet said, "I'll leave you to my friend."

"No, Yves, no! I will write everything down. Sign it and seal it with my blood."

Pruet smiled. He had been a man of almost infinite forbearance with Nicolette, but she never should have touched his guitar.

"Very well." He lifted the phone receiver from its answering machine base and tapped in the code that opened the safe room.

A minute later, Nicolette sat in Pruet's study writing out her confession.

And narrating it for the magistrate's audio recorder.

Georgetown

37

Try as she might, and Margaret Mary Sweeney tried mightily, she didn't live a life as free from sin as she would have liked. She was having serious second thoughts about bringing Deke Ky into the case. There was no question in her mind that either

Horatio Bao or Ricky Lanh Huu would kill a federal officer if he thought it necessary. If Deke were in top form, he'd be more than a match for either or both of them. But the question nagging Sweetie was whether she was bringing Deke back into the field too soon.

She had taken the task of tracking down the identity of the young woman she had seen doing Horatio Bao's mail run from Deke and given the job to Welborn. Maybe she should have the two of them work as partners. The young Air Force captain was soon to be married, and Sweetie feared that if she put him in harm's way he might not make it to the church on time, or ever. But if she didn't use Welborn, Deke would have to take more risks.

She could back up Deke, of course, but that would take her away from working the clerical angle—Father Francis Nguyen and Bishop George O'Menehy—and she didn't want to do that.

The dilemma was enough to make her curse or at least want to.

On top of all that, there was Putnam and his crack about being abandoned by his family. The remark had been off the cuff, but she had the feeling he was telling the truth. Probably about being raised by black people, too. Her feelings for her landlord, despite her best intentions, were becoming increasingly ... unplatonic. He was too young for her, too glib, likely too kinky if she let things develop in that direction, but he was smart, caring, and occasionally courageous. If she were ever to have a man in her life at all, she could do far worse.

Sitting alone in the offices of McGill Investigations, Inc., Sweetie thought it would be comforting to have Jim to talk to.

And just then the phone rang. But it was Welborn.

"Margaret," he said, "are you there?"

Sweetie said, "Sorry. I was expecting someone else."

"You want me to clear the line?"

"No, we've got call waiting. I'll let you know if I have to interrupt."

"I got the information you wanted," Welborn said.

Sweetie brightened. "The young woman from Horatio Bao's office."

"Calanthe Bao, age twenty-six, single, only documented child of Horatio Bao, Georgetown alumna, executive assistant to her father, part-time yoga instructor, part-time dance teacher, regular traveler back to the mother country, and to Hong Kong, Paris and London."

Sweetie was genuinely impressed by the number of databases Welborn must have accessed to gain all that information; the federal government didn't know all, but it came close.

Sweetie's first question was: "Calanthe?"

Jim had gotten her hooked on the meanings of names.

"French via the Greeks," Welborn said. "Western given names are not uncommon for Viets, what with their history as a French colony. The name means beautiful flower. Looking at the woman's DMV photo, it wasn't misapplied."

Welborn was getting into the case; Sweetie could hear it. That tilted her thinking in an unholy direction. "Did you get her address?"

"Lives with Dad; it's a big house." He gave Sweetie an address in Arlington, Virginia.

"Is there a mother?"

"Violette Bao died of ovarian cancer twelve years ago."

Leaving a widower and a young daughter to forge on alone, the two of them close enough that they still lived together. Probably close enough that Calanthe knew all of Horatio's secrets. Doubtless, she'd rather die than reveal them. But if a newcomer were introduced into their little world, who knew what he might see, even in passing.

Sweetie said, "Tell me if I'm prying—"

"Which means you're going to."

"Okay. So tell me if my prying isn't too far out of bounds. But how are you feeling about your upcoming wedding to Ms. Fahey?"

Welborn took a beat. "I didn't fully understand how much I could love someone before I met Kira. I'm greatly looking forward to having her as my wife and to being her husband. As to the ceremony and all its attendant details, it's funny you should ask, because I have a question about that for you."

Surprised by having the tables turned on her, Sweetie asked, "What kind of question?"

"Kira and I hadn't settled on a clergy member to perform the ceremony, not until you gave Kira her little assignment recently."

Sweetie made the jump quickly. "She wants Father Nguyen to marry you?"

"She's so taken with the man," Welborn said, "if he weren't a priest, I think she might throw me over for him."

"Is either of you a Catholic?" Sweetie asked.

"No. Kira is Episcopalian. I've heard them described as Catholics with money, but I wasn't aware they exchanged liturgical blessings like interlibrary loans."

"They don't. What's your religious affiliation?"

"My branch of the Yates family started out as Baptists. When Mother came home from England unwed but pregnant with me, we migrated to Methodism. Currently, I just pray to make it through another day."

"Divine pragmatism," Sweetie said. "Under normal circumstances, a Catholic priest wouldn't marry you unless you both converted. That would mean months of study first. Then being baptized."

"That's what I was afraid of," Welborn said with a sigh.

Sweetie understood perfectly: the things we do for love

She told the young officer, "With Father Nguyen, though, you might catch a break. He's something of a freethinker, and he might soon be looking for a less hierarchical church."

"Blessed be," Welborn said, sounding relieved.

"Glad I could lift your spirits. Earns me one more question. If I were to ask you to do something potentially risky, would you have any reluctance because you're getting married soon?"

"You mean, am I superstitious? No. You know my story, right?"

A car in which Welborn had been riding with three friends, all of them soon to be Air Force fighter pilots, had been hit broadside by a drunk driver. Of the four in his car, Welborn had been the sole survivor. The drunk not only lived, he got away clean, identity unknown. Although Welborn's life had been spared, an injury to his inner ear took away his chance to fly fighters. He had moved on to become a federal officer with the Air Force OSI.

"Jim and I talk," Sweetie said. "I know your story."

"My accident left me with a sense of fatalism, Margaret. You don't die a moment before your time is up, and you don't live a second longer. Personal plans have no bearing on the matter."

That wasn't the way Sweetie saw things, but she said, "Okay."

"What you have in mind for me, it has something to do with Calanthe Bao, doesn't it?"

"Yes, it does," Sweetie said. "Maybe Ricky Lanh Huu, too."

The Hideaway, Paris

38

McGill and Gabbi didn't have to worry about sleeping arrangements because they had decided to sleep in shifts: one would snooze in the bedroom while the other watched the door with the shotgun. But neither of them felt like sleeping anytime soon. It turned out they both had a craving for a late night snack.

"The pub's kitchen is closed," McGill said. "So which one of us is going to whip up something?"

"You cook?" Gabbi asked.

She'd emerged from the bathroom dressed in a white track suit she'd found downstairs, her hair glistening, her face scrubbed pink. She looked like a coed to McGill and he told her so. When she objected, he said okay, a grad student. That was a compliment she could accept.

"Before I married the president," he said, "I was a part-time single dad. I cooked for my kids."

"Anything fancy?"

"Chocolate lava cake."

"You're kidding."

"Eggs, sugar, butter, flour and chocolate," McGill said. "Cook for ten minutes at 350 degrees. What's the big deal?"

Gabbi grinned. "You're really something."

"Yeah, but you know what I feel like now—if they're not illegal in France, if there's any chance at all we can find the ingredients—Rice Krispies Treats."

Gabbi beamed, beckoned McGill to follow her.

"One of the many reasons my brother, Gianni, is so good to me?" she said. "From the time he was little right up to the next time I see him, I always make Rice Krispies Treats for him. He claims he gets all his best ideas while eating them."

They entered the flat's kitchen. Gabbi opened a cabinet and took out an unopened box of the cereal and a fresh bag of marshmallows. From another cabinet, she produced a sauce pan and a cookie sheet. From the fridge came a block of butter. From a drawer the necessary utensils.

"*Allez-y, chef,*" Gabbi said. Go for it, chef.

"You think Harbin would like any?" McGill asked, setting to work.

"With the right wine, sure."

"Okay if I have mine with milk?" McGill asked.

Gabbi nodded. "You and me, both."

McGill's phone sounded. *Take Me Out to the Ball Game.* Sweetie.

He told Gabbi, "I can cook and talk, but..."

She nodded and took the shotgun. "I'll be just outside the apartment door. Won't hear a thing unless you yell for help."

McGill winked and she left. He clicked the talk button.

"Hello, Sweetie."

"Didn't wake you, did I?"

"No. I was just about to make some Rice Krispies Treats. In fact, I'm doing it as we speak."

"If I was the kind of person to say so," Sweetie said, "I'd say darn that sounds good, only I wouldn't say darn."

"Are you at home or the office?" McGill had the feeling there was something more important going on than a case of sugar envy. He turned on the oven to preheat.

"The office."

"I'll call the White House kitchen and have some sent over."

"You can do that?"

"I'm just beginning to understand my super powers."

Sweetie laughed. "Jim, more often than not, you make me glad I know you. Hey, listen, before I forget, I'm doing something for Caitie because her agent couldn't reach you." She told him about the movie script coming her way. "That okay with you, requiring it to make the grade with me first?"

"What could be more Hollywood?" McGill asked. "A script always has to climb a mountain before it gets greenlighted." Or so he'd heard from Patti. "I'll make a note to call my little starlet tomorrow. Her sister and brother, too. Now, Margaret, please tell me the real reason you called."

She brought him up to date on McGill Investigations' domestic case.

"I have this nagging doubt, uncharacteristic of me, I know, that I might be putting Deke back into action too soon."

McGill responded by telling Sweetie where things stood on his side of the ocean.

"This guy's supposed to wrestle bears?" Sweetie asked. "And he smells like one, too?"

"Yeah. I got to telling Magistrate Pruet about Grizzly Adams. Which put me in mind of another American frontiersman, Davy Crockett. You remember the stories about him?"

"Wore a 'coonskin cap," Sweetie said. "Kilt him a b'ar when he was only three."

"Yeah, but if you ever read about him you know *how* he killed bears."

"Sorry, never got beyond reruns of that old Disney TV show. Fess Parker."

So McGill filled her in on Crockett's history and what he had in mind for The Undertaker when they caught up with him.

If they didn't shotgun him that night.

"Wow," Sweetie said, after hearing the idea. "French cinema." Then she added, "Would be a lot simpler if you could just shoot him in the knee, but I can see where you wouldn't want to cause a big fuss in someone else's country."

"Yeah. So I've got these two guys Odo and Harbin, very tough, know more than a few things about fighting. I'm counting on their help, but my question is, do I invite Ms. Casale to the dance?"

Sweetie said, "I'd be in on it, if I were there, wouldn't I?"

"Of course."

"So you're not a sexist. But is your concern about her qualifications or something else?"

"She told me she's thinking about leaving the foreign service soon. Seeing if she can make a go of it as a painter. I'd really hate it if she got hurt, or worse, right before she took herself out of the game."

"Huh," Sweetie said, and told him of her concern about using Welborn to back up Deke and what he had said. "Ask her if she's a fatalist. If she is, you're set to go. If she's not, just pretend she's one of the guys and decide if she's good enough."

"Thank you, Margaret."

McGill dumped the marshmallows in the pan and stirred..

"Yeah, I've solved your problem, but what about mine?"

"You remember how we decided you were ready to return to duty after you took that bullet for me?" McGill asked.

He could imagine the grin on Sweetie's face.

"Yeah. You made me arm-wrestle you. I almost won and you said close enough."

"My arm was sore for a week," McGill said. "I couldn't do without you at that point."

"So I should challenge Deke to arm-wrestle me?"

"Why not? It worked for us."

Sweetie took a moment to consider. "You're right. Thanks. Say, Jim, can you have those Rice Krispies Treats sent to my place? They always taste better when you share them."

"No problem," McGill told her.

He called the White House and placed the order as he stirred the Rice Krispies into the mix of melted marshmallow and butter. When the cereal was well covered, he coated the serving pan with a glaze of butter. He took the sugary mass out of the sauce pan, pressed it into a neat rectangle of uniform height. The chef on duty at the White House told McGill he'd have his Treats on their way to Ms. Sweeney *tout de suite.*

McGill, Gabbi and Harbin chowed down as soon as their treats were cool.

The president's henchman stood the first watch.

Saturday, June 6th—Paris

1

McGill had finished showering and shaving and was brushing his teeth when Gabbi knocked on the bathroom door.

"You decent?" she called out, a tone of urgency in her voice.

The president's henchman was completing his toiletries in his boxer shorts. He checked to make sure his fly wasn't gaping but decided, in the absence of hearing a door ripped from its hinges, that it would be more discreet to slip into the navy blue sweat pants and white T-shirt Gabbi had provided for him.

"Ten seconds," he replied.

On the count of ten, he opened the bathroom door. He was barefoot, but felt sure no one could make anything inappropriate of that.

Gabbi handed him her mobile phone. Whispering, she said, "A gypsy woman, forwarded from the embassy."

McGill nodded and said, "Hello."

An older woman with an accent McGill guessed to be middle-European said, "My name is Madam Mystère. A young man came to me. He told me of an American who asked him to find a woman. A woman with blonde hair who was beneath a certain bridge on a certain night. Do you know of this?"

"I do," McGill said.

"You are the American?"

"I am."

"I will not mention a name, but you are a man of great importance."

So the gypsies had somehow found out who he was.

Celsus was right; the world was closing in.

"Of some importance." That was as much as McGill would concede.

"You spoke of a reward to the young man."

"Two hundred euros."

"This is a fair price, you think, for such a prominent man?"

"You give discounts to poor men?" McGill asked.

There was a moment of silence and then a gleeful cackle.

"I have never given a discount in my life," the woman said.

"So what would you think is a fair price?"

"A thou—"

"Five hundred tops," McGill said. "With at least half going to the kid."

"He is my grandson; he will take less."

"Half," McGill said. "That's the deal."

"Payable in advance."

"Upon delivery. I give the money to the kid. When he brings the woman."

"He is too young to control her."

"Madam Mystère," McGill said, "forgive me if I am wrong, but in my experience with these things most hostages are so drugged they could be shipped UPS without waking them."

There was another moment of silence.

McGill filled it. "It would be a very bad idea to drop Ms. Martel into the Seine. You and your grandson would have to leave the country. So would anyone who helped you. The French magistrate working this case is a very stubborn man. He would give the name of Madam Mystère to Interpol, and if you don't leave France, he has this mean Corsican who—"

"Enough," the woman snapped. "I could put a curse on you right now."

The threat made McGill think of Chief of Staff Galia Mindel.

"You wouldn't be the first," he said.

Undeterred, the woman muttered something sibilant in a language McGill didn't come close to recognizing.

The president's henchman responded in Latin. "*Ego loco meus fides, quod, vita in manuum Deus omnipotens.*" I place my faith, trust, and life in the hands of almighty God.

Sweetie would be proud of him. Rebutting the diabolical with the divine.

For her part, Madam Mystère seemed to recognize that her thrust had been parried, even if she had understood McGill's words no better than he'd understood hers. The fight went out of her.

"Five hundred, then, half for the boy," she agreed glumly.

McGill threw her a bone.

"One hundred more, if you can deliver the woman within the next hour."

"Done!" Madam Mystère agreed, her humor much improved.

McGill gave her the delivery address.

Winfield House, London

2

Sir Robert Reed called on Galia Mindel and they took tea in a sitting room. Sir Robert wore a dark blue Savile Row suit and brought with him a wafer thin attaché case. Galia wore a skirt and jacket from Bergdorf's. Her garb, also dark blue and summer weight wool, was the feminine duplicate of Sir Robert's. The two of them might have been doing a stage act. Sir Robert pretended not to notice and Galia did her best to keep any color of embarrassment off her cheeks. They said little before their tea was served, and both made sure the sugar they put in their cups was thoroughly stirred before looking up.

Sir Robert asked, "May I inquire as to the president's health this morning?"

"She's on the mend," Galia said. "Still sore but less so than yesterday. The White House physician believes rest and conservative treatment will suffice." Galia sipped her tea before asking, "And how is Prime Minister Kimbrough?"

"A bit worse off. He's suffered a hairline fracture of the mandible as well as the fractured cheekbone and the damage to his nose. His jaw has been wired, one nostril has been packed, and he has two black eyes."

"My sympathies," Galia said, sounding not the least bit sympathetic.

"I'm told he's quite a sight," Sir Robert added.

"Probably best not to let any press photographers get a bead on him."

Sir Robert almost smiled.

He said, "He won't be able to speak publicly for months."

"I'm sure there are those who will step forward in his place."

Hesitating as he raised his cup, Sir Robert agreed, "Yes, that will doubtless be one of his foremost concerns. The United States may, in fact, have effected a change of government in the United Kingdom."

"Karma," Galia said, "after the prime minister tried to intrude on our election. But you do think the special relationship between our countries will survive."

"I daresay it will."

"Is there anything else I might help you with this morning, Sir Robert?"

The knight put his cup and saucer down and picked up his attaché case. He opened it and withdrew a sealed manila envelope. He handed it to Galia.

She saw that it was addressed to Captain Welborn Yates.

Sir Robert said, "Her Majesty, with regrets, must decline the invitation to attend the marriage of Captain Yates and Ms. Kira Fahey. She expresses her hope that the happy couple will understand. A gift will be delivered at the appropriate time."

"I'm sure they'll understand. I'll see that Her Majesty's message reaches them."

A twinkle appeared in Sir Robert's blue eyes.

"Have you found me out yet, Galia?"

She didn't even pretend that she hadn't had him investigated back to the day he was born.

"You cover yourself very well, Sir Robert, but, yes, I know you're Captain Yates' father."

"A very proud father. The young man has done quite well for himself. I do admit I aged an extra ten years when I learned of his accident. It was quite the task not to rush to his bedside."

Galia nodded. She understood why he'd been unable to go.

"You couldn't embarrass Her Majesty. Making public your affair with Captain Yates' mother."

"Yes, exactly." He paused for a moment's reflection. "I don't think I'll be giving away anything to say that my place in the firmament will be changing shortly."

"The president and I have guessed that things are in flux."

"Speaking only for myself, I'll be at something of loose ends. For the first time in my adult life, I'm a bit unsure of where I belong. I have to say, without any deprecation to you, that was why I behaved impulsively when I brought you home after dining with you."

"That was why you kissed me," Galia said.

Sir Robert nodded.

"It was quite a kiss anyway," she told him.

He smiled. "For me as well, and motivated as every kiss should be, by an irresistible impulse to be close to someone you find compellingly attractive."

Galia felt the sudden need to blink rapidly.

"Thank you," she said through a constricted throat.

"When she left England, Marian—Welborn's mother—told me to forget about her, get on with my life, find someone proper to marry. I was never able to do that. Never gave it any serious consideration. But the night I dined with you, that was the first time I was tempted."

"Then you thought about it," Galia said, "and you decided you wanted to attend your son's wedding with his mother on your arm."

Sir Robert nodded. He gestured to the envelope Galia held.

"There's something in there from me as well. Something to help Welborn with a case he's working on. I worked through the night to get the information."

The knight smiled when he saw Galia grow tense.

"Please, Galia, don't worry that I've planted a mole in one of your intelligence agencies. The lad talks to his mother; his mother speaks to me. A person of interest to him travels here to London and to Hong Kong on a regular basis. I've documented that person's activities for him."

The tension drained from Galia.

"I really wouldn't put you in a bad spot with the president," Sir Robert said.

"She isn't the one who worries me."

"Then who? Oh, yes, of course. Mr. James J. McGill."

The Hideaway, Paris

3

There was a big Irish-looking guy, wavy black hair, blue eyes, and pink cheeks, standing inside the front door of the pub when McGill and Gabbi came downstairs that morning. Neither of them had ever seen him before.

"And you are?" McGill asked.

He moved slightly to the man's left. Out of the corner of his eye, he saw Gabbi flank the man to his right.

"I might ask the same of you, only I was told not to."

"Your name," McGill repeated. He didn't reach for his gun, but he was already planning attacks and defenses. He sensed Gabbi was, too, and made allowances to coordinate with what he thought she likely might do.

The guy saw what they were doing. He held up his hands. Which might be a gesture of placation. Or it might be the first move of his counterattack.

"Me name's Ronan Walsh," he said.

"Where's Harbin?" McGill asked.

"Takin' a kip in the back room."

Reasonable if he'd been up all night. Perfectly acceptable—if they'd known the guy.

"You use escrima sticks, too?" McGill asked.

"I'm not particular. Anything that comes to hand, or me hands alone."

McGill nodded. A kindred spirit. But still an unknown quantity.

"Harbin called me," Walsh said. "Asked me to stand in while he rested a bit."

"Did he warn you a big, ugly sack of shit might come calling? McGill asked.

"He did."

"And you're ready for that?"

"I am." But he didn't have Harbin's shotgun.

At first glance, McGill couldn't see that Walsh was carrying any kind of weapon, but blades were easy to conceal. As were piano wire, caustic crystals ... and pins? The guy wore a button on his blue nylon jacket with an image on it of the Irish rocker Bono flashing the peace sign. The pin holding the button in place had to be two inches long. Dip that in something toxic, stick it in somewhere soft and...

McGill said, "You like U2?"

Walsh knew what he was being asked.

"Oh, yeah," he replied. "They're deadly."

"Let's take a walk to the back room," McGill said.

"I was told not to leave the door. Not even to empty meself."

"Every plan calls for adjustments," McGill said.

That was the decisive moment. Conflict or cooperation was about to ensue. Without seeing it clearly, McGill had the impression Gabbi had taken a half-step back and had gone up on her toes. He stayed right where he was.

"And what if the big divil in need of a bath comes callin'?" Walsh asked.

"I'll shoot him," McGill said. His tone left no doubt he was telling the truth.

Gave Walsh a clear idea what might happen to him as well.

"Would ye like me to lead the way?" he asked.

"That would be best for everyone," McGill told him.

Walsh shrugged and moved forward, slowly, as McGill and Gabbi stepped back to give him room, but not too much. He knocked on the door to the room where he'd said Harbin slept and opened it a crack.

"Hey, Harbin, ye didn't tell me there'd be a bloke an' a bird threatenin' to muss me hair."

Harbin's groggy voice responded, "*Merde.*"

McGill told Walsh, "Step away from the door."

He had his gun on the man now. The two men gave Gabbi room to step forward. She looked into the room and saw Harbin stretched out on a cot, a blanket draped over him.

"*Comment allez vous?*" she asked.

How are you? McGill knew that one.

"*Trop fatigué pour ètre utile à vous, ma chere.*" Too tired to be of use to you, my dear.

McGill didn't catch that, but he was reassured when Gabbi smiled and closed the door. He put his gun away. He saw Gabbi remained alert in case Walsh had taken offense.

"Sorry," McGill told the man, "but you can't be too careful."

"Not a problem. You can buy me a pint somewhere down the road."

He smiled at Gabbi, telling her she could relax. But she didn't, not entirely.

"Tell Harbin to give me a call when he wakes up, will you?" McGill said.

Gabbi gave him the number for her mobile. Walsh opened the door for them and locked it behind them. He was back on the job.

They got in Gabbi's Peugeot and drove off, heading to Pruet's office.

"Harbin never mentioned that guy to you before?" McGill asked.

"No."

Gabbi stopped for a red light, and McGill looked at her.

"What's your training in self-defense?" he asked.

"Aikido and Krav Maga." The latter being the Israeli end-a-fight-fast discipline. Before McGill could ask if Gabbi was any good, she told him, "I watched the way you put Glen Kinnard down. I would've done it pretty much the same way."

The light turned green and Gabbi put her eyes on the road and her foot on the gas.

McGill asked, "You ever do any work with escrima sticks?"

"I've worked out with Harbin a bit," she said.

Sounded like an understatement to McGill.

"That's good," he said.

Gabbi's skills fit in with his plans. He felt better about asking her to join him, Odo and Harbin. Made him think, too, if he approved of Gabbi knowing how to defend herself, and to take part in an assault on a giant, he really shouldn't be so reluctant to teach his own girls Dark Alley.

Magistrate Pruet's office

4

It looked to McGill and Gabbi as if the magistrate were putting up a jigsaw puzzle on the wall. That or doing the installation of a mosaic, Odo handing him one piece at a time which he affixed to the wall with some adhesive goo that had been given the scent of lemons. The impression McGill got was that a young Pete Townshend had wound up and smashed a delicate guitar into a million pieces. From which Pruet was trying hard to restore some sense of order.

Only this instrument was never going to be whole again.

Pruet turned to his guests and told them, "If the government objects or assigns me to a new space, I will have this section of wall removed and take it with me."

"Maybe donate it to a museum after you die," McGill suggested.

The magistrate's face, which had been dour, brightened.

"The thought had never occurred to me, but I know just the curator. *Merci.*"

He gestured to his visitors to sit. He took the seat behind his table.

Odo remained standing.

"The Undertaker?" Gabbi asked, gesturing to the vandalized guitar.

"*Ma femme,*" Pruet said.

"Your wife?" McGill asked, not sure he had it right.

But glad he'd never made Patti or Carolyn that angry. Patti, especially.

"Soon to be ex-wife, on very favorable terms," the magistrate said. Looking at Gabbi, he added, "But you are right; The Undertaker did visit my apartment last night. Fortunately, he had departed before I arrived."

Pruet told them of finding the monster's reek throughout his home, and his wife in the safe room. He did not detail his discussion with Nicolette and neither McGill nor Gabbi was gauche enough to ask for specifics.

"You summoned M'sieur Sacripant, of course," Gabbi said.

The magistrate shook his head. "I had given Odo the night off. After I put Nicolette in a taxi to the Ritz, I returned to my apartment and threw open every window. I turned on every light and collected every piece of my guitar I could find."

McGill saw that Odo was now the one shaking his head.

But the president's henchman understood Pruet.

"You had a gun," he said. "You hoped someone would come to your door and give you the excuse to shoot him."

"A number of candidates came to mind," Pruet admitted.

Wondering if he'd been one of them, McGill asked, "You still want me to go?"

"I have reconsidered," the magistrate said. "Examining the failure of my marriage, I came to have a sense of the success of yours. For your wife, the most powerful woman in the world, to accede to your choice of occupations, there must be an intuitive bond between you. She must know the risk inherent in what you do, as you must realize the danger of her position. I do not think she would hold anyone else responsible should..."

Pruet did not finish the thought, only shrugged.

But McGill gave it voice. "Should I get it in the head."

"As you say."

McGill turned to Gabbi. "Will you and Odo please give me a moment alone with the magistrate?"

Gabbi got to her feet and looked at Odo, who, after receiving a nod from Pruet, accompanied her from the room.

"My sympathy on the guitar," McGill said. "It's clear how much it means to you."

"You play?" Pruet asked.

"I sing." Off the magistrate's look of surprise, he explained, "My mother is a voice teacher."

Pruet smiled. "You are not at all what I expected."

"It's useful to have people underestimate you, but you know that, don't you? When you looked at the file on Diana Martel you saw something that bothered you. Something more than just having an oversized thug in the picture. I didn't call you on it at the time, but I bet you saw ... well, someone *politically* big. Someone who could tell The Undertaker where you live. And give him reason to think a street criminal like him could get away with going after a magistrate."

Pruet steepled his hands and stared at McGill.

"My guess," the president's henchman said, "you're looking at another scandal. Maybe not exactly an interior minister stealing government money, but something of that scale. Another guess is it could clear Glen Kinnard, if you could ever make it public"

"M'sieur Kinnard was moved once again this morning, to better quarters, with more freedom of movement, and the satellite television system he requested."

McGill took a moment to ponder that.

He said, "Creature comforts are fine, but until you put him on a plane to the United States, don't reduce the number of cops guarding him."

"No?"

"No. He's the kind of guy who could get himself into more trouble."

Pruet picked up his phone and made a call, his French far beyond McGill.

"Is there anything else you wish to tell me, m'sieur?"

The president's henchman looked at his watch. "Diana Martel should be delivered out front within the next fifteen minutes."

Pruet chuckled. "You are a marvel."

"That's just the half of it. I've got an idea how to bag The

Undertaker, too. That'll help with whatever your big problem is, won't it?"

Pruet stood without saying a word. He went to his filing cabinet and from the top drawer took a bottle of cognac and two snifters. He poured for both of them and handed a glass to McGill.

"*Vive l'Amérique*," he toasted. Long live America.

McGill didn't like cognac, but to refuse the drink would have been unfriendly.

Unpatriotic, too. He stood and took his cognac like a man.

Quai d'Orsay, Paris

5

"That crafty old bird," McGill said with a smile.

By the time he, Gabbi, Pruet and Odo had stepped out the front door of the magistrate's office building, there was a UPS truck parked at the curb. There was no driver anywhere to be seen, but the kid who had tried to sell him the gold ring was nervously shuffling back and forth in front of the truck. When he saw McGill he did a double-take at his new look, realized McGill was still the man he wanted, and hurried his way.

Then, as if remembering a critical step in a hastily memorized script, he stopped abruptly and bent over as if to pick up something from the sidewalk. Eyes wide now, he held up a key.

"Look what I have found, m'sieur," the kid exclaimed. "Who knows what it might unlock? A vault of treasure perhaps."

McGill plucked the key from the kid's hand.

"That was the case," he said, "you'd have to sell me a treasure map, too. So I could know where the vault was."

The kid couldn't keep a grin off his face; he'd have to remember that one.

"Lucky for us," McGill told him, "this key is stamped UPS. Think that could be a coincidence?"

The kid shrugged. "You could look. Perhaps someone has sent you a package."

Odo started to close in, but McGill shook his head. That slowed the Corsican down. Another shake of the head from Pruet brought him to a stop.

McGill said, "Let's hope the package hasn't been damaged."

The kid almost said something but bit his tongue.

McGill walked over to the back of the truck. The kid followed, not wanting to be far from the cash he expected to come his way. The president's henchman looked at the boy, decided it was safe to proceed, put the key in the lock and turned it. Opened the back of the truck.

As he'd predicted, the hostage was unconscious, bound hand and foot with duct tape, but alive, breathing easily, and showing no signs of abuse.

"Oh, look, sir," the kid said. "The lady even has her purse with her."

There was not a centime to be found in that purse but there was a photo ID card, conveniently showing that the unconscious woman was indeed Diana Martel.

McGill took six hundred euros out of his pocket and handed the money to the kid.

"The deal," he told him, "is half for you, half for grandma."

The boy smiled. "She is giving me four hundred."

"How come?"

"She said you were the first *gadjo* ever to make her laugh, asking if she gave discounts."

Gabbi stepped forward.

"You better go," she told the kid. "Your girlfriend's getting nervous."

Gabbi nodded to the corner of the block where a young girl stood watching, ready to run at the slightest provocation.

The kid stuck the money in his hip pocket and struck a proud pose.

"Not my girlfriend," he said, "my wife."

"Congratulations," McGill said.

"*Bonne chance*," Pruet added.

Winfield House, London

6

SAC Celsus Crogher knew something was wrong the moment he stepped into the office the president was using at Winfield House. When he'd been summoned, he thought it had something to do with Holly G's meeting with the queen that afternoon. Some item of royal protocol had probably clashed with Secret Service procedure, calling for a compromise on his part. Crogher hated security compromises. But the longer the president kept him waiting, standing mutely before her desk as she finished writing a note on presidential stationery, the more he thought he'd been summoned to answer for a personal fuckup. Normally, he'd have tried to sneak a peek at the contents of the presidential message, but just then he had the feeling he'd better keep his eyes front.

At two minutes and forty-two seconds, by his internal count, the president looked up. "Please take a seat, Celsus."

He did as instructed, maintaining an erect posture.

"I'd tell you to relax, if I didn't know that would make you uncomfortable."

"Yes, ma'am," the SAC said.

"So I'll get right to the point. Did you enjoy your trip to Paris?"

A normal person might have blushed. The SAC himself had even shown a hint of color recently. But this time Crogher only grew more pallid.

There should have been no way Holly G could know about that … unless McGill had ratted him out. It would be just like—

"No one betrayed you, Celsus," the president told him, as if she were reading his mind. "Not any of your people. Not Jim, either, if I'm correct in assuming that's who you went to see."

As the president hadn't addressed a direct question to him, Crogher remained silent, still trying to work out who—

"Galia," the president said, doing her clairvoyant thing again. "Among everything else the chief of staff does for me, she counts noses. She takes inventory of everyone who's in his place and everyone who isn't. When someone as prominent as the SAC of the White House Security Detail vanishes for the better part of the day, she brings it to my attention. I made a phone call and learned where you went. Would you care to explain your absence in detail, Celsus?"

Crogher went as white as a week-old corpse. What the hell was he supposed to say? He was worried that the president of the United States was philandering with the president of France and her husband ought to know about it? If only so McGill could give the frog the boot and the SAC could reestablish his normal security routine for POTUS.

He couldn't bring himself to say that, but he had to say something.

Crogher went with a partial truth. "I felt compelled to tell Mr. McGill that as risky as his insistence on a minimal security presence is at home, it is far more hazardous abroad."

The president straightened in her seat, and Crogher saw her wince as the pressure increased on her bruised bottom.

"Do you have any credible information of a specific threat against my husband?"

Now, they were back on familiar ground. Crogher felt a swell of anger. He answered bluntly, "Ma'am, Mr. McGill's rejection of a sufficient Secret Service detail constitutes a daily threat to his well being. By extension, any misfortune that might befall him could distract you from the optimum execution of your office, and that would be a disservice to the nation."

The president's eyes narrowed and her face hardened.

"SAC Crogher, I assure you that I will never fail either my husband or my country. If the day should ever come that I cannot be true to both my wedding vows and my oath of office, I will invoke Section Three of the Twenty-Fifth Amendment. Vice President Wyman will act in my stead and, I'm sure, perform with distinction."

Crogher thought to himself, Christ Almighty, that's why this woman was president. He was the guy who carried an Uzi, but she made him feel as if she could jump across that desk and rip his heart out. Which, in the very next minute, she did.

"You have my apology, Celsus."

"Ma'am?"

"When you wanted to leave the White House, I should have accommodated you."

Crogher did something he couldn't remember ever doing before, he let his body go limp.

"When you leave this office," the president continued, "please write your letter of resignation, send it to the director, and have him forward a copy to me. By presidential order, you will receive a year's severance pay in recognition of meritorious service. I'm sorry things didn't work out, but the world has changed, and you seem wedded to the past. Jim McGill is only the first man to be married to a president. Some of his successors may well be malleable fellows, but others are bound to be ... henchmen. The people doing your job—and mine—will have to learn to deal with that."

The SAC sat motionless until the president told him, "You may go now, Mr. Crogher.

En route to Hôpital Saint-Antoine, Paris

7

Pruet rode in the Peugeot with McGill and Gabbi to visit Arno Durand at the hospital. In the magistrate's Citroën, following behind, Odo transported a laboriously revived, and handcuffed Diana Martel. The stripper was happy to be freed from the bastards who had kidnapped her—she couldn't remember who her captors were; they'd drugged her and the whole experience was a blur—but she was not pleased to be informed that she was being held as an accessory to the death of Thierry Duchamp.

She remembered Thierry quite clearly, but refused to say a word about him or anything else. Except to mutter *cochon*—pig—in Odo's direction at regular intervals. Every time she did,

Odo would glare at her. He gladly would have beaten the *putain* for her insolence, had he not been working for Yves Pruet.

In the Peugeot, McGill asked Pruet if the magistrate would mind if he made a call home from the car. McGill didn't think a conversation with his youngest child would require privacy. Caitie was an early riser and if he had the time difference right, she should just be getting out of bed, taking that day's step in her plan for world conquest.

The magistrate said, "By all means."

As McGill hit speed dial and waited for the call to be routed, Gabbi paid attention to her driving. Pruet, sitting in back, courteously gazed out the window.

Reaching his ex-wife's home in Evanston, Illinois, McGill said, "Hello, may I please speak with Miss Caitlin Rose McGill, heiress to the cinematic tradition of Shirley Temple."

After a laugh, his ex-wife, Carolyn, said, "You're dating yourself, bud. Not one kid in a hundred would recognize Shirley Temple's name, including our little Miley Cyrus."

"Shirley has become Miley?" McGill asked. "Let me make note of that."

"How's London?" Carolyn asked.

As far as the general public knew, McGill was keeping Patti company in the UK.

"Very English," he said, "you hardly need any subtitles at all."

He'd tell Carolyn the truth afterward, when spilling the beans wouldn't matter.

"Is that Dad?" a voice piped up. Caitie.

"We have a princess here, too," his ex told him. "She'd like to speak with you."

"You and Lars are well?" McGill asked.

"Healthy and happy, thank you."

"And how come I haven't heard from Kenny lately?" McGill wanted to know.

"That would be the doing of Miss Liesl Eberhardt."

"*Kenny* has a girlfriend?" McGill asked in wonder.

"Come on, Mom," Caitie intruded. "Nobody cares about

that mushy stuff."

McGill said, "God help us all when *she* gets a crush on somebody."

Carolyn laughed again, but said, "I better surrender the phone before she stares a hole in me."

A half-second later, McGill's youngest child said, "Dad, did you read the script? Can I do the movie, pleeeeeeease? Annie said they won't wait much longer."

McGill knew when a batter was expecting a fastball, it was time to throw her a curve. Likewise, when a child expected to be treated like a child, it was time to ask her to imagine herself as an adult.

"Caitie, I'm wondering something, as I haven't read the script yet."

"You *haven't?* Oh, Dad!" Caitie stopped in mid-whine. She was sharp, realized they hadn't gotten to the important part yet. "What are you wondering?"

"I'm wondering when you go off to college, will you think it's cool to have your friends see you in this movie or will you be embarrassed if they see it? And a little farther into the future, how would you feel about having your kids see it?"

"*Kids?* Dad, I'm eleven years old."

"Now, but not forever. I guess what I'm thinking is, do you really like this script or is it the *idea* of being in a movie you like?"

There was a moment of silence. Then: "You asked me *three* things."

McGill thought, as he had many times before, Caitie should be a lawyer.

"Pick one," he said.

"I ... think it's the idea." She continued in a defeated voice. "By the time I get to college, this story probably will seem lame. But does that mean I shouldn't do anything now because it'll be dorky later?"

"Not at all. In fact, I'm a little reassured you might consider this movie lame. It makes me more inclined to let you do it."

"Great. Caitie McGill, lame-o actress."

McGill had to stop himself from laughing out loud.

"Sweetie's going to read the script," he said. "She might think the part is a classic, will hold up for a hundred years."

"But if she's right, Annie said there isn't much time."

"Honey, let me have your agent's phone number. I'll call her."

"You will?"

"We'll work something out. If these movie people have a real interest in you, this won't be your only opportunity. But I wouldn't worry too much. You're going to make your mark in this world, one way or another."

"I know, Dad. I'm still going to be president. But I thought I should get my start in the movies, like Patti."

Thank God she didn't want to start in modeling, like Patti, McGill thought. But, who knew, that might come, too.

"Trust me, things will work out. I heard about Kenny, but how's Abby doing? Is she around?"

"No, she's at Jane Haley's house. They're looking at college websites. Since they finished last year at Saint Viv's tied for number one in their class, they're thinking of going to the same school, like a team. One won't go unless the other's accepted, too."

"That's interesting," McGill said.

Made it tougher for a school to unduly favor Abby.

He wondered if such a notion would fly with an admissions officer.

"Oh, and Sweetie got Abby not to change her last name."

McGill smiled. "That's good. What about you? If you get into the movies, are you going to change your name?"

"Heck no," Caitie said. "If they want me, they can take me the way I am."

Eleven years old, and Caitie wasn't going to let anyone push her around.

McGill couldn't have been happier. He told Caitie he loved her.

She gave him her agent's phone number.

A moment after the call ended, Pruet addressed McGill. "If I am not being impolite, m'sieur, may I ask a question or two about your family?"

McGill took a look over his shoulder at Pruet. "Go ahead. I'll let you know if your questions are out of bounds."

"You spoke with your daughter and her mother, your ex-wife?"

"That's right."

"You maintain a civil relationship with your former wife?"

"We were childhood friends. Now, we're adult friends. The marriage and the kids happened in between. I love my children more than life, but the farther away I get from my marriage with Carolyn, the more I ask myself how it ever happened. We should have stayed just friends."

The magistrate nodded and said, "Quite a candid answer, m'sieur."

Gabbi gave McGill a look. She had thought so, too.

"Yeah, I've got to watch that. Next thing you know, I'll be on Oprah."

Gabbi laughed, but Pruet missed the meaning of the reference.

"*La première présentatrice de télévision des États-Unis*," Gabbi said.

McGill didn't catch that mouthful, but he figured it took a lot to explain Oprah.

With that cleared up, Pruet moved on.

"Your relationship with your children..."

The magistrate let the question hang, perhaps thinking it too personal.

But McGill said, "What about it?"

"Does your concern for them ever weigh on you as you go about your work?"

McGill looked at the magistrate again. He knew Gabbi, too, was paying as much attention as she could without running into the back of a tour bus.

"You mean will I worry about my kids when we go after The Undertaker? Not in the heat of the moment. There's no time then. But before ... thinking of my children, my wife, and even my ex-wife makes me one very careful fellow. I do my best to plan ahead."

"*Je suis heureux de l'entendre,*" Pruet said.

McGill looked at Gabbi for help.

She told him, "Magistrate Pruet is glad to hear that."

Annandale, VA

8

Enid Crowther, the housekeeper at the rectory of St. Magnus's parish, knew Father Nguyen's schedule to a fare-thee-well. After saying 6:30 a.m. Mass, he took refuge in his office for thirty minutes of prayer and personal reflection. Only then did he think of corporal sustenance and take a breakfast of fruit, cereal, and a cup of lightly honeyed tea. When he hadn't emerged at the usual time, Enid gave him an additional five minutes. When he still remained inside his office, she gave him five more minutes.

At that point, Enid began to worry. She pressed her ear lightly against the door. Not a sound to be heard. Father Nguyen was a relatively young man, she knew. But of late she'd also seen an unusual degree of concern written into his normally serene face. Maybe Father had a medical condition he was reluctant to share with anyone.

Enid would never forgive herself if Father was lying on the floor in need of aid, unable to call out for help, and she left him there to expire.

She knocked gently on the door, and got no response.

She knocked harder and—

"If that's you, Enid, please come in."

Father's voice sounded absolutely normal. Her heart slowed. She sighed quietly in relief and opened the door. Father was seated behind his desk, apparently not praying at all. He had a pen in his hand and a sheet of paper in front of him.

Francis Nguyen was writing his letter of resignation from

pastoral duties, but not the priesthood. He put the sheet of paper in a desk drawer before his housekeeper could read his words.

"How may I help you, Enid?" Father Nguyen asked.

"I'm facing a bit of a puzzle, Father."

"A question of faith?"

"No, Father, a question of laundry."

The priest regarded his housekeeper with a look of incomprehension.

Then he smiled. "Well, I'm not sure I can help, but I'll do what I can."

"Father, have you taken up drawing?"

He was back to being puzzled.

"No."

"Then I'm at a loss," Enid said.

"As am I. Why don't you start from the beginning?"

"Yes, Father. I was doing your laundry. Followed my laundry routine exactly as I always do. Used the same detergent and, of course, I used the washer and drier here at the rectory."

Father Nguyen nodded, but he didn't see where Enid's story was leading.

She showed him, taking a dust cloth from her pocket.

"Father, this looks to me like the cloth you always use to tidy up the altar. It was among your clothes in the laundry basket. I noticed nothing unusual about it when I put it in the washer, but look at it now."

She unfolded the cloth and there was the likeness of a man's face. It was masterfully done, a composition of line and shading. The work was of such sensitivity that Father Nguyen half-expected the man's likeness to start speaking to him.

"Father, I rewashed this cloth three times, with bleach," Enid said, "and this drawing won't come out. In fact, I'd swear each washing only made it more ... beautiful. I thought maybe you had done it and I'd better stop trying to get it out."

Father Nguyen extended his hand and Enid gave him the cloth.

As soon as he had it in hand, it did speak to him. At least insofar as keying his memory. The young woman named Kay, new to his church, soon to be married, despairing that her father, dead many years, would be unable to see her wedding. She'd been crying and he'd offered her the dust cloth to dry her tears.

She had asked him if he had a miracle up his sleeve.

She had needed a sign that her father would see her wedding.

Looking at the image Mrs. Crowther said was indelible, Francis Nguyen could see the resemblance between the man's likeness and the young woman, Kay. Doing his best to control himself, he thanked Mrs. Crowther for bringing the cloth to his attention. But by the time the housekeeper left his office, he was trembling.

How, he wondered, could something be both a miracle and a mistake?

He was certainly unworthy of receiving such a clear example of God's grace.

If only his well-being were involved, he would have burned the cloth.

But if the image were indeed a likeness of Kay's father … he would have to show it to her.

Hôpital Saint-Antoine, Paris

9

Walking into Arno Durand's hospital room a second time, seeing him with all four limbs in casts, his head bandaged, and a white cotton shirt covering his torso, McGill thought he resembled the "soldier in white" from *Catch-22*. Only Durand's face wasn't covered, except in bruises, which had ripened colorfully overnight. So much the better, as far as McGill was concerned. Also, unlike Joseph Heller's character, Durand was not mute.

He saw McGill, smiled, and said, "*Mon ami*."

The reporter was about to say more, but the rest of McGill's entourage crowded into the room, and Durand fell silent. He regarded Gabbi appreciatively, but his eyes came to linger on the handcuffed Diana Martel. He examined her at length. She bore the inspection stoically, someone who'd been through the exercise too many times to remember.

Growing bored, the stripper asked, "*Est-ce que je peux fumer?*" May I smoke?

Odo replied, "*Seulement si vous ètes en feu.*" Only if you're on fire.

Diana gave Odo a dirty look, but Durand had enjoyed Odo's riposte, and the stripper's reaction only made it funnier for him. He laughed aloud, revealing several broken teeth. Diana recoiled from Durand's gruesome jollity.

Better and better, McGill thought.

Pruet and Gabbi watched impassively.

Switching to English, Diana asked McGill, "Why have you brought me here?"

"This gentleman," McGill said, declining to name the reporter, "had an unfortunate encounter with a friend of yours, The Undertaker."

Diana shrank from the name, but immediately bumped into Odo, and moved quickly away from him, bringing her near Durand's bedside. The reporter looked up at the woman and, despite his injuries, was excited to have her so close. Maybe he liked women in handcuffs.

McGill said to Durand, "Will you please tell Ms. Martel what happened to you?"

The reporter nodded slowly, as if reluctant to visit the terrifying memory. Some of the hesitation had to be real, McGill thought. Even so, he also saw a flicker of glee in Durand's eyes. The reporter knew he'd been given a starring role, and he meant to make the most of it.

He began in English. "The boom came first, a sound like a blast of heavy artillery, as the downstairs door was smashed free of its hinges. Tortured creaks and moans came from the staircase. Each step cried out as it fell under the weight of the monster's heels; each wail brought the beast ever closer to me. Then, even before the door to my apartment was battered to splinters, in rushed the smell: the stink of an open grave occupied by a rotting corpse..."

Diana Martel, her face deathly pale, retreated, backing up once more against Odo. She remained pinned fast to the Corsican as Durand continued his narrative in French. McGill caught only a few words, but the tone was unmistakable. The reporter was doing his best to scare the stripper witless and succeeding brilliantly.

Likely for McGill's benefit, Durand concluded as he began, in English.

"Then with the monster's hands grasping for me, only inches away, I flew from the window, sure the embrace of the Grim Reaper would be far kinder than the crushing clutches I had so narrowly escaped."

Reliving the moment of high terror, an involuntary tremor ran through Durand, making his plaster encased arms and legs bounce alarmingly in their slings. The reporter, his eyes wide, his mouth open in a silent scream, had succeeded in horrifying himself.

Causing Diana Martel to scream and turn to be comforted.

But Odo was not about to provide succor. She sidestepped quickly and laid her head on McGill's shoulder. He patted her back gently, his manner paternal, his voice filled with concern.

"If you help us, we'll lock this guy up. Somewhere he'll never leave, never be able to pay you a visit. Because, you know, unless he's locked up, he'll have to dispose of everyone who could testify against him."

The stripper looked up at McGill, scared but already starting to calculate. In her world, there was a bargain to be made in every situation, even the most desperate. She was looking for an angle. McGill interrupted her silent scheming.

"I'm just a visitor here," he said. "I can't make any promises, except this: Things will go better for you if you cooperate than if you don't."

Platitudes were all very well, but Diana Martel wasn't about to roll over for a *flic*, American or not. Not until McGill gently turned her around for another look at Durand.

"Play it cagey," he said, "and who knows, *you* might get out of jail soon. Now, how do you think that would make us feel? Maybe as if there were no point in going after The Undertaker. Then where would you be? Possibly without even a window to throw yourself from."

McGill felt the woman's shoulders tremble under his hands.

He asked softly, "What is The Undertaker's real name?"

The whispered answer was only a heartbeat in coming. "Etienne Burel."

With the dam breached, McGill turned the woman over to Pruet and Odo. Things would go better now in their native language. Pruet began speaking quietly to Diana, one conspirator to another, as he led her from the room. Odo shut the door behind them.

The president's henchman turned back to the reporter.

"Are you all right?" he asked.

Durand drew a deep breath and let it out slowly. "I will need a moment to compose myself, m'sieur. Then I have something I must tell you. Something I must show you."

10

"You remember Pierre?" Durand asked McGill.

Gabbi had just returned to the reporter's hospital room after conducting a successful fifteen-minute search for a DVD player and a television. She had rolled a stand holding the two pieces of electronics to the right of Durand's bed, made the connections between them, and plugged the works into an electrical outlet.

"The guy on the motorcycle?" McGill asked. "The one you had spying on Ms. Casale and me outside that café?"

Durand offered a small nod. "Pierre is what an English reporter would call his legman. You have such people in America?"

"Yes," McGill said, "though sometimes we call them go-fers."

Durand frowned and turned to Gabbi. "Gophers?"

"*D'aller pour*," she explained.

The reporter smiled. "*Très bon*. Pierre is my go-fer. This morning he brought me something I had not known existed." He turned to Gabbi. "It is under my pillow, if you please."

She stepped forward and gently placed her hand under the pillow, came out with a DVD in a paper sleeve. Crudely printed on the sleeve were the words: *Enterrement numéro un*.

"Burial number one?" McGill asked.

Gabbi and Durand both nodded.

The reporter added, "Pierre said this came by courier to my office yesterday. He opened the package only this morning. Watched the disk. Brought it straight to me. He wanted to call the police. Pierre is young."

"It's that bad: what's on the disk?" Gabbi asked.

"I have not seen it, but Pierre says it shows The Undertaker killing a man in some sort of unsanctioned fight. There is no sound, for which Pierre was grateful, but the titles explained both parties understood in advance that the fight was to the death. The other fellow was given the opportunity to deliver the first five strikes without response. If he had won, he would have been given ten thousand euros."

McGill thought about that and shook his head.

"My conclusion also, m'sieur," Durand said. "Death is the point at which such barbarity must ultimately arrive. There is, of course, an underlying message in the timing of this disk's release."

The president's henchman had already reached the same conclusion.

"It's a warning," McGill said. "Back off or this could be you."

"*Exactement*."

"Are you sure you want to see this, Arno?" Gabbi asked.

"Upon reflection, no. I have had enough excitement today."

"You mind if we take a quick look?" McGill asked.

"If you like. Then perhaps the disk should go, as Pierre suggested, to the magistrate."

"Sure," McGill agreed. "Just as soon as we're done."

He turned the stand and the TV screen away from the bed. Durand closed his eyes. His lips moved silently. A prayer, perhaps. Thanking God he'd had the courage to jump and the luck to survive.

Gabbi slipped the disk in the machine and pressed the play button.

She and McGill both shared the same thought.

One man's warning was another's scouting report.

Georgetown

11

Sitting in Jim McGill's office, Sweetie felt like Mother Superior weighing the fates of two malcontents and a motorhead: Deke, Welborn and Leo. Serious matters weighed on the minds of the first two; Leo, unruffled by being called back to work, was absorbed by something he was reading in *Road & Track*, nodding his head, smiling, even uttering a soft, "*zoom*."

"Leo," she said, "what I need from you is reassurance that if either Deke or Welborn gets in trouble and needs a fast get away, you can scoop them up."

"Of course, I can," Leo said, not looking up.

"And no one will catch you."

Now, Leo looked at Sweetie. "Not unless it's Dale Jr. driving number 88. Even then, I like my chances. He doesn't have the street experience I do."

"Thank you, Leo. Why don't you wait in the outer office where our conversation won't disturb your reading."

"Yes, ma'am," Leo said, leaving, his nose back in his magazine.

"All right, gentlemen. You can tell me what's bothering you or you can tell me to mind my own business, but I need to know if I can count on you."

Deke and Welborn nodded in unison. She could count on them.

Sweetie was unpersuaded.

She looked at one and then the other and asked, "Okay, who wants to share?"

Welborn started. "Kira called from the White House. She told me an envelope containing documents that have a bearing on our investigation has been sent from London and will be available for pickup later today."

Sweetie said, "London? One of the places Calanthe Bao visits regularly?"

Welborn nodded.

"But Jim is in Paris, not London. So who—

Deke said. "Maybe the president found a few minutes to lend a hand."

The special agent was kidding, but Sweetie didn't find the idea that farfetched.

Welborn, however, shook his head. "It didn't coming from the president."

"How do you know?"

"My mother called me this morning. She asked if it would be all right if she brought my father to my wedding." Off Deke's puzzled look, Welborn explained. "I've never met my father; I didn't even know his name until today."

Deke nodded, and as if it explained everything said, "Families."

"Yeah. My mother told me my father was sending something helpful for me. And, oh, by the way, the queen won't be able to make the wedding."

"Queen?" Deke asked. "Of England?"

"That would be the one."

"Maybe, if you have a good band, things will still work out," Sweetie told him. "Anything else on your mind?"

"Kira heard from Father Nguyen. Something so important—she didn't say what—she had to go see him."

That tidbit hit home for Sweetie. Piqued Deke's interest as well. What was the priest up to and how did it involve the vice-president's niece? Sweetie had been thinking of going to see Bishop O'Menehy before she visited Father Nguyen, but now she thought she would reverse the order.

"What about you, special agent?" she asked Deke. "What's your problem?"

"I heard from my mother's lawyer. He wants me to come in and talk about taxes."

"You owe the IRS?"

"I didn't yesterday. But my mother transferred the titles to her house, her Florida condo, and her car to me."

Sweetie and Welborn exchanged a look.

Sweetie asked, "I didn't notice, but is your mother in failing health?"

Deke laughed. Then he said, "My mother is on the lam."

"*What?*" Welborn asked.

"Back to Vietnam," Deke said. "No extradition."

"Your mother was our client," Sweetie said. "If she's skipped, I suppose we could stay here and play cards."

"Just forget about the people who shot me?" Deke asked.

"Well, there is that. If you feel strongly about it, I suppose we could carry on."

"Mom knew when we got close to the bad guys we'd find out she was in business with them," Deke said. "She planned all along to be far away when Bao and Ricky get the chop."

Sweetie nodded. She saw things the same way.

And Welborn echoed Deke's earlier sentiment. "Families."

12

Ten minutes after the two federal agents left the offices of McGill Investigations, Inc., just as Sweetie was about to make her own departure, Putnam called. He said Deke had asked him to follow up on that detail Margaret had mentioned when they were last together.

Sweetie said, "You mean—"

"Yeah. The kids living in the other houses purportedly owned by Bao's thugs, they all go to parochial schools, too."

Putnam, in his thorough, lawyerly fashion, provided Sweetie

with the names of all the kids, their parents, and the schools they attended.

Sweetie then tested the degree of Putnam's attention to detail.

"Did you happen to make note of any school that has a nun as its principal?"

What with the shortage of young women in the Catholic Church who possessed a religious vocation these days, she knew that was a reach.

But Putnam had not only checked that point, he'd come up with one.

"Remind me to buy you dinner," Sweetie told him. "Somewhere fancy."

"In your company, Margaret, a hot dog stand becomes Lutèce."

Sweetie had heard of the famous French restaurant in New York, of course, but...

"Hasn't that place closed?" she asked.

"So it has. Well, you'll just have to come upstairs and let me cook for you."

And she thought, all right, maybe it was time. He'd come down to her place to share the Rice Krispies Treats the White House had sent over—still warm— and been a gentleman.

"Okay," Sweetie said. Maybe they'd take things further than a goodnight kiss.

Putnam said goodbye, but before he clicked off she heard him shout, "Yippee!"

It was only when Sweetie got down to her car that she remembered: She hadn't challenged Deke to arm wrestle with her. Initially, she'd been reluctant to do so in front of Welborn and Leo. Then hearing the news Deke and Welborn had to share, and revising their plans, she'd gotten distracted. Now, it was too late.

Ah, well. Some things you just had to take on faith.

Falls Church, VA

13

Sweetie rang the doorbell of the modest apartment on John Marshall Drive and wasn't surprised when the woman who answered the door wasn't wearing a habit. Not many nuns did these days. Sweetie wondered, though, if the dispensation of traditional garb hadn't been one of the reasons why Catholic girls were less inclined to dedicate themselves to a religious life.

"May I help you?" the woman asked.

She was a strawberry blonde, her hair cut short. She was slender but not toned, and wore no make-up. She was dressed in jeans, sneakers and a Mount Saint Mary College sweatshirt. Sweetie put her age in the neighborhood of fifty.

"My name is Margaret Mary Sweeney. I'm a former novice. I used to be a cop in Chicago and Winnetka, Illinois. Now, I'm a private investigator in Washington."

The woman smiled broadly, taking ten years off her appearance.

"Well, don't you have the colorful history, sister?"

"I suppose I do," Sweetie said. "Are you Sister Angela Edwards? They told me at the convent I could find you here."

"You found me, all right. But like you, I've left the convent."

"You're no longer the principal of Saint John the Baptist School?"

"No. They didn't tell you that?" Angela Edwards smile was much tighter this time. "I suppose that's to be expected. But you're a surprise. I've met some police officers before, but you're my first private investigator. I thought people in your line of work always wore fedoras."

Sweetie smiled. Former Sister Angela was having fun with her.

"Only in Bogart movies," Sweetie said.

"But you would like to ask me some questions?"

"If you have the time, and don't mind."

Angela Edwards' smile grew large again.

"Well, this is certainly an interesting way to begin my secular life. Please come in."

14

Aside from a card table and two metal folding chairs, her bed and a print of the Sacred Heart on the wall, Angela had yet to furnish her new home.

"Would you like some refreshments?" she asked. "I can offer you lemonade, Coca-Cola or Kool-Aid, and your choice of chocolate chip or macaroon cookies, both store-bought, I'm afraid."

Sweetie gave the former nun an inquiring look.

"Some of my former students have been bringing me care packages the past two weeks. I must admit I haven't been out much, certainly not to shop for groceries, but I do like to take walks as the day begins. There's something reassuring about seeing the sun come up."

Sweetie said, "A sign God is still in his heavens."

"Yes, exactly," Angela said with a smile. "May I ask you a question?"

Anticipating her, Sweetie said, "I left because of a boy."

"He called on you at the convent? Came to plead his love beneath your window at night?"

"No, neither of those things. In fact, I never saw him again. He died. But I couldn't get him out of my mind."

Angela took Sweetie's hand in hers. "I'm so sorry." She paused before asking, "Did you ever marry?"

"No. I ... I think the Lord played a little trick on me for leaving the religious life. He let me meet a man I care for more than any other, but I could never see relating to him in any way other than platonically: as a friend and a colleague. But in the past year, I've met a very unlikely guy who just might amount to something more."

"Well, good for you," Angela said. "I'll pray that it works out."

"Prayer might be what it takes," Sweetie said.

She eased her hand away from Angela and said, "May I begin?"

"Of course," Angela said with a nod.

"Why did you leave your vocation, your school?"

Angela's face sagged. A mist of tears blurred her green eyes. She wiped them with the cuff of her shirt. When she looked at Sweetie the sadness she had felt was replaced by indignation.

"After being faithful to my vows for thirty years, I was asked to write a letter declaring that I was a Catholic in good standing."

Sweetie knew this was a profoundly serious matter to Angela, but she couldn't suppress a grin, and had to ask, "A good Catholic as decided by whom?"

"His Excellency, Bishop O'Menehy. The request came from the diocesan office."

Sweetie shook her head. "Those guys. Most of them just don't have a clue."

"No, they do not," Angela confirmed. "With all the trouble they've caused the church over the years, *they* should be the ones to declare their piety and their purity. Nuns aren't the ones who've brought so much shame on the church, not the ones who cost the church so much money that could be better spent in so many other ways."

"So you politely declined to write the letter?" Sweetie asked.

"Oh, no. I wrote one, all right. I said I viewed myself as a good Catholic, and I suspected Pope John XXIII would agree with me, if not his successors or their bishops."

Sweetie smiled broadly. John XXIII was her favorite pope, too. *Il Papa Buono*. The good pope. He was to the papacy what John F. Kennedy was to the presidency: beloved. The men who followed him in the Chair of Saint Peter were more likely to recall Richard Nixon, to Sweetie's mind anyway. As for Angela's crack about the bishops, that was just a hard elbow to the ribs of the ruling class.

"Were you asked to recant or at least revise your words?" Sweetie asked.

"I was. I informed the diocesan office I had made my first

and last statement on how I regarded my faith and my relationship to the church. They bided their silence until the school year was finished."

"Didn't want to cause an uproar among the parishioners," Sweetie said.

"That thought occurred to me as well. The day after the school year was completed I was informed that I was no longer the principal of Saint John's. I was to confine myself to my quarters as much as possible, spend my time in prayer and reflection, and await the decision of my superiors as to where I would serve the church next."

Sweetie asked, "Did you renounce your vows by letter or phone call?"

"E-mail," Angela said. "Somebody once told me e-mail is eternal; I felt that was apt."

Sweetie smiled. Angela Edwards was a tough woman, and she'd caught her at just the right time. "Angela, did you know a third-grader at St. John's by the name of Mai Vanh?"

"Of course. I know all my children by name, appearance, and family."

That didn't surprise Sweetie, even though Angela's claim would likely include hundreds of children and an even greater number of parents, siblings, and other relatives. Only top politicians had memories equal to those of good educators.

"What can you tell me about Mai and her family?"

Sweetie might have shared confidences with Angela, but that didn't mean the former principal was going to give away information about her students—her *children.* Sweetie had no doubt that Angela still felt an obligation to all the young souls whose temporal and spiritual welfare she had once safeguarded.

"You haven't told me whose interests you represent, Margaret."

"Primarily, I'm working for a friend who was shot and almost killed by criminals in the Vietnamese immigrant community. In a larger sense, I think there's a threat to ... well, the diocese. I hope you won't hold that against me. In fact, I think the demands the bishop's people made on you might be related to a priest I met in Annandale."

Angela sat up straight in her chair. "Father Francis Nguyen?"

Sweetie nodded. She wasn't surprised Angela knew of him. Religious communities, like any others, had their grapevines.

"Do you know what will become of him?" Angela asked.

"No, but my guess is, like you, he'll soon be taking a new path."

The former nun put a hand over her eyes. Despairing for the church that had driven her away, Sweetie felt sure. After a moment, Angela looked back at Sweetie.

"Will any of your actions have an adverse effect on Mai?"

Sweetie had considered that question herself. Not just for one little girl, but for all the children involved in Horatio Bao's machinations.

"There's going to be some anxiety for a number of children and their families. Could be disruption. Even displacement. But I've been paid a considerable fee to do this job. I'll donate it to the families who suffer."

"Will your fee be enough to make things right?"

"Probably not. But I know some people who ... have connections. I'm sure they'll help."

Angela meditated on the situation.

"If I don't help you, will things only get worse?"

"Likely, they will. My friend, the one who got shot, was a federal agent. They take care of their own."

"I'm glad someone does." Bitterness had crept into Angela's voice. She pushed it aside. "I have some money of my own." She laughed. "You wouldn't know it to look at this place. But my father set up a trust fund for me. He let me have only 10% of the quarterly disbursals, knowing I'd give it to the church. The rest was rolled over into treasury bills. If you can donate your earnings, how could I do any less?"

"So what can you tell me about Mai? Is there anything unusual?"

"She's a lovely little girl. Perfect attendance. Immaculately groomed and dressed. A good student. Not exceptional in her academics, but fiercely determined. She'll be a success someday on the strength of her will alone."

Sweetie hated to ask her next question, but did so anyway.

"Did you see any signs of abuse?"

"You mean molestation?"

Sweetie nodded.

"No, none at all."

"Let's give thanks for that," Sweetie said. "But was there anything at all that struck you as unusual about Mai's behavior?"

There was: Sweetie saw it in Angela Edwards' frown.

"Mai was a transfer student. Came to Saint John's from a public school. If you asked her about her old school or where she had lived before coming to Falls Church, there was a pause of a second or two before she answered. And after she did, she would nod to herself and smile."

Sweetie had seen variations of that behavior any number of time in adults.

Ones who were being interrogated by her or another cop.

Happy when they got their lines of bull laid out just as they'd been rehearsed.

"Thank you, Angela. You've told me everything I need to know."

Buckingham Palace, London

15

The presidential motorcade arrived at the palace, punctual to the second. Palace staff deferred to the Secret Service in the matter of opening the door of the president's limousine. Once that issue had been disposed of, Sir Robert Reed stepped forward and extended his hand to Patricia Darden Grant. The president took it and looked Sir Robert in the eye.

"A pleasure to meet you, Sir Robert."

"The pleasure is mine, Madam President."

He released the president's hand and bowed slightly.

"I'm very fond of your son," Patti said.

"As am I, ma'am. I look forward to meeting him."

"Before the wedding ceremony, I trust."

"His mother is working out the details. Will you please follow me?"

Patti gestured and a fit, conservatively dressed young woman in her thirties stepped forward. "This is Special Agent Hernandez. She'll be happy to chat with you, Sir Robert, while I speak with Her Majesty."

Sir Robert smiled. "Thank you for your consideration, ma'am."

They both knew the president was telling him the Secret Service had insisted she have an agent nearby, even at Buckingham Palace. Sir Robert would have the obligation to seat Special Agent Hernandez out of earshot of the president's conversation with the queen, but with a clear sightline on Holly G.

Patti had no doubt Sir Robert would accomplish his task with élan.

He gestured toward the Palace.

"Her majesty," he said, "expresses the hope you will enjoy tea with her in the garden."

Arlington, VA

16

Welborn stood with his face pressed against the window of the strip mall dance studio like a kid staring into a candy store. He was dressed in a butter yellow polo shirt, beautifully faded jeans and new TopSiders. Parked behind him in a slot just to his left was Kira's new show car, a red Porsche Cayman S. She had hinted that she would buy him a matching model as a wedding gift. He'd teased her, saying he wanted a Honda Civic hybrid. But after driving the Porsche, Welborn thought maybe he'd ask for a Tesla Roadster. Electric eye candy with plenty of zoom and no carbon footprint.

In the mall's mid-afternoon lull, there was no one around to pay attention to Welborn.

After two minutes of diverting himself with automotive thoughts, and staring into the dance studio, Welborn heard a car pull into the lot, taking the parking space right behind him. As if slow on the uptake, he turned around only when he heard the newly arrived car's door open.

His effort was rewarded by his first look at Calanthe Bao. Right here, he thought, was a serious example of supermodel talent scouts falling down on the job. If this woman didn't belong on magazine covers, no one did. Long, shining black hair. Golden skin. Features symmetrical to the nearest millimeter. Tall and slim, but he'd bet she could do half as many pull-ups as he could, and he could do a hundred.

"May I help you?" she asked. Great voice, too. Throaty alto.

A hundred replies jostled for the head of the line. None of them as witty as he would have liked. None of them in character.

So he said, "I'd like to take some dance lessons, but I don't see the hours posted anywhere."

"It's not that kind of dance studio."

"No?" Welborn asked, puzzled. "What other kind is there?"

She smiled and, if possible, looked even more gorgeous.

"The kind for gypsies," she said. "Dancers who work on stage."

"Oh," Welborn said. "Lessons for people who already know what they're doing."

She smiled again. "Maybe not as much as they should know."

He sighed. "Well, they certainly have to know more than me." With a wave, he said, "Thanks." He started for his car. With his pilot's peripheral eyesight, he saw her studying him.

"Wait a minute," she said. "What kind of dance do you want to learn?"

Welborn stopped with a hand resting on the roof of the Porsche and looked at her.

"Wedding," he said.

"I beg your pardon."

"You know, the kind you do at a wedding. I'm getting married in a month. My fiancée is a terrific dancer. I'm not any kind at all. I thought it would be a nice surprise if I could get through our first dance without stepping on her toes. Maybe even lead a little."

"What a thoughtful gift," Calanthe Bao said. Looked like she meant it, too.

When Welborn had suggested the idea to Deke as the ruse to approach their target, he'd said, "What a crock." Welborn hadn't taken the criticism to heart. He'd soon be marrying his own beautiful woman, and until recently the Secret Service agent had been living with his mother.

"Maybe you know some other place," Welborn suggested. "You know, open to us non-gypsies."

Calanthe paused before answering, clearly weighing a decision. Taking in Welborn's appearance. He didn't think it hurt her appraisal that he wasn't driving a Honda Civic.

"I'll give you lessons," Calanthe said, deciding.

"You're a gypsy?"

"No, I'm the one who helps them get their choreography right."

"That's very generous of you. How can I thank you?"

"Oh, there will be a bill for services rendered. And I'd appreciate it if you try not to step on my toes."

"Do my best," Welborn said with a smile.

"I'm Callie," she said, extending her hand.

He took it, felt the strength he'd suspected, and said, "Welborn."

She liked that: a name denoting money. It added to her appraisal.

Callie told him she had to run an errand.

To the post office, he knew. Closed early on Saturday. Deke had used his tin to question the manager of the PO Sweetie had seen Calanthe use. It wasn't surprising the PO guy knew when Callie came by every day but Sunday.

Welborn had taken his spot at the dance studio window minutes before Callie was scheduled to drive past. A good-looking guy with a red Porsche had both caught her eye and proven to be acceptable bait.

"Should I wait in my car?" he asked.

She handed him two keys. "The studio will be more comfortable. I'll be right back."

With a wave, she got in her car and drove off. Welborn watched until she was out of sight. Then he looked off into the middle distance. There was a small park across the street. On the far side of it, Deke was sitting in his car and watching.

Ready to move fast if Welborn gave a distress signal.

Welborn just gave him a grin and held up the keys.

That was when Ricky Lanh Huu pulled into the lot in a Nissan sedan.

He popped out and asked Welborn with a sneer, "What're you smiling at, pretty boy?"

17

In both flight school and federal officer training, Welborn had been taught to identify enemies swiftly. All of that was superfluous in Ricky's case. Welborn would have recognized him as a troublemaking twit back in his playground days.

Ricky started to run his mouth some more, but Welborn had stopped listening. He needed to make a move. Not just because Ricky might precipitate a scuffle, but because Deke was certainly already in motion, coming to swoop down on the punk everyone credited with shooting him. Welborn couldn't blame him for that, but he didn't want Horatio Bao to be alerted that he was being targeted. So Welborn opted to use the keys he'd been given. He opened both locks with no wasted motion. Before Ricky could grasp that Welborn wasn't hanging on his every word, the young Air Force captain had let himself into the dance studio and relocked the door.

Tactical retreat, Welborn thought. He'd be happy to get up close and personal with this punk another time. For his part, Ricky didn't like being dissed. People weren't supposed to walk out on one of his performances. He marched up to the studio door, leaving his car door open and the engine running. Welborn didn't think that was too smart.

Told him a thing or two about the guy. Impulsive to a fault. Overly sure of himself.

"Hey, asshole," Ricky yelled, trying the door and finding it unyielding. "I asked who you are? You fuckin' deaf or something?"

Welborn went with, "Something."

Ricky tried the door again, rattled it hard. Got angrier that the door remained unimpressed by him, too.

"Broken glass can cause terrible cuts," Welborn warned.

Over the punk's shoulder, Welborn saw that Deke had arrived on foot and recognized that his colleague in off-the-clock law enforcement was safe for the moment. He amused Welborn when he stepped back to eavesdrop from behind a tree.

Ricky had no idea he was being observed. He banged the glass door hard, as if to test the truth of Welborn's warning. The glass fooled them both and stayed intact.

The punk pulled a knife out of a pocket, flipped it open with a flick of his wrist. Neat trick, but once again Deke drew Welborn's attention. Welborn hoped the Secret Service agent hadn't thought he was threatened by the blade. He shook his head to warn him off.

Ricky thought Welborn was reacting in dread to his weapon.

"Oh, yeah, man. You gotta come outta there sometime and when you do..."

He moved the tip of his blade in a small circle and finished with an upward jab.

Getting bored with the creep, Welborn flipped him off. He wanted to get rid of him before Callie came back. Ricky went to rattle the door again, but even his learning curve wasn't that high. He turned to look at Kira's Porsche, and in particular its tires. If Ricky had rotated his head a few more degrees, he would have seen Deke sitting behind the wheel of his own car, quietly closing the door, but he didn't. Ricky turned back to Welborn to make sure he got the idea.

"Gonna slash your tires," he said. "All of them."

Michelins, costing $370 apiece. Welborn didn't see Margaret reimbursing him. He wasn't keen on having to explain the situation to Kira either. She might buy him a Honda after all.

As Ricky turned back to the Porsche, Welborn rapped on the door.

Ricky stopped and looked back. Welborn gestured with his index finger. Wait a minute.

He took a pen and a small notepad out of a back pocket.

He wrote two sets of numbers on a page and held them up for Ricky to see.

The first set was: 911. The second was: 4AXT219. Ricky's license plate number.

By now, Welborn had his cell phone in hand.

Ricky had no trouble comprehending the police emergency number, but recalling his own tag number was an exercise in memory that required verification. He turned and ...

Saw someone driving off with his car.

Deke had his head dipped and his shoulder raised. With the speed he had the car moving, it was unlikely Ricky had gotten a good look at him. But he ran down the street after his car nonetheless. Didn't have an efficient stride, Welborn observed.

Two minutes later, Callie Bao returned.

Buckingham Palace, London

18

Members of the household staff set out scones, strawberries and cream, and poured tea for the queen and the president. It was assumed the two eminent ladies were up to adding and stirring their own sugar, if they so desired. Neither did.

After making perfunctory but sincere observations about the beauty of the royal gardens, the president asked, "You're feeling well, Your Majesty?"

The queen offered a polite smile but couldn't hide the sadness in her eyes.

Patti knew that Galia had been right; something was seriously amiss.

"My physical constitution is as sound as ever, Madam President ... even though my heart bears a heavy burden."

"Is there any way I might be of service?"

"You already have. I very much appreciate your making time for me. I know how very busy you are. I've watched the start of your administration with great interest. It has been a unique opportunity to observe a woman wield such immense power."

"How am I doing?" Patti asked with a hint of mischief.

"Brilliantly," the queen replied, joy now filling her face. "I can't tell you how much I envy you young women. The world has become a much different place for you."

"Thanks to the women of your generation, Your Majesty."

"Yes." The light in the queen's eyes dimmed. "I wish I'd had more to do with that."

Patti wanted to suggest otherwise, but you didn't contradict the queen.

Her majesty continued, getting to the point of the visit, "The Duchess of Cornwall is mortally ill."

There it was, Patti thought. The Prince of Wales' second wife was dying. Patti ran the possible consequences through her mind, without forgetting her manners.

"I'm terribly sorry, Your Majesty."

"As am I, thank you. The prince has informed me he is withdrawing from the line of succession. He will be attending to his wife in her final days, and then he will withdraw from the public eye for an indefinite time. He feels he would no longer be fit to accept the throne."

After seeing a second wife die, and waiting to be crowned well into the second half of his own life, Patti could understand that. The question now became—

"I've spoken to the Duke of York and the Earl of Essex." The queen's two younger sons. "I've explained to the duke that I feel the monarchy would best be served by a younger king; the earl has never been interested in the crown."

After the monarch had let all three of her sons grow into middle age or older waiting for their mother to abdicate, that must have been a tough one for the duke to swallow, Patti thought. Even the earl might be having second thoughts. But what did she know about being a queen?

Well, she had a pretty good idea who the next king would be.

"My elder grandson will accept the crown."

Better him than his younger brother, the president thought.

The queen averted her eyes for a moment, as if to gather strength, then looked directly at the president.

"My grandson's willingness to claim his birthright did not come without conditions. He will not wait indefinitely to become king."

Patti kept a straight face, but thought good for him.

"That is why I shall abdicate one minute before midnight on the thirty-first of December. The new monarch shall be crowned on the first day of the New Year."

That tied things up with a ribbon and a bow, the president thought. But the queen was not finished.

"My grandson informs me that he will model his reign after The House of Orange and Nassau." The Royal Family of the Netherlands. The queen frowned in displeasure. "Wilhelmina rides a bicycle in public; my grandson proposes to do so as well."

As gently as she could, the president said, "Please remember, Your Majesty, the world *is* changing. In many ways."

"Directly to that point, Madam President, my grandson also intends to speak out on the politics of the day, whether it discomfits our politicians or any others. If Whitehall doesn't like that, he says they can pension off the lot of us."

For the first time since they began their conversation, Patti put down her teacup and sat back to think of political implications for the United States.

"If your grandson's opinions resonate with his subjects," she said, "that will make him very popular, far more powerful, all but impossible to displace."

The queen showed a rueful smile. "The monarchy ascendant."

"That's quite an idea to conjure with," Patti said. "Thank you for giving me fair warning."

The queen said, "I know the prime minister meddled in your election; I was too reticent to say anything, of course. I should have, and I'm sorry I didn't. Please accept my apology."

"If you wish, Your Majesty, of course."

"I'm also aware of Norvin Kimbrough's reputation for being less than genteel in his treatment of women, especially those who dare to involve themselves in governance. You must have been the ultimate affront to him. So I must confess no distress as to what happened to him at your hand. In fact, I thought what you did was beautifully played."

Patti felt a chill. The queen knew what she had done? The president doubted her majesty had a working knowledge of Dark Alley, so she only said, "I hope the prime minister recovers quickly."

"Not too quickly. Without ever saying so publicly, I hope his party replaces him. For reasons of health, of course."

The president wanted him to be replaced for any reason.

"In any event, Madam President, I think you've served notice to your male counterparts, including my grandson should it ever come to that, not to trifle with you. My only wish now is that I might be of help to you in some way."

Patti picked up her teacup, sipped, and pondered.

"There is one thing, your majesty."

"What might that be?"

"The woman who killed my first husband has petitioned our Supreme Court to have her death sentence imposed without delay. Should the court rule in her favor, it becomes my decision whether to let the execution be carried out."

The elder woman smiled once more. "Life or death, now there's a decision worthy of a queen. What does your heart say?"

"My husband, Mr. McGill, said everyone involved in the crime should be strapped to gurneys. Given lethal injections, that is. I've never told anyone, including Jim, how many moments there have been when I've come to agree with him."

"What other considerations do you face? Moral questions? Political ones?"

"Politics be damned," Patti said, "but morality, there's the rub. If I let Erna Godfrey be executed, I become a passive accomplice to her death. But there's more to it: That woman is still too close to what she did. She hasn't admitted in any way that taking Andy's life was wrong. That's what galls me most. If she were to die soon, it would be without ever feeling any remorse."

"Then give her the opportunity to reconsider," the queen said.

"Let her live?"

"I've read many commission reports regarding how dreadful our prisons are. I imagine yours are of a similar nature."

"So I've been told."

"Is this Godfrey woman in good health?"

"As far as I know," the president said. "Her legal case is the one issue from which I've distanced myself."

"Well, were she to be ill, I would let nature take her instead of the state. If she's physically well, why not give her any number of decades to think about how gruesome her crime was, how feeble her excuses for committing it are?"

"I should commute her sentence then?" the president asked.

"Think of it as *extending* her sentence," the queen answered.

Magistrate Pruet's office, Paris

19

Yves Pruet watched the DVD of The Undertaker's snuff match on a television set up directly in front of the table he used as his desk. McGill stood at his side and watched the action from an oblique angle. It was the third time he'd seen the fight, if it could be called that. The first two times he'd been both nauseated and infuriated. Now, he was getting into the metaphysical realm. What kind of mutant could do what The Undertaker had done? For that matter what kind of sociopath could hold a camera steady and record the savagery?

Pruet sat and watched stoically until the end, then clicked off the television.

He looked at McGill, his silence an invitation to his guest to speak first.

McGill said, "I've heard of American mobsters doing that, but not *like* that."

Pruet sighed, lowered his head, still trying to comprehend what he'd seen.

McGill moved around to the other side of the table, moved the TV and video disc player aside and pulled up a chair.

"You've got the guy," he said. "Committing murder on camera. You know his name. Ms. Martel must have told you everything she knew, so you should have some idea where he can be found. Now, it's just a matter of sending enough cops to bring him in ... right?"

McGill sat and waited for the magistrate's response.

It was some time in coming, but McGill understood why and was patient.

Looking up, Pruet finally said, "Had I returned home earlier, that might have been me."

"But it wasn't," McGill said. "God or fate, whichever you prefer, must have other plans for you."

"It might have been Nicolette as well."

"But she skated, too."

"What do you think we should do with this creature, M'sieur McGill?"

The president's henchman suspected it might come to this. For whatever reason, Pruet couldn't play it straight. Send a couple dozen cops out and bring The Undertaker down—alive—with a hail of rubber bullets. That wasn't an option.

"If you want me to help, you'll have to put your cards on the table," McGill said.

"I would be most surprised if you haven't guessed every card I hold."

"Okay. I'll tell you the way I see things, now. I was wrong

thinking Thierry Duchamp's death might have been a mistake, that the intent was only to injure him, so crooked gamblers might make a—pardon the expression—killing."

"You are correct," Pruet said, "that was never the case."

"But you let me think so," McGill said.

The magistrate only shrugged.

"Because if I helped you succeed without really understanding the true nature of the case that would be as good as it gets for you," McGill told Pruet.

"We would all prefer to be seen in our evening wear not our underwear."

McGill smiled. Saw no reason to hold a grudge.

He said, "The more I learned, the surer I became that once you send Etienne Burel out to start pounding on someone, there's going to be only one result."

Pruet nodded, his expression grim.

"That being the case, I have to wonder why this thug wasn't locked up or buried a long time ago. He makes an easy target, and there are rounds big enough to bring him down."

"And your conclusion?" the magistrate asked.

"Someone with clout is protecting him."

"Clout?" Pruet asked.

"Political muscle."

The magistrate nodded, adding the word to his vocabulary.

"So you think politics are involved?"

McGill nodded. "Has to be. Just on the bad guys' side, there are hardliners and people who want to cut their losses."

Pruet was intrigued by McGill's analysis. "And how do you know this?"

"Simple. The hardliners sent The Undertaker to visit first Durand and then you. The ones who want to cut their losses are the people who sent the video that show the Undertaker killing a man. Damning evidence in any nation, I would imagine."

"It certainly would be here," Pruet told McGill.

"Might even go farther than that," the president's henchman said.

"What do you mean?"

"I mean," McGill said, "where there's one incriminating video disk, there might well be another. And the second disk might be used as justification for someone to kill The Undertaker. Not only that, it might be used to criticize you, *m'sieur le magistrat,* for not eliminating him first. Those two things would put a crimp into your investigation of Thierry Duchamp's death, wouldn't they?"

Pruet was silent, but the look in his eyes acknowledged McGill's point.

"Your insurance against something like that happening," McGill said, "is to hang on to Glen Kinnard as long as you can. If you let Glen go, you're telling the bad guys they better move fast."

Pruet sighed. He said to McGill, "You have undoubtedly deduced your own usefulness in this affair."

McGill nodded. "Sure. I saw that before leaving home. Things go to hell in a handbasket, I get to be the scapegoat. But who decided that, you or *m'sieur le president?*"

Pruet was silent for a moment. Then he said, "Jean-Louis. I insisted if there were a disaster to be borne, it would be mine alone."

"*Merci, m'sieur,*" McGill said. "But your friend, Jean-Louis, could not accept that."

"Why not? You think our bonds of friendship are that strong?"

"I do. But there's more than that, as we both know."

"What do we both know?"

"That you're the French president's henchman." McGill saluted the magistrate.

Pruet saw any pretense that McGill was wrong would be futile.

"Actually," he said, "Jean-Louis calls me *le compagnon du bourreau.*"

McGill arched an eyebrow. *Qu'est-ce que c'est?* Say what?

Pruet said, "In idiomatic English, the hangman's companion."

20

It was one of those moments where two men with a common background and a shared task might share a drink, and the magistrate was heading for his filing cabinet. McGill feared Pruet was about to bring out more cognac.

"You have anything without alcohol?" he asked. "I'm going to need both my wits and my reflexes soon, assuming I'm right in thinking that if you call in the gendarmes they might be the ones to shoot Etienne Burel on sight."

The magistrate closed the file drawer. He returned to his table and picked up the phone. "*De l'eau du minérale de Perrier?*" he asked McGill.

"That'll be fine."

Pruet put in his order.

"I asked Odo and Ms. Casale to join us for our refreshments."

McGill nodded and said, "You've been sorting things out for your friend Jean-Louis for a long time, haven't you?"

"We met at the *lycée*. Got along famously from the very beginning. Truly enjoy each other's company. More than meet each other's needs."

For a moment, McGill almost thought—

Pruet saw his misconception and shook his head. "No, m'sieur, not that way."

"*Désolé,*" McGill said. Sorry.

"*C'est rien.*" No problem. "What I was getting at ... Have you a friend who understands you better than anyone else? To whom you need never explain yourself? Who naturally sympathizes with you, but does not hesitate to tell you when you are in error? Never intending any malice when he does."

"I do," McGill said, thinking of Sweetie. "She looks like she could be Ms. Casale's elder sister. My former wife is also like that to a certain extent. The president and I are more and more like that every day."

Pruet had to laugh, and shake his head.

"I envy you your ease with women," he said.

McGill replied, "A matter of luck, and not trying too hard."

"I will do my best to remember that: not to try too hard. In any event, Jean-Louis and I met at a time of greater than usual social ferment in France. We, like everyone else with a spark of ambition, decided we would change the world. It went without saying that he would be the face of our effort; I would be the strategist. Over the years, our efforts have met with a certain success."

McGill smiled. "I'd say so, if reaching the Elysée Palace was on your to-do list."

"Not just to reach the palace, m'sieur, but to remain there long enough to do meaningful things for *La Belle France*, and to some extent the world at large."

"When you first read Diana Martel's police file," McGill said, "you saw something in it you didn't like. Something that told you Thierry Duchamp's death had far larger implications than anything I was thinking. You saw something that threatened President Severin."

"And by extension President Grant," the magistrate said.

McGill thought about that for a moment and said, "The new defense doctrine they are championing?"

"Without Jean-Louis, there is no champion in Europe. The British prime minister opposes the plan; the German chancellor, for historical reasons, would not be permitted to lead."

"So what are we looking at? Your president's political enemies have set out to sabotage him? The Undertaker kills Thierry Duchamp, France's biggest football star, on the eve of an international tournament. It's chalked up as a street crime. Then what, the president is blamed? The opposition claims he can't even keep the streets safe for a man who's a national treasure?"

Pruet nodded. "Jean-Louis is demonized. He is called upon to strictly enforce law and order. Provocateurs spark riots in the immigrant communities. Portions of the capital are set ablaze. *M'sieur le président* is required to forsake the G8 meeting or, if he goes, is reviled further, and the government rejects anything he might try to accomplish there."

McGill sat back in chair.

"You saw a name in Diana Martel's file that gave it away?"

"The owner of the strip club, Paradis Trouvé."

"Where Etienne Burel works."

"*Oui.* The owner is a friend, a henchman if you will, of Jean-Louis' most serious political enemy. Only this fellow, the underling, was reported lost at sea, having fallen from a yacht sailing off Tahiti. A massive search was organized but his body was never found."

"Could be he drowned," McGill said with a shrug. "If nobody gets around to updating the deed on a strip club, that's going to be a surprise?"

The magistrate opened the one drawer in his table, took out a photograph, slid it over to McGill. He saw a middle-aged man with thinning sandy brown hair, a sun-browned face, a prominent nose and a cigarette dangling from his mouth.

"That's your guy, huh?" McGill asked. "And the picture's current."

"Odo took it yesterday."

McGill had an insight. "A man who's supposed to be dead could be your hardliner, the guy who sent The Undertaker to visit you and Durand. Why not? Who's going to suspect someone who's been lost at sea?"

Pruet nodded, finding McGill's reasoning plausible.

"As soon as possible, I will send Odo to collect him."

The door to Pruet's office opened.

"Did I hear someone mention my name?" the Corsican asked.

Gabbi was a step behind him. She closed the door behind them.

"I was showing Mr. McGill your photo of Charlot Karel."

Odo nodded and placed the tray with the drinks he carried on Pruet's table.

McGill took the glass he was offered and sipped.

"So, in his own way, Glen Kinnard screwed up the bad guys'

plans," he said. "A visiting American, here to scatter his French-born wife's ashes in the Seine, couldn't be portrayed as a street thug."

Pruet sampled his own glass. "For which we are most grateful. As for those of us here today, we are left with the task of capturing and questioning not one but two villains without help from the police."

"Because you really do fear the cops might kill Burel?" McGill asked.

Odo gave it away. "We are dealing with another interior minister."

McGill thought maybe the French should reorganize that office.

Then something Pruet had said popped into McGill's head.

It might explain how Thierry Duchamp had become the target for assassination.

"I bet the interior minister likes old-fashioned, low-scoring French football teams."

Pruet sighed. "M'sieur McGill, you are coming to know us too well."

St Magnus rectory, Annandale, VA

21

Sweetie slowed the Malibu as she approached the parking area adjacent to the rectory of St. Magnus Church. A flash of familiar red hair caught her eye. Kira Fahey was coming down the back steps of the rectory in tears—and smiling ear to ear. In her right hand, she clutched what looked like a white cloth to her chest. She ran in the direction of a Lexus SUV, but stopped halfway and looked at the cloth or something on it. Sweetie could hear the sob that came from Kira.

Sweetie pulled into a parking slot and put the car in neutral. Deciphering the sound she'd just heard coming from Kira was problematic. The mix of emotions it had contained was hard to read. There was a note of desperate loss, but also a distinct undertone of joy. Almost a laugh. That mitigating happiness was what kept Sweetie from rushing to Kira to see if she needed help.

Apparently, she didn't. She continued on to the Lexus and after a moment of sitting behind the wheel—and holding the cloth up in front of her—she drove off. Waiting until Kira was out of sight, Sweetie shifted to park and shut down the engine.

She climbed the back steps of the rectory and rang the doorbell.

22

A frowning housekeeper admitted Sweetie to Father Francis Nguyen's spartan office. The priest's wooden desk and chairs looked like they might have come from the WPA. Adding to the early 20th century feel of the space was a portrait of Pius XII on the wall behind the priest. Sweetie wondered about that choice. Pius XII was the pope criticized—condemned, even—for his failure to take a stand against the Nazis. The Vatican had rationalized his conduct, but the pontiff remained a flashpoint of controversy to the present day.

Addressing the housekeeper, Father Nguyen said, "Thank you, Mrs. Crowther. That will be all."

When Sweetie didn't hear the woman leave, she turned to look at her. Gave Mrs. Crowther her best cop stare. Worked like a charm. She left forthwith.

When Sweetie heard the door click shut, she said to the priest, "Thank you for seeing me, Father."

The priest raised his hands and let them fall: a gesture of conciliation not blessing.

"I came to your office unannounced," he said.

"But never unwelcome. Jim and I can always use guidance."

"As can we all."

Sweetie didn't want to get into a humility contest.

She was about to speak when the priest preempted her.

"Would you happen to know the young woman who just

visited me? You may have crossed her path on your way in; her name is Kay."

Having conducted many an interrogation in her day, Sweetie was familiar with the use of the unexpected question. She also knew how to answer one truthfully, if incompletely. Keeping the extent of her knowledge to herself and her sin of omission venial in nature.

"I saw her. She looked familiar. But the woman I know isn't named Kay."

All true, and she didn't rat out Kira, Sweetie thought. But she was sure, despite her best efforts to live a good life, she would spend a long time explaining herself to Saint Peter. Assuming she made it as far as the Pearly Gates.

Father Nguyen wasn't done with his inquiries.

"Do you believe in miracles, Margaret?"

"I do," Sweetie said without hesitation.

"Have you ever been the beneficiary of one?"

She thought of her cousin Patrick coming home safely from the war, and she thought of walking among Reverend Burke Godfrey's agitated followers with Caitie McGill and both of them coming away unharmed.

"More than once," she said.

That got the good father's attention.

"Would you mind if I told you a story then?"

"I'll listen to yours," Sweetie said, "if you'll listen to mine."

23

Sweetie had to admit Father Nguyen's miracle was more impressive than either of hers. "Have you spoken to anyone in the hierarchy of this?" she asked the priest.

He shook his head. "I only confirmed with Kay just now that the image on the cloth is indeed that of her late father."

Sweetie had a question on that point. "Did the young lady ever tell you how old she was when her father died?" Kira had never mentioned it to Sweetie.

"Quite young. Six years old."

"That had to be some time ago. How could she recognize his likeness?"

"She told me she has been studying family photo albums as the date of her wedding approaches."

Okay, Sweetie thought. She could buy that.

Father Nguyen continued, "She said the image of her father on the cloth is exactly the same as a picture in which he is standing next to Kay's mother. It was taken on their honeymoon."

"Whew," Sweetie said. "If this is a miracle, it's a good one. There's no chance anyone with artistic talent could have spent some time working on the cloth?"

The priest didn't take offense; he was looking for a critical point of view.

"What would an artist use as his model? I don't even know Kay's last name, much less where she lives or keeps her photo albums."

"Maybe the artist saw Kay herself. Is there a resemblance between her and her father?"

"Yes. But not so strong as to be exact. She has promised to bring the picture in for me to compare. Then there is the question of which medium an artist might have used for his work."

"Medium? You mean, oil, tempera, fabric paint?"

The priest told Sweetie of Mrs. Crowther's efforts to wash the image out of the cloth, including her use of bleach in a third attempt.

"She said laundering the image only made it more beautiful, to use her word. That was when she thought she should bring the cloth to me. Asked me if I had drawn it."

"Had you?" Sweetie the ex-cop asked.

"No. It's all I can do to write my name legibly."

Sweetie sat back, folded her hands in her lap. Shrugged.

"I'm not an expert in the field, Father, but if it's not a miracle, you've got me stumped."

"It would have been helpful," the priest said, "if the portrait had come with a signature."

Sweetie laughed. "Not even with the Ten Commandments did He do that."

Father Nguyen smiled broadly. Sweetie, as she did with most people, had won him over.

"Miracle or not," she said, "you can't take this story to Bishop O'Menehy."

"No," Father Nguyen said.

"It would look self-serving for a priest at odds with the hierarchy. There would be a big investigation, an ecclesiastical circus. The Vatican would demand to take possession of the cloth. Years of debate would follow. And in the end—"

"I would be denounced. The cloth would be burned or simply disappear."

"Martin Luther can never be made a saint."

"No, that would never do," Francis Nguyen said. "And it would never do to ask Kay to part with the cloth."

With that, the priest won Sweetie over, too.

"Now, what is your story, Margaret?" he asked.

She said, "Did you ever hear the one about the priest, the bishop, and the two gangsters?"

Father Nguyen clearly didn't think a joke was about to follow.

"Don't worry," Sweetie told him. "I might have figured out a happy ending."

Magistrate Pruet's office, Paris

24

Gabbi was off on a shopping trip. Odo was out arresting Charlot Karel, the interior minister's supposedly dead lieutenant. Pruet was off securing the use of some private dungeon in which to stash Karel, Diana Martel and eventually, they all hoped, The Undertaker. McGill was by himself in the magistrate's office once again watching the DVD of The Undertaker doing in his victim. This time it was to find the mountainous thug's weaknesses.

There were always some. McGill had a pad and pen to make notes.

Of course, the man who had died at The Undertaker's hands had thought he could find weaknesses, too. Exploit them with his five free blows. End the fight and win ten thousand euros before he broke a sweat.

The setting for the fight was indoors. Harsh blue-white light created an illuminated square perhaps twenty feet on a side and showed a concrete floor speckled red. Not with blood, McGill thought, more like an automotive fluid of some sort. Some of the stains looked to be wet. McGill had the feeling the site was some sort of warehouse. The square of light was surrounded by deep shadows, but in an early frame McGill thought he caught a glimpse of a lowered overhead door, giving him the suggestion of a loading dock.

From his earlier viewings, he knew there were at least two eyewitnesses to the killing that was about to happen: the camera operator and a man with a handgun. If the video's producers were smart, those were the only two spectators present. If there were dumb mutts behind the grisly exhibit, they had sold as many tickets as they could.

While the lighted square was still empty an opening title appeared.

Un combat à la mort. A fight to the death.

The challenger stepped out of the darkness.

Jean Martin was supered on the screen.

Gabbi had said the name was the French equivalent of John Smith.

McGill estimated the soon-to-be-dead Smith stood maybe six-three and weighed at least two-forty. Wearing only a wrestler's singlet, Smith didn't look the least bit fat; his musculature and supporting skeletal structure were round and dense. He was a brute power guy. In most cases, he probably got his way with one hard shove. Put a guy flat on his ass and stand over him glowering, daring the poor sap to get up.

The Undertaker stepped into the light, also in a singlet, and by comparison Smith suddenly looked slight. Smith didn't have a face fashioned by kind thoughts and good deeds, but compared to the mug on The Undertaker, he looked like Truman Capote.

A new super appeared. *Le champion final.* The ultimate champion.

Having only visuals for reference, McGill couldn't tell if The Undertaker's trademark cloud of stench hung about—No, wait. Looking for a reaction now, he saw Smith's nose wrinkle in disgust and his mouth fall open so he could breathe through it. Yeah, the big guy was doing his best impression of a 400-pound skunk.

McGill had a better understanding now of how terrified Arno Durand had been when The Undertaker had kicked in the reporter's door and didn't let a little thing like a cast iron skillet bouncing off his skull bother him. The president's henchman didn't see himself jumping out a window, but in the absence of having some major firepower in hand, he would try to beat feet rather than try to take the guy on alone.

Smith clearly saw that even with five free shots he was going to have his work cut out for him. Trying to shove this monster off his feet wasn't going to work. The Undertaker stood unmoving, his hands at his sides, as Smith moved to one side of him and then the other, to see what he might see. From behind, the camera followed Smith, giving McGill the challenger's point of view. The Undertaker looked completely unconcerned that Smith might launch a sneak attack on him.

Still, the monster kept watch. When Smith moved to The Undertaker's left, he followed the movement with his eyes. When Smith moved to The Undertaker's right, though, the monster had to turn his head to keep track of him.

McGill paused the disc and made a note. *Limited, if any, peripheral vision on right side.* He hit the play button.

Smith started to move behind The Undertaker, see what might be of interest back there, but a hand suddenly projected itself from shadow into the light. The hand, masculine and holding a gun, waved Smith off. He was not permitted to walk behind The Undertaker. The interdiction made McGill wonder if Smith might have seen an Achilles' heel of some sort from that point of view or if the gunman simply didn't want Smith getting too close to him.

Perhaps fearing Smith might knock the gunman on his ass and make a break for it.

Couldn't have a fight to the death if one guy ran away.

Smith took the warning to heart and backed off. He went back to inspecting his target from permissible angles. Having gotten somewhat past the horror of what would soon happen, McGill now appreciated what Smith was up to: He was trying to wear out the monster's patience. Get him to relax, maybe get exasperated and look away. Appeal to someone in the shadows to get the show on the road.

And that's just what The Undertaker did, insofar as he turned his head to his left. The moment his eyes were off Smith, the smaller man attacked.

McGill hit the DVD control for slow motion and watched what followed closely. Smith threw a roundhouse left hand, real haymaker. McGill knew exactly the spot Smith was trying to hit: the hinge of The Undertaker's jaw, the temporomandibular joint. The same spot McGill had hit to turn Glen Kinnard's lights out.

Smith's punched carried more than enough power to knock out anyone in his weight class; it might even have dropped The Undertaker to his knees where it might have been followed by a nice kick to the teeth that would have settled matters in Smith's favor. Well, after Smith had stomped the giant's head, as the promoter insisted on someone dying.

The problem for Smith wasn't The Undertaker's bulk, it was his height. Most likely, Smith had never thrown a punch at someone over seven feet tall. He overcompensated and missed the monster's jaw, catching him flush on his right ear. The Undertaker stayed on his feet. In fact, he stood straighter than before, as if he'd been jolted by electricity. His mouth opened wide in what must have been a nightmare-inspiring scream.

McGill paused the video. He looked at the monster's teeth. Most of them were present and approximately in proper alignment but The Undertaker plainly didn't brush after every meal. His tooth color ranged from gray to black. From decaying to dead.

McGill wrote: *A good shot to the mouth will really hurt this guy.*

He returned the player to slow motion. Like any good street fighter, Smith immediately pressed his advantage. He kicked The Undertaker in the crotch. Again, however, he hadn't properly accounted for the monster's height; the giant's family jewels dangled a good foot higher than most men's and it looked to McGill as if Smith's foot just grazed his target rather than drove into it. And for all McGill knew The Undertaker was smart enough to wear a cup.

In any event, Smith's kick was still enough to make the monster bellow in pain once more; it even drove him back a step or two. Smith did not relent, but he lowered his sights to more accessible targets. He kicked the beast smartly on his right knee and then his left knee.

McGill paused the video. *Make this guy move as much as possible, especially try to make him pivot.*

If The Undertaker were at all human, those knees would never be the same. Just carrying all his weight should make them sore. Get him to make a sudden change in direction and one of his legs might buckle. If he went down to his knees, they could throw a net over him.

He set the player back to slow motion. Smith still had one free shot left and what he hoped—or at least what McGill would have hoped in his place—was for the monster to lean forward and put a hand over each knee, to try to rub the pain out of them. That would present The Undertaker's head like a football, the American kind, to be punted the length of the field.

The giant did bend forward, but either instinctively or as a result of experience, he knew enough to cover his face with his massive forearms, taking away a straight-on kick. McGill thought what he would have done in Smith's place was to take another good shot at the monster's jaw. Follow that up with a kick to the side of the knee. If the leg joint was unstable already, another kick should have collapsed it. But that was when Smith made his fatal mistake.

He stepped back. Probably thinking he had one more free shot and a better opportunity to use it was bound to present itself. He'd have been better off if he had decided he'd done all the damage he could and there would never be a better time to take everyone by surprise and run.

All he did, though, was back off and study his outsized opponent from a distance of maybe eight feet. McGill clicked the video to normal speed. Twenty seconds later by his count—a length of time he noted—The Undertaker began to rise ever so slowly. It made McGill think of mountain building. When he was fully upright he turned his gaze on Smith. Where there had been cruel indifference in The Undertaker's expression before there was now loathing and a measure of fear. Smith, though much smaller, had hurt him, might possibly best him if given another chance.

Looking at the monster through the camera's lens, it was clear to McGill the beast was never going to give Smith that chance. But being there in the flesh, adrenaline surging, maybe with sweat in his eyes, Smith hadn't noticed that the rules had changed. Now, there were no rules.

The Undertaker didn't give away his hand. He stood as he originally had.

Unmoving. Seemingly indifferent to both his own pain and to Smith.

The smaller man really should have seen through that, McGill thought.

Nobody, no matter how big and bad, bellowed in pain one moment and shrugged it off the next. It had to be a fakeout. The giant was making his own plans.

Smith, laboring under a terminal misapprehension, began

another inspection of The Undertaker. Adding to his miscalculation, Smith moved to the monster's left, his visually superior side. Smith didn't close the distance with his opponent, the mountain came to him.

In an intuitive maneuver, the camera operator had moved in counterpoint to Smith. He caught the look of horror on Smith's face as The Undertaker fell upon him like an avalanche. But the giant didn't drive him to the floor, crush him, and pummel him. He twisted the smaller man around so they both faced the same direction. His massive arms crushed Smith against his chest.

The camera operator rushed to get the two combatants' faces in his lens. The Undertaker turned to meet him halfway. Facing the camera's bright red light, seeing it as a sign of what awaited him in the next life, Smith furiously drummed his heels against the monster's shins. He might as well have thrown wads of paper at the beast. The Undertaker began to squeeze and bones began to break. Visibly.

It was Smith's turn to scream.

Had it been The Undertaker's choice, he could have ended it all right there. Snapped the smaller man's spine and been done with him. But when he calculated Smith would no longer be able to raise his arms in his own defense he relaxed his crushing embrace. But only long enough to place a gargantuan hand on either side of Smith's head. He lifted the man off the floor and—

McGill had seen more than enough. He clicked off the machine.

The Undertaker had his vulnerabilities.

But the cost of making a mistake with him was unspeakable.

Upton Hill Regional Park, Arlington, VA

25

His Excellency, Bishop George O'Menehy, cleared his schedule for Margaret Sweeney and rode in the back of her Malibu. Father Francis Nguyen rode shotgun. They found an open picnic bench in a sun-dappled glade at Upton Hill Regional Park, and Sweetie bade the clerics to sit. They did, side by side, but with a good foot of space between them.

Sweetie looked down at them. Francis Nguyen looked calm and composed, as usual. Bishop O'Menehy seemed anything but serene; he looked as though he was bracing to hear the worst news of his life. For all Sweetie knew, he was right.

She had persuaded the bishop to accompany her and Father Nguyen by telling him, "I know how Horatio Bao is blackmailing you, Your Excellency. I know how he's keeping you quiet about it, too."

The bishop had lost all color in his face when he heard that. He took his glasses off and for a moment looked as if he might pass out. Both Sweetie and Father Nguyen had to steady him. He regained enough self-possession to tell his secretary, Mrs. Novak, he would be unavailable for the rest of the day. From the look Mrs. Novak had given her, Sweetie knew she had made another enemy among the diocesan support staff.

Sweetie had seated the clerics so they were in sunlight and she had her back to it.

She started bluntly: "There's a cancer eating away this diocese and his name is Horatio Bao. I know both of you gentlemen are constrained by the seal of the confessional so I don't expect you to admit anything. All I want you to do is listen … and then tell me, yes or no, whether you'll agree with my plan to help you."

Bishop O'Menehy stiffened his spine now. "Nothing you propose may contravene Church law, if you expect my help."

"Of course not, Your Excellency," Sweetie said.

"And you'll not expect us to break Caesar's law either?" Father Nguyen asked.

"No. There will be some risk to the plan, however. Not a lot, if I'm right. But both of you will have to show some physical courage."

The two clerics looked at one another, each assessing the other man's character.

"I agree," Father Nguyen said, turning back to Sweetie.

Bishop O'Menehy said to Sweetie, "I heard your confession, but are you, in fact, Catholic?"

"I am."

"And what you are about to propose, will it be of benefit to the Church?"

"It will put an end to your being blackmailed, Your Excellency. Is that beneficial?"

The bishop nodded. "If that's what will happen, my personal safety is of no matter."

So the old guy could be brave, too. Whatever their doctrinal differences, Sweetie admired him for that.

"Okay," Sweetie said, "keep straight faces, gentlemen, so you don't give anything away, and I'll tell you what's going on and how we're going to fix it."

Callie Bao's dance studio, Arlington, VA

26

"You conned me," Callie Bao told Welborn Yates as he held her hand and waist. The two of them were moving through basic swing steps, a recorded percussion track keeping the beat. "You already know how to dance."

"One and two, three and four, five-six," Welborn responded. "Small and big, small and big, rock-step."

He gave her his most winning smile and a shake of his head.

"I had one lesson when I was nine years old. I told my mother if she made me try to take any more I'd run away from home. You're just a great teacher, a great dancer."

She gave him a look, assaying the BS content of his words. Decided what he'd said was close enough to the truth not to matter. Maybe he was a natural, and as good looking as he was, she was not going to quibble.

"What this reminds me of a little," Welborn continued, "is my job."

"Your job?"

"I fly fighter jets. I'll grant you the speeds are different. But the two of us moving as one, the responsiveness, the maneuverability, it's very similar. Maybe that's why I'm picking it up fast."

Thing was, that was how he actually felt.

His only fib was referring to flying jets in the present tense.

"You're military?" Callie asked.

"Well, I certainly hope we're the only ones who fly F-22s."

Callie Bao moved closer to him. The scent of her perfume intensified. Her hand was suddenly warmer in his. Another military thought occurred to him: She'd armed her weapons.

He'd have to be very careful here.

"You know something?" she asked, her voice more breathy than before.

"What's that?"

"I'll give you all the lessons you want for free, if you do one thing for me."

He was almost afraid to ask: "What's that?"

"Take me up. Take me flying in one of your fighter jets." She was pressing against him now. "Don't say you can't because I've seen it on television, celebrities getting rides in fighter jets. I've always wanted to do that, to feel all that incredible power, to rocket straight up into the sky."

She put her mouth on his neck, took little nibbles.

Damn woman had gotten him going. Reminding him of his own excitement in flying jets. Working him up pretty good on her own, too. There was only one way to preserve his virtue: Lie.

Clearing his throat, Welborn told her. "Okay."

Callie pulled her head back and Welborn feared she was about to kiss him.

Wouldn't be able to explain that one to Kira.

He held up an interdictory finger. "No civilians get to joyride in F-22s, but I can take you up in something that will be a real thrill. That good enough?"

It was good enough to get him a kiss on the cheek instead of the lips.

And an invitation of sorts.

"Take me out for something to eat. Tell me what it will be like."

"I'll pick you up for dinner at seven," Welborn told her.

The law offices of Horatio Bao, Arlington, VA

27

It was only after Ricky stepped into Bao's office and got a dead-eyed stare that he remembered what was expected of him. Already repressing the anger of having had his car stolen out from under his nose, and the yellow-haired dog giving him the finger, he now had to choke back a further indignity. Ricky ground his teeth and bowed to his boss.

Bowing had become a pain in the ass and a point of real controversy among the younger generation of Viet Kieu. Who the hell did these old pricks think they were? Little emperors?

Of course, Ricky's ambitions were such that he saw himself reaching heights even Bao could only dream of, and then every-damn-body had better bow to him.

"Why are you here?" Bao asked. "Why did Calanthe admit you without buzzing me?"

Ricky was supposed to keep his distance from Bao's official place of business.

"Your daughter is not at her desk," Ricky said.

Bao's already dark mood clouded further. His daughter was as dutiful as the thug in front of him was impulsive. The lawyer had seen the hope in Ricky's eyes that he would one day marry Calanthe as the first big step in whatever fanciful climb he imagined to be his future. Bao would sooner have his daughter marry a *danh tu*.

A hulking white American.

The lawyer made his impudent underling wait before he addressed the situation of his missing daughter. He picked up a picture postcard from his desk. It featured a photo of the Golden Gate Bridge half-shrouded in fog. It had been delivered that morning by FedEx in an overnight envelope.

When Bao had opened the envelope, the first thing he had wondered was: Who paid for the overnight delivery of a postcard? Flipping the card over, he'd seen who had sent it and it had chilled his heart. Written in Vietnamese were the words: *On my way to Hanoi. Hope you will join me. If you dare.* More colloquially, if you have the balls. *Musette Ky.*

The woman was telling him many things: that she was no longer within easy reach; that she was fleeing from imminent legal danger of her own; that if he chose to follow her, she would have already subverted those who had been paid to give Bao refuge. Returning to Vietnam, thumbing his nose at any American authorities who might pursue him, had always been Bao's default retreat. Calanthe had overseen the construction of two mansions for him in his native country, one north and one south. She had spent a fortune in bribes to smooth over Bao's past connection to the fallen government in Saigon. He had always taken comfort in having such a foolproof refuge.

Now, the damnable Madam Ky was saying she had taken that away from him. He knew, of course, that her father had been a double-agent during the war, working for both the Americans and the Communists. What she was telling him in her card was the old man's first loyalty had been to Hanoi. Her connections would trump his. If Bao fled to Vietnam, he would be returned to the Americans. Worse, he might be imprisoned in his homeland.

Charges could always be manufactured.

Not that any need be contrived. Bao's agent, the young fool with the insolent sneer standing in front of him, had shot the Secret Service agent assigned to guard the president's own husband. Washington would consider being given the culprits of that crime a great favor. Should Hanoi punish Bao directly, that might bring even greater appreciation.

The Communists might make a slave laborer of Bao, have him assemble Nike shoes for the rest of his life, all the while envying the peasants next to him who earned a dollar a day.

Ricky lost patience cooling his heels.

"There was this guy waiting outside your daughter's dance studio," he told Bao.

"What guy?" the lawyer asked.

"Some American asshole. I wanted to know what the hell he was doing. When I went to grab him, he let himself inside Calanthe's place. He had the keys."

Bao took in the implications of that, not liking any of them.

"Why didn't you call me?" he asked.

Ricky's belligerence suddenly disappeared.

"I couldn't," he muttered. "My phone was in my car, and somebody stole my car."

"What?" Bao asked, not believing what he was hearing. "Who would do that?"

How the fuck should I know, Ricky wanted to shout.

All he said was, "I didn't get a good look. But he was Asian not white."

"Viet?"

"Maybe." Thinking about it. "Probably."

"Look for word on the street. Someone will know."

"How am I supposed to get around?" Ricky asked.

He'd already run and walked for miles. His feet were sore.

"Buy a bicycle," Bao said, dismissing him.

Ricky ground his teeth even harder now, but did not forget to bow before leaving. It was only after he hit the street that he growled, "*Du ma.*" Fuck you.

Buy a bicycle. To hell with that. Someone stole his car, he'd steal someone else's. Something a lot nicer than the damn Nissan that old turd said he had to buy. Then he'd find that blonde bastard. Couldn't be a coincidence that guy was in his face when Ricky's ride got lifted. He'd get even with that white boy real soon.

28

In his office, Horatio Bao called Hanoi for the second time that day. His worries were vastly increased now. He had the feeling things were falling apart. It was the same sense of dread he'd felt when the time had come to flee Saigon. He was very careful to press every digit of the phone number correctly, make sure each was in the proper sequence. He had to talk to the government minister who would be his protection when he went home.

When he had tried earlier the call had gone unanswered for twenty rings. Now, a voice answered, but it was recorded. The message was, "The number you've called has been disconnected."

Horatio Bao dropped the phone. It was time to run again, he knew. First, though, he'd have to get rid of Ricky. The young fool was one of only two people who could tie him to the shooting of the Secret Service agent. The other was his daughter.

He trusted Calanthe. She was the light of his life, the image of her departed mother. He relied on her to do his banking and investing around the world. She would know where they should now seek refuge

He called his daughter's cell phone.

Got her voice mail.

Upton Hill Regional Park, Arlington, VA

29

Sweetie told Father Nguyen and Bishop O'Menehy, "Each of you is being held hostage by the seal of the confessional. I thought a confession had to be sincere and the penitent's feeling of remorse had to be genuine for the seal to be valid, but I was mistaken. At least that's what my research told me. Or do I have that wrong?"

"You do not," Bishop O'Menehy said. "The seal is inviolable."

"Do you see it the same way, Father?" Sweetie asked.

The bishop turned to look at the priest, concern written deep in his face.

He needn't have worried. Father Nguyen was not about to rebel on that point.

"Exactly the same way," he said.

The older man sighed in relief.

"Fine," Sweetie said. "Remember what I said about not giving anything away, gents, because I'm going to tell you what's going on. Father, last Thanksgiving, you were having dinner with your aunt, Musette Ky, and your cousin Donald Ky. At some point in the evening, the doorbell rang and—"

"I'm not sure I should hear this," the bishop said.

"My guess is you already have, Your Excellency. I saw Horatio Bao and Ricky Lanh Huu go into your confessional. I've heard from Special Agent Ky that Father Nguyen kicked Ricky out of his church. So, I bet, he's heard both Bao's and Ricky's confessions, too. That's the way a lawyer with a belt-and-suspenders mentality would do things. Each of you knows the bad guys' secrets, but they've fixed it so neither of you can ever make that admission."

Despite Sweetie's admonition to the clerics not to give anything away, they glanced at one another. Couldn't have said more clearly she had it right.

"Anyway, the doorbell rang at the Ky house. The hope of those outside the house was that Ms. Ky would open her own door. If that had been the case, she would have been the one who got shot, not her son. But Deke Ky took the bullet and almost died. Musette ran to her son, held him in her arms. Father Nguyen also rushed to see what help he might render. Arriving at the doorway, standing over his aunt and his cousin, he looked out and got a glimpse of the man who had shot his cousin: Ricky Lanh Huu.

"Thing was, maybe Father Nguyen didn't know Ricky at the time. Which would have made it harder to identify him to the police. But Ricky saw that he'd been spotted. If he'd kept his cool after shooting the wrong person, he would have taken out both you and your aunt, Father.

"But Ricky's a punk, so he ran. He went to Bao and reported what happened. Bao knew who the men in Musette's life are; a guy like that does his homework before he does business with someone. Bao pieced it together that his punk had shot Musette's son, a Secret Service agent, and the other guy on the scene, the one who had spotted Ricky, was Father Francis Nguyen. Bao knew silencing a priest didn't require violence. All you had to do to shut him up was confess to him. So that was just what Bao sent Ricky to do."

Sweetie stepped directly in front of the priest. "I won't ask if you saw Ricky enter your confessional, Father, but if you had any feeling something was wrong when he first arrived, like maybe the devil had dropped in for a chat, you should have cut him off at his first word."

Now, the priest had his poker face on.

"Of course, there could have been problems with that," Sweetie continued. "If Ricky actually had been sorry for what he'd done, how could you turn a true penitent away? And if he just wanted to shut you up, and you tried to dodge him, he might have shot you right there. Might have shot any witnesses who were in the church, too."

Francis Nguyen's expression hadn't changed a millimeter, but Sweetie saw in his eyes that she'd found the truth. The priest had been ambushed just like Deke.

"Now, I'll have to mention something that was confessed to me," Sweetie said. "Not being a priest, I can do that. Deke Ky told me his mother was something of a business consultant to certain criminal enterprises. I'd bet my pension she had worked with Horatio Bao before. So he came to her with a new idea. Only this time she wanted no part of it. Which meant it had to be something pretty awful."

Try as he might to not show any emotion, Bishop O'Menehy winced and lowered his head. His dismay was shared. Father Nguyen put a hand over his eyes. Even Sweetie sighed.

She said, "The greatest stain on the Church's name over the past generation has been its tolerance of pedophile priests. Over the last ten years, this disgrace has been exposed to the world. Dioceses across the country have had to pay tens of millions of dollars in damages. Finally, after suffering years of condemnation, the Church hoped it had put the whole sorry episode behind it. But then along came Horatio Bao."

Both men looked up at Sweetie, the anguish clear in their eyes.

"Bao had this idea," Sweetie said. "He knew a lot of guys like Ricky. A lot of them were doing prison time. And some of them had been locked up with pedophiles—some of who were former priests. So Bao had his bad guys approach these child molesters with a proposition. They told the ex-priests they could either protect them or kill them. Being weak, the pedophiles cooperated, but what did Bao want from them? He wanted them to say they had committed molestations that had never been discovered. A claim a great many people would be inclined to believe."

Sweetie didn't say so, but her expression made plain she would be among the credulous.

Tears fell from the bishop's eyes.

"The Church couldn't have that," Sweetie went on. "It had already lost an untold number of communicants and a good deal of its moral authority. More stories of kids being molested might damage the Church beyond repair. So Bao came to you, Your Excellency, with bad news and good news. The bad news was another scandal was about to erupt; the good news was for the right amount of money he could keep it quiet. Of course, he told you this in the confessional, and, worse, he probably told you it was all a scam and asked your forgiveness for his sins, too."

The older man began to sob. Father Nguyen moved close and put an arm around him.

Sweetie said, "But blackmailing her church was an idea Musette Ky couldn't abide. Bao had told her his plan, at least in outline. She could wreck the whole thing. But if Musette were killed, and Bao made his scam work in this diocese, he could take it to parishes nationwide."

Both clerics were aghast. The mass marketing of evil was an idea that had never occurred to them.

"You've got a game that plays," Sweetie told them, "you play it for all it's worth. The rollout was probably where Bao wanted Musette to help."

To Sweetie's surprise, the two men clasped hands and began to pray together in Latin. Call and response, bishop to priest. Sweetie waited patiently until they finished.

Addressing both men, she continued, "Having guaranteed your silence via the confessional, Bao thought he was safe. Public speculation about the shooting of Deke Ky said it had to be connected to his job protecting James J. McGill. So Bao had no worry there. And by Ricky shooting Musette Ky's son, even inadvertently, he thought he had intimidated her into silence. But then word of the troubled relationship between Father Nguyen and the diocese reached Bao. He must have felt threatened by the possibility that Father Nguyen might be expelled from the priesthood. If that happened, would a former priest still be bound by the seal of the confessional?"

Bishop O'Menehy started to speak but Sweetie cut him off.

"I know, Your Excellency, the seal is inviolable, but that's not how a crook would think."

Sweetie looked at Francis Nguyen. "That was probably why Bao sent Ricky to your church. To warn you there would be consequences if you *ever* talked about what you'd heard, priest or not." Sweetie hesitated, but decided this was no time to hold back. "That or Ricky was supposed to bring you somewhere out of the way and shoot you."

Now, Bishop O'Menehy's put an arm around the younger man.

Sweetie went on with her story. "After nursing her son back to health, Musette Ky hired me to investigate Deke's shooting. She knew, if I was any good, I'd learn of her involvement. Ms. Ky wasn't at home the last time I visited. Deke says she went back to Vietnam."

Francis Nguyen nodded: He could see that.

"I wouldn't be surprised," Sweetie said, "if Musette Ky eventually sends me something, say a recording incriminating Bao, just in case I'm not the detective she hopes I am. But with a little help I did find a number of Vietnamese immigrant families of modest means who have experienced sudden gains in upward mobility. All of them have moved into properties owned by pawns of Horatio Bao; all of them have young children in parochial schools. At least one of these kids has been coached how to explain the changes in her life. And if a kid tells a story often enough, she comes to believe it.

"Stories like how she was molested by a priest. The whole thing is despicable beyond words, but if the kids are well coached, and the pedophiles in prison fear for their lives, it would probably work. Because the public is preconditioned to believe it.

"Given the absence of any new public accusations, Your Excellency, I have to believe you found enough money to make at least a down payment on Bao's demands."

George O'Menehy might have been dead a week for how ashen he looked.

"So what do we do now?" Sweetie asked. "Because you know blackmailers never stop until they've taken everything you have."

Neither Father Nguyen nor Bishop O'Menehy had an answer. But Sweetie did.

"What we do is get them to attempt a new crime and catch them in the act." She smiled. "Then the only people they'll get to confess to will be cops."

Rue de Lille, Paris

30

McGill's team gathered in the basement where he'd clocked Glen Kinnard. He was joined by Gabbi, Odo, and Harbin, who had consented to joining the team. McGill had insisted they do a dress rehearsal. They all wore black unitards and sneakers.

Magistrate Pruet, in his everyday attire, looked on with a measure of unease.

"Please put your masks on," McGill said.

He and the others slipped on their masks. Each of them bore the face of a black dog with blood red eyes and gleaming white fangs. Gabbi had done a great job of finding masks for the job, McGill thought as he caught sight of the others on the team.

No, the other members of the pack.

"Turn to face the magistrate, *s'il vous plait*," McGill said.

They turned in unison to face Pruet.

Confronted by the pack, the magistrate involuntarily retreated. He bumped up against a support pillar. The fear of suddenly being trapped showed on Pruet's face.

McGill took pity and turned to the others, breaking the tension.

"Can everybody see all right? Have a full field of vision?"

They all did.

"No problems breathing?" McGill asked.

None.

"Okay, let's get the sticks. Do a little high-low timing practice. Gabbi, please start with Harbin. I'll start with Odo. Each of us will go through the drill with all the others."

Each member of the pack picked up two escrima sticks, usually made of bamboo, but in this case hardwood. The sticks were smooth black cylinders an inch in diameter and thirty inches long. Paired off, the pack members faced each other, grasping the sticks close to the bottoms, the tops resting against their clavicles.

"Gabbi, you and I will strike first, on three. One, two, three."

With the stick in his right hand, McGill took a slow easy swipe at Odo's head. Gabbi did the same with Harbin. Both defenders easily parried the blows with the sticks they held in their left hands. *Clack.* McGill and Gabbi followed with slow head swipes using the sticks in their left hands. The defenders parried with their right-hand sticks. *Clack.* The same pattern was used to attack and defend their opponents' legs, right and left. *Clack-clack.*

To Pruet, it all looked like some macabre dance.

Until McGill said, "Okay, pick up the tempo."

Suddenly the din of stick striking stick filled the room. The only thing that kept Pruet from covering his ears was a fascinating rhythm to the noise. The percussion of combat. If a stick were to hit a head, a skull would fracture; if a kneecap were struck, it would shatter. After a moment of watching the sticks flash through the air, Pruet realized he could discern other sounds. The *whir* of the sticks displacing air; the pull and thrust of anaerobic respiration.

For the moment, the magistrate concentrated on McGill's battle with Odo. It seemed to him that the president's henchman was too quick for the Corsican. Odo's parries were arriving only at the last possible instant. Pruet's heart rose to his throat, thinking his friend would soon be killed or disabled.

But McGill called out, "Break!"

And the combatants stepped back and returned their sticks to their resting positions against collarbones. After what Pruet thought to be far too short a time, McGill asked, "Everyone ready to go? Good. Odo and Harbin attack. On three. One, two, three."

Neither pair started slowly. Speed had already been established. Pruet found himself drawn to watch Gabbi now. He didn't want to see harm befall a woman and would call a halt himself, if he deemed it necessary. But *la femme Américaine* was equal to her opponent. A fact that was not lost on the brawny man attacking her. He did his best to outpace her, but—*merci à Dieu*—he wasn't able to get past her defenses.

A new sound caught the magistrate's ear.

He turned to look at the other combatants. Odo was setting upon McGill, swinging his sticks at fantastic speeds. Fear filled the magistrate's heart anew. If one of Odo's strikes were to land—

That was when Pruet identified the sound he'd heard: McGill was whistling.

He couldn't identify the tune, not with all the furious *clacking* going on, but it was something in time with the parries the president's henchman used to defend himself. Odo heard the whistling, too, and took it as an insult that McGill could deflect his best efforts so casually. The Corsican became infuriated, spurred on to try even harder to brain McGill. Should he succeed, the fate of nations would be altered.

Gabbi and Harbin ceased their own contest to stand beside Pruet and watch.

The magistrate knew he should shout an order to desist.

But he didn't. He feared his voice might be the distraction that would cause disaster.

As Odo's attack rose to fever pitch, McGill's whistling grew in volume. As if to be a further taunt. Finally, Pruet recognized the tune. "I Love Paris," Cole Porter's famous song. The composer had been American, but every Frenchman of a certain age knew the song.

And even a Corsican or two. McGill's emphatic intonations made his position clear to Odo: Here was a visitor who had developed a great affection for the City of Light and its people. Odo didn't stop swinging his sticks. Rather he slowed the tempo, and the volume of McGill's whistling dropped. Eventually the combatants returned to the lazy pace at which McGill had begun the exercise.

The two men stepped back and raised their masks.

McGill smiled, sweat running down his face, and said to Odo, "Don't let anyone put you off your game, M'sieur Sacripant."

Gabbi translated the idiom. "*Ne laissez pas n'importe qui vous distraire.*"

"The Undertaker uses his stench as a distraction. None of us can afford to be distracted," he told the pack. "Thirty seconds, then we change partners."

31

They watched the death match video again; Harbin seeing it for the first time, keeping his expression impassive. McGill pointed out the giant's weaknesses, as he saw them. Pruet added the one he'd discerned that couldn't be gleaned from the video.

The magistrate said, "This fellow has a further weakness. He has a hearing deficit on his right side, as well as his vision problem."

He cited The Undertaker's inability to locate the source of...

Pruet didn't want to say the sound of his soon-to-be ex-wife whimpering.

...a sobbing woman hiding in his apartment, he said.

"That's good to know," McGill said. "What strategy does it suggest?"

Odo answered, "A blow to the left ear. Leave the *bàtard* deaf."

"The same could be said for his left eye," Harbin added. "Leave him blind, too."

McGill nodded. "Anything that makes him easier to bring down."

"We've got to stay on our toes," Gabbi cautioned. "This prick might not be fast, but within a radius of a couple meters, he's got a burst. That's how he grabbed the poor fool in the video."

McGill agreed. "Can't forget that for a second. If he does manage to grab one of us, the others all close in and attack immediately. Head shots." McGill looked at Pruet. "I know the reason we're not just shooting this guy is so you can use him as a witness, but—"

"Other imperatives must prevail," Pruet agreed.

"As long as that's clear." McGill turned back to the pack. "If one of us is grabbed, the man or woman holding the position immediately clockwise delivers the first two blows; the person to the left follows with two; the next to the left finishes up with two."

It wouldn't do to have them all swing at once and deflect each other's strikes.

"And if we need to go around again?" Harbin asked.

"God help us all," McGill answered. "But we'll do encores upon demand."

There was a knock at the door. The four members of the pack looked at the magistrate. Pruet went to see who had come calling. A man in a dark suit whispered something to him. Pruet nodded and closed the door.

McGill gave it a second in case the magistrate had something to share. When he didn't say anything, McGill continued talking strategy. They would also target The Undertaker's teeth, hands, wrists, elbows, and knees. Any areas covered by masses of flesh, muscle, and fat would be secondary targets. But better to get in some kind of hard blow than forgo one altogether.

Harbin brought up a salient question: "When do we attack, m'sieur?"

"Tonight," McGill said. "I'm expected to be at dinner with the queen tomorrow."

An appointment, Pruet silently prayed, that McGill would keep, undamaged.

"The queen, m'sieur?" Odo asked.

"The one in London."

The Corsican looked at Pruet to see if he was being mocked again.

The magistrate said, "We will all do our best to see you are on time, m'sieur."

McGill told Pruet he was happy to hear that and suggested how the magistrate might be of help. He had Pruet stand on a crate to approximate The Undertaker's great height. The magistrate was given his own pair of sticks to hold out and simulate the giant's reach. Then everyone practiced reaching the targets previously discussed. Stopping short of actual contact.

When McGill called a halt, everyone was breathing hard, but not overworked.

Harbin had another question, "Why the dog masks, m'sieur?"

"The Undertaker is supposed to stink like a bear. In my country, a great frontiersman named Davy Crockett hunted and killed many bears. He did so by using dogs."

Gabbi added, "Also you can put a scent of your preference inside the mask to obscure The Undertaker's stench."

"That, too," McGill said.

"Did your countryman hunt with sticks?" Odo asked.

"No, he was happy to shoot and eat his prey. And if worse really comes to worse, I expect Magistrate Pruet to shoot The Undertaker."

Yves Pruet nodded solemnly.

Everyone was given the time and place where they would rendezvous.

The magistrate asked McGill to remain behind a moment.

When the others left, he said, "The mask also allows the American president's husband to remain anonymous."

"Yes, it does," McGill said, "but that's not why you asked me to stay behind."

"No, I have news for you. Your client, Glen Kinnard, was not content to watch satellite television. He has taken advantage of his relaxed security to escape."

St. Germain-des-Prés, Paris

32

McGill ran up the steps of the Église-de-Saint-Germain-des-Prés. He'd asked Gabbi if she knew an English-speaking priest who would hear his confession. Preparing for the hereafter was as important to McGill as getting ready for the here and now. She'd given him the name of her own confessor, Père Hébert Clavel—and after McGill looked at her inquiringly, she told him she'd made her own visit to the good father after completing her shopping trip.

"*Très bon*," McGill had told her.

Father Clavel was waiting for McGill outside the confessional. It was the first time a priest shook hands with him *before* he forgave McGill's sins. Going into the confessional, the president's henchman bared his soul, and received his absolution and penance. Then the priest made a personal observation.

"I am not one to involve myself in politics, m'sieur."

"Yes?" McGill said.

"But I have been fascinated by your wife's rise to power."

"It's been a remarkable story."

"Please tell *Madam la Présidente* that I include her daily in my prayers."

"*Merci, Père Clavel.* I will."

"And, *M'sieur le Henchman,* never come to me with an admission you have failed her."

"Won't happen, Father."

When McGill got back into Gabbi's car, she asked, "You have that much to forgive or were you handing out autographs in there?"

"Tending to my immortal soul inclines me to think about my all too mortal body," McGill told her.

"Meaning what?"

"Well, what if The Undertaker has a big brother?"

Gabbi snorted. "You're kidding, right?"

"Hard to imagine, I know. But what if he has friends or at least minions? Somebody who can help out. If that video we saw was shot recently the big gorilla might not be at his best. But what if he's smart enough to suspect he's being set up and brings backup?"

Gabbi thought about that.

"Wouldn't do to bring sticks to a gunfight," she said.

"Not at all. Pruet will have his gun, but I don't see him coming out on top in a shootout."

"Me neither. You think the four of us should carry guns?"

McGill shook his head. "Wouldn't want Big Boy to grab one of our pieces."

"What are you thinking then?"

"Who do we know locally," McGill asked, "people who are sneaky enough to avoid easy detection and slick enough to act as lookouts for us?"

Gabbi saw right where McGill was going. "Gypsies."

"Yeah, them," he said.

The Hideaway, Paris

33

Harbin was back working the door when McGill returned.

"M'sieur," Harbin said to McGill, "your wife called."

That one stopped McGill. He gave the doorman an inquiring look.

Harbin nodded. "*Oui, m'sieur.* I have never spoken to my own president, but now I have spoken to yours."

"Did she want anything in particular?" McGill asked.

"We chatted pleasantly for a moment; her French is exquisite. Then she asked if I am a handy fellow with my sticks. I could only guess she heard of this from you."

"What did you say?"

"I told her in all modesty I am very, very good."

It was true. Harbin had the edge over both Odo and Gabbi. While Gabbi was as quick and fluid as Harbin, he brought a lot more muscle to his game.

"I also told her in truest modesty you are perhaps a little better than me."

McGill got the feeling Harbin had never admitted that to anyone before. As to the accuracy of his assessment, McGill would have said there wasn't a ray of daylight between them.

"You didn't tell her what we have planned?" McGill asked.

Harbin rolled his eyes.

"Sorry," McGill said. "I should have known better."

"*Oui, m'sieur,* you should. But I will be this indiscreet. If I were you, and I didn't speak French, I know who I would ask to teach me."

McGill smiled.

Patti giving him French lessons. There was an idea.

34

"I dismissed SAC Crogher," Patti told McGill when he called her from his borrowed apartment.

"Huh," McGill said. He added, "So you found out."

"About his little trip to Paris? Yes."

"I didn't rat Celsus out, so..." McGill came to the only logical conclusion. "Galia did."

The president didn't rat out her chief of staff.

"I won't comment on that," she told her husband.

"I won't ask you to. It's also not my business to ask you why you canned Celsus, but I am curious."

"I thought you'd be pleased to see him go."

McGill would have thought so, too. Now, he wasn't so sure.

"Somebody has to take his place," he said. "Might be someone more agreeable to me personally, but I have to tell you, Madam President, I don't see anybody making me feel more comfortable that my beloved wife is as safe as anyone can make her."

"I'm not the problem," the president said.

"What?" McGill asked. "I stepped in it again?"

Patti gave her husband a précis of her discussion with Celsus.

McGill said, "You make some very good points. There will be more First Gentlemen, and undoubtedly some of them will make the Secret Service gnash their teeth more than I do. I've been having some thoughts of my own on that matter."

"Such as?" the president asked.

"Maybe I should set a better example for those who come after me. I was thinking I could continue using Deke and Leo when we get home, but maybe someone like Crogher, if not Crogher himself, could give me a daily summary of threat assessments against me. If tensions get elevated, we could put a few more agents in play as an outer perimeter, with Deke coordinating them. If there were evidence of an actual plot against me, then I'd have to play an active part in the takedown effort."

"Rather than retreat to a safe place while the Secret Service does its job," the president said.

"Would you have married a fellow given to retreat?" McGill asked.

"No. You're right. I married the man who catches the bad guys."

"And has mastered the entire California Pizza Kitchen cookbook, too."

The president laughed and said, "And has certain other talents as well."

"Including the ability to speak candidly to the world's most powerful woman."

"You're going to tell me something I don't want to hear?" Patti asked.

"I'm going to tell you Celsus lied to you."

A long moment of silence followed. McGill would have been dumbfounded, too, if someone had told him SAC Crogher had lied to him. He would have said there wasn't a line of code in the man's operating system that would allow for deceit.

"How did he lie?" Patti asked.

"Celsus came to see me in Paris because he thought you were carrying on with the president of France. He wanted me to travel to London and give Jean-Louis Severin a boot to his backside. If only because extramarital hanky-panky upsets Celsus's security protocols."

"Jim, there's really nothing going on, I swear."

"I know. That's not who you are. But we all have our histories, and that's what Celsus saw. Someone you were close to in your past. Not being fully human, Celsus misunderstood."

"You're terrible. Celsus is human enough that he felt he couldn't confront me."

"Tough to tell the boss to stop fooling around. Even androids get that."

"Stop it ... should I apologize and ask SAC Crogher to return?"

"Skip the apology; take credit for wringing those concessions out of me."

"I'm very glad you're the man I married. You will be here for dinner with the queen, won't you? Her Majesty told me she's very much looking forward to meeting you."

"I'll be there."

"You'll have Glen Kinnard off the hook by then?"

"I'm past all that. Right now, I'm trying to keep President Severin's political enemies from doing him in. Politically, of course."

Patti was quiet again, before saying, "You'll tell me all about it?"

"Next time I see you," McGill said.

Washington, DC

35

Sweetie didn't give Putnam enough time to cater a meal. When she, Welborn, Kira, and Deke gathered in the living room at the lawyer's townhouse, all their host could offer them were drinks and snacks. Of course, his Snickerdoodles came from the Munchies Organic Natural Store in Cumberland, Maryland, were made with quail eggs, and cost $30 a box. Putnam washed his cookies down with champagne; everybody else drank Jasmine Green Honest Tea, which Sweetie thought was good, but not a match for the ice tea coming out of the White House kitchen.

Welborn and Kira needed a few minutes whispering to each other in a corner of the room before they joined the others, taking a love seat that had been left vacant for them.

"Sorry to keep you waiting," Welborn said.

He'd felt the need to explain privately to Kira his role in what they were about to do. He didn't want her to think his dinner date with Callie Bao was anything but a ruse engineered by Margaret Sweeney. He definitely wasn't getting cold feet as their wedding day approached. Kira accepted his explanation with a sense of serenity he'd never seen in her before … and that made him wonder how much he really knew about his fiancée.

But then she told him about her late father's image miraculously appearing on Father Nguyen's dust cloth. How her mother had wept when she'd seen it. How both of them were happy beyond words that the late Desmond Fahey would indeed be at their wedding in spirit.

So, Welborn thought, the Queen of England couldn't make their little affair, but a man dead almost twenty years would be in attendance. As would his own father, the man he'd never met. He could only wonder what other surprises might crop up.

"Welborn," Sweetie said, "you're cleared for landing."

He snapped out of his reverie, saw everyone was looking at him.

"You did make a date with Ms. Bao, right?" she asked.

He nodded. Before he could go on, Putnam raised his hand.

"Before we go any further," he said, "I have to ask if this conversation should be privileged? Would it be worth a dollar from each of you to formally become my clients, and put anything we say here off limits to law enforcement snoops?"

Deke Ky cleared his throat.

Putnam said, "Yes, I know you're Secret Service, but you're in protection not investigation, aren't you?"

Welborn cleared his throat.

"Office of Special *Investigations*," he said.

Putnam frowned. "Maybe I'm out of my depth here. Are we about to enter a conspiracy here or not? If we are, we need to give ourselves whatever cover we can. If not, I might as well call for pizza."

Sweetie grinned. "What we're doing here is setting up a sting. It's all perfectly within the bounds of the law."

Deke gave Sweetie a look, then handed Putnam a dollar.

Welborn, who'd seen Deke steal a car, also forked over a buck.

Kira, in solidarity with her betrothed, gave Putnam a dollar, and took a Snickerdoodle.

Sweetie looked around and asked, "What's going on here?"

Before anyone could answer, Welborn raised a legal point.

"What I learned about attorney-client privilege, the communication's confidentiality is obviated by the presence of a third party. If you count noses here—"

Putnam waved away that concern. "If you don't tell, I won't." He looked at Sweetie. "Are we causing moral problems for you,

Margaret?"

"Probably, if I knew what you were all talking about."

"I have no idea," Putnam said. "I'm simply operating on the principle the thought police have no right to know the content of any of my conversations."

Sweetie could see both Deke and Welborn had trouble with so sweeping a statement, but Kira nodded in agreement.

"How about this, Margaret?" Putnam asked. "We'll discuss what we can with you here, and then at a certain point you can—"

"Go downstairs and say my rosary," Sweetie said.

"Exactly," Putnam agreed. "Chances are we won't get caught for anything anyway."

Famous last words, Sweetie thought. Her inner Mother Superior wanted to banish any notion of impropriety ... but the cop in her understood the value of deniability.

So all she said was, "Where's your date with Ms. Bao going to be, Welborn?"

"Krung Thep. Thai place on the Columbia Pike in Arlington."

"Time?"

"Table's booked for seven o'clock."

"Putnam," Sweetie said. She told him what they needed.

The lawyer nodded, accessed his iPhone and booked another table for two at the restaurant.

"Do we have to worry the tables might be in different rooms?" Sweetie asked.

Welborn shook his head. "I swung by the place to take a look. It's small. One room. Every table should be in view of every other table."

"Good. Let's hope we can spoil Ms. Bao's appetite," Sweetie said. "Make sure you get the young lady to the restaurant five minutes late. We want to have the stage set when you arrive."

"Okay," Welborn said.

Sweetie detailed the plan as she'd conceived it. "It shouldn't take more than a few minutes before Ms. Bao asks you to excuse her, Welborn. If necessary, act offended. In any case, put her in a cab, don't drive her home. Your job is to shadow your man and make sure he stays safe. I'll do the same with mine."

Turning to Deke, she said, "Is this where the plan takes a new direction and I should excuse myself?"

Deke nodded. Sweetie gave him a look, gave them all a look. She wanted to rap their knuckles with a wooden ruler. But she left without another word.

Putnam sighed as the door closed behind Sweetie. "I was getting so close."

"She'll be back," Welborn told him. "The good ones have staying power."

Kira liked that and kissed his cheek.

Welborn asked Deke, "So, after you stole Ricky's car, what did you find in it?"

Arlington, VA

36

"Fuckin' LoJack," Ricky muttered as he backed away from the Corvette.

After spending hours looking for a cool ride to steal, he was confronted by the harsh reality that he'd never get away with stealing the kind of car he wanted. Seemed every asshole who could afford 50K or more for his ride had installed some godzilla security system that would chew Ricky up and spit him out. If he tried to get over on one of those things, the cops would grab him before he got the car out of its parking space.

It was demoralizing to think the straight world had gotten the upper hand on an enterprising young criminal like him. Fucking yuppie scum.

Two prime examples of which were standing on the sidewalk out in front of a coffee shop up ahead of him. Two dudes with a bicycle. Pretty cool looking bike, if he wanted to be honest about it. Black, sleek, had the name Leopard on it. One guy was showing it to the other.

The guy with the bike was all dressed up like he was going to compete in the Tour de France, right down to his yellow jersey. Only his hair was going gray and his belly bulged. Still thought he was cool, though. Ricky was close enough now to hear him tell the other guy he'd paid three thousand for the bike.

Shit, 3K for a bike? Ricky might brag on that himself.

Except Ricky remembered Bao's sneering voice tell him, "Buy a bicycle."

He had the money to do just that, *buy* himself a black Leopard. But that would only confirm what a limp dick he was. Ricky had a better idea. *Steal* a bicycle. He blitzed the guy in the yellow jersey, knocked him on his ass and grabbed the bike in one motion. He was on it and gone in a heartbeat.

Three grand bike for the straight world; free for him.

Thing was, the other guy—who it hit Ricky now—was probably twenty years younger than Yellow Jersey, started chasing him. Ran pretty damn fast, too. If he knocked Ricky off the bike, he might draw out a scuffle long enough for the cops to come.

Time to give the hero something to think about. Ricky pulled his Custom Chris English knife and popped the blade open. Five inches long, as sharp as a scalpel, glistening in the sunlight. Ricky held it up where the guy chasing him couldn't miss seeing it. He continued to pedal; the footsteps behind him slowed and fell back.

Ricky got away, but it had been a close thing. Damn, he couldn't even steal a bike without turning it into a nail-biter. He could almost hear Bao laughing at him. And right there was the problem: He was working for the wrong fucking guy. Bao was never going to teach him anything good. He'd just use Ricky for muscle, and someday when Ricky got popped by the cops, Bao would find another young guy who'd bow to him, work for small change, drive some bargain basement sedan, and not complain because he got his giggles scaring and hurting people.

He needed a new mentor, someone who could teach him how to get past LoJack; someone who could teach him stuff that made money, like identity theft. Teach him all sorts of ways to get over on the straight world.

He had to move on, but not on the damn bicycle he was riding. The yuppies he'd robbed had probably called in the theft already. He doubted either of them got a good look at him, but Yellow Jersey probably knew the bike's serial number by heart. He rode into an alley, stopped halfway down, behind a house with a high white fence. The fence looked like it was made of plastic, but it didn't have any openings. Good for privacy. Or hiding a stolen bike.

Ricky listened for a minute, didn't hear any sounds coming from anywhere nearby. He heaved the bike over the fence ... and heard a splash. Jesus, he must have thrown the thing into a swimming pool. Which he immediately realized was a stroke of good luck.

Dumbass that he'd been, he probably had left fingerprints all over the bike. Now, though, sitting at the bottom of a pool, he didn't have to worry about that.

He did a fast walk out of the alley, feeling better now. Things were turning his way. And he had an idea of just what he should do. Split for Southern California. Yeah. Nice weather. Big Viet Kieu community out there he could slide into and do his thing. Find somebody smart, close to his own age, to work for. Someone who'd never think of asking him to bow. Someone who'd set him up with a cool ride right off.

Maybe a Porsche like that blonde prick at Callie's studio was driving.

Callie Bao. Before he left town, what he ought to do was go see her. Ricky knew she did her old man's banking. He'd bet the old fuck kept a pile of emergency cash on hand, in case things got hot and he had to di-di. Callie would know where it was; she probably kept her own emergency pile, too. He'd take whatever money he could find and consider it his severance pay. He'd take Callie's car while he was at it.

In fact, if she gave him any shit about taking whatever he wanted, he'd tell her he'd rat out her old man. The cops would love to hear about the scam Mr. Respectable Lawyer Horatio Bao had cooked up, using all those kiddy-diddling priests in prison.

Once Callie heard him say that, she'd settle right down.

Of course when Ricky told Callie he wanted a taste of her, had from the first time he'd seen her, she might resist. Say that wasn't part of the bargain. They'd just have to see how much she loved daddy.

Ricky strode along briskly now, a young criminal with a sense of purpose.

Magistrate Pruet's office, Paris

37

McGill sat on a corner of Yves Pruet's table. He was alone for the moment, and took the opportunity to place a call to Muro de Alcoy, Spain. The young man he spoke to was pleasant, helpful, and told him it would take only a minute to see if the item señor requested was in stock.

Within the promised length of time, the young man came back to the phone.

"Yes, we have it, señor. Would you like express shipping?"

"I would," McGill said, and provided the address.

"You wish to have the shipping insurance also, señor?"

"Yes, and please light a candle to see it arrives undamaged."

The young man chuckled. "My mother goes to church far more often than I do. Would it be acceptable if she lights the candle?"

"Yes. Please give my thanks to your mother."

With that, McGill provided his name and credit card number. The young man read back the information for confirmation, giving no sign he thought McGill was anyone special, beyond a new customer to be valued for his patronage.

It reassured the president's henchman that there were still places he might travel without causing a fuss—provided he wasn't accompanied by the missus.

"*Gracias, señor*. Please let us know if we may ever be of further help."

McGill said he would and clicked off. He looked out the door of Pruet's office, went back inside and made another call. This one was to Chicago and Emilie LaBelle, Glen Kinnard's daughter, the young woman who had hired him to go to Paris.

She answered on the second ring.

"Hi, Emilie. This is Jim McGill. How are you?"

"I ... I'm fine, Mr. McGill."

She was surprised to hear from him. He could hear tension in her voice. Just as he'd expected.

"Your dad make it home yet, Emilie?"

There was no immediate answer. He heard muffled whispering, as if a hand had been placed over the instrument. Then Emilie came back.

"Mr. McGill, I feel really bad saying this, but I can't answer your question."

"On the advice of a lawyer?"

No hand over the phone this time, but somebody in the background whispered again. Emilie disregarded the *sotto voce* instruction and said, "Yes, on legal advice."

McGill thought he heard the sound of a lawyer's hand hitting a lawyer's forehead.

Limiting himself to a smile, McGill said, "Tell everyone not to worry. As long as your dad stays out of the public eye until I give him the word, everything should work out fine."

Emilie couldn't help but ask, "You mean he won't be arrested?"

"Not unless he returns to France. Or visits a French possession."

Tongue in cheek, Emilie asked, "So a trip to Tahiti's out?"

"Did the best I could," McGill told her.

"Thank you, Mr. McGill. You did great."

"Hope you and your dad get along. Tell him I'm sorry about busting his jaw."

A moment later, Pruet entered his office, a gentle hand on the shoulder of Diana Martel, easing her forward. Odo brought up the rear, cutting off the possibility of an impulsive retreat.

McGill picked himself up off the corner of Pruet's table.

Nodding at the stripper, McGill asked, "Is she ready?"

"She has been persuaded," Pruet answered.

Odo rolled his eyes at his boss's gentle tone.

McGill looked at the woman. He could see she was still afraid.

He told her, "You won't be able to hide your fear, so use it. Make him think you're afraid of the police, not him. He's the one who has to save you."

She didn't meet McGill's eyes, but nodded all the same.

"Diana was most helpful," Pruet said. "She gave us additional information about her friend, how we might have to deal with him."

"What kind of information?" McGill asked.

Pruet looked at the woman, taking his hand away, letting her stand on her own.

Now, Diana looked at McGill. "One night, a wrestler comes to the club. Romanian. Very big. Close to one hundred fifty kilos." McGill converted to English measure: three hundred and thirty pounds. NFL lineman size. "His jacket has Olympic rings on it. For first time, I see fear in Etienne's eyes. The Romanian is very loud, gets very drunk. Wants six girls at his table. Says he'll pay for every *putain* in Paris. So all the girls dance for him. He puts his hands on all of us. When time comes to pay, he takes Lili and Nina by the neck." The memory made Diana briefly close her eyes. "He say he has no money but we must all kiss him goodbye, ask him come back soon, or Lili and Nina..."

She made the motion of someone breaking a stick.

"We all look for Etienne, but he has vanished."

Good trick for a guy that size, McGill thought.

"So we all kiss the Romanian, beg him to visit us again. He laughs. Tells us we are good girls. He walks toward door. Then Etienne steps from behind curtain. He has pitcher of vodka. Throws on Romanian. Throws match. Wrestler flambé."

Diana smiled now, that memory far more pleasant for her.

"Etienne not want to burn club, so he hits wrestler's head

with pitcher, jumps on him, smothers flames. Wrestler not so strong now."

McGill could see how being set ablaze and hit on the head could take the starch out of a guy. So they'd have to watch The Undertaker for any sign he was carrying an accelerant and matches or a lighter. That and how he might improvise with any found objects.

"Good to know," McGill told Diana. "Thank you. Are you ready now?"

With a shrug, she nodded.

She was the lure. The Undertaker had to know Diana was a weak link. She could testify against him. So despite any affection he might feel for her, she would have to go. There were always other strippers with which he might console himself.

McGill understood only a few of the words Diana used during her call.

But he thought her tone of desperation was pitch perfect.

The Undertaker would show up that night.

Under the Pont d'Iéna where the whole thing began.

Winfield House, London

38

As soon as the president got off the phone with McGill, she summoned her chief of staff. Galia appeared at Patti's private quarters within minutes. Her face was a picture of concern. An urgent summons from the president portended serious matters, especially when the Commander in Chief was visiting a foreign land.

Galia began to assess the situation at its most basic level.

"You're feeling well, Madam President?"

The question took Patti by surprise. But now that it had been raised...

"Still recuperating," she said. "Please have Aggie prepare a press release. Let the media people know that following my appearance at the Queen's dinner tomorrow, I'll be taking a week's vacation here in Europe. Resting from my labors. Easing my aches and pains."

It was, of course, the president's prerogative to take a holiday when and where she pleased, but Galia had always assumed she would be given proper notice of such a decision, if not consulted on it in advance.

The president deciphered her chief of staff's bemused expression precisely.

"Something the matter, Galia?"

"No, Madam President. I'll adjust your schedule accordingly. If the press asks for more specifics as to where you'll be..."

"Press Secretary Wu will tell them Europe. That's all they need to know."

Galia understood the president's natural desire for privacy, but not sharing her vacation plans with the American public might not sit well politically. One look at the president's face, though, told Galia not to push the matter.

Seeing that she'd preempted debate on that topic, Patti said, "Galia, who is Jean-Louis Severin's worst political enemy?"

"Foreign or domestic?" the chief of staff inquired.

"Domestic. Who is his Roger Michaelson?"

"The interior minister, Jules Guerin."

"The French interior minister controls the national police?"

"Yes, Madam President."

"Could he force the deportation of someone holding a diplomatic passport?"

"He might have to consult the Foreign Minister. I'd have to check on that. But even diplomats declared *personae non gratae* are given forty-eight hours to organize their departures. They're hardly ever given the bum's rush, if that's what you have in mind."

What Galia couldn't keep from thinking was: *What had McGill done now?*

Had he created an international incident that would hurt the Grant administration?

The president, though, didn't seem intent on damage control. Rather, she persisted in her original question. "Work with me on this one, Galia. Could Jules Guerin, if he took it in mind, grab someone and put him on a plane, boat or train out of France?"

Galia nodded. "If it was important enough to him that he didn't mind taking the political heat for overstepping his bounds, I imagine he could. After all, he's got the cops; the cops have the guns. There are long-term institutional checks on his power, but in a moment of madness, maybe he could." The chief of staff paused momentarily before taking the plunge. "Madam President, are we discussing Mr. McGill here?"

"Yes." Patti gave a brief laugh. "But almost certainly not in the way you think, Galia. Will you please find the president of France for me, and tell him I must see him immediately."

Galia paused before hopping to it. Hoping for an explanation.

The president went so far as to tell her: "I'm about to do a big favor for Jean-Louis. So I can collect one later."

The collection of IOUs from fellow heads of state was always an agenda to pursue, Galia knew. "I'll find *M'sieur le President* right away, ma'am."

39

Indeed, Jean-Louis Severin rushed to Winfield House like a lovesick adolescent. He sat next to Patti on the sofa where he found her, and took her hands in his. Looked into her eyes.

"*Qu'est-ce qui ne vas pas, ma chère?*" What's wrong?

Patti reclaimed her hands and gently patted his.

"I'm afraid your interior minister is about to kick my husband out of France."

Jean-Louis drew back. "Guerin? Why would he do such a thing?"

"Because Jim is about to do some dirty work for you with your friend Magistrate Pruet. You know, the fellow you wrote to about your romances with American girls at Yale."

The president of France sighed and slouched back into the corner of the sofa.

"There was but one girl at Yale," he said, "and we both know who she was. Your husband has learned of this?"

"He has."

"And how did he receive the news?"

"With great maturity and understanding. He's been married before himself. Had a romance or two in his time."

Patti thought Jim had mentioned another girl besides Carolyn to him one time. But only one time. She'd like to know ... but now wasn't the time.

"I am very glad to hear that," Jean-Louis said. "He really should know that a treasured friendship is all that remains between us."

"Erika Kirsch should be clear on that point as well."

Her former boyfriend laughed.

"You have always been the smartest one in the room, Patricia."

She smiled. "In many ways, I've met my match in Jim McGill. But this time he's overlooked something I've seen."

"And what is that?" Jean-Louis asked.

"That if Jim is helping Pruet do some heavy lifting for you against Guerin, then it is in Guerin's interest to give Jim a quick ticket out of France."

The president of France leaned forward, the better to examine that idea.

"You are right, of course. I should have seen that myself."

"New romances can be distracting," the president of the United States said.

Jean-Louis nodded. "*Mais oui*."

"Please be careful, old friend. I need you to remain in the Elysée Palace. But after the former Madam Severin has falsely accused me of being your mistress, perhaps she will be more reluctant to accuse anyone else."

Patti suspected Jean-Louis' friend, Magistrate Pruet, might have been deliberately careless in letting his estranged wife browse his old correspondence with the present president of France. But she didn't say so.

Jean-Louis leaned forward and took Patti's hands again.

"I will be very careful. And I will do anything for you."

"Remember those words," she told him. "Because the day will come when I'll need your help with something you won't want to do. But after alerting you to what Jules Guerin is likely thinking, and letting my husband save your derrière, you're going to owe me a very large favor."

It was ironic, Patti thought.

Jim always did his best to eschew politics, but here he was again.

Helping her to succeed in her job.

Arlington, VA

40

Horatio Bao hadn't killed anyone since he'd immigrated to the United States, and he was proud of that. He had *ordered* the deaths of a dozen people, but had always kept a safe interval, physically and legally, between himself and the blood that had been shed to advance his interests. There was no moral distance between the taking of a life and causing one to be taken, but then morality never had a place in any of Bao's calculations. Efficacy was everything.

Holding to that ideal, and having no idea what boobytraps Musette Ky had set for him before fleeing the country, Bao spent hours shredding and burning every piece of paper in his law offices.

Any record he needed to preserve for future use was encrypted and resided under another name in a server on the far side of the world. Periodically, the lawyer would take a pause from his labors to try to reach his daughter, Calanthe. He tried her cell number, the number at the home they shared, and the number at the townhouse his daughter kept for the times she entertained young men she didn't wish to introduce to her father.

Bao understood his daughter's need to have such a retreat. She was a vibrantly healthy young woman; she required the company of young men. He thought it wise that she indulge herself in casual dalliances before finding the right man to marry. He suspected most of the men Calanthe brought to her townhouse were American. Possibly European. But white, one way or another. He didn't see her with a non-Vietnamese Asian. The Chinese and Japanese were both historic enemies. The Koreans were … much too fond of garlic.

Having finally destroyed all the tangible records of more than thirty years of his law practice, Horatio Bao sat down and poured himself a shot of Macallan whisky. He'd learned to appreciate single malt scotch while working with the Americans in Saigon. But he never took more than one drink per day. That built anticipation, made each drop more pleasurable, created a warm glow but didn't blur his thoughts.

He tried all three of his daughter's phone numbers again; got voicemail at each one. It was completely unlike Calanthe to remain unavailable for contact from him for so long. Try as he might, though, he couldn't bring himself to worry about her. She was too intelligent, too strong, too well trained to fall prey to any common criminal.

Some sort of automobile accident was possible, a random instance of mischance that even an alert and nimble driver would be unable to avoid, but Bao thought that possibility too unlikely to give much credence.

Far more likely, he thought, Calanthe had seen a sign she was being observed by the police, or the FBI, and was now on the run. The damnable Madam Ky might have thought it amusing to attack his daughter after he'd set in motion the shooting of her son. God curse her if she had actually caused Calanthe's death. If that were the case, he would spend the rest of his days hunting down the vile creature.

But if Calanthe were merely evading the authorities, she would know to turn her cell phone off or dispose of it so they couldn't track her electronically. Eventually, she would buy a disposable phone and get in touch with him. They would make their plans for a rendezvous and map their futures from there.

In the early days, Bao and his late wife had a precise evacuation plan, but by the time Calanthe had become his confidante it had become outdated, and he'd become foolishly secure in his status as a prosperous American. He'd come to think he was invincible. It gave him a new insight as to what a huge psychological advantage the Communists had had in their fight against the United States for his homeland.

Even so, his confidence in his daughter remained complete.

He never would have imagined she'd spent the entire time he'd been purging his office getting massaged, waxed, styled, and manicured at SomaFit in D.C. The spa, of course, requested its clients to turn off their phones.

Callie Bao hadn't decided that Welborn Yates was *the* man for her—there really was no right man for her—but she thought it would be fun to make his head spin, take him away from his fiancée, and get as many rides in his fighter jet as she needed before growing weary of him.

How could her father ever have guessed that?

What had been easy for Horatio Bao to see, though, was that he had to get rid of Ricky Lanh Huu. Now, given the urgency of the situation, Bao realized he'd have to take care of his underling himself. He called Ricky's cell number. Heard the first ring.

As long as he was going to bloody his hands on Ricky, Bao thought, he might as well do the same with Francis Nguyen and Bishop O'Menehy. The seal of the confessional, he realized now, was a second-best guarantee.

On the second ring, Ricky answered Bao's call.

"What?" the young goon asked in a surly voice.

The lack of deference angered Bao, but he pushed his ire aside.

"I need to see you," the lawyer said in a normal tone.

"Yeah?" Ricky said, his tone of insolence obvious, "Soon as I get myself a bicycle, I'll be right over."

He clicked off, leaving Bao to glare at the mute phone in his hand.

Magistrate Pruet's office, Paris

41

McGill's pack of attack dogs was all but ready to leave for the hunt when he took Gabbi aside and handed her a small black metal squeeze flask and a black elastic band with which to bind it to a leg, and told her what he wanted her to do as a last resort if things started to go badly for their side under the Pont d'Iéna that night. She gave McGill a long look, seeing now there was a much darker side to the man who made Rice Krispies Treats.

"You're asking me to do just the first part, right?" she asked.

The president's henchman nodded. "We don't want it to come to this, but if necessary, I'll finish it."

"Pruet knows?" Gabbi asked.

"I got what I needed from him. He used to smoke a pipe."

"All right," Gabbi said. "Good thing I'm leaving State. This wouldn't look good on my record."

"Yeah," McGill said. "You got the gypsies ready to go?"

"For two thousand euros, half up front."

"Good. We want all the insurance we can get."

They were about to head out the door when McGill's ring tone sounded: "Take Me Out to the Ballgame." His cell phone along with everyone else's mobile, save Pruet's, was lying on the magistrate's table. There were no pockets in the unitards they wore.

"Always something," McGill said.

He told the others to go downstairs; he'd join them directly.

Picking up his phone, he saw that he also had a text message from Sweetie.

We go tonight. Ora pro nobis. Pray for us.

McGill answered the call. "Don't have a lot of time here."

He was thinking it might have been one of his children, hoping it wasn't. He didn't want to have one of them on his mind in the next few hours. Luck was with him. The caller was Celsus Crogher.

"This won't take a lot of time," Celsus said. "I'm only calling to confirm what Holly G told me about the security concessions she got you to make."

McGill was surprised Celsus hadn't taken the president at her word.

"Confirmed," he said. "If you come back."

"I'm thinking about it."

"Celsus, I really don't have time now." McGill had an idea. "Listen, where are you now?"

"D.C."

"Good. I'll tell you what. You promise to come back, I'll see to it you get to put the cuffs on Deke Ky's shooter."

"Sonofabitch," the former SAC said. "You can really do that?"

"Yes or no, Celsus?"

"Yes."

McGill gave him Sweetie's cell number and told him to call.

"When?"

"Tonight."

"Sonofabitch."

"Goodbye, Celsus."

McGill turned to leave, to catch up with the others, but—

Gabbi, Pruet, Odo, and Harbin were herded back into the magistrate's office by a squadron of men dressed in black paramilitary uniforms, each holding an automatic weapon. They looked like French special ops soldiers or cops to McGill.

A man in civilian clothes moved to their front. His garb was a designer suit, but he had closely cropped hair and the look of a soldier, too. A senior officer.

He stared directly at McGill.

"M'sieur James J. McGill, I am Colonel Gaetan Millard of the Interior Ministry. Special Security Department. I have an order for your immediate deportation from France."

Gabbi stepped forward and launched a torrent of French at Millard that made the rims of his small round ears turn red. The only words McGill caught were *coup d'etat*, but whatever else she was saying was definitely getting under the man's skin and she showed no sign of letting up.

Out of the corner of an eye, McGill saw a grim smile appear on Odo's face. He knew just what it meant. The Corsican was preparing to take a run at the guys with the guns. For that matter, so was Harbin. He couldn't see Pruet, but it wouldn't have surprised him if even the magistrate was ready to go out in a blaze of glory.

Millard was about to touch off the bloodbath when, having taken all the lip from Gabbi he intended to, he raised an open right hand to smack her. McGill moved in on the man before anyone could blink. He caught Millard's wrist with one hand, levered the French officer's elbow with the other hand, twisted hard, forced the colonel's arm behind his back and held it there in an arm lock.

The sounds of safeties being clicked off a dozen automatic weapons filled the room.

McGill addressed Millard and his men, "If you're all feeling suicidal, there's nothing I can do about that, but I guarantee this: you and whoever sent you will suffer worse than we do."

The president's henchman wondered how many of the men pointing guns his way understood English. He was hoping someone, Millard maybe, would translate for him. But then a phone sounded.

The ring tone was *La Marseillaise.*

Arlington, VA

42

Nobody had ever given Ricky the address of Callie Bao's apartment. As far as he was supposed to know, she lived with daddy, and that fact alone was thought sufficient to keep the likes of him away—and for a long time it did. Then Ricky got to thinking: A hot chick like Callie had to be getting some action somewhere and he didn't see her taking boyfriends home to Horatio Bao. So being very careful, and glad for once that he had a piece of shit economy sedan that was invisible in traffic, he began to follow Callie around after work.

One Friday night, she led him to a yuppie condo complex. Red brick, four stories high, manicured lawns and mature trees and plantings. Good lighting on the perimeter, the interior walkways, and the underground parking. Security cameras everywhere. He wasn't going to sneak into that place, but with the leverage he had on daddy, he didn't need to. He'd press her directory number on the visitor's phone, tell her what was what, and she'd buzz him in.

That thought pleased Ricky. Being let in just like invited company.

He couldn't have felt any better if—

Damn! There was his car, parked right out front at the curb. Looked like his car anyway. So many of the damn things on the road, he couldn't tell for sure. Maybe if he could ever keep the number on his damn license plate straight he'd know, but reading always gave him a headache. Didn't matter, though, he had the feeling it was his ride. How many times had his hunches ever been wrong? A few times maybe, but not many.

Ricky looked around. A car was coming out of another residential complex across the street. A couple of white yups in a BMW. They didn't give him a second look as they drove off. Now he had the street to himself. He crept up to the car and confirmed it was his. The windows were cracked an inch; he could smell the interior. Smell himself in there. He took another look around. Nobody close. Nobody even looking out a window.

Could Calli Bao have hired someone to swipe his car, he wondered. What would be the point? Why would she leave it parked in front of her place? A sign she wanted him to come by? Like she knew all along he'd been following her and it turned her on? No, that was bullshit. He wasn't the kind of fool who believed in shit like that. If Callie Bao knew he'd been tailing her and wanted to lure him someplace, it would be because she'd have people waiting to give him a beating.

If he wanted anything from that girl, he'd have to make her give it to him.

Ricky looked at the car's door locks. They were all up. From the curb side, he could see the keys were in the ignition. Whole thing felt like a trap to him. Maybe he opened a door, the damn car blew up. Best thing to do was just walk away.

It was the walking part of that idea that was hardest to take.

His feet were killing him.

Then there were things he'd like to get out of the car, too. Five thousand in cash tucked up under the dashboard. The list of Bao's HBA clients and the amounts of monthly tribute they paid. Pictures of Callie Bao, too. Getting into and out of her car. Always nice views of her legs. Sometimes more than that when her skirts were short enough. Shots of where she lived, right up on the top floor there at the corner of the building.

Ricky had wanted to see what the inside of the place looked like ever since he first followed her there. Fuck it. He was done walking. Far as he knew, neither of the Baos had ever hired anyone who did explosives. It was his damn car, legal title and all. He wasn't ever going to walk one step more than he had to again.

He scrambled around to the driver's side and popped the door open, closing his eyes just for a second. When he didn't get his ass blown away, he slid inside. Oh man ... his piece of crap car never felt so good. His feet tingled with relief. He reached under the dash and—yes!—his money was right where he'd left it. He opened the glove box, got Bao's client list, and the pictures of Callie—quickly counted—were all there.

Still, he didn't believe for a minute that his car had been stolen for a joy ride and just coincidentally left outside Callie Bao's love nest. But he didn't see any danger in reclaiming the use of his car. Not unless a bomb was wired to the ignition. With a respectable ride, he could have used a remote control to turn on the engine, but, no, not...

Ricky thought he better stop having bad thoughts about his car. That might be what had jinxed him. He reached out for the key, closed his eyes once more, and started the car. No big bad bang. If anything the engine seemed quieter than before, almost purred. He gave the steering wheel an affectionate pat. Maybe the car deserved to be washed and waxed. Get a cool new paint job even.

He thought his own needs could use some tending, too. Now, that he was finally off his feet, his stomach was demanding attention. Hell, he was fucking starving. He knew just the place, too. Good cooking, quick service, quiet. He could eat and figure out what was going on and get back to Callie Bao. Her stash of cash had to be a lot bigger than his.

Ricky pulled out, headed for Krung Thep on the Columbia Pike.

Krung Thep restaurant, Arlington, VA

43

Except at public dinners where the faithful were gathered for fundraising purposes, Bishop George O'Menehy no longer said grace before taking his meals. Well, maybe sometimes, silently, if he'd had a particularly good day. Mostly, his prayers of late involved themes of forgiveness and redemption. Giving thanks had fallen to a seldom visited third place.

When he saw Francis Nguyen fold his hands and lower his head. after the waitress had brought appetizers to their table, however, he did likewise. Even so, he kept his eyes open and looked around. The dining space was a simple rectangle with large windows that looked out on the strip mall's parking area. Only half of the eighteen tables were occupied, Asian diners slightly outnumbering their Western counterparts. Nobody that he could see seemed to be paying any particular attention to the two men in casual attire about to say grace over their meal.

Father Nguyen said, "Lord, we give thanks for this food that will help sustain us, but more than that we rely on thy grace and mercy. May we never lack for the strength to do thy will."

"Amen," the bishop said. He'd never heard that iteration of grace before, doubted it had been written by any official Church body, but he found the humble words comforting.

Both men made the sign of the cross and began to eat.

After a moment, O'Menehy looked up and said, "We're destined to go our separate ways, aren't we, Francis?"

The younger cleric nodded. He hesitated, then said, "I've been asked to help form a new parish."

O'Menehy sat back stunned, fork dangling from his hand. "A new parish? In which diocese?"

At the invitation of which cardinal, he left unsaid. Was the hierarchy at some level far above his own taking his troublesome priest away from him? Why hadn't he been informed?

"No diocese," Father Nguyen said.

The bishop was even more shocked now.

"Outside the Church?"

"Yes."

"A Protestant parish then?"

"No."

Father Nguyen's answer left O'Menehy confounded. Outside of Catholicism or its Protestant counterparts, what else was there for a Christian? There were the Orthodox churches, of course, but the bishop didn't see Francis Nguyen in an Eastern Rite church.

"Francis, I'm at a loss here. Please help me."

"In Massachusetts, the local diocese closed a parish, after the parishioners raised the money to construct a beautiful new church. That left a great many people very angry, especially as the diocese wanted to sell the new building and the several acres of scenic land on which it sits to help pay ... to help pay damages awarded by a court in a matter of child abuse."

O'Menehy dropped his fork on his plate, his appetite gone now. He would have left the restaurant at that moment, if he hadn't had to remain and play his part in the drama Sweetie had contrived for him and Francis Nguyen.

"The parishioners sued the diocese," Father Nguyen said. "They claimed they had been defrauded, allowed to pay for the new building so the diocese could get a better price from an Evangelical group that made an offer on the property. The parishioners said they would better any other offer for the new building and the land, but their suit claimed they shouldn't have to pay twice for the property. I imagine you would have heard of all this, if you hadn't been preoccupied with your own problems."

His problems. Recalling them made the bishop shake his head.

"The court has ruled for the parishioners?" the bishop asked.

"The judge required an additional payment of one dollar, but yes."

"And now these angry people want you to be their priest?"

"Their pastor."

The conversation was brought to a momentary halt as their dinners arrived.

As the meal was being served, Welborn Yates and Callie Bao arrived. A striking couple combining the good looks of both East and West, they drew far more notice than the two men who had quietly prayed over their food. They were seated at an oblique angle to the clerics, at a distance of no more than twenty feet.

Callie paid direct attention to her date. But the presence and the identities of the bishop and the priest sitting nearby had not escaped her. She was unable to focus on Welborn's conversation and also hear the specific words Bishop O'Menehy and Father Nguyen were speaking.

But she had no trouble discerning the intensity of the two men's dialogue.

Sweetie had told the clerics to put on a good show for Callie Bao.

Without giving her a moment's thought, they were succeeding brilliantly.

Magistrate Pruet's office, Paris

44

Colonel Millard used the distraction of the phone playing

the French national anthem to try to wrest himself free from McGill's armlock. McGill not only resisted the effort, he tightened his hold on Millard's arm. The conflicting pressures resulted in the colonel suffering an acromioclavicular dislocation—aka a shoulder separation. It was a good one, too. The pop of Millard's arm coming out its joint was louder than some small caliber gunshots McGill had heard.

The resulting pain made the Frenchman's knees wobble. McGill was not about to let his human shield drop and leave himself exposed to a squad of guys with machine guns. Guys who had to be losing their patience with him. McGill clamped his free arm around Millard's upper chest, trying hard not to look like he was choking the colonel. If the guys with the guns thought he was doing that, there'd be no reason for them not to try a fancy shot to take him out.

Before any of the soldiers could misinterpret McGill's restraint of their CO, a new voice was heard from, speaking French in a commanding tone. It boomed from Pruet's mobile phone.

"*Chacun, reste absolutment immobile.*"

Gabbi quietly translated for McGill: "Freeze."

He gave her a puzzled look: All that for freeze?

She responded: "Everyone stay absolutely still."

He nodded, pleased to see that the opposition was following orders.

"*C'est le Président Severin.*" This is President Severin.

McGill was far enough along in his French to understand that. He wondered how ... Patti was looking out for him, that's how. She'd foreseen a problem he'd overlooked, and of course she had friends in a high place who could sort things out fast.

The French president continued, "*Pruet, expliquez-moi la situation. En Anglais.* Am I making a fool of myself here? Are you and M'sieur McGill sitting in your office sipping cognac?"

With that Jean-Louis Severin broke the tension in the room. Half the paramilitary guys understood English well enough to chuckle. Responding quickly, McGill took advantage of the moment to return Colonel Millard to two of his men. He got some hard looks, but nobody tried to grab him.

Pruet told Severin, "*M'sieur le Président,* your instincts are flawless. You averted a very serious situation, for everyone in this room and for two great nations." The magistrate went on in French to detail the scene in Paris.

Then Severin spoke in French, using a tone of absolute command. Gabbi provided McGill with whispered simultaneous translation.

"*M'sieur le Président* is offering the troops over there a choice. Years in prison or a month's paid leave in any French possession in the world."

McGill knew which choice he'd take.

Gabbi continued, "The colonel, if he plays ball, will find himself promoted, otherwise things won't go so well for him, either."

Even through his severe pain, Millard was able to make the right choice. His men followed his lead. Odo took everyone's name, and then they left.

"*Laissez-moi parler avec le partisan de la présidente, en privé,*" Severin told Pruet.

The magistrate took his mobile off speaker and extended it to McGill.

"He would like to speak with you confidentially."

McGill accepted the phone and moved to a corner of the room.

"Thank you, sir," he told Severin. "You prevented a very bad situation."

"I am only too happy to do so, and please call me Jean-Louis."

"My pleasure, Jean-Louis. My friends call me Jim."

"I hope I will be able to meet you soon, Jim. Patti has told me she would like to spend a week in Paris with you. A private visit. I said I would do everything I could to help."

"That's very kind of you, Jean-Louis."

"You have no ... no misconception of my relationship with your wife?"

"None at all," McGill said.

"*Bon*. May I ask you a favor?"

"Sure. I owe you one."

"Please be very careful with what you and Pruet are about to attempt tonight. There is only so much I can do to help you, and I would hate to see Patti's heart broken again, as it was with Andy Grant."

"Me, too."

The two men said their *au revoirs*. McGill turned to the others. "*M'sieur le Président* says we're good to go."

Krung Thep restaurant, Arlington, VA

45

Ricky was so focused on sating his hunger he didn't see the unmarked police car following him. The cops were so intent on following Ricky they didn't see Sweetie tailing them. To her credit, Sweetie had a gift for following a car through traffic. She had excellent vision so she could hang back a good distance; she was alert to intervening vehicles and pedestrians; most of all, she an intuitive sense of what the target driver was likely to do: turn left or right, pull into a parking space or jackrabbit if he somehow sensed the tail.

Occasionally, she lost someone. She wouldn't endanger the lives of innocents to keep the target vehicle in sight. But for the most part she got the job done. Tonight was easy, a series of long straightaways and gentle curves. There were just two turns and long green lights made sure everyone got through the intersections legally.

Deke had told her where to find Ricky's car and to take up her observation post well back as there would be cops watching the car, too. The only way Deke could know all that was if he had set up his own sting in collusion with friendly local cops. The Secret Service agent might simply have known where Ricky usually parked his ride, but Sweetie had seen the surprise in Ricky's body language when he spotted his car. He hadn't known it would be where he found it.

That told Sweetie someone else had parked the car where Ricky found it, and who could that person be except Deke? Circumstances would incline a former cop to think the federal agent had stolen a bad guy's car—then left it where he would find it. After planting two dicks in an unmarked car on the bad guy's tail.

In the course of tailing both cars, Sweetie saw how Deke had rigged the game to allow the cops to make a legitimate traffic stop. The right brake light on Ricky's car didn't work. More than one serious felon had been apprehended due to trivial traffic violations.

Sweetie had the distinct feeling that when the cops pulled Ricky over they were going to find something in Ricky's car he had no idea was there. Say, drugs or guns. Something that possessing would put him in front of a judge for a lengthy sentence.

It was a setup, start to finish. As a former cop, Sweetie could admire the craft that went into contriving the trap. As a former novice in a convent, she was clear on the immorality of it. Two wrongs, as every parochial school child learned, didn't make a right. But if you shot a fed, you couldn't expect a lot of Christian charity from him in return. And she was in no position to judge Deke.

It wouldn't be long before she took Bishop O'Menehy into her safekeeping, knowing that she had stage-managed the circumstances to have Horatio Bao or one of his minions seek to do the man harm. If all worked according to her plan, she would have to defend the bishop, even at the cost of putting a bullet into a bad guy.

What was the moral jeopardy for her in planning something like that? Sweetie didn't have a precise reckoning, but she intended to confess her actions as sins.

She saw Ricky's car turn into the parking lot of the Krung Thep restaurant, and a moment later the unmarked cop car swooped in for the ... traffic violation.

The whole thing was going down in full view of the people enjoying their Thai dinners, including Welborn Yates and

Callie Bao. Ms. Bao, Sweetie thought, already should have seen the bishop and Father Francis Nguyen engaging in a spirited public debate of matters theological. Add Ricky getting busted in front of her eyes, and things should start popping soon.

The smart thing for both Baos to do was run.

But, Sweetie knew, bad guys rarely did the smart thing when the net was closing.

46

"You prick," Callie Bao said, glaring at Welborn.

The picture of innocence, Welborn asked, "Who, me?"

Callie looked out the window adjacent to their table. The cops who had stopped Ricky had him out of the Nissan now. His hands were on the roof of the car. One cop had his gun on Ricky while the other cop was looking through the car's trunk. The second cop soon held up a large plastic bag filled with a white substance. Ricky got very agitated.

"Oh, fuck no!" Everyone in the restaurant heard Ricky's shout.

Ricky pushed off the car and spun around with a knife in his hand. He might have actually lunged at the cop holding the gun on him, provoking a justifiable shooting, except Ricky froze when he saw Callie Bao staring out at him from the restaurant. He dropped the knife and extended an accusatory finger at Callie.

"She did it!" Ricky yelled at the top of his voice. "That bitch set me up!"

The cop holding the bag tased Ricky. His erratic behavior lay outside the cop's comfort zone. The cop's partner gave him a thumb's up as Ricky writhed on the ground.

Callie Bao turned to Welborn. Turned her face away from the cops. Who just might be curious to see who their prisoner was accusing of a setup.

"You were saying?" Welborn asked.

"Meeting you was happenstance. Seeing them here," Callie

nodded her head in the direction of Father Nguyen and Bishop O'Menehy, "that was coincidence."

Welborn knew where she was going; he'd read Ian Fleming, too.

"And the guy getting busted out there, that was enemy action?" Welborn said. "But he pointed the finger at you, not me. Why would he do that? And what's he going to tell those cops when they get him back to the station?"

Callie took a knife in hand now, not a switchblade, a piece from the table setting, but it had a pointed tip and a serrated edge. It could do damage. As mad as Callie was, she might have made the attempt in front of a roomful of witnesses. Only she saw that Welborn had taken something off the table, too. His linen napkin. He'd twisted it for strength. A thrust from Callie might be intercepted, her wrist encircled, pressure applied until bones fractured if necessary.

She put the knife down and stood up.

Glaring some more at Welborn she said, "We're not done, you and me."

"You're still up for dance lessons?"

Callie looked at the knife again, but thought better of it. She headed for the door. Didn't look back when Welborn asked if she wanted him to call a cab for her. Didn't look at Father Nguyen, Bishop O'Menehy, or any of the other diners who were staring openly at her.

Welborn saw her take off her pumps when she got outside; she put them in her handbag. She walked barefoot past the cop car with Ricky now ensconced in the back seat. Seeing her pass by, Ricky began to vocalize with great animation. He even began to bang his head against the window. Both cops turned to look at him, but neither seemed to notice Callie.

She moved off into the night with the rhythmic stride of the dancer she was.

Welborn thought Kira would approve of his behavior with Callie.

But he sure hoped some cop somewhere arrested her soon.

His mother had warned him about women scorned.

Under the Pont d'Iéna, Paris

47

Not that it was unpleasant, especially when the weather was mild and clear, but few tourist guides advised spending the night under a Paris bridge. The *flics* of the Metropolitan Police actually discouraged it, verifying Anatole France's famous observation: "The law in its majesty makes no distinction between rich and poor; both are forbidden to sleep under the bridges of Paris."

Despite that longstanding policy, no one tried to shoo McGill and his pack of attack dogs from the shadows under the Pont d'Iéna, adjacent to M'sieur Eiffel's tower. One member of the pack, Gabbi, paced the walkway just east of the bridge's protective cover, sans mask, doing her best impression of Diana Martel. Gabbi wore a cloth coat over her black unitard. The coat belonged to Ms. Martel. It had been packed in a bag the gypsies had returned with the woman. Pruet had thought to have Gabbi put it on.

"The proper costume for the proper occasion," he'd said.

McGill had thought: *How French.* And: *How right on the money.*

In the lamplight coming from the nearby empty BatoBus depot, the others saw Gabbi's blonde hair drape over the coat's upturned collar. Her general resemblance to the stripper, helped along by the sunglasses she wore, was really quite good. At least, they all hoped so.

"Maybe I should have worn my wonderbra," Gabbi whispered as her pacing brought her close to her lurking companions.

Odo and Harbin had no idea of what she was talking about.

McGill understood the reference, and that Gabbi had cracked wise to keep her nerves settled. He said, "Don't worry about your bust-line. Remember, the guy has only one good eye."

Gabbi laughed softly. McGill smiled. The two Frenchmen looked at each other and shrugged.

They'd arrived two hours early, not wanting to let The Undertaker arrive first and deprive them of the advantage of surprise. They had considered two hours to be a sufficient precaution; maybe the bad guy might come one hour early if he was feeling enterprising; no way would he be there two hours early.

He wasn't. Nor one hour early. In fact, he was now ten minutes late.

Odo whispered, "I'm very glad I gave up smoking … but right now I could do with a cigarette."

"Pruet talked you into giving up the smokes?" McGill asked quietly.

"*Oui.* At the time when he gave up his pipe."

Nobody spoke for the next ten minutes. The men just watched Gabbi pace. She kept any further thoughts to herself. The city slept all around them. McGill hadn't heard a pedestrian pass by overhead for half an hour.

He wondered if Pruet had fallen asleep in his car parked over on the *Rive Droite.*

He also wondered if, despite *M'sieur le Président's* intervention, someone in the enemy camp had tipped off The Undertaker. Or put him down. Maybe the sun would rise and they'd all fall in their beds, sore from crouching and pacing and being thwarted.

Not that McGill would be able to sleep.

He had to find his way across *La Manche*—the English Channel to Anglophiles—and get fitted for his eveningwear and the fancy dinner with the Queen. Try not to fall asleep in his soup at Her Majesty's table.

Thoughts of what he might be doing in the future ended when McGill saw Gabbi stop pacing as she came their way. There was a look of concentration on her face. After a moment, she glanced at her companions.

"He's coming," she said. "From the east. Alone. He's a kilometer out."

All that intel had come from the mobile phone in her pocket. It had been set to vibrate and her hand had been on it. The number of buzzes provided by gypsy observers told her everything she needed to know.

Now, Gabbi would speed dial Pruet and relay the information.

The curtain was about to go up.

Horatio Bao's house, Arlington, VA

48

Horatio Bao was in his home office, his wall safe open, packing his last bag when Callie returned. He was filling the suitcase with banded stacks of hundred dollar bills. It was a carryon bag, so it held only a half-million dollars. He could have stuffed more in, but he didn't want any hassles about the bag being too big to bring on board.

So when he saw his daughter arrive he had another reason to be glad to see her; she could bring another bag filled with cash. They'd both have to declare the money since they would be taking more than ten thousand dollars in cash out of the country. If anyone asked what they intended to do with the money, a one-word answer would suffice: gamble.

Asian and Latin American high rollers were known to travel with huge amounts of money because, after all, nothing earned a warmer welcome from a casino than cold cash. Lavish suites, limos, and any form of entertainment imaginable were all comped for the gambler who arrived with seven figures of legal tender to risk. Happily for Bao, the credibility of posing as a gambler was helped by the fact that a number of Viet-Kieu had moved to the front rank of poker players in the past ten years.

So he had the right appearance. He had the money. He had a tailor made smokescreen. He could even pass off his daughter as his young trophy wife.

To complete the illusion, he really should have chartered his own jet. But Horatio Bao had entered the world desperately poor, and no matter how much money he'd made, banked, and invested since, he couldn't escape his fear of losing it all. Which left him a penny-pincher. Flying first class was as far as he could go to indulge himself.

"Where have you been?" he asked his daughter.

Callie had put her shoes back on and called a cab once she'd been out of sight of the restaurant. But her feet still hurt and her bruised pride was even more painful. She heard the anger in her father's voice and her first impulse was to lash back, but she knew he was right to be displeased with her. She'd have been far better off if she'd been a dutiful daughter.

Using her dark mood to suit her own purposes, Callie let tears well up in her eyes.

"I've been made a fool, father," she said, the tears rolling down her cheeks.

Bao interpreted his daughter's words and tone flawlessly.

A man had misused her. For a moment, he doubted that was possible. But looking at his only child's face he saw that it was true. His ill temper vanished.

"Tell me what happened," he said quietly.

She did, in reverse order. Ricky had been arrested; Father Nguyen and Bishop O'Menehy were arguing in public; she had been deceived by a *danh tu*. Not only that, the young woman embroidered, the American had had his way with her.

Horatio Bao took his daughter in his arms.

"He forced you?" Bao asked.

Aside from her abraded feet, there wasn't a mark on Callie, and she knew her father would never believe a man could take her by force without battering her.

"He took me by guile," she replied.

Bao found that notion hard to accept, too, but when he felt Calanthe tremble in his embrace, he allowed for the possibility.

"This American," he asked, "he has yellow hair?"

Callie stiffened now. She pulled her head back to look at her father.

"How did you know?"

"Ricky saw him. He said the *danh tu* let himself into your dance studio."

Those pricks, Callie thought. Ricky for ratting her out, Welborn, for never saying a word to her about Ricky.

To her father, she said, "He told me he needed dance lessons for his wedding."

"Hardly your usual client," Bao said.

Callie lowered her eyes. "He is handsome ... he has a very nice car."

Bao stepped back from his daughter.

"And perhaps you sought to disillusion him with his fiancée?"

Callie gave her father a chilly smile.

"Only for my amusement, nothing more."

"But then he outwitted you."

Callie's anger returned, but it was leavened by shame.

"Yes."

Bao moved on to another topic.

"You said the police stopped Ricky in his car, and found drugs in it."

Callie nodded.

Bao told her. "This afternoon, Ricky told me his car had been stolen outside your studio, stolen by an Asian man. Then he has the car back, only now it has drugs in it."

The lawyer held his hands out, indicating Callie should tell him what had happened. She knew her father had nothing to do with illegal drugs, would never allow anyone to work for him who was a user much less a dealer. As for Ricky, he got off on *being* Ricky. If an Asian man had stolen Ricky's car and set him up for a drug bust, it could only be...

"Donald Ky," Callie said.

Her father nodded and began filling another suitcase with money.

"No doubt Ricky is telling the police all about us right now."

No doubt at all, Callie silently agreed, not after his public accusation of her setting him up. But she didn't share that detail with her father.

"His word alone isn't enough, is it?" she asked.

Bao looked over at her, not stopping his work.

"To arrest us, you mean? Only if they think we're about to run. So..."

Speed was of the essence. Callie helped her father load the bag.

Bao, to his great financial dismay, knew that chartering a plane would now be unavoidable. He'd have to use one of his false identities to arrange it.

As the two of them worked in tandem, Bao said, "Even if we were to be arrested, Ricky's claims alone wouldn't be enough to convict us. Bishop O'Menehy, I would prefer to silence, but I think he's more likely to keep holy the seal of the confessional."

"Father Nguyen, though," Callie said, "if he were to talk along with Ricky..."

"We would never see each other again after we were imprisoned. Even fleeing this country, after what we have done, we wouldn't be safe in any country where the Church has influence."

That was, any place where they would care to live.

Bao closed the top of the suitcase and Callie zipped it shut.

"Father, as one who has admitted her own mistake, I am sorry to remind you of your own error. You really should have let me be the one to shoot Musette Ky, not just ring her doorbell."

Bao kissed his daughter's cheek.

"The past is past. But before we run one of us must kill Francis Nguyen."

Her father's assessment was shortsighted again, Callie thought.

They'd have to be rid not only of the priest, but his cousin, Donald Ky, as well. She had no doubt he would hunt them down if he were allowed to live.

"Father," Callie said, "I know how we can dispose of the bishop, Father Nguyen, and probably Donald Ky, too."

Bao looked at his daughter with the appreciation any good parent would show a bright child. "Tell me," he said.

Callie did, watching her father smile and nod in approval.

It was a good plan, Callie agreed. But a great one would have included Welborn Yates.

Under the Pont d'Iéna, Paris

49

They saw The Undertaker coming from a long way off. At more than seven feet tall and heavier than four hundred pounds he was hard to miss. He wore a workingman's jacket and baggy pants. Moving along the Seine, from one pool of light to the next, it looked like he was getting bigger in stop-action increments. Damn, but the sonofabitch was huge, McGill thought.

He, Odo, and Harbin crouched in the deepest shadows under the Pont d'Iéna. McGill could feel the tension rise in his companions. No doubt they, too, were wondering if they were about to bite off more than they could chew. Then McGill noticed something encouraging.

"Look at the way he's walking," he said quietly to Odo and Harbin. "His legs are stiff. That guy he killed in the video, his kicks must have left the big jerk hobbled."

Odo nodded, but he reminded the others, "That may be so, but we must not forget Ma'amselle Casale's caution: He may well remain quick over a short distance."

"*D'accord.*" Harbin agreed.

"Yeah," McGill said. "*D'accord.*"

All three of them started breathing in unison. Taking in all the oxygen they could without being noisy about it. Psyching themselves up. Getting ready to fight.

Gabbi, for her part, displayed no sign of pre-game jitters.

She stood with her back to The Undertaker's approach, giving him a view of a blonde woman wearing a coat that should look familiar. In another piece of stagecraft arranged by Pruet, Gabbi lit a cigarette, Diana Martel's brand, using the stripper's personal lighter.

Draw the target in. Let him think everything was going his way.

On the other side of the river, a car horn sounded briefly. It drew The Undertaker's attention. But the sound was not repeated and there was no way for him to determine where it had originated. He turned his attention back to...

Diana had removed her coat. Now she wore something black and tight. She started to walk under the bridge. Etienne Burel watched the way she moved: *très sexy*. The costume she wore looked like a sheen of paint applied to her skin. More than that, it seemed as though Diana had somehow lost the weight he'd been nagging her to shed. She'd always taken his comments as insults, telling him she would become sleek as soon as he did.

But Etienne had never been trim or elegant. He'd always been as he was: mammoth, towering, grotesque. Shunned and shamed when young, he came to embrace his monstrous appearance. He learned to take delight in the fear he inspired, pleasure in the pain he caused.

The world would never love him, but there were other satisfactions to be had.

Following behind Diana, he thought she looked like the young girl he had met ten years ago. From the start, she had been the one woman who had never been afraid of him. *Vraiment*—truly—she had been the only woman who had ever bent him to her will. Lavishing him with sex such as he had never imagined, much less experienced, she had persuaded him to commit his first murder.

The victim had been her own brutal father. The man who had abused her since she was a child. Diana had not only watched Etienne destroy the man, she had directed each blow, each kick, the breaking of each bone. It was only when she wearied of her father's screams that she had Etienne finish him. Then she rewarded Etienne as she had motivated him.

The experience of that night was so powerful he had asked Diana to marry him.

She laughed bitterly at the idea. Wives were to be beaten. To be impregnated and then to turn deaf ears to the pleadings of their abused children. She would be no man's wife, no child's mother. Tubal ligation insured she would never bear a child, but the simple fact of living with Etienne, sharing his bed year after year had made her his wife in his mind.

He'd even bought her a ring. Never showed it to her. Kept it in a corner of a drawer in the wardrobe of their bedroom. Not the same as on Diana's finger, but close enough.

Which meant he was entitled, as any husband might be, to beat her when given good reason. She'd been right about that. He'd only taken a hand to her twice, and then with great care, despite his anger, because he did love her, and the last thing he wanted to do was kill her.

Now, here he was, ready to take her life. The truth was, he had tired of her.

So it was ironic that seeing her tonight reminded him of the old times, brought back old thoughts. If he could believe those feelings would be more than temporary, he might have looked for another way out for them. Without turning to look at him, Diana stopped under the bridge.

He halted ten feet away from her. If she ran and eluded his first charge, he would have a hard time catching her. But he had the feeling she wouldn't try to flee. She knew why he was there and accepted her fate. She flicked her cigarette butt into the river, but still didn't look at him.

He told her, " *Je le ferai rapidement et indolorement, ma chère.*"

I will make it quick and painless, my dear.

Looking at her, seeing her so slim, so youthful, so sexy in her black outfit, he wanted her one last time. The idea of taking her life caused a pang of regret, one of the few he'd ever felt. He actually thought he might defy the men who had hired him, who had told him he must kill her. He might disobey them even at the risk of his own life. He was so intent on Diana he failed to see other dark figures emerge from the shadows.

"S'il te plait, Diana, laisse-moi te voir l'une dernière fois."

Please, Diana, let me see you one last time.

He decided that if she smiled at him they would run away

together, danger be damned. He held his breath as she turned to regard him.

And staggered back, gasping, when he saw she had the face of a snarling dog.

Still groping for understanding, The Undertaker saw a man, also dressed in black, also wearing the mask of a vicious dog, appear beside Diana. He was growling, and he held two long black sticks in each hand. As he handed two of the sticks to Diana, Etienne understood he had been betrayed, had walked into a trap.

His face flushed with anger. Did the two of them really think—

The giant heard more growls coming from behind him. These sounded like they might actually be ... no, they were not real dogs. He saw two more men in black wearing dog masks and holding sticks. So there were four of them, then, including Diana.

That was when The Undertaker had his epiphany: the woman standing before him was not his wife. She was someone who looked as Diana had years ago. Someone who had sparked old feelings and memories. Someone for whom he'd almost made a fool of himself. She was the one at whom his rage now pointed.

He lunged at her with startling speed.

Gabbi knew he would come for her first. She'd heard his words of endearment. He'd kill her painlessly, but for old time's sake how about one last peek, darling? What a guy. Then a gentle breeze had brought his scent to her. He hadn't bathed in skunk pee; he'd put on cologne. Dolled himself up to break her neck. You made a guy like that look like a chump and...

She darted to her left and ducked, moving to The Undertaker's right, his bad side both visually and aurally. His massive arm swiped at her but passed a foot over her head. He might have reached back and grabbed her, but Gabbi heard a sound like a baseball bat hitting a pumpkin and then a scream.

McGill moved in to attack the moment he saw The Undertaker start for Gabbi. If the colossal SOB had only feinted in Gabbi's direction, he would have had McGill cold, wrapped him up in a lethal bear hug while the escrima stick in his right hand was still drawn back. But The Undertaker never gave McGill a glance, and the president's henchman delivered a forehand strike that split the giant's left brow. Blood gushed into The Undertaker's good eye.

Etienne howled in pain. Reflexively, he swung his left hand out in a backhanded blow. It barely connected, fingers only, but that was enough to draw a grunt of distress, and to cause a body to fall hard to the concrete. His satisfaction was fleeting. He felt a sharp blow to the outside of his right knee that almost brought him down. The woman, the faux Diana, had attacked him. He turned to his right, but all he could see was the blur of the Seine flowing by, and then the back of his head was battered by two stunning blows.

He bellowed again in pain and covered his head with his hands and arms.

No sooner had he done that than his ribs on both sides and his elbow on the right came under attack. Hard sticks were battering him all over, the blows repeated in flurries as if he were some enormous drum. Each bash was accompanied by a growl or a snarl. Even more daunting than his terrible pain, The Undertaker began to drown in a riptide of panic. Maybe he was under attack by real dogs after all. Maybe he'd only imagined they were people in masks. Soon he would be felled and devoured. Eaten alive in the middle of Paris.

His screams rose to a shriek of terror. He threw his arms wide and spun counterclockwise on his left leg. Though his vision was blurred by his own blood and the gray veil that had hung over his right eye for years, he was still able to feel his hands connecting solidly with flesh. He heard two cries of pain that weren't his own, and felt immense satisfaction.

He had been seriously hurt, but he was not yet defeated.

The two enemies he'd just struck, they had been men. He could tell by their heft. But chances were, as solidly as his hands had struck them, they were out of the fight, if not altogether unconscious. And the first blow to his head, that one had come from the side opposite where he had charged at the woman.

He'd barely made contact with his first attacker, but even a glancing blow from him was usually enough to make a man's head spin. If he was lucky, the woman would be the only one left. Just let him get hold of her and he would wake half the city with her screams.

But first he had to be able to see his hand in front of his face.

McGill had been lucky enough to land on his backside. He'd kept his head from striking the concrete by thrusting his arms backward. Abraded the hell out of his elbows, but he could live with that. For just a second he remembered Patti had taken much the same kind of fall. But unlike her, nobody would be rushing to his aid.

Gathering himself, he saw the others beating a fearsome tattoo on the giant. The growling, howling, and smacking of wood on flesh and blood was a sight to behold. For a moment, McGill thought The Undertaker would have to collapse beneath the fury of the assault and the fight would be over. But then the giant spun, arms outstretched, like some Brobdingnagian ballet dancer doing a pirouette. He caught both Odo and Harbin by surprise, delivering stunning blows to each of them. The two men were left sprawled on the walkway.

Gabbi only barely sidestepped the behemoth's battering limbs.

McGill got unsteadily to his feet. Not wanting to give himself away by speaking, he gestured to Gabbi to pull back. They'd take a moment to gather themselves, to work out some advantageous positioning. Coax The Undertaker away from their fallen comrades.

All the bastard would need to do to finish Odo and Harbin would be to raise an enormous foot and stomp them.

Gabbi saw McGill gesture for her to step back. But she remembered the video of The Undertaker's fight to the death with the brawler McGill had called Smith. She had reached the same conclusion the president's henchman had: Smith could have won, could have lived, if he'd pressed his advantage. Gabbi wasn't about to make the same mistake Smith had made.

While The Undertaker was still trying to rub his eyes clear, she charged him.

Gill saw what Gabbi was about to do and yelled, "No!"

He tried to run at the giant to give Gabbi help, but he didn't have his equilibrium back and fell to his knees. All he could do now was watch.

Etienne Burel heard McGill's shout, and turned his head in that direction.

He never saw Gabbi coming at him from the other side.

Gabbi wanted to hit the big bastard smack across his ugly face, but he still had his hands up around his head, and being close now she thought the worst she could do if she went up high was to get him on the hands or wrists. A better idea, it came to her quickly, would be to whack him again on his knee. Maybe that would bring him down and Magistrate Pruet could put in his appearance and throw his net over the beast.

All she'd have to do would be get out of the way of the tree as it toppled.

Using all her might, she bashed The Undertaker on his right knee. Actually, the strike landed just below the right knee, as she couldn't see his patella under the baggy pants he wore. The blow unexpectedly produced a reflex action. Anchored by his relatively sound left leg, The Undertaker's right leg shot out. His massive boot caught a retreating Gabbi squarely on her left hip.

An awful cracking sound mixed with screams from both the giant and the State Department's Regional Security Officer.

McGill saw Gabbi rise into the air like a football kicked off a tee. Her mask flew off, showing her face twisted in agony. The sound of the giant's foot making impact with her hip had been louder than that of Colonel Millard's arm being pulled out of its socket. McGill could only imagine the pain Gabbi was feeling, but he saw it was sufficiently great that her eyes closed as she lost consciousness at the apogee of her flight.

And then she dropped into the Seine.

Magistrate Yves Pruet, dancing back and forth across the Pont d'Iéna, above the battle going on below, felt as if he were the sole listener to a radio play that even Orson Welles at his most fiendish would have been hard put to devise.

He'd heard words of love spoken by a man to a woman he intended to kill.

He'd heard the slap and crack of hardwood sticks colliding with flesh and bone.

He'd heard the impact of punches thrown in retaliation.

He'd heard the thuds of falling bodies hitting concrete.

He'd heard moans, groans, and screams. Many screams.

But all of the drama had occurred where he'd been unable to see. It was maddening. He'd raced back and forth across the bridge, following the sounds of the battle below, all the while carrying a large net meant to throw over The Undertaker should he emerge from the shelter of the bridge.

McGill had told him it was too bad he wasn't up to carrying an anvil to drop on their quarry, especially if The Undertaker were the only one to leave the battlefield. Pruet had hoped that one of his colleagues would dash out from under the bridge to be followed by the lumbering villain. He would then literally drop the net of the law over The Undertaker, saving one of his friends from a terrible fate.

But fantasies, as was their nature, often went unfulfilled.

Sometimes, however, reality substituted an event beyond one's imagining.

Pruet heard a splash, a body hitting the water.

The Seine flowed to the west, and as luck would have it he was on the proper side of the bridge to look down and see who had fallen into the river. The magistrate's heart lodged in his throat when he saw the blonde head of Mademoiselle Casale pop to the surface of the water. She'd lost her mask and he could see her eyes were closed; the magistrate could only hope she was simply unconscious. Pruet had never fished a day in his life, but he did exactly the right thing when he cast his net. Holding one end in his left hand, he threw the other end of the net into the air … and gave thanks to a God he hadn't addressed since childhood that he'd snagged one of Mlle Casale's arms and her head in the latticework.

He exerted all the restraint he could on the loop holding her arm while applying just enough upward pressure to keep Mlle Casale's head out of the water, lest he strangle her. The task might have daunted a master marionettist. Pruet also had to struggle against the pull of the river's current. He had to strain against the dead weight of the woman's body. Above all, hold onto his catch without doing any fatal damage.

Odo had been after him for years to begin a simple fitness program.

He'd replied that as long as he was able to play his guitar he was fit enough.

Now, having renewed his acquaintance with the Almighty by giving thanks, the magistrate turned to supplication.

Pruet prayed for strength, and for Mademoiselle Casale's deliverance.

It wasn't often that McGill lost his temper. The last time had been when Sweetie got shot, taking a bullet that should have been his. He might have beaten the teenage punk who had pulled the trigger to a pulp, if he hadn't seen the terror in the eyes of the girl the shooter had taken hostage—terror directed at him after his first punch had lifted the punk off his feet and made his eyes roll back in his head.

There was no chance of him clocking Etienne Burel like that, but once McGill saw Pruet's net snag Gabbi, saving her from the immediate prospect of drowning, saving him from having to put his dubious lifeguarding skills to the test, he intended to give The Undertaker the beating of his life. The pain and unsteadiness McGill had felt a moment ago had vanished. The adrenaline rush that came with seeing Gabbi splash into the Seine left him feeling like he'd been plugged into the city's main power grid.

He had lost his own escrima sticks in his fall, but Odo's were lying next to his body. He scooped them up and hopped over the inert Corsican. The Undertaker was preoccupied rubbing his battered leg when McGill tore into him. He hit the giant hard across the back of both of his hands. For any normal man, the blows would have been disabling, breaking several bones, causing blackout pain. With this monstrous bastard, though, McGill felt like he'd smacked his stick against the arm of a well-upholstered sofa.

The Undertaker was human enough to bellow in pain, but he kept his hands up, pulling them alongside his head. Then he began to advance on McGill, hate in his eyes, hobbling forward on his one functional leg like a boxer who didn't mean to quit this side of the grave.

Determined sonofabitch, McGill thought. The old line Joe Louis had used to rebut Billy Conn popped into McGill's head: "He can run, but he can't hide."

Thing was, McGill didn't intend to run or hide. The sticks gave him a reach equal to the giant's, and he was ten times quicker. McGill attacked The Undertaker's elbows. When Burel howled and dropped his hands, McGill battered his wrists. The giant tried a clumsy swipe at McGill's head and he ducked under it. He delivered a shot to the big bastard's ribs, and...

He broke something. Not bone. Glass.

McGill danced back and saw a large stain appear across the

side and front of The Undertaker's jacket. He'd cracked open a bottle holding some—Jesus! He'd busted the giant's bottle of stink juice. McGill had dabbed the inside of his mask with Old Spice Classic aftershave. The company's ads said it smelled like freedom. At that moment, though, freedom was overwhelmed by the stench of the devil's outhouse.

The olfactory assault drove McGill back, made him gag and cough.

He didn't see how he was going to get within striking distance of The Undertaker now. But the big bastard didn't have any problem with the way he smelled. It made him smile, and he came at McGill again, seeming to move better than before, as if the stink was to him what spinach was to Popeye.

And when it rained, it poured.

McGill heard Pruet's strained voice call out.

"Whoever is down there, I beg you to hurry. I cannot hold on to mademoiselle much longer." He repeated his plea in French.

Hearing the magistrate's voice brought to McGill's mind the only alternative means of attack he had available. He pulled Pruet's lighter, formerly used for the magistrate's pipe, from where he'd Velcroed it to his left arm. He flicked the cap open and was immediately chagrined that he hadn't thought to test it before now. Didn't know if it was charged with fluid. He said a one-word prayer, "Please," and thumbed the ignition wheel.

A high, steady blue flame appeared immediately.

McGill didn't know if The Undertaker's stink juice was flammable but from the sudden look of fear that appeared in the giant's eyes, he guessed that it was. The big SOB tried to turn and run, but McGill was too quick. He tossed the lighter and the flame kissed the stain.

The big man went up like a sheaf of hay. As he burned, he shrieked and hopped in place, looking to McGill's eyes like a demon doing a jig. The torment of the flames kept The Undertaker from seeing the obvious solution to his problem.

Only because Pruet needed the bastard alive, McGill yelled, "*La fleuve!*"

The river. Good thing he'd been studying the language.

Still, The Undertaker hesitated, as if he were hoping for another alternative. Finding none, he hopped to the edge of the walkway and tumbled into the water.

McGill, who also wasn't overly fond of water that rose above his chin, raced over to where Gabbi bobbed on the Seine. He lowered himself into the river while holding on to a boat stanchion. He immediately felt the pull of the current. But he was able to extend his right arm and grab a floating loop of net. Pruet let go of his hold, and McGill took care to neither dislodge nor asphyxiate Gabbi as he pulled her in.

Getting Gabbi and himself out of the Seine without losing hold of the stanchion required an effort the likes of which McGill could not recall. It left him panting as the two of them lay side by side on the walkway. He doubted he'd be making an appearance on the dance floor at Buckingham Palace. Catching his breath, he removed his mask, sat up, and disentangled Gabbi from the net. He pressed his fingers to her throat and found a pulse. He looked up at the bridge and saw Pruet staring expectantly at him. He gave his new friend a thumb's up.

The magistrate beamed, then abruptly became anxious again.

"*Les autres?*" he called.

McGill looked to where Odo and Harbin lay unmoving beneath the bridge.

He could only shrug. Pruet took that as a sign he should call for help.

After the magistrate had departed, McGill noticed the blackened, steaming bulk of The Undertaker floating downstream, his face in the water. Just then a boat motored by, moving in the same direction as the giant's body, crewed by his friends the gypsies.

One of them called out, "Shall we take that whale aboard for you?"

"*S'il vous plait,*" McGill said.

"We will add the charge to your bill."

"Naturellement."

McGill felt Gabbi take his hand. He looked and saw she had opened her eyes.

In a raspy voice, she asked, "Did we win?"

Thinking of Odo and Harbin, he answered, "Remains to be seen."

Arlington, VA

50

Bishop O'Menehy looked at Sweetie across the rectory's kitchen table.

"Do you really think they mean to kill me?" he asked.

Sweetie told him, "If they have the time, yes."

The cleric put a hand over his eyes. It was always a sobering moment to learn someone wanted you dead, and might try to achieve that ambition. Sweetie had been threatened with death by thugs in Chicago when she'd been on the CPD; she'd been shot by a punk in Winnetka. Neither experience had been any fun. Both had caused her to rely more heavily in her faith.

Ego loco meus fide...

The bishop looked up and told her, "I wish I'd kept Father Lonnigan here a bit longer."

The bishop had sent the rectory's young cleric home to his parents in Maryland; he'd sent the housekeeper to visit her sister in Virginia Beach. The idea was to get the innocents out of harm's way. Now, the bishop and Sweetie had the house to themselves.

Sweetie told O'Menehy, "Say a good act of contrition. God will understand if you can't get in a confession with Father Lonnigan tonight."

"You take your faith so lightly?" the bishop asked.

Sweetie said, "I take my faith seriously. I just wear it lightly."

The bishop suspected heresy lay within that notion, but decided now was not the time for debate. His point was confirmed when Sweetie's cell phone beeped. She had a text message.

It was from Jim: *Kinnard cleared. Bad guys bagged. Three friends hurt. I got bruised. Not badly. Keep me posted.* Sweetie lowered her head and offered a small prayer of gratitude.

Jim also told her to expect a call from SAC Celsus Crogher.

"Something wrong?" the bishop asked.

Sweetie looked at him and smiled.

"Just the opposite. The good guys won a round. Makes me feel confident."

"About our situation?"

"Yes."

Sweetie's cell intoned another call. Crogher.

"Please excuse me a minute, your excellency. I have to take this."

The bishop looked uneasy at the prospect of being left alone.

"I should alert you if I see anything threatening?"

Sweetie nodded. "Duck under the table and give a yell."

Margaret Sweeney took Crogher's call in the rectory's living room, sitting in a big overstuffed armchair. Made her feel like she'd be speaking *ex cathedra*. She knew who Celsus Crogher was, of course, had even seen him lurking on visits to the White House, but never had occasion to speak with him before.

"SAC Crogher," the man announced himself.

"This is Margaret Sweeney."

"Holmes told me you'd give me the man who shot Special Agent Ky," Crogher said, getting right to the point.

"That man was taken into custody earlier this evening by the Arlington, Virginia police."

"Damn."

Sweetie got the unmistakable impression the fed had wanted to do the honors himself.

She said, "There was no way Jim could have known that would happen."

"Yeah, if you say so."

Sweetie knew that McGill didn't worry about keeping SAC Crogher happy, but neither did he go out of his way to antagonize the man, if only to make things easier on Patti. So she told Crogher, "We're still working on grabbing the people who hired the shooter, if you're interested in that."

"Hell, yes!" Crogher said.

Sweetie decided to chastise the man about his language another time. Right now, there was a more important point to be made.

"What we're doing here isn't your standard federal law enforcement exercise, Agent Crogher. You try to make it fit the mold, you'll mess things up."

Sweetie heard a grunt, and then Crogher said, "That's your way of telling me I shouldn't try to run things?"

"You might not even want to be present, if your career is what matters most to you."

Crogher laughed. Not a pleasant sound.

"I almost blew my career out of the water with the president twelve hours ago. So what do you want me to do, follow your orders? Holmes's orders?"

Crogher's attitude brought out the Mother Superior in Sweetie's nature.

"Agent Crogher, you should know that Jim McGill has no knowledge of or supervisory capacity in the matter at hand. If you'd like to be involved in tonight's activities, where you might possibly be helpful, I'll give you the information you need. But only if you promise me you'll be able to work constructively with others."

Sweetie had been tempted to say "play well," but pulled back.

Crogher still got the message. He said flatly, "Yeah, I'll be a team guy."

"Fine," Sweetie said.

She told him where he could find Deke, Welborn, and Francis Nguyen.

The bishop was pouring himself a cup of coffee and looking out a window to see if the forces of darkness were gathering nearby when Sweetie returned to the kitchen. Apparently, the devil's minions were working another neighborhood at the moment. He turned to Sweetie.

"What if no one comes for me?" he asked.

"Odds are they won't," she told him.

Her words left O'Menehy nonplussed.

"Then what are we doing here? Why did I send Father Lonnigan and Miss Meehan away? Why are you armed?"

Sweetie had shown his Excellency that she was packing.

She said, "There is a *chance* some mugs might try to break down your door and shoot you, but it's a small one."

The bishop visibly relaxed; Sweetie didn't want him to think he was in the clear.

"What's far more likely, Your Excellency, is they'll try to get you to come to them. That way they control the situation. They lure you somewhere they can get an easy shot at you and then get away clean."

The bishop set his coffee cup on the countertop. He leaned back against it and supported himself with both hands.

"How do you know this?" he asked.

"I was a cop for a long time. That's how these guys work. They never want a fair fight; they want the deck stacked in their favor."

"Why would anyone ... why would I accommodate them?"

Sweetie said, "Because they know how to stack the deck. They're pretty good at coming up with compelling reasons."

"I can't imagine any reason that would compel me to sacrifice myself."

Sweetie looked at O'Menehy. He had his back up. He was scared. And it bothered him greatly to see Sweetie knew just how the villains planned to manipulate him.

"You think there is a way to make me complicit in my own demise?" the bishop asked.

"I do," Sweetie said.

The bishop set his jaw, seeking refuge in Irish stubbornness. But his resolve crumbled under the weight of Sweetie's patient stare. She wasn't trying to goad him. She simply knew the way things would be.

"What is it, damn all sinners to hell. What are they going to do?" O'Menehy demanded.

"As I mentioned to you before, Your Excellency, you've already been manipulated through a perversion of one of the sacraments. Guys like Horatio Bao and his people, when they find a weakness, they keep poking at it."

The bishop still didn't see what Sweetie was getting at.

So she said, "What's the one sacrament that involves a cleric making a house call?"

Now the bishop understood. "The anointing of the sick and dying."

Sweetie still thought of it as Extreme Unction, but at least they were on the same page.

"Bringing spiritual aid and comfort to those in pressing need," she said. "Perfecting spiritual health, including the remission of sins if necessary. If you get a call to attend to one of your parishioners, with Father Lonnigan gone, would you really refuse to go?"

The anguish on the bishop's face was stark.

To his credit, though, he said, "Of course not. If called, I must go."

No sooner were his words spoken than the phone on the kitchen wall rang.

And a heartbeat after that, Sweetie had a terrific idea.

The Novak house, Arlington, VA

51

Like any successful predators, the Baos made a careful study of the game animals in their hunting range. Long before they launched their blackmail scheme against the Church, it was necessary to evaluate the character of not just the bishop of the diocese, but all the priests close to him. All it would take would be one fearless cleric to go to the local cops or, worse, the FBI to ruin the whole plan. The fallback for Horatio Bao was to have his people in prison kill the former pedophile priests who had been ready to "come forward with further tales of molestation," but that still would leave a taint of suspicion on the Viet Kieu lawyer. The authorities might start looking into his other activities, and those investigations wouldn't be stopped with a convenient death or two. If anything, further suspicious deaths would bring even harsher scrutiny.

Calanthe was the one who had suggested to her father that they investigate the lay people who provided clerical support in the diocese. She knew that secretaries and other functionaries often had a far greater understanding of their superiors' doings than upper management ever would have guessed. It would be unforgivable, Callie said, to be undone by a flunky.

As a result of Callie's precautionary measure, the Baos came to know Bishop O'Menehy's personal secretary, Eva Novak. A childless middle-aged widow, devout in her faith, she had come to regard every Catholic in the diocese as a member of her extended family.

She helped work out payment plans for parents who fell behind on parochial school tuition; she advised travelers on the best times of year to hear His Holiness speak to audiences in St. Peter's Square; she always accepted invitations to be a guest at baptisms and weddings. At wedding receptions, she would coax the band into playing at least one polka, and showed the people of other cultures, and an unsuspecting partner plucked from a handy table, how the dance should be done.

The only time she ever resisted the will of the faithful was when either the clergy or the laity tried to honor her service to the diocese. She told everyone it was blessing enough simply to be allowed to do her job. It was enough for her to serve the Lord and live life the way her mother, Agneta, had taught her.

When Agneta's heart began to fail, offers of help came from every corner of the diocese, but medically there was nothing to be done for an ailing woman well into her nineties. Her body had given its all and soon it would know eternal rest. The offers were more a show of moral support for Eva than anything else.

But when Bishop O'Menehy asked Eva what he might do for her, his secretary asked that Father Francis Nguyen be allowed to say Agneta's funeral mass. That was not only Eva's wish, it was her mother's as well.

The bishop could not deny such a heartfelt request from someone who had served the Church so selflessly, so joyously, and so long. From the bishop's point of view, Eva and Agneta Novak were the people responsible for Francis Nguyen's continued standing as a Catholic priest.

That the Church was at irreconcilable odds with one of its most inspirational clerics was a tragedy in Eva's eyes. Almost as great as that of losing her mother. Maybe it was worse. Mom was as sure of salvation as anyone could be. Father Nguyen's fate remained uncertain.

As for herself, Eva was sure she was on the brink of damnation.

She put the phone in her living room down after making the second call.

She turned to Horatio and Callie Bao and said, "They're coming, Bishop O'Menehy and Father Nguyen, both."

The two silent figures in black suits and Roman collars approached the Novaks' modest ranch style home in Arlington walking side by side. The younger one was slim, Asian and bareheaded. The elder one was Caucasian, bulkier, and covered his white hair with a black fedora. His eyeglasses had slipped halfway down his nose. He was the one who stepped forward and rang the doorbell.

Eva quickly came to the door, in tears, distraught that her life had come to this, and the two men stepped inside. The door closed behind them. For ten seconds, the approach to the house was the sole province of a chorus of crickets.

Then Sweetie, Deke, and Welborn crept out of the darkness.

No sooner had the two visitors entered her humbly furnished home than Eva Novak embraced each one of them. She knew this was inappropriate behavior. When a priest arrived at the home of a sick or dying person he carried with him blessed oil signifying the grace of God that would cleanse the stain of any sin. He was on a mission of redemption not a social call. Nonetheless, Eva put her arms around Francis Nguyen and before releasing him went so far as to whisper in his ear, "Father, forgive me, for I have sinned."

Without any explanation of her transgression, she went on to hug ... Eva Novak did her best to blink away the curtain of tears that hung over her eyes. When she managed a partial clearing of her vision she saw the man she held in her arms, the man who held her, was not His Excellency Bishop George O'Menehy. He was a man with a hard face she had never seen before.

Eva's first impulse was to pull away, but without apparent effort the man held her close and whispered into *her* ear, "Count to five slowly, then step behind me."

Such was the authority of SAC Celsus Crogher's voice that Eva Novak followed his instructions without demurral.

Agneta Novak had all but departed the life she had known for so long when she had a vision. An angel appeared, entering her bedroom through its window. The apparition looked to be exactly what Agneta thought an angel should resemble. Tall and strong with a crown of golden hair and the kindest eyes she had ever seen.

The old woman's heart filled with joy and her mind knew the greatest peace. Surely, here was her escort to the Kingdom's Throne. They would kneel together before the Almighty.

It never occurred to her to wonder why an angel would be dressed in black Lycra.

Deke and Welborn arrived at the back of the house. A low wattage bulb glowed in the kitchen. The two men, also dressed in black, their federal credentials dangling from lanyards around their necks, looked at each other. The agreement had been Deke would enter the house. Welborn would wait out back in the small yard, watching for anyone to make an escape attempt in that direction. If Welborn thought things were going the wrong way, he'd follow Deke inside.

Welborn gestured to the house and raised his eyebrows.

You up to this?

Deke gave him a thumbs up.

Welborn nodded, took partial cover, going down on one knee behind a willow oak, leaving himself a direct line of fire on the back door. Father Nguyen said the Novaks never locked their doors, but that didn't mean two characters of a more suspicious nature like the Baos couldn't have locked them. But they hadn't. Which boded well, Welborn hoped. The bad guys weren't expecting any unpleasant surprises.

Once Deke slipped inside, he turned off the light in the kitchen.

Gave him better cover, but if the Baos noticed...

Welborn debated the wisdom of Deke's move as he waited.

The old lady smiled at Sweetie and in a thready voice said, "You've come for me?"

"I have," Sweetie whispered. She stroked Agneta's cheek. "Your time is close, good mother, but not quite here."

Agneta looked confused. A glint of trepidation entered her eyes.

Sweetie said, "I will keep you safe. To see your daughter one more time."

The old woman smiled and nodded. "Yes."

"There might be someone with your daughter when she comes. Leave that to me."

"Close my eyes?"

"If you like," Sweetie said.

Then she retreated to a shadowed corner of the room.

As soon as Eva Novak took shelter behind Crogher, Horatio Bao brought his gun out, and there it was, the SAC thought, the irrefutable threat of violence. Eva had been held against her will, coerced into summoning the priest and the bishop.

Peeking out from behind Crogher, Eva asked Bao, "May I see my mother now, please?" She could only hope her mother hadn't passed on before Father Nguyen could give her the Church's final sacrament.

Bao nodded.

Father Nguyen didn't ask for permission; he followed Eva.

Bao raised no objection. With a nod of his head, he detailed Callie to keep watch over them. She took a gun out, too, let it dangle alongside her leg, and fell into line.

Horatio Bao looked at the man he took to be Bishop O'Menehy and said, "I was sure you'd know I'd be waiting for you. I doubted you'd have the courage to come."

Crogher kept his head down for the moment, saying nothing.

Deke Ky heard Bao's words, but he couldn't see him. What he could see was a middle-aged woman, his cousin Francis, and Callie Bao approaching a door just off the kitchen where he crouched behind the L of a counter. The older woman knocked gently on the door, opened it and entered the room. Francis followed silently. Callie Bao stopped before going in. Deke could see the look of uncertainty on her face.

She was trying to remember something—hadn't a light in the kitchen been left on?

Sweetie saw Eva Novak enter the room, go straight her mother's bed and kneel next to it. The old woman had her eyes closed and a smile on her lips.

"Oh, Mama," Eva sobbed, thinking her mother dead.

Francis Nguyen kept his eyes on the two women in front of him, but hooked the thumb of his left hand, gesturing to indicate he was being followed. Sweetie moved soundlessly toward the door and waited.

Deke saw Callie Bao step into the bedroom. From what he could tell, she hadn't resolved the question of whether the kitchen light had been left on, but she had a more pressing demand on her time. Or she suspected someone unaccounted for had entered the house, and she intended to lie in wait for him.

"You have nothing to say, Your Excellency?" Horatio Bao asked. "You don't wish me to abjure my evil ways? Save my immortal soul?"

Crogher was getting tired of this asshole. The time came, and it wouldn't be long now, he was going to have a hard time not killing him. That would mean having to explain himself to a lot of people, probably a disciplinary hearing, maybe even a judge, but he was beginning to think it would be worth it.

What kind of fucking guy would kill a priest, a bishop, and two women?

On top of ordering the shooting of one of Crogher's own men.

With his right hand, Crogher removed the eyeglasses he'd been peering over. He slipped them into his coat pocket. That tensed Bao up a little, but when his hand came out empty, the creep relaxed. With his left hand, Crogher took the hat off his head, brought it down to his chest, and used it to cover his right hand.

Then he raised his head and let Bao have a good look at him.

Callie Bao was sure something bad was about to happen. She was certain the light in the kitchen had been left on. She had wanted the illumination as a precaution against an unexpected visitor dropping by, a neighbor stopping by with an offer of help or a gift of some foodstuff. Eva Novak was the kind of person who might receive friends through her kitchen door.

If that were to happen, Eva had been instructed to send the visitor away. And do so without giving any signs of warning. Something Callie would need light to see.

But now the light was out.

Still, Callie hadn't heard anyone knock. No doorbell had sounded.

The bulb could have *burned* out.

A new thought skittered across Callie's mind, chilling her. Was Eva Novak one of those ridiculous people she'd sometimes read about? The ones so oblivious to the realities of life they never locked their doors. Callie had double dead-bolt locks on all her doors.

If Eva did leave her doors unbolted someone could have entered and *turned off* the light. She was about to ask the woman just how stupid she might be when the priest spoke.

Tracing the shape of a cross in oil on the ancient woman's forehead, he said, "Through this holy anointing—"

That was as far as he got because the old woman opened her eyes.

Her voice was weak but joyful. "Oh, Eva, you're here. And Father Francis has come. The two of you … and my angel."

Angel? Callie thought.

She clicked the safety off her Beretta.

Crogher hoped Margaret Sweeney wouldn't get into a shootout with the Bao woman. For once, though, he wasn't worrying about procedure. He just didn't think that was the last thing a dying old lady needed to see.

Horatio Bao was still gaping at him, the lawyer's jaw actually slack. He couldn't get over how a slick, superior motherfucker like himself had been duped. Crogher was reassured by the way the guy stared at his face; he almost certainly hadn't noticed the SAC was wearing a Kevlar vest under the priest outfit.

Crogher was tempted to tell Bao, "Surprise, asshole."

But he knew this whole thing, at the very least, was going to be written up as a report to reside in Treasury Department files until Doomsday; those jerks at Justice might even find a way to snag a copy of it; and unless the Baos opted for suicide by cop, there would be depositions and cross-examinations by defense attorneys.

So Crogher went with, "Federal officer. You're under arrest. Put your weapon down."

Crogher held in his right hand the .22 he'd taped inside the bishop's hat. He felt comfortably in control of his situation. But he would have liked some reassurance as to what Margaret Sweeney's situation was.

Deke Ky combat crawled from the kitchen to the open doorway of the nearby bedroom. He intended just to take a quick look inside, assess the situation, and pull his head back. But he arrived just at the moment Margaret made her move.

Callie Bao had a semi-auto in her right hand, swinging it in an arc, looking for a target in the dimly lit room. Francis was using his body to shield both Novak women. And then Margaret pounced.

She slapped her left hand onto the top of the gun. A semi-auto couldn't fire if the slide was prevented from moving. Margaret's right hand encircled Callie Bao's narrow wrist, pushing the gun arm away from Margaret in case her grip on the slide was imperfect. The disarming technique was well under way. Now it was only a question of…

Deke smiled as he saw Margaret kick Callie sharply on the point of her left knee. Heard Callie's gasp as the pain reached her brain. A dislocated knee made it a lot harder to keep someone from taking your gun. Now if Margaret had learned the same procedure he had…

Yes, with her left hand she snapped the barrel of the semi-auto to point toward the floor. In the process, the trigger guard fractured Callie's trigger finger, snapping it like a twig. Then for good measure Margaret followed through with her right elbow, catching Horatio Bao's daughter solidly on her jaw. Good night, dark princess.

Deke got to his feet and eased toward the living room.

Crogher heard a thud come from the old lady's room. Sounded like a punch to the jaw, if he heard it right. His money said the blow came from Margaret Sweeney, and he'd bet McGill's big blonde packed a wallop.

The sound drew Bao's attention from the SAC. Crogher's eyes never left their target, but he did drop the bishop's hat and extended his weapon in a two-handed grip.

Then Margaret called out, "Clear!"

She had taken the young Bao woman under control. Crogher grinned in appreciation. McGill's partner was a pro—not that he'd ever give her or the president's henchman the satisfaction of acknowledging it. The SAC's smile disappeared as if it had never existed.

When Bao looked back all his saw was a grim-faced white guy with a gun in his hands, a guy who looked like he still did all his own shooting rather than hire it out. It was plain to Bao that all he had for a future was a life sentence in a prison. He turned his weapon toward his mouth.

But then he felt a gun pressed against the back of his skull.

"Allow me," a voice said. "Mom would want it that way."

Musette Ky's son, Bao knew at once.

Having her brat shoot him would give her years of great joy.

Bao decided to take his chances in court, after all. He dropped his gun.

"I surrender."

He may have, but Deke clubbed him unconscious anyway.

On a personal level, SAC Crogher approved.

Professionally, though, he hated the idea that he was going to have to fudge his report. Possibly commit perjury. It would either be that or admit that one of his own agents had assaulted a suspect who had disarmed himself. That was the kind of goddamn problem you got when you played cops 'n' robbers instead of following procedure.

Crogher blamed the whole mess on creeping McGillism.

Then, as if some supernatural agency had detected his treasonous thought from the other side of the Atlantic, he got a text message directly from Holly G.

Jesus. Could Holly G read his mind?

The president wanted him back in London forthwith.

Sunday, June 7th—Buckingham Palace, London

1

The queen's speech was brief, gracious, and to the point. She told the heads of state and other assorted dignitaries seated around the glittering table at Buckingham Palace that she would be abdicating her throne in favor of her elder grandson one minute before the stroke of midnight on January first of the coming year.

Her Majesty raised her eyes from the notes she held in her hands, looked at her guests, and said to them, "I may have to develop an interest in gardening."

Everyone at the table laughed. Then the queen looked directly at McGill, sitting to her right, one chair beyond that of the president of the United States.

"I believe, sir, you have found ways to occupy your time after retiring from government service. May I rely on your advice?"

McGill inclined his head respectfully. "It would be my pleasure, ma'am."

Ma'am, he'd been told, was an acceptable form of address.

Patti discreetly squeezed McGill's hand to let him know he'd done well.

Her majesty concluded her prepared remarks and offered an apology on behalf of Prime Minister Kimbrough for his absence that evening. He was still in hospital, but sent his warm regards and best wishes to all present.

Mr. and Mrs. James Jackson McGill both managed to keep straight faces.

During the course of the evening, the queen inquired about McGill's children.

"I understand you have two daughters and a son. I trust they are all doing well."

"They are, ma'am. I couldn't be happier with them."

"President Grant tells me your younger daughter would like to follow in her footsteps."

McGill smiled and said, "With Caitlin, you never know, ma'am. She's recently spoken to me about playing a part in a movie. Should she visit Europe, she may well decide that becoming a queen would suit her better than being elected president."

The fanciful notion amused Her Majesty.

"She's a young lady with spirit then," she said. "Please inform me if Caitlin should ever plan to travel to London. Perhaps she and I might have tea. I might be able to offer her a suggestion on marrying a prince with prospects."

McGill could only hope the queen was kidding.

Winfield House, London

2

That night in their suite, McGill heard of the advice the queen had offered to Patti regarding the fate of Erna Godfrey.

"Her Majesty suggested I could *extend* that woman's sentence," Patti told him.

As far as McGill could remember, Patti had never referred to Erna by name.

"She's right, you could."

"But do you think I should?"

McGill was sitting by himself on a love seat. He'd removed his dinner jacket and white tie, kicked off his shoes. Patti was standing five feet away, still looking ready to appear on the cover of any fashion magazine in the world. He gestured to the seat cushion next to him.

Patti sat close to her husband, rested her cheek against his shoulder.

"You have to understand," McGill said, "you are the only one whose feelings about Erna Godfrey run deeper than mine."

"I know," Patti said.

McGill sighed. "It was a lot easier for me to want her dead right after."

He didn't need to say after what.

"Now," he continued, "I have feelings that almost make me

ashamed. I mean, if it weren't for a hateful woman committing a murderous act, I'd never have become your husband, and right now I can't imagine being anything else." McGill looked at Patti. "Even so, please don't ever think I didn't do my absolute best to keep Andy alive."

Patti's eyes filled with tears, and McGill put an arm around his wife.

She said, "I know you did. If anyone was at fault, I was. I didn't trust your judgment. Because of my doubt, Andy and I let our guard down." McGill watched a tear slide down each side of her face. "I love you with all my heart, Jim McGill, but I still miss Andy. Hardly a day goes by that I don't wish he could have seen that I actually made it to the White House."

"And now you're shaking up the whole world," McGill said, a grin returning to his face.

The president's laugh still held a measure of rue.

"Yes, and beating the hell out of anyone who gives me trouble. Just like my henchman."

McGill's laugh was more joyful. The two of them held onto each other, rocking in each other's arms, ending the moment with a kiss.

"I think the queen is right," McGill said. "Commute Erna's sentence to life without parole. Let her have a good long time to reflect on what she's done. Maybe she'll come to serve some useful purpose, other than bringing us together."

Patti nodded. She stood and pulled McGill to his feet. Led him off to bed.

3

The call from Sweetie came after Patti had fallen asleep. McGill whispered to Sweetie to hold on a minute and took the phone into the sitting room, closing the bedroom door behind him.

"Everything all right?" he asked, taking a seat.

"As much as something like this can be," Sweetie said.

"Let's start with the basics. Are the bad guys behind bars?"

"Yeah, the principal ones. The local coppers are still rounding up foot soldiers."

"But this guy Bao, the lawyer, and his daughter..."

"Yeah, I disarmed Ms. Bao, kicked her on the knee and broke her pretty jaw. Deke clubbed Daddy after he pulled a gun on SAC Crogher."

McGill was amazed. "The guy drew down on Celsus and he's still alive?"

Sweetie gave him the official version of what had happened.

McGill chuckled again, still amused. "Celsus dressed up as a bishop. Wish I could have seen that."

"I was glad he agreed to play along. Anyway, we're hoping that the Virginia prosecutors will charge the Baos with kidnapping the Novaks and conspiring to murder them and Father Francis Nguyen and Bishop George O'Menehy. We've got them cold on weapons charges."

McGill said, "Good to hear."

"Ricky Lanh Huu is talking. Gave away Bao's plan to blackmail the church in exchange for some drug charges being dropped. The prison authorities are putting the ex-priests in protective custody, there are two of them, and the cons working for Bao are being segregated, too. Nobody's talking yet, but it looks good that somebody will, if only the pedophiles."

McGill said, "So it's going to be another black eye for the church."

Sweetie sighed. "Yeah. Father Nguyen and Bishop O'Menehy are going to co-celebrate Agneta Novak's funeral mass. After that, the bishop will retire and Francis Nguyen will leave the Church."

"Deke's coming back to work?" McGill asked.

"I expect so."

"Patti and I are taking a week to ourselves."

"She can do that?"

"She's a Republican president," McGill reminded her. "They're famous for taking vacations."

Sweetie snorted. "You twisted her arm, didn't you?"

"Just a little. We're going to see Paris together, but don't tell anyone."

The admonition made Sweetie think of the seal of the confessional.

"Your secret's safe with me," she said.

"One more thing," McGill said. "Patti's going to announce she's decided to commute Erna Godfrey's sentence."

"Life without parole?"

"Yeah."

"You all right with that?"

McGill said, "I am."

"Me, too. Give the Lord a chance to work a little redemption."

"Stay well, Margaret."

"Bring me something from Paris," Sweetie said.

June 8-14, Paris

1

Magistrate Yves Pruet arrived at the *Hôpital Saint-Antoine* before visiting hours. He came as soon as the gendarmes standing guard outside the room Odo and Harbin shared had called to tell him the two men were awake. As it turned out, he was the second visitor they received that morning.

Hearing this news, Pruet asked, "Who preceded me?"

"The American ambassador," Odo said with a grin.

His expression revealed gaps in his smile caused by the loss of three teeth. Both men had suffered concussions and there was a question whether Harbin might have suffered a degree of hearing loss. He would be tested after his ears stopped ringing.

"We have been invited to dinner at the White House," Harbin said, holding up his invitation. "Our presence is requested by *Madam la Présidente.*"

Pruet could see how proud of themselves Odo and Harbin were.

"I hope you will know which forks and spoons to use," he said with a straight face.

Odo looked at Harbin. "I think *M'sieur le Magistrat* has yet to receive his invitation."

"Quel dommage," Harbin replied. What a pity.

Odo said, "At the risk of depressing you further, Yves, President Grant has offered a two-week vacation for each of us and a companion to see any part of America we choose."

So, Pruet thought, McGill was behind this. He had told his wife what had happened beneath the Pont d'Iéna and his wife was expressing her gratitude in the same fashion Jean-Louis had used to co-opt Colonel Millard and his squad of paramilitaries.

Pruet nodded. "No doubt the two of you will seek centers of cultural edification."

"I am taking Marie to Hawaii," Odo said.

"And you, m'sieur?" Pruet asked Harbin.

"New Orleans," he said.

Being single, Harbin had decided to travel alone.

See what companionship a traveling Frenchman might find in the Big Easy.

2

Arriving at his office that morning, wondering how best to pursue the investigation of yet another interior minister, Magistrate Pruet saw a large package wrapped in brown paper lying on his table. His first thought was: *Bomb.*

Such was the state of mind in contemporary France. In Paris, public trash bins had been replaced by transparent plastic bags to eliminate the concealment of explosives. Unattended luggage at airports was secured and disposed of on the spot by controlled detonations. All such parcels were presumed guilty until proven otherwise.

As for the one in Pruet's office, who but the minions of Interior Minister Jules Guerin, the intended target of Pruet's investigation, had the authority to breach the security of the building and enter the magistrate's personal environs?

Guerin must have decided the way to short-circuit Pruet's snooping was to eliminate the magistrate. *Sacre bleu.* Guerin might even have it in mind to mount a full scale *coup d'état.* That would mean everyone involved in the Kinnard-Duchamp Affair would be in jeopardy, Frenchmen and Americans alike.

Then the magistrate's fevered imagination ran headlong into a wall of logic. Jean-Louis Severin was no fool, and his security was *plus que parfait.* There was very little chance any French president would ever be assassinated. The government security forces knew their jobs too well, having learned from the thirty failed plots to assassinate Charles de Gaulle.

That cordon of protection, of course, didn't extend to Pruet himself. But it was the magistrate's job to do the president's political dirty work. Even with Odo laid up, Pruet had assumed his old friend, *m'sieur le président,* would certainly have extended some measure of protection to him.

Wouldn't he?

Finding his thoughts turning once again to a merciful God, the magistrate crept forward to examine the package. Yes, the shipping label was addressed to him by name. Then he saw the return address: Muro del Alcoy, Spain. The town's name brought a smile to Pruet's lips.

Looking at the package with fuller understanding now, he saw that it was just the right size. If an assassin could be so clever as to bait him with something like this, at least he would die happy. The magistrate ripped off the wrapping paper, pulled open the shipping container, and saw the guitar case. He lifted it gently from its bed of excelsior.

A truly sadistic killer might have brought him safely to this point, knowing there was no chance he would ever leave the guitar case unopened. Fatalistically, Pruet unlatched the case and...

There it was, its beauty timeless, its gleaming perfection making him feel as young as when he had first set eyes upon its predecessor: an Alhambra classical guitar, the very image of the one he had loved for years. The instrument whose shattered remnants now hung on the office wall behind him.

He had never named that martyred masterpiece. As a young man he'd thought such an idea to be bourgeois sentimentalism. Well, he was a good deal older now and admittedly bourgeois in his tastes. He would take his time and find the perfect name for his new guitar.

An envelope lay across the strings. The magistrate opened it and read the card.

Un cadeau de votre ami Américain. Le partisan de la présidente.

A gift from your American friend. The president's henchman.

Pruet picked up the instrument and held it close, as if embracing a lover.

In the coming days he would have to interrogate everyone from a senior member of the government to a grotesquely burned behemoth. Instinct told him, having a written agreement in hand or not, he would also face a vicious divorce battle now that Nicolette was no longer in fear of imminent death. He would be attacked in the media. Protestors were likely to jeer his name in the streets. It was possible someone might even try to use an actual bomb against him. That or some other lethal device.

Had his American friend foreseen all that?

Provided him with his one true source of comfort.

Pruet put the guitar down, went to his file cabinet, poured a glass of cognac, and raised his glass. Whether McGill had known of the trials he would face or not, it was time for a toast.

"*Vive l'Amérique! Vive le partisan de la présidente!*" said M'sieur le Magistrat, drinking.

Yves Pruet returned to his table, tuned his new guitar by ear, and began to play.

3

That afternoon, *Le Monde* carried a story with a Washington, DC dateline. President Patricia Darden Grant had issued an executive order commuting Erna Godfrey's sentence of death to life in prison without the possibility of parole.

Unknown to the public, however, she issued the order only after heeding McGill's advice to have a suicide watch instituted on Erna. Just in case the infernal woman didn't want to go on living on Patti's terms.

4

That same afternoon, McGill called his daughter's talent agent at William Norris. He didn't have a direct number for Ms. Annie Klein; he had to go through her assistant, Patrice, just like everyone else. Unlike most callers, however, after identifying himself and stating his business, he wasn't told Ms. Klein was in a meeting, on another call or otherwise unavailable.

The agent came on, sounding almost giddy, within five seconds.

"Mr. McGill, sir, it's a pleasure to finally speak with you."

To McGill's ear, Caitie's agent sounded barely older than his daughter.

"The pleasure is mutual, Ms. Klein. Have you had a chance to speak with Caitie recently?"

"Yes, sir. She told me about your concern, and hers, regarding the role I originally suggested for her, and you're both absolutely right. She should do something more substantial."

"How about getting a little training first?" McGill asked. "An acting lesson or two."

There was a moment of silence from New York.

"Not a good idea?" McGill inquired.

"No, no. It's a terrific idea, Mr. McGill. I was just trying to think who might be right for Caitlin as a drama coach."

"I was thinking of my wife."

"The president?"

"Exactly."

"Would she ... have the time?"

"If I ask her nicely, she might find the time."

The agent digested that, resulting in another silent moment.

"So you're saying, sir, we should take our time with this?"

"You don't have a great script in hand for Caitie, do you?"

"No."

"And surely your interest is a long-term thing. You're not simply looking to exploit Caitie's appearance in Lafayette Square last year."

"No, sir. Not at all."

"If you don't mind my asking, Ms. Klein, are you relatively new at your job?"

To her credit, the young woman didn't hesitate in answering.

"Yes, I've only recently been promoted from ... administrative duties."

"The legendary mail room?" McGill asked.

"Yes, sir."

"But you're an intelligent, well-educated young woman."

"Summa cum laude from Smith." The note of pride was clear in Annie Klein's voice.

"My congratulations to you and your parents."

"Thank you, sir."

"Is Caitie your first client?"

"I don't know, Mr. McGill. Is she?"

McGill thought about it. The young agent had already made a favorable impression.

He told her, "Caitie is blessed, Ms. Klein. She has many fine female role models in her life: her mother, her older sister, her stepmother, her godmother. But I think the addition of a young professional woman as a mentor could be valuable. Of course, you'd have to hold Caitie in the same high regard the rest of us do. In addition, any acting she might eventually do has to be a companion piece to becoming as academically accomplished as you are. Are you up for all that?"

"Mr. McGill, with all due respect to your daughter Abigail, I'll look out for Caitie like another sister. I'll give her the benefit of my best advice whether that means comforting her or giving her a firm shove in the right direction."

McGill liked the young woman's attitude.

"All right, Ms. Klein. I'll call you in a week. We'll set up an appointment for Caitie and me to meet with you. Please have a long-range plan for Caitie in hand. One that will bring her to your current age. One that will make me as proud of her as your parents must be of you."

"May I ask you something personal, sir?"

"You may."

"Is your attitude toward me, personally, going to be paternalistic?"

"More like fatherly, I'd say. Will that be a problem?"

"Actually, no. That's what I was hoping you'd say. My dad is a great guy but he does research in a lab. He's not exactly worldly. In this business, I wouldn't mind having another older man in my corner. Would you be up for that?"

McGill reckoned that turnabout was fair play.

"Sure," he said.

5

A light knock sounded at the door the moment McGill ended the call. Almost made him think someone was eavesdropping. Galia? No, Patti had sent her home to keep an eye on things.

"Who's there?" he asked.

"Je recherche le partisan de la présidente," a sultry female voice answered.

Not only did McGill recognize the voice, not only did he understand the message, "I'm looking for the president's henchman," he even knew the proper French response.

"Me voici." Here I am. Gabbi would be proud of him. *"Entrez."*

The door opened and for just a second he thought it was Gabbi standing there.

But she was laid up in the American Hospital in Paris, letting her fractured pelvis heal.

The stunning blonde wearing sunglasses was his wife.

The president told McGill, "Your mouth's hanging open, sailor."

She slid the shades halfway down her nose and gave him a smile.

"Fooled ya, huh?" Patti asked.

McGill said, "Only for a minute. Never told you, but I have a tattoo of you as a blonde."

Patti threw her stylish Parisian clutch purse at him. McGill fielded it neatly.

"Not a chance," she said, walking toward him. "I have eyes-only clearance on that material."

McGill got to his feet and kissed his wife. "Still the same great kisser," he said. He looked at her closely. "A wig, right?"

"A very good one, quite expensive."

"Courtesy of the taxpayers?"

The wisecrack earned him a sock on the shoulder.

"From my personal account. It was suggested to me that for security purposes during our sojourn to Paris I alter my appearance. So I thought a man who frequently works with fair-haired women—Sweetie and now Ms. Casale—might like the same look from me."

"You wear it well," McGill said. "Red hair would be nice, too."

"I'll keep that in mind. For now, though, I thought if you could play Belmondo, I should assume the image of an icon of French cinema, too."

McGill regarded his wife again, and guessed, "Bardot?"

She shook her head. "Jeanne Moreau."

McGill said, "I know the name, but I'm not familiar with her work. Did she ever do a movie with Rory Calhoun?"

"No."

McGill tried again. "How about with Belmondo?"

Patti smiled. *"Moderato Cantabile.* Moreau is a rich, bored wife. Belmondo is a blue-collar guy who catches her eye."

"Très français. Do we have a script?"

"We'll improvise. Now, I want you to see someone else who'll be in character as he watches over us." She picked up McGill's phone and summoned SAC Crogher.

Celsus appeared a minute later and McGill beamed when he saw him.

The SAC was wearing wire rim glasses and a beret.

His sneer of disgust at the entire world was perfect.

"Magnifique," McGill said.

6

McGill and Patti took in all the Paris tourist sites. The costumed Crogher directed a ring of Secret Service agents also dressed in a casually French style. The agents stayed close but not oppressively so. Orbiting around the Americans was an undercover legion of gendarmes provided courtesy of *M'sieur le Président* Jean-Louis Severin.

The French security people never heard Patti speak anything but their native tongue. Anything that needed to be said in English went directly from the president's lips into McGill's ear. Given this conduct, the French thought the blonde woman was McGill's French mistress, and he had a thing for having his ears stimulated. Both of which met with their approval.

McGill and Patti stayed in the top floor apartment of a building in Saint-Germain owned by August Pruet, *M'sieur le Magistrat's* father. The lower stories of the building were occupied by the Secret Service. The French government provided air patrols in the skies above the flat when the First Couple was in residence.

7

At Patti's request, Yves Pruet joined her and McGill for a private dinner. He brought his new guitar with him. After dessert and cordials, he played the Pathétique movement of Beethoven's Sonata Number Eight in C Minor. Patti and McGill applauded the performance *con brio*. The president asked Pruet if he had anything in his repertoire that would allow McGill to accompany him vocally.

McGill wondered aloud if Pruet knew "Puff the Magic Dragon."

The magistrate turned to the president and said, *"Si vous devenez jamais fatigué de cet homme, je serai bientôt disponible."* If you ever grow tired of this man, I will soon be available.

Patti laughed, but declined to translate for McGill.

He gave each of them a dubious look and said, "Okay, if the two of you don't appreciate Peter, Paul and Mary, we can always do Elvis."

To McGill's great surprise, Pruet played the opening riff of "Heartbreak Hotel."

And the president's henchman followed with a credible

knockoff of Presley.

Patti told McGill that night in bed she was sorry the performance hadn't been recorded.

He said, "Maybe after Yves and I leave our day jobs we can work up an act."

8

The only time Patti took off her wig while in a public place was when she and McGill visited Gabbi in her hospital room. The curtains were drawn and two agents barred the door. Patti thought it was important to meet the State Department officer looking like the president of the United States, not a Jeanne Moreau impersonator.

Patti took Gabbi's hand in both of hers.

"Thank you for your service," she told her.

"It was my pleasure, Madam President. Except for winding up here."

"You're being treated well?"

"VIP all the way. I'm just a little worried my tap dancing days are over."

The president let go of Gabbi's hands and looked at McGill inquiringly.

"She's pulling your leg, I think," he said.

Gabbi grinned and said, "You don't often get a chance to kid the big boss."

McGill said, "She can be cavalier because she's planning to retire."

"Are you?" the president asked Gabbi.

"Yes, ma'am. I was going to resign. Now, I've been told I might qualify for a disability pension."

"What will you do with your time, now that you've given up beating giants with sticks."

"I'm a painter, a graduate of the School of the Art Institute of Chicago."

"Really? I used to be on the school's board."

"I thought you looked familiar."

"She's doing it again," McGill said.

The president bent over and kissed Gabbi's cheek. "She's earned the right. Ms. Casale, if you don't mind, I'd like to see your portfolio."

"Ma'am?" Gabbi asked.

"Mr. McGill and I will need our official portraits painted before I leave office. I'd like you to be considered for the commission."

Gabbi was stunned.

"I'd be honored, ma'am. Where should I send my portfolio?"

Patti took out a business card and wrote on the back.

"Straight to the Oval Office," she said. "This'll do the trick."

She gave the card to Gabbi.

On their way out, McGill bent over and kissed Gabbi's cheek, too.

"Can't make any promises on the president's portrait," he said, "but for mine the fix is in."

9

The First Couple boarded Air Force One for the trip home before dawn. The vacation in Paris had surpassed their fondest imaginings. They sat side by side holding hands in the president's private suite.

McGill said, "I'm not trying to rush things, but after this past week, when we leave the White House and the kids are off on their own, I'm really going to enjoy traveling with you."

Patti seconded the sentiment by kissing her husband.

She might have lingered but there was a knock at the door.

A sharp knock.

McGill tensed as the president turned toward the door.

"Yes," she said.

Colonel Michael Kuharich, the pilot of Air Force One entered.

"An urgent message for you, Madam President, from Chief of Staff Mindel. The call was initially held because we're about to rotate." Pilot jargon for take off.

"Thank you, colonel. You may proceed with our departure."

The Air Force officer saluted and backed out, closing the door.

Patti picked up the phone. "What is it, Galia?"

The past week, everything had gone smoothly. Patti had received her daily briefings, relayed her decisions, and the government and the world rolled on without her being present in the Oval Office.

But now…

Galia came directly to the point. "Madam President, Erna Godfrey was found unconscious in her cell this morning."

The president listened to the remainder of her chief of staff's report and told Galia, "We'll be taking off immediately. Keep me abreast of any further developments while we're in flight."

She broke the connection and looked at McGill.

"What is it?" he asked.

"Erna Godfrey attempted suicide."

"How the hell did that she do that? Wasn't she being watched?"

"She was. That's why she's still alive. A visual check was being done every quarter-hour. A guard found her collapsed on the floor of her cell."

"What did she do?"

The president shook her head, still trying to comprehend what she'd been told.

"No one is sure how she managed it, but she swallowed her tongue."

McGill recoiled at the very idea.

"But she's not dead?" he said.

It was easy to see what kind of uproar there would be if the Reverend Burke Godfrey's wife had managed to kill herself while in federal custody. The accusations that she'd been murdered would be swift and inevitable. The political fallout would be enormous.

The fact that the president was out of the country when the

incident occurred would only add to suspicions. Patti's absence would be construed as an attempt to provide complete deniability. And if the public ever learned Patti had been cavorting about Paris disguised as a blonde, God help them all.

"Not dead," Patti told him. "Surviving on a ventilator. No one knows if she'll ever come off it."

"Does she show any signs of brain function?" McGill asked.

The president's answer was lost to the thunder of Air Force One climbing into the sky.

ABOUT THE AUTHOR

Joseph Flynn is a Chicagoan, born and raised, currently living in central Illinois with his wife and daughter. He is the author of *The Concrete Inquisition, Digger, The Next President, Hot Type, Farewell Performance, Gasoline Texas* and *The President's Henchman.*

You can read free excerpts of Joe's books by visiting his website at: ***www.josephflynn.com***

CPSIA information can be obtained
at www.ICGtesting.com
Printed in the USA
LVOW03s1500170717
541649LV00012B/1033/P